The Serpentine Detective:
An Inspector Gaston Lafarge Thriller

PIRA

To Jo-Jo whose words of comfort gave me the will to hang on when aged five through a rash act of bravura/showmanship as my life was in the balance.

First published in 2021.

CONTENTS

Chapter One

Nuremberg, October 16, 1946

"How did you get the capsule to Goering, you Nazi loving collaborator?" growled the burly military policeman.

Not being blessed with the same amount of brains as his brawn he followed it up by wielding his truncheon and brought it down with such force on the rickety wooden table the legs almost gave way completely.

"Your behaviour leaves me completely indifferent Sergeant, I am quite used to being intimidated, having lived under the Nazis and without wishing to give them too much praise, they were masters in that particular art. And by the way, you will address me as Chief Inspector," said Gaston Lafarge.

Lafarge wished he felt as cool as his insouciant remarks had sounded, but truth be told, having experienced many a tight corner this situation surmounted all of those.

Here he was in a dank dark room and accused of aiding Hermann Goering, Chief of the Luftwaffe and Hitler's Number Two, to escape the hangman's noose by taking poison.

Needless to say, Goering's suicide hours before being escorted to the gallows, had been a huge embarrassment to the Americans. They had been charged with guarding those of the Nazi leadership who had not taken their own lives in the dying days of the regime and afterwards.

Goering's suicide had been the second major embarrassment for the Allies.

For Heinrich Himmler, the former chicken farmer who had been the architect of the death camps, had also committed suicide when he had been captured and realised he would be tried as a common criminal. His delusions of being a man the Allies would deal with over building a new Germany shattered.

The unscheduled departure of Goering, the most highprofile defendant, exacerbated Lafarge's plight, as the Americans sought someone other than one of their own on whom to lay the blame.

The stocky Military Policeman who was doing such an unsubtle job of interrogating Lafarge had been the one who swung by his hotel room and arrested him, leaving his two juniors to rifle through his meagre possessions.

Lafarge had crossed the sergeant's path on several occasions at the courthouse and had enjoyed cordial relations with him while exchanging cigarettes. The Frenchman appreciated the real American tobacco and not the cheap ersatz type he made do with more often than not in Paris, unless a friendly black marketer passed on a few cartons purloined from US stores.

Now all cordiality had disappeared and he did not dare ask for a cigarette, fortunately he had some of his own and trying to build on his impression of not being intimidated he took one from his overcoat pocket. It was so cold that he had preferred to keep it on even though it was threadbare and offered little protection from the freezing conditions that prevailed both indoors and outdoors in Nuremberg.

The Bavarian city, like most of Germany, was a pile of rubble but it had been specifically chosen for the trial owing to its significance to the Nazis, most notably the passing of the 1935 Nuremberg Laws which amongst other things declared Jews were no longer entitled to be German citizens.

"You do not have permission to smoke and for the record your title means nothing anymore, you are a prisoner Lafarge just like those degenerate sons of bitches that we hanged earlier on today. They lost their rank and privileges once they became our property," said the sergeant with a malicious edge to his voice.

Lafarge shrugged and lit his cigarette anyway but the sergeant whipped it from his mouth and took a puff of it himself before screwing his face up in disgust and grinding it out with his boot.

"Jesus that is shit you are smoking, I saved you some minutes of your life there," he remarked.

Lafarge sighed in exasperation, hugged his coat round him and stared straight ahead with not the slightest inclination of engaging in conversation or answering questions. He hoped that someone from the hotel would have noticed him being taken away and notified the French delegation, which would mean he could be a free man again within hours.

The sergeant, though, wasn't going to let up with his questions, limited as they were.

"So Goering paid you?" he asked as he circled round behind Lafarge, smacking the truncheon into his hand.

Lafarge was damned if he was going to give the Sergeant any information and played for time.

"Sergeant Miller I don't give a damn for your rules or regulations, furthermore I do not recognise them and being a Chief Inspector from an ally of your country I demand to be released or have access to a lawyer, who will no doubt secure my freedom within minutes," said Lafarge.

Miller laughed mirthlessly and bent down so close to Lafarge that the Chief Inspector could smell the stale odour of bourbon on his breath and ascertained the sergeant hadn't taken a bath at the very least that day, if not longer.

"You speak pretty good English for a Frenchie, prisoner Lafarge. But that isn't going to be enough to see you argue your way out of here…or for that matter get you a lawyer," said Miller.

Lafarge did indeed thank his late father for having sent him and his brothers and sister to England at different times to learn the language, it had served him well in the past and he hoped it would do so this time too, contrary to what Miller thought.

"You think you are sitting pretty and not obliged to answer my questions, just waiting for me to get bored and that I won't resort to giving you some rough treatment because you are a citizen of an ally – a questionable one I might add after the things that went on in your country during the occupation," said Miller.

"But I reserve the right to treat you as a hostile should I believe that is what will serve me and the best interests of the United States Army."

"Now we have evidence against you and plenty of it. Your unwillingness to answer the questions is pointless and does your cause no good at all," added Miller.

Lafarge held out his hands and said: "Where is the evidence? I see no thick file. I have heard nothing from your lips that suggests concrete testimony to my guilt. The most important remaining member of Hitler's circle of criminals has succeeded in securing and concealing a poison capsule and committed suicide on *your* watch. All I see is a sergeant who has been humiliated.

"Instead of you owning up to your responsibilities you charge off after a high-ranking policeman from an ally in a vain attempt at a cover-up.

"I have to say I have no truck with the Nazis, whom I had the misfortune to be captured by and then had to serve. I detest them. However, I congratulate the Reich Marshal on outwitting his enemies…and ultimately what does it matter how he perished? He saved you the job of doing it yourselves," added Lafarge.

Miller bristled at Lafarge's remarks which pleased the Chief Inspector no end. The thickset American rubbed his chin as if thinking over whether he could he resort to outright violence, not to gain any information but simply to punish his prisoner for his impudence.

Lafarge hoped he would opt not to but he had experienced pain before – an almost near-death experience in the dying days of the Vichy regime with the now extinct Bonny and Lafont gang or the French Gestapo as they were known – so he knew his threshold for absorbing beatings was high.

Lafarge ran a hand through his thick wavy blond hair and pondered another thought that had suddenly come to him. He must have been in this room for several hours now and yet no one apart from Miller had seen fit to interrogate him or at least come and observe.

He was not an authority on US Military legal procedure but a rough guess told him that they operated like other armies, uniformed police picked up the suspects and then they were interrogated by their superiors.

This thought both encouraged and alarmed Lafarge.

He was alarmed because if no one else higher up knew he was in the building then he was totally at the mercy of the unpredictable behaviour of Miller -- who was evidently intent on securing a confession out of his scapegoat to save his own skin -- but encouraged because it meant he could use this to his advantage if he made the sergeant aware he realised the game he was playing.

"Sergeant I would like to see your superior officer please, someone who is of similar rank to me," said Lafarge who before Miller could respond went on: "I think you could at the very least do that even if you deny me a lawyer."

Miller shifted uneasily from foot to foot confirming Lafarge's suspicions that he was acting alone. The two young Military P had been only too happy to please their sergeant and certainly would not have questioned his authority.

Lafarge grinned and this time he shielded the cigarette he pulled from his crumpled packet as he lit it, and then took great joy in inhaling the revolting tobacco deep into his lungs before exhaling – the smell at least blocking out the Sergeant's body odours.

Miller was too busy thinking to react to Lafarge's small gesture of defiance this time.

"Let's have a race Sergeant Miller, see if I finish my cigarette before you come up with a response," said Lafarge teasingly.

Miller did not appreciate Lafarge's remark or the fact that the tables were turning and his prisoner had outsmarted him, which truth be told the Frenchman was not going to take a lot of credit for. There was a reason a forty-something man like Miller had risen only to the rank of sergeant and in the Military Police to boot.

Miller sighed and looked at Lafarge with disdain.

"Lafarge you simply do not get it. You are correct in that you can ask to see someone of similar rank but that request is not granted and is out of my hands in any case," said Miller.

"What do you mean out of your hands?" asked Lafarge, who tried to hide a sudden surge in anxiety.

It was Miller's turn to smile triumphantly at Lafarge, labouring the point by lighting up a Lucky Strike and slowly exhaling before removing the stray strands of tobacco from his lips.

"My orders are to keep you isolated and under interrogation until you finally admit it was you who furnished Goering with the cyanide capsule," said Miller.

As if to emphasise this Miller removed his finely-polished white helmet -- MP emblazoned on the front -- and placed it on the table whilst he pulled up a wooden chair opposite Lafarge and swung his legs up on to the table, the heels of his boots almost in the Frenchman's face.

Lafarge's confidence had been stripped away. All thoughts of outsmarting Miller and obtaining his release evaporated. He could discount any possibility of a speedy return to Paris, which was of the utmost importance both on a personal level and professionally.

It was all the more painful and frustrating as Lafarge had wanted to turn a page in terms of proving himself reliable and not always placing the job above his personal life.

Hence his solemn promise to his wife to be Aimee that he would wrap up his business as quickly as possible and return to marry her.

Aimee needed some consistency and happiness in her life. After the trauma of giving birth in Ravensbruck she was forced to leave her son in care in Cologne, and denied access to him by the couple he had been placed. She then returned to Paris with her fellow liberated prisoners.

They had managed to resolve that problem when Lafarge had accompanied her to Cologne. He used charm and when that failed he had threatened the man with exposure for having been a member of the Gestapo. He complimented himself on his meticulous research but his joy had been diluted due to the emotional strain the obfuscation of the couple had placed on Aimee.

Miller listened intently while Lafarge related this part to him, the Chief Inspector calling on his last reserves in dealing this card to try and sway the sergeant in at least appealing to his superiors to allow him to return to Paris.

He was even willing for an American, why not Miller himself, to accompany him to the French capital. That guard could enjoy the colourful nightlife -- Lafarge didn't think the sergeant was the daytime sightseeing type -- in the City of Light. It would compare favourably to the limited attractions in Nuremberg which consisted of scrambling down to a cellar of a bombed out building to savour a few flat beers and be pawed at by some local women, largely war widows, who would sell their bodies for a bar of soap.

The professional reason for his desire to return to Paris Miller knew already , which was why he was in such an unholy mess right now.

Miller stood up and paced the room as if he was giving serious thought to Lafarge's proposal.

He returned to the table and offered a cigarette to Lafarge. That's a good sign thought Lafarge as he accepted it.

"Lafarge I sympathise with your dilemma, I really do, but I have my orders. Before you start citing the 'only obeying orders' defence has been dismantled at the trial of the war criminals, these are the orders that I have to abide by otherwise I will be sent back home to my dusty small town in Tennessee," said Miller.

"Believe me you wouldn't wish it upon an ex-wife who had cleaned you out. Apologies for the comparison by the way given you are due to get hitched."

Lafarge shrugged aside Miller's effort to pat him on the shoulder, the sergeant sighed and withdrew some papers from his inside pocket and laid them down on the table.

Miller jabbed his finger -- Lafarge noticed how dirty the fingernail was, re-enforcing his low opinion of Military Policemen in general and their apparent lack of regard for cleanliness.

Lafarge tried his best to appear nonchalant as he picked up the paper as if he remained sceptical of Miller's story but there was no doubting the sergeant's veracity or the trouble he was in when he read the signatures.

Whether it had been for his benefit or not the text was written in French and English authorising the arrest and detention of Chief Inspector Gaston Lafarge on the charge of being an accessory to the suicide of Hermann Goering and was signed by Professor Henri Donnedieu de Vabres and Auguste Champetier de Ribes

This ended any hope Lafarge entertained at appealing to the French to have him released for the two signatories were the lead French judge and the prosecutor at the Nuremberg trial. Gone was the nonchalant air as he was now completely disheartened but also furious at his stupidity in becoming embroiled in the whole story.

The irony was he had come to Nuremberg to save a Jew. In the end in order to achieve that he had colluded in ending the life of one of the architects of the genocide of the Jews.

Lafarge ran a hand though his hair, stroked his unshaven chin -- he didn't know how long he had been incarcerated in the room as it didn't possess a clock and his watch had been removed -- and decided there was only one thing for it, rely on his gambler's instinct that had thus far got him through immeasurable scrapes and tough situations.

"I want to make a confession."

Chapter Two

The long and unlikely road to Lafarge's imprisonment in Nuremberg started innocuously enough with a call to a break in at an art gallery on the Avenue Montaigne.

Ordinarily such a crime would not have been in Lafarge's remit, however, two dead bodies elevated its importance and entailed that the Chief Inspector was lured away from a mountain of paperwork and dull administrative duties to attend the scene of the crime.

The gallery was called Albert Zilberstein and was large – a double fronted building – with a Monet in one of the windows and a Sisley in the other. Lafarge whistled softly to himself as he pushed open the bullet-marked door and stepped inside to find a scene of utter carnage.

One of the corpses lay on the steps leading down into the main emporium, the victim, well dressed in a camel hair coat, which now looked a tad shabby as it had two bullet holes in the back, was facing the door as if he had been trying to escape when he came to grief.

Lafarge lifted his head up by the hair – the curly mop of blond identical to his own – and recognised him immediately as Gilles Le Vaillant, a former muscle for the notorious Bonny-Lafont gang who had styled themselves as the French Gestapo during the Occupation.

There was no copyright on villainy and thuggery in those times mused Lafarge, but the Bonny crew had profited the most from collaborating and inflicting the worst violence and humiliation on their victims as long as there was money or art to be gained from such brutality.

Le Vaillant was one of the more cultured and intelligent of the group, although he too was renowned for his ability to slip from civility to sadism within seconds. That was one less thug to worry about thought Lafarge, who had come close to death at the hands of the gang during the Occupation.

Lafarge went down the steps and was greeted by three

colleagues all from the local precinct, one of whom he knew, Inspector Bruno Giraud, who was a rotund fellow of around 50. Despite his physique there was nothing lazy about his mind, although he was reputed to have been sleight of hand too when he was stationed in Pigalle during the Occupation, taking backhanders from the club owners as protection money.

Lafarge, though, liked him and he was not one to be casting stones in anyone's direction given his record during the Occupation. He smiled warmly at Giraud, who introduced him to his two colleagues. One was a spotty-faced young man called Laporte, the other middle-aged, suavely dressed and called Lalande.

*

Giraud swept his hand round the large double-roomed space – they were linked by an archway – and Lafarge followed it taking in the bullet marks in the white-washed walls although it appeared the artworks, save two sculptures, had miraculously escaped the fusillade.

The second corpse lay by a large Louis XV desk, behind which sat a smartly-dressed man. Although not as thickset as Giraud, he was of portly frame with a waxed moustache and pig-like eyes. Lafarge surmised this was Zilberstein, but did not ask to be introduced quite yet.

Lafarge knelt down and ran an eye over the dead body. He was smart in appearance, wearing a black leather coat with a natty chalk pinstripe suit and patterned tie. The trouble was that the man who owned the smart apparel had what looked like a letter opener sticking out of his left eye.

Lafarge flinched but it didn't prevent him from also recognising the man, Patrice Romain, another hoodlum who had not been a member of the Bonny gang but had nonetheless profited well from the Occupation, enjoying favour from both the Nazis and the French police.

He had briefly been a member of the hated and feared Brigades Speciales. They had been effective at breaking up Resistance cells and had played a major role in the infamous rounding up of the Jews in the sickeningly named 'Spring Breeze' Operation in July 1942, orchestrated by Lafarge's bitter enemy Rene Bousquet, now incarcerated in Fresnes Prison.

Lafarge rose to his feet, largely unmoved by the deaths of two hardened criminals, and was ready to speak to the man he took to be Zilberstein. He regretted that it being just after nine in the morning he could not avail himself of the fine looking cognac that rested on the desk. He compensated by lighting a cigarette and introduced himself to the man behind the desk, who remained seated but confirmed he was indeed Zilberstein.

Giraud gave a rundown of what he had gleaned had happened, but Lafarge interjected and said he wanted to hear it from Zilberstein.

The gallery owner didn't look best pleased. Indeed Lafarge observed he became rather flustered.

Lafarge waited patiently, although he felt like clicking his fingers to hurry the man along. Instead he looked at his watch to register his impatience.

"What do you wish to know exactly Chief Inspector?" asked Zilberstein, his voice gravelly, a smoker surmised Lafarge.

Lafarge gritted his teeth realising that co-operation from Zilberstein would be hard-earned. Zilberstein had not offered Giraud or himself a seat, but undeterred Lafarge sat down in a large green covered Louis XV chair, one of a pair, that faced the desk and suggested to Giraud to also sit.

"Well Mr Zilberstein, you could tell us the exact train of events. Did you come in to find them, or did they burst in?" asked Lafarge.

Zilberstein ran his finger along the edge of the desk.

"I had come in early to catch up on some sales paperwork, when there was a knock on the door," said Zilberstein.

"A knock on the door, but there is a bell isn't there?" said Lafarge.

Zilberstein smiled, although it was smug more than warm.

"Ah I am still waiting for the workman to come and fix it. As you know too well Chief Inspector if there is one regret since the Liberation it is that we have lost the Germans' habit of getting things done sharpish," he said raising his arms to emphasise the point.

Lafarge nodded, but stored the remark away and made a note

to double check about the bell.

"Anyway my business partner Otto Meissner was not here yet, nor the other staff members. I went to the door thinking perhaps it was one of them," said Zilberstein.

"It wasn't them, though, and yet you still opened the door," said Lafarge, leaving the implication hanging in the air.

Zilberstein shrugged it off.

"I saw a well-dressed man, and before you ask the one in the leather coat, and so I wasn't in the least bit suspicious. Besides I have always gone on the theory that most criminals don't arise early," he said, the smug smile back again.

"Criminals don't keep to any particular schedule, Mr Zilberstein," said Lafarge testily.

"I imagine once you opened the door the other one burst in?"

"No, I left the door unlocked. I felt safe, the staff would be arriving soon enough, and other gallery owners would also be opening up," he said.

"So I was showing the man in the leather coat round the gallery and was about to leave him to have a longer look whilst I returned to my paperwork when the other fellow walked in."

Lafarge listened attentively whilst Zilberstein recounted how the two had then threatened him and roughed him up a bit, pinning him against the desk. This, though, had worked to his advantage as it meant he could reach behind him and grasp the letter opener which he had then stabbed Romain in the eye with.

Le Vaillant had made a run for it but Zilberstein had shot him down.

"I am still rather shaken Chief Inspector, hence why I am seated at my desk and did not stand up to greet you. Killing men in such a fashion is not something I am accustomed to," said Zilberstein, mopping his brow as if to add weight to his statement.

Lafarge remained silent, lit another cigarette for himself and Giraud, and tapped his cheek with his non-smoking hand. He was far from satisfied with Zilberstein's account and he did not appreciate being taken for a fool.

He wondered whether Giraud had continued his old habits of offering protection for a price. He thought this because the lack of detail in Zilberstein's account intimated he had been coached. A smart detective would keep the script to a bare minimum. Perhaps Zilberstein was waiting for Lafarge to make him an offer, a price for accepting his account of events.

After all this was how things had operated during the Occupation and there was no reason why people's mentality should change even after the bad guys had been expelled. A successful formula can be adapted to all circumstances. Every person after all has a price right?

Wrong in Lafarge's case, he had left that all behind him in the wake of a rather bloody spree in 1944, and not even members of his own family had succeeded in buying him off in 1945 – so Zilberstein was in for a rude awakening if Lafarge had judged the situation correctly.

Lafarge rose and walked round the room, taking in the masterpieces that hung from the walls – he applauded the manner in which none of them were damaged as the shots had miraculously hit the walls. It was all too perfect for him.

He turned and stared at Zilberstein, who held his gaze. Was that a note of defiance from the gallery owner thought Lafarge, was he daring the Chief Inspector to challenge his account?.

Lafarge pondered this as he took in the bare wall behind Zilberstein, and then a smile came to his lips. A look of confusion, or was it panic, flitted across Zilberstein's face. Lafarge strode across the room to the far right hand corner and pushed against it. His instinct had been right for a cleverly disguised door swung open to reveal a corridor leading to several rooms.

Lafarge said nothing but looked at Zilberstein, who had not bothered to turn around and was staring into space. Lafarge motioned to Giraud to go and take a look, the Inspector ordering the younger detective to accompany him.

Lafarge walked behind where Zilberstein was sitting, he could sense the gallery owner was increasingly uncomfortable and uncrossed and then crossed his legs, not once but twice.

The Chief Inspector walked over to the archway and peered round to the left seeing that there was no damage to the walls.

He returned and sat down, ran his hands down his face and

then an imaginary crease on his grey suit trousers. He lit another cigarette, looked at his watch which told him it was almost 10 in the morning and then tapped his knee with a finger waiting for the return of Giraud and his subordinate.

Ten minutes went by before they re-emerged, and with them they had a stern looking youngish man, who had a duelling scar running down his left cheek which skirted his mouth. He looked none too pleased at having been discovered, he had been engaged in some work when he was disturbed as his white shirt sleeves were rolled up to his elbows, the expensive looking cufflinks dangling precariously from their holes.

"Herr Meissner I take it," said Lafarge laconically.

The man nodded, though, his clear blue eyes flashed a look of annoyance. Lafarge indicated for him to take the seat beside him. Meissner looked at Zilberstein, who nodded.

"Right Herr Meissner and Monsieur Zilberstein, perhaps we can go through what really happened here this morning, or rather last night," said Lafarge staring at Zilberstein.

"I have no idea what you are talking about, and by the way it is Monsieur Meissner, I am Alsatian not German. I would be extremely foolish to have remained here if I was German," said the high-pitched guttural voice from beside him.

"I apologise, foolish of me indeed especially as those good Germans who fled here seeking sanctuary from the Nazis before the war were deported to the east, with the help of the French police force ," said Lafarge.

"Yes all very regrettable," said Meissner, rather too hurriedly for Lafarge's taste but he let it pass as time was moving on and he wanted to clear this up once and for all.

After all the people who could claim to have had a good war in France were few and far between, and what Meissner may have got up to was not his concern, unless of course it pertained to this incident.

Zilberstein remained silent, as if this would make Lafarge pack up and go. Instead Lafarge instructed Giraud to telephone for someone from forensics to come and dust for fingerprints, as well as a pathologist to run a preliminary examination over the corpses, even though it was patently clear how they had died. A rough time of death, though, would help. Lafarge was perplexed that whilst Giraud had been conscientious in contacting him, he had not done anything else one would routinely do.

"How long will this take Chief Inspector?" asked Zilberstein finally breaking his silence.

"All day," responded Lafarge, barely able to conceal the pleasure he took in seeing the look of annoyance it provoked in Zilberstein.

"Now gentlemen, I would like you to also hand over the weapons these two hoodlums had on them. I would also like an explanation as to why you both appear determined to keep the fuss to a minimum by inventing a story that is so lacking in credibility," said Lafarge.

Zilberstein shot Meissner a glance, the latter may have been technically an employee but to Lafarge's eyes he clearly was the dominant character.

"They didn't have any weapons Chief Inspector. Like I told you one of them pinned me to the desk…." said Zilberstein, stopping mid-sentence when Lafarge held up his hand.

"Where was the other man while you were being pinned to the desk?" asked Lafarge.

"I don't know, I think he was in the room through the archway," said Zilberstein.

"Where were you Meissner?"

"I was in the back, unpacking some paintings we had delivered yesterday. I didn't hear anything, the first thing I knew was when I heard the shots, and came to see what was happening," said Meissner.

Lafarge rubbed his chin as if deep in thought.

"What did the men want? It doesn't look to me that any of the pictures have been disturbed or taken down. Also if as you claim they didn't have weapons what caused all the damage to the walls? I doubt that was you Mr Zilberstein as you made a pretty good mess of Le Vaillant's back," said Lafarge.

Zilberstein shrugged and smiled apologetically.

"Those bullet marks are from the dying days of The

Occupation Chief Inspector. We thought we would leave them as we felt it would attract the curiosity of the customers and add to their interest in the paintings encircled by them," said Zilberstein with a chuckle.

Lafarge got up and went over to double check the veracity of this strange man's story. He ran his fingers over three of them and admitted that part of the account was true, giving them due credit for a bizarre but inventive bit of marketing.

"Alright, but you still haven't told me if you knew these men and what they wanted," said Lafarge.

"No we did not know them. I can ask the staff if they did, but we will need photos in order to do so," said Zilberstein.

"As for what they wanted, the man lying there demanded I accede to his demands and pay protection money."

"I laughed at him and refused, saying I had all the protection I needed, and his type of offer would not flourish in an area such as this. It may work in Pigalle, Pere Lachaise and Montparnasse but not here in Avenue Montaigne."

"That is when he became aggressive, retorting that he had made fortunes during the Occupation in St Germain des Pres, adding that he already had several of my rivals in his pocket."

"Even though he was getting increasingly angry I laughed at that too, for I know for a fact my rivals are too mean to pay a penny for such services. That was when he became physically aggressive."

"The rest you know."

Lafarge nodded and felt he had been telling the truth, or at least a more truthful version than the first one, which wasn't hard but he wondered what Meissner's role had been. Was he telling the truth about being in the back, it would be hard to argue if they went there and found paintings and the crates they had come in. Although he had a fair idea that was what he had been working on when Giraud had found him.

Meissner looked at Zilberstein and then at Lafarge.

"So we hope that answers your questions," said Zilberstein.

Lafarge made to get up but then sat down again, catching the odd couple off guard as he hoped he would.

"I would like their weapons. I just don't see two professional hoodlums, who have made their careers based round carrying guns, coming here unarmed no matter how genteel the area is compared to others," said Lafarge.

"It would also serve your interests Mr Zilberstein that you hand them over, because otherwise I will be obliged to arrest you for murder."

A look of alarm and astonishment crossed Zilberstein's face, he glanced at Meissner, who shrugged and looked away.

"You can't be serious Chief Inspector," said Zilberstein, his voice trembling.

"I am deadly serious. I can understand, if your version of events is true, that you acted in self-defence with Romain, but whilst I have little sympathy for Le Vaillant you shot him in the back and that there is no defence for," said Lafarge.

Zilberstein flinched, his bottom lip quivered, he looked for help from Meissner, but the bullet-headed Alsatian didn't offer any so Lafarge decided to throw a grenade in his direction and hopefully shake him out of his comfort zone.

"You will be coming along as well Meissner, as an accomplice," said Lafarge.

"That's ridiculous Chief Inspector. I told you I was down the back working. I am not responsible for what took place in here," protested Meissner.

"What price loyalty hey Zilberstein?," said Lafarge.

"I just want you to hand me the weapons, then we can perhaps sort something out," he added, throwing in a sweetener.

Neither of them bit, though, which surprised Lafarge. Suddenly a thought, and not a very appealing one occurred to him. Perhaps they were telling the truth after all, and he was being taken for a ride but not by them.

"Giraud, how long did the people from forensics say they would be?" asked Lafarge, turning round in the chair to address Giraud.

Giraud, who was standing over by a fireplace halfway to the entrance looked at his watch and shook his head.

"They said 30 minutes, but perhaps they are stuck in traffic," said Giraud.

Lafarge rose and stretched before moving towards the door

that led to the passageway.

"Mr Zilberstein do you have an office?" asked Lafarge.

Zilberstein still in his sedentary position nodded.

"Right then I suggest you and Mr Meissner go and wait for me there, until I have spoken with the pathologist and forensics," said Lafarge.

"I need one of your men Giraud, to keep an eye on them."

Giraud appeared to hesitate, but then reluctantly ordered the younger of his men to escort the two men. Lafarge was surprised to see that Zilberstein had little difficulty in moving, for he had begun to think perhaps he was disabled as he had sat in the same position for a couple of hours.

Lafarge kept the door slightly ajar, saw that the three men went into the room to the right of the passage, and then placed himself behind Zilberstein's chair.

"They aren't coming are they, Giraud?" Lafarge asked, though it was more rhetorical.

Giraud laughed and shook his head.

"You're being a bit neurotic, no Chief Inspector? Why on earth do you think they aren't coming?" asked Giraud.

"You know very well why they aren't coming Inspector, can you tell your other colleague to come through from the other room please," said Lafarge.

Giraud glared at Lafarge and told his colleague to stay put.

"There is a very good reason why neither Zilberstein nor Meissner could hand me the weapons of Romain and Le Vaillant," said Lafarge, who moved towards the corner of the room to the left of the desk so he could have a better vantage point if the other detective came through the archway.

"It is because one of your men shot Le Vaillant after you Giraud had stabbed Romain. Zilberstein could not have stabbed him as I noticed he had neither blood on his jacket nor on his hands, and even if he had the time to wash it off it would have left traces.

"So I would like you and your colleague who appears to prefer to stay out of sight, itself a sign of guilt, to hand over your service revolvers to prove neither of you fired the bullets."

Giraud grinned and rubbed his forehead, vigorously enough

that he dislodged his trilby.

"You know Chief Inspector there have been rumours you are becoming increasingly erratic and delusional, I dismissed them as I have always held you in the greatest of respect even if you were responsible for having me transferred from Pigalle," said Giraud.

"However, this wild claim of yours, some would call it slanderous, proves the rumours are true after all."

Lafarge sighed, his patience was wearing thin, but he was also aware the likelihood of this stand-off ending peacefully was small and it was at times like this he regretted not having a partner. His previous partner had been killed the year before and it still pained him that they had fallen out just prior to his death.

"You are wrong Giraud. I had nothing to do with your removal. I don't know who fed you that line but such decisions are not in my power, and in any case I deal with murders and not vice," said Lafarge.

"However, even if you hold me responsible for that and breaking up your nice little earner, this is not the reason you called me down here."

Giraud shrugged his shoulders and turned to retrieve his trilby but at the same time clicked his fingers.

Suddenly from the archway spun the other policeman who fired off three shots in Lafarge's direction, but the Chief Inspector had registered the clicking of the fingers and taken evasive action throwing himself behind the desk.

It came at a price as he hit it hard with his left shoulder and though he was right handed and wincing in pain, he was able to pull his service revolver from his shoulder holster.

He did so just in time as the younger detective burst through the door leading to the passageway, this move betraying his inexperience as a veteran would have used the door as protection and fired from the small gap which was available to him.

Lafarge wasn't complaining at his rookie like error and loosed off two shots, both connected with him and he crumpled to the carpet, moaning in agony. Lafarge couldn't tell though whether he was out of the game yet, and he couldn't risk peering round the desk to see how badly wounded he was.

"You've only got four bullets left Lafarge, and there are two of us," Giraud shouted, his voice calm and confident.

"We can come to an arrangement. We can kill the Jew and his Alsatian lover boy, think of it Lafarge a yellow star and a pink star all in one package…and pin these on them.

"I will retire from the force and disappear so you don't have to worry about our paths crossing on the job."

Lafarge was repulsed by Giraud's terminology, harking back to when the Nazis compelled Jews to wear yellow and homosexuals to wear pink stars in the camps. One of the few saving graces of Marshal Petain's collaborationist government was that they refused to impose that law, but more importantly he knew the offer was meaningless.

Giraud would kill him and the other two – that had been the intention from the start he guessed, Meissner and Zilberstein had been kept alive only so long as they were useful in keeping Lafarge in the gallery – and in the most optimistic of possibilities Giraud would, in an act of generosity, hail him as a hero who died in the course of performing his duty.

"No deal Giraud. I will take my chances with four bullets rather than on taking your word for anything," said Lafarge.

"Besides, you and your hoodlum buddies came here to kill me, and whatever your many faults you are renowned for being zealous in pursuit of your goals."

Lafarge took a quick look through the hole in the centre of the desk and cursed himself for Giraud had bought time by disappearing from view. The only consolation was that the wounded detective had stopped moaning. Lafarge could see his only option was to make a go at getting to the door to the passageway and shutting it.

He made a dash for it but he hadn't taken into account that the young detective's feet were blocking him from shutting the door and now he was out in the open. He opted to kick at the feet rather than look up and face the other two detectives.

"Say your prayers Lafarge," growled Giraud and cocked his revolver.

Lafarge did look up at the Inspector but his firing arm also came up at the same instant and he loosed off before Giraud. In one of those fortuitous moments that occasionally entered the Chief Inspector's life Giraud's colleague had spun round into the room not realising how close to the archway his boss was and knocked him off balance.

Giraud and Lafarge swore as two precious bullets were wasted, for being knocked off balance had saved the former's life by inches, one nicking his neck. He still lay on the floor holding a hand to the wound, whilst Lafarge turned his attention to the other man, who had made the error of turning to Giraud instead of firing at him.

Lafarge was grateful that the two colleagues Giraud had enrolled into his criminal scheme had been so badly trained, and fired one bullet into the man's chest killing him instantly.

Lafarge turned the revolver on Giraud, who was climbing to his knees but had left his gun on the ground. Lafarge shook his head as Giraud trailed his arm to the ground reaching for the weapon. The Inspector might have been corrupt and a murderer but he was not a quitter, though, although Lafarge might have added that he was dumb.

Giraud grabbed for the gun and picked it up but Lafarge was ahead of him, and fired the remaining bullet which hit his target in the stomach.

Lafarge bent down over him and could tell he would die before an ambulance reached the gallery.

"Why did you go to all this trouble Giraud?" Lafarge asked the dying man.

Giraud spluttered, blood coming out of his mouth, beads of sweat covering his face.

"Old scores to be settled Lafarge," he gasped.

"But Bonny and Lafont are dead as are most of their gang, and the others have fled," said Lafarge.

Giraud grimaced, although it could have been a smile, one that a gargoyle might make.

"You have plenty of enemies Lafarge, ones who pay well, even from behind prison bars," said Giraud, his voice now barely a whisper.

"That is part and parcel of our job Giraud, we all make enemies, even those of us who pass over to the other side," said Lafarge trying to sound relaxed.

Giraud laughed but it provoked a coughing fit, blood sprayed out of his mouth, some of it splattering Lafarge's jacket.

"Maybe, but it's not something I have to worry about now. You by contrast better watch out every time you take a step outside Quai des Orfevres, or turn the key to your apartment.

"We may have failed but there will be others, for your enemies are not the type to give up. You are a Jew loving Vichy turncoat detective and you deserve to die very slowly, the price is the same however long it takes."

That was the final straw for Lafarge. His always fragile temperament snapped and believing there was little other information Giraud would be willing to give up he put his fingers round the Inspector's nostrils and held them tight ensuring his last few moments on earth were as painful as possible.

Chapter Three

"Three dead policemen and two gangsters, when I wished you a Happy New Year and hoped you would bring it in with a bang I did not mean it literally Gaston," remarked Lucien Pinault, commissaire of the Brigade Criminelle and Lafarge's superior.

Lafarge, who was sat with a large glass of Pinault's cognac in the commissaire's large office overlooking the Place Dauphine at his headquarters in the Quai des Orfevres, chuckled.

Pinault took a sip from his coffee cup as he had yet to have lunch so it was a bit early for cognac.

Lafarge had not had lunch but he never passed an opportunity if there was a cognac on offer –he found as it helped him at least to dull the pain of the constant misery he had to deal with whether they were the families of the victims or occasionally the culprits – and he knew Pinault's Courvoisier was excellent.

Ironically it was one instance where he had a German soldier to thank for him still being able to drink his favourite tipple, as a Lieutenant Gustav Klaebisch, whose family had been involved with the cognac region in between the wars, had ensured that not all the stocks were snaffled by his comrades.

He was one German whose hand Lafarge would not hesitate to shake, he would have more of a problem in shaking Klaebisch's brother-in-law's hand, former German Foreign Minister Joachim von Ribbentrop who probably wished he had stayed in the wine sales business as he was now imprisoned awaiting trial for war crimes in Nuremberg.

"Do you have any idea who could have ordered this hit on you?" asked Pinault bringing Lafarge back to the real world.

Lafarge shook his head.

"All Giraud said was there are plenty of enemies of mine both inside and outside prison who had collaborated, probably the operative word as some would have profited under Vichy and the Nazis, to have me killed," said Lafarge.

"Do you think Zilberstein and Meissner are involved in any way?"

"I don't think so sir. The way they acted throughout the charade played out by Giraud they appeared genuinely petrified. Even when I pulled them out of the office I had told them to go to so as to make them safer they didn't register anything approaching disappointment that it was me and not Giraud who had survived," said Lafarge.

Pinault contorted his large pink lips – a sign he was in reflective mood though rather disconcerting for his interlocutors – and ran his thin fingers through his greased back black hair, before withdrawing them and then looking at them rather distastefully.

"Okay well who is top of your list, three will do," Pinault said as he wiped his fingers free of grease.

Lafarge scratched his chin, a rather more conventional way of thinking things through.

"You may groan but I think Bousquet is certainly involved and as for others, well the metals guy Joseph Joanovici and any number of who remains from the Bonny Lafont gang," said Lafarge.

Lafarge had a good idea who else might wish him dead.

He wasn't going to mention Pierre-Yves de Chastelain, partly because he still wasn't certain the lawyer survived the war but mostly due to the fact it would take them back to the murder of the starlet Marguerite Suchet in 1942 and he did not wish any part of that investigation to be revisited.

Their antipathy dated back to before The Occupation when they had regularly crossed swords in the court room. De Chastelain's overzealous defence of his clients had often led to fiery exchanges with the lawyer accusing Lafarge of corrupting witnesses. Their confrontations became so notorious the public queued to watch them and even took to betting in the local cafes as to who would emerge victorious.

To Lafarge it was no game as he felt he was having to defend the honour of the police whilst de Chastelain appeared to believe that Lafarge epitomised endemic corruption in the force..

"Hmm that would be a collection of real beauties," said Pinault.

"However, Bousquet is in prison awaiting trial on a charge which carries the death penalty if found guilty, so I am not sure he would want to make matters far worse for himself by being part of a plot to murder a senior policeman," said Pinault.

"Well you can't be hanged twice sir," interjected Lafarge.

"Erm yes quite. Anyway as we learned Bousquet was not involved in the murder of your father in Fresnes, and there he had much more opportunity. The only people I am told who visit him are his lawyer and his wife and children and whilst they are faithful to him I don't see them being the go-betweens with a gang of killers," said Pinault

"I would still like to go and see him sir. He hates me so much and fears what I could say in court in his trial that I am certain he is the driving force behind it," said Lafarge.

Pinault nodded.

"I would love to put Joanovici behind bars, the fat swine deserves the death penalty as much as anyone," said Pinault.

"One obstacle sir, he pays us hush money," said Lafarge, knowing his bluntness would irritate Pinault but he had seen it happen with the Moldovan-born metals magnate, who had escaped the fate of his fellow Jews due to his ability to enrich the Nazis and Vichy members during the war, passing an envelope to the Prefect of Police Charles Luizet.

"Yes I know your feelings on that topic Chief Inspector, but I thought we had moved on," Pinault said testily.

Lafarge held his hands up.

"However, I have trouble in believing Joanovici would join forces with the remnants of thc Bonny and Lafont gang. If there is one person they would prefer to see dead ahead of you Chief Inspector, it is Joanovici," said Pinault.

"It was him after all who ratted out their bosses by telling us where they were in hiding as a means of buying more life insurance for himself from de Gaulle. As you can see he got it, but I would wager the fools who have stayed behind are looking to get back at him when they can.

"Joanovici for his part I doubt gives a damn about you with the greatest respect. All he cares about is Joseph Joanovici and staying alive and out of court, the latter he may find harder and harder to avoid."

Lafarge took Pinault's point for whilst each of those he had mentioned had good reason to want him dead, there appeared little logic in Joanovici teaming up with a group of people who also wanted him dead. Rumour had it as well that Joanovici's coffers – which had overflowed during the Occupation with his handsome rewards for supplying metals to the Nazis – were running dry.

"Well then sir I am a bit stumped, you have done a superb job on shooting down every one of my top three," said Lafarge smiling.

Pinault also smiled and gestured for Lafarge to have another glass, which he willingly accepted.

"Not at all, there is no harm in you going to see Bousquet. You can read him very well, although he may refuse to see you which is his right. As for the Bonny Lafont thugs, I am afraid there you will have to rely on grasses to root them out," said Pinault.

"If it is them acting as the muscle then it is more likely they will find you rather than the other way round."

Lafarge acknowledged that Pinault was right. He could ask his grasses if they had heard anything but if they had been threatened they were more than likely to take his money and lie to him. A bit of time inside was worth it more than a bullet in the back of the head if they were caught grassing – he didn't think him telling them about the way he dispensed justice a few years back would have the same effect.

Nope, all he could console himself with was going and taunting Bousquet, which was always a good way of getting something out of one's system.

Firstly, he returned to the gallery as he wished to question Zilberstein and Meissner, who he had left in a state of shock after they emerged from the office and saw three further corpses in the show room.

Despite Lafarge believing they were innocent parties they could also provide invaluable firsthand eye-witness testimony. He hoped that Zilberstein having been liberated from the bristling menace of Giraud and his men would be more forthcoming, the Chief Inspector also counted on the two men being indebted to him for saving their lives.

He found Zilberstein fussing over the fingerprint man daubing too close to a Manet whilst Meissner was remonstrating with a gendarme demanding he be allowed to call their cleaner so she could come and start the arduous task of trying to make the gallery presentable so they could re-open.

The gendarme shrugged his shoulders, pointed to Lafarge and walked off to smoke outside.

Meissner glowered at Lafarge but could see any further protestations would be fruitless.

"I am sorry Monsieur Meissner but the gallery will remain closed until we are satisfied we have gathered all the information we require," sad Lafarge, silently enjoying the simmering fury and frustration of the stern Alsatian.

"I think this is preposterous. The gangsters are all dead and have been taken away. No one else was here, so any other fingerprints will be of the staff, us, you and clients who were here yesterday," said Meissner, who despite his best efforts could not quell his natural pugnacity.

"I understand your concern but a major crime has taken place, the attempted murder of a senior police officer, and five people have been killed. Unfortunately for you it took place here and as a result like any crime scene, it has to be gone over meticulously as other clues may be thrown up," said Lafarge.

"You and Monsiour Zilberstein can help in speeding up that process by answering some questions."

Meissner nodded and called over to Zilberstein to come over. Lafarge earned a look of gratitude from the fingerprint man, who resumed his careful dusting of the wall.

Lafarge ushered them into the office, a large room with three comfortable soft-backed armchairs seated round a marble-topped coffee table, and a large desk with a Louis XV chair behind it. They all sat in the armchairs, Zilberstein rather more composed than he had been when pestering the fingerprint man, and asked Lafarge if he would like a drink to which the Chief Inspector replied by asking for a cognac.

Meissner and Zilberstein both opted for Scotch and lit cigars,

Lafarge declining their offer of a Cosechero, made of the finest Nicaraguan tobacco, preferring his French brand of cigarettes Gitanes.

Both men said they were non-plussed by why their gallery should have been chosen when they were one of many in the street, though Meissner conjectured perhaps it was because they were considered one of the best. Zilberstein nodded sagely, taking brief comfort from such a thought.

Lafarge learned that the two hoodlums had shown up first, followed 10 minutes later by the detectives. The quintet barely talked to each other and did not appear to be on good terms. Indeed Giraud remarked that he had sought for years to arrest Le Vaillant and now fate had put them in the same room.

Le Vaillant had got increasingly angry at being needled by Giraud, and said but for the money he would have walked out. Romain had begun to get riled too but instead of confronting Giraud he had made anti-Semitic remarks and waved his gun in front of Zilberstein's face.

He had pushed Zilberstein into the chair behind his desk and it was at that point Giraud had seized the letter opener and as Romain turned round he stabbed him in the eye. Le Vaillant had made for the door but as Lafarge had seen from the corpse he had been shot twice in the back by Giraud.

It turned out that had always been the plan, the two gangsters had been set up as the victims – Lafarge grinned sardonically at the thought of them being considered as such – for Giraud had said as much to his two subordinates.

Giraud then had got Zilberstein to ring the Quai and ask specifically for Lafarge and thus the trap had been set.

Lafarge found Zilberstein's account convincing, and it was chilling the lengths this syndicate who wished him dead would go to in achieving their goal. He had more or less emerged unscathed from previous attempts on his life but he had not encountered such professionalism before – in the planning if not the execution.

"Did you overhear Giraud say anything to his men about who had paid them?" asked Lafarge.

Both men shook their heads, Meissner adding that aside from instructions as to where they were to position themselves before Lafarge turned up and Giraud feeding Zilberstein the story, he was to tell the Chief Inspector there was little conversation.

Lafarge took a sip of the excellent cognac, which went some way to suppressing his rising anxiety over his safety, and thought except for the drink it had largely been a wasted journey. However, his ever suspicious mind told him something about the two men was not quite right.

He couldn't put his finger on it but being experienced in the vagaries of human nature - they made him feel uncomfortable.

He decided he would ruffle their feathers a bit and see what fell from the tree. He was not sure Giraud had been correct in thinking they were close in the sexual sense, but there was to Lafarge's mind something unusual in their relationship.

"How long have you owned the gallery?" asked Lafarge, not specifying as to who the question was directed.

He noticed an exchange of looks, Meissner seemingly directing Zilberstein to respond, although the latter did not look too happy at being ordered to do so.

"We bought it two years ago, soon after the Liberation," replied Zilberstein.

"Who did you buy it from?" Lafarge asked deciding now to solely address Zilberstein, because he felt one of the reasons he was terse in his responses was that his nerves were taut and if he exerted enough pressure he might prompt him to divulge more information than he wished to.

"I don't see what business this is of yours Chief Inspector," retorted Zilberstein, and Lafarge heard a barely audible hear hear from Meissner.

"Answer the question Mr Zilberstein, I am here as part of the investigation into an attempted murder of a senior police officer, a double homicide and perhaps for good measure throw in an attempted armed robbery of your premises. So I think my questions are pertinent," said Lafarge evenly.

"There was no attempted robbery Chief Inspector," protested Meissner.

Lafarge held his arm up to cut him off.

"Listen if I were here to look over your paintings as a prospective buyer I would not attempt to second guess your expertise, so kindly do the same with regard to my being the expert in criminal matters and what I say is law," said Lafarge.

"That is well put Chief Inspector but I think you are going too far, you know very well there was no intent to rob the gallery," said Meissner, his eyes glinting with a determination and strength that Zilberstein's lacked.

There was little doubt Lafarge had sized them up correctly but that was counter-balanced by having both in the same room, for Meissner's defiance could only serve to stiffen Zilberstein's resolve .

He cursed himself for not having questioned them separately, it had been with the good intention of giving the forensic man a bit of peace and quiet and also he thought it would be a mere formality.

Lafarge decided to ignore Meissner's protestations without saying as much, thinking this might hit home to Zilberstein that there was only one boss in the room and it wasn't his Alsatian partner.

"Who did you buy it from Mr Zilberstein?," asked Lafarge, keeping his tone amiable but firm.

Zilberstein looked distinctly flustered, realising that there was no avoiding answering the question now that Meissner had been put in his place by Lafarge.

"We bought it from Hal Rosenberg," said Zilberstein.

Lafarge could not believe it. That was a name he had not expected to hear of again, although he thought of Hal Rosenberg and his beautiful wife Evelyn a lot, the latter rather too much even though he had only met her once under the most dangerous of circumstances.

He knew Rosenberg was an art dealer but when he had rescued them from their apartment– such discussions had not been at the top of the agenda.

They had been lucky in that Lafarge had been feeling in a courageous and rebellious mood and offered to safeguard them in his flat when two fellow plainclothes detectives from the

Brigades Speciales had come to the building with uniformed gendarmes to sweep up the Jews living there.

He had been unable to save either the Horowitz's or the other Jewish family as they lived on floors above him but the Rosenberg's had salved his conscience – that and a fair amount of cognac since.

They had disappeared soon afterwards and he had not heard from them since the Liberation, but if Zilberstein was telling the truth then this was the first piece of evidence they had survived and also a rare bit of good news on a thoroughly shocking day.

He hoped neither Meissner nor Zilberstein had remarked on his look of surprise, for he did not feel inclined to impart that he knew them. He did wonder, why Rosenberg, having survived the war, would wish to divest himself of his gallery and a prime piece of real estate.

That riddle he would have to try and solve for himself, provided Pinault would allow him to.

He did allow himself one probing question around the sale, he hoped without revealing too much of why he would be taking an interest in the vendor.

"Did you know Rosenberg from before the Occupation?" asked Lafarge.

Zilberstein nodded.

"What were you, friends, rivals, colleagues perhaps?"

"We were shall one say friendly rivals," he smiled.

"Where was your gallery?"

"I had mine in the Marais. It was a more modest affair than this one, but I did well enough and occasionally I would even sell to Rosenberg, though he lacked for little in terms of paintings and artists.

"However, when you get as high as he did there is always the need for more and I possessed some of the newer painters that he felt could be the future for his gallery," said Zilberstein, suddenly warming to the task of answering questions.

Lafarge mused Zilberstein had done remarkably well to be able to purchase the gallery in Avenue Montaigne regardless of however many paintings he had sold to Rosenberg.

"You are Jewish I take it Mister Zilberstein," said Lafarge.

"I would say your powers of observation are remarkable," replied Zilberstein, displaying a hitherto hidden ability for sarcasm.

Lafarge did not bat an eyelid, he was far happier with a Zilberstein who was growing in confidence and liable to fall into a trap than the timid mouse he had first encountered. Meissner must have sensed this as he tried to intervene.

"Careful, you do not want to rile the Chief Inspector," said Meissner trying to sound jocular but his warning to his partner was implicit.

"So being Jewish I imagine you spent the Occupation abroad or worse hiding in France. The latter must have been a terrible experience for your nerves," said Lafarge.

Zilberstein reached for his drink, Lafarge could not miss that his hand shook ever so slightly as he raised it to his lips.

Zilberstein swore and with his silk handkerchief wiped the lapel clean.

"You should mop your brow too," said Lafarge.

Zilberstein looked askance at the Chief Inspector and then did so.

"I was joking Mister Zilberstein," said Lafarge.

Zilberstein clearly did not find the joke very amusing, Meissner even less so.

"If that is all Chief Inspector, or at the very least if you could finish up soon it has been a very long and tiring day and we would hope to be able to open tomorrow," said Meissner.

"I am still waiting for an answer from Mister Zilberstein," said Lafarge icily.

"I spent part of the Occupation hiding in Paris, some French friends looked after me, but then with the Rafle it became too risky for them and I was passed down a line of Resistants," said Zilberstein.

"I ended up in Bordeaux and then eventually made it to Algeria after it had been liberated."

"You did not waste any time," said Lafarge.

Zilberstein looked confused and stared at him seeking clarification as to what he was implying but Lafarge was not going to give him any.

"Algeria was not to my taste and besides I wanted to return and reclaim my apartment and my gallery," said Zilberstein.

"I can understand that Mister Zilberstein, and as it turns out your speed was fortuitous as you ended up with this gallery. If you had dallied a bit longer the opportunity might have passed to someone else," said Lafarge with his most disarming tone.

Zilberstein nodded appreciatively.

"Yes indeed, I was most fortunate that Rosenberg came to my gallery on the first day of my return and after a good lunch – what passes for decent these days although the rationing is nothing compared to the Occupation – we drew up an agreement of sale," said Zilberstein.

"You said during the Occupation?" asked Lafarge.

"Oh did I, my apologies a slip of the tongue!" said Zilberstein with a little chuckle, though Lafarge observed it seemed a nervous one.

"Did he offer you a reasonable price? It must have been, for disappearing during the Occupation did not come cheap," said Lafarge.

"I had enough saved," said Zilberstein defensively.

"Don't worry Mister Zilberstein I am not going to ask you how much you paid. After all you experienced during the Occupation I am pleased things have turned out well for you," said Lafarge smiling, though he felt anything but warmth towards the man.

"I am sure Mr Rosenberg would not have sold to you unless he felt he was getting the price he felt he merited, so I will not be looking into that."

"I should hope so Chief Inspector as I do not see that it has anything to do with you in any case," said Meissner, prickly as ever.

Lafarge for once turned to Meissner and looked straight into his eyes. He was not someone to mess with surmised Lafarge, or at least that was the impression he tried to project.

Lafarge, though, had never been a respecter of people and their reputations, only their acts could earn them his respect, and that came by being tested.

"So Mr Meissner how did you become involved in the gallery.

Did you too know Mr Rosenberg, or were you part of the furniture?" asked Lafarge, judging such a colloquialism could annoy Meissner's prissy nature.

He laughed inwardly as he saw Meissner bristle.

"No Chief Inspector I was not a staff member here before the Occupation, I was an art dealer in Strasbourg," said Meissner.

"I did, however, know both Mr Rosenberg and Mr Zilberstein, the latter rather well. We stayed in touch until the military and their British counterparts betrayed the country and allowed the Nazis a free run and for obvious reasons explained by Edouard we lost contact.

"However, he got back in touch with me when he learned I had moved to Paris and suggested that the gallery was too big an entity for him to run on his own and invited me to run it with him," said Meissner.

There was a tone of finality to Meissner's response, that their patience had run out and the Chief Inspector should pick up his hat and be on his way. Lafarge was for once in complete agreement with them.

He bid them farewell, leaving them behind to clear up what remained of the mess – forensics had finished too – and with looks of relief on their faces as he shut the door and disappeared into the cold misty night.

Their belief that they could get on uninterrupted with their lives would be swiftly dispelled for Lafarge didn't believe their story one bit and once he had the scent of wrongdoing in his nostrils it was as magnetic to his persona as that of cognac -- it had to be tackled.

Chapter Four

Hal Rosenberg played on Lafarge's mind on the journey home.

He would be very happy if Rosenberg – whose anglicised first name came from his American mother according to Zilberstein – and his wife had survived the Occupation but then if that was the case surely they would have come and reclaimed their apartment.

He could have sold his gallery to Zilberstein for any number of reasons but if he really needed money – many returning Jews who had evaded the security forces during the war found that their protectors did not do it all out of the goodness of their heart but demanded a high price to do so – surely selling the apartment would have been his priority so he could keep his business and generate some capital.

Lafarge admitted to himself he was hardly one to judge what was good business sense given his own possessions were so meagre, his father had not left much when he died the year before and his step-mother had unsurprisingly cut him out of her altered her will prior to her execution as he had been responsible for her predicament.

Fortunately though, he had not sold his flat as he had kept an open mind on whether Rosenberg would return at some point and it appeared he had been wise to do so. The question was, how did he try and find him?. The Hotel Lutetia, which had been perhaps chosen by someone with a dark sense of humour as the centre for welcoming back those who had survived the camps and forced labour , as it had also been the headquarters for the German secret service the Abwehr, had returned to being a business concern.

He sighed as he entered his apartment building near Pere Lachaise – he was a few blocks down from the grand entrance to the massive cemetery – realising that if he is to track him down it will take a lot of sifting through papers and legwork in the displaced persons camps where they must have lists of those who had been through the system.

The trouble as always with Lafarge was he didn't know whether he was going down a particular path due to altruistic reasons or because he had taken a dislike to a particular person, in this case persons plural in Zilberstein and Meissner. He doubted Pinault would be willing to dispense man hours on a hunch even if his hunches usually proved to be correct.

The policeman's lot appeared to be reactive not proactive, which had a certain logic to it because if one was stepping in before a crime was committed there would not be much call for detective work and indeed arrests would be superfluous as no crime had taken place. It was all rather Kafkaesque thought Lafarge.

He could see the concierge Madame Grondon was at home, but he did not think it worth disturbing her on such a cold night by calling her out and asking her if she had seen the Rosenberg's, and besides he was looking forward to spending a rare evening en famille with Aimee and their baby boy Ancil.

Aimee had wished to call him that because it meant 'God's protection' and whilst Lafarge was far from being a devout Catholic – he understood his beloved's reasoning.

Aimee was putting Ancil into his cot when he arrived. Aimee looked stunning even dressed modestly, blue trousers, a cream shirt and a scarf knotted round her throat with her blonde hair tied back.

To his relief she appeared to be in a good mood this evening. Her mood swings had become more frequent when Lafarge had hoped they might decrease as time slowly moved on from her appalling experiences in Ravensbruck. There were days when even getting out of bed was a challenge for her and talking was out of the question. On those occasions Lafarge was loathe to leave her, fearing that she might do herself and Ancil harm.

Madame Grondon remained as loyal as ever – she had certainly had to put up with enough drama and violence surrounding Lafarge in the past few years but always made it appear as if it was no bother to clear up afterwards – and would occasionally step in and look after Ancil. She said it prepared her well for becoming a grandmother, though she was getting increasingly impatient as her three daughters and one son had yet to produce a grandchild.

Quite often Aimee would sleep in the same bedroom as Ancil leaving Lafarge to snore away on his own, another hangover from Ravensbruck.

He was in two minds whether to tell her about the attempt on his life and that it was unlikely to be the last if Giraud had been telling the truth. But if he was in danger then so was she and Ancil. So once she had come out of the bedroom and he had poured them a glass of red wine each he told her.

She took the news calmly. As Aimee had experienced being totally powerless and waking up every day for a year with the possibility of being picked at random to be put to death, then she considered he was in a better position for at least he knew he was a marked man. Plus he carried a gun.

"That is awful Gaston. What are you going to do about it? You have been involved in some close shaves before, but this is the first time I can recall you are the actual target," said Aimee.

"That is true," he said, cursing that despite his best efforts to try and move on it was hard to banish from his mind the lengthy list of family who were either dead or incarcerated.

"I have told Pinault and we will take measures in as much as we can to prevent another attempt and also endeavour to find out who is behind this. I was going to go and see Bousquet as I am sure he is involved but it is probably a waste of time and will only end with me wanting to save the executioner an early morning rise," added Lafarge.

"Good I am relieved you are not going to spend some much needed funds and petrol to go to Fresnes just so you can get your monthly fix of gloating over Bousquet," said Aimee, a note of frustration in her tone.

"I think he has rather more on his mind than concocting plots from there to get rid of you. I imagine like me he knows with your powers of self-destruction you will implode all by yourself."

Lafarge bristled at her remark, which carried a fair amount of truth in it. Pinault too thought Lafarge had an unhealthy obsession with Bousquet.

Yet they had not seen his preening opportunism and cold blooded determination to rise as high as possible within Vichy, trying to be more German than the Germans in compiling the lists of the Jews – even children whom the Nazis had neither asked for nor were particularly happy to have on their hands -- and drawing up the plans for the Round-up.

Lafarge, though, would leave him be for the moment, hoping that they would succeed in arresting those responsible and as a bonus they might admit Bousquet had also been involved.

"I would like you to take extra care Aimee when you are out for a walk with Ancil. These bastards will probably consider you fair game," said Lafarge.

"They will be furious their plan this morning failed and will want to strike fast, no doubt aiming for the most exposed and innocent parties.

"Despite our meagre resources in terms of personnel, Pinault has organised to have a gendarme stationed outside the building and someone in plainclothes to follow you when you take Ancil out.

"I can take care of myself. Hopefully this whole business will be sorted out soon enough, one way or the other but my primary concern is for you and Ancil.."

Aimee looked alarmed but Lafarge's assurances calmed her nerves – her anxiety understandable in normal circumstances but in her case even more so, having thought she had found a safe haven from the horrors of Ravensbruck to be told there could be imminent danger was not what she needed to hear.

She walked over and kissed him on the lips and poured them both another glass whilst informing Lafarge that she had made a cassoulet – made up of the ingredients he had procured from his black market snitch as rationing was still firmly in place and causing the populace great hardship made worse by it being a foul winter.

Lafarge did not feel any great remorse that he was able to prevail upon an outside source for such thing. As far as he was concerned he had a family to feed and he was at least keeping the streets safe or trying to.

"Well I have some news for you too Gaston," said Aimee once she settled back having put the cassoulet on the stove.

Lafarge sat forward on his ageing and increasingly tatty leather armchair, which was the only piece of furniture in the apartment that belonged to him. Despite Aimee's constant pleas for him to throw it out he held on to it as he felt it was the one constant in his life and had been for years. It reassured him every time he walked into the apartment to see it in all its battered faded elegance.

"I was hoping you could perhaps stay here tomorrow and look after Ancil, I asked Madame Grondon but she has to go to hospital for a check-up."

Lafarge groaned as he wanted to track down other acquaintances of Rosenberg's and find out whether Zilberstein's story really held water.

"I have an audition for a film at midday and I don't think bringing Ancil would gain me many bonus points even before I have opened my mouth."

That changed it for Lafarge, he could not have been more delighted both for Aimee's morale and also that she had perhaps started to get her life outside the apartment back on track, for she had not indicated an interest in acting since she returned.

"Aimee that is fabulous. What is the film and who is the director?" asked Lafarge smiling broadly.

Aimee too looked genuinely happy for once, no wonder she had looked radiant when he returned.

"The title of the film is 'L'assassin n'est pas coupable' and the director is Rene Delacroix," said Aimee.

"I have not heard of him, has he got a good reputation?" asked Lafarge, who went to the cinema a lot.

Aimee looked not in the least disappointed that Delacroix's name failed to register with Lafarge.

"I am not surprised as it is only the second film he has directed, the first came out in 1939. However, he appears a decent chap, even if he is somewhat lacking in humour due no doubt to his being a devout Roman Catholic," she said.

"Anyway it looks as if Albert Prejean will star in it so that is a good sign. It is a subject you would like very much too as it revolves round murder.....sadly for my profession it is the murders of actors on a set."

"Well I seriously hope I won't be called to your set to investigate a murder! Life imitating art and all that," Lafarge joked, to which to his relief Aimee laughed.

"That is fantastic though Aimee. Prejean is a decent actor so this chap must be alright. Even for a devout Catholic, just remember your rosary beads and go to confession before you go to the audition, but lay off the communion wine," Lafarge added with a grin.

*

Aimee left early the next morning wearing an all tartan red and black check ensemble with a pill box green hat and green gloves. He occupied himself with feeding Ancil, played with him a bit, throwing a ball at him and then recovering it as at two-years-old he wasn't fully tuned in to the reciprocity part of the game.

It did not take Lafarge long to get bored of the game and it dawned on him that retirement or at least leaving the police and becoming a private detective held few attractions if he were to be at a loose end for days.

Fortunately Ancil too grew tired of clapping his hands together and failing to catch the ball, so Lafarge thought of putting him back into his cot and reading to him. It was just as he was on his way to do this there came a knock at the door.

Wary given the events of the day before, he placed Ancil in the cot, shutting the door behind him. He went and fetched his service revolver and called out asking who was there.

"Hal Rosenberg."

Lafarge had to make up his mind as to whether this was a ruse, he could not recall Rosenberg's voice as he had only engaged in conversation with him once before and that was four years ago.

He looked through the peephole but could not see the visitor clearly as the passageway as usual was badly light and the man was cast half in shadow. Finally his curiosity and a desire to get to the bottom of the Rosenberg story over-rode his prudence so he opened the door with the chain still attached.

To his relief it was indeed Rosenberg, though, he was an emaciated version of the vibrant good looking if nervy man he had saved the day of the Rafle. Lafarge smiled – though the warmth of that was countered by the gun he was holding in his free hand and which was protruding through the gap of the open door.

He quickly withdrew it and unchained the door, shaking Rosenberg's hand.

Rosenberg on first appearance to Lafarge aside from his shrunken physique did not look like someone who had come into money of late. His grey suit was crumpled and there was mud on the hems of his trousers, the collar of his blue shirt was frayed at the edges and his striped tie had stains on it.

Lafarge knew instantly that he would be paying another visit to Zilberstein, for the man had clearly been lying.

Firstly they exchanged pleasantries and Lafarge explained he had been lucky to find him at home as his wife had had to go to an audition.

"I know I was watching the building from across the street and have been for several days," said Rosenberg.

"I observed this morning your wife leaving alone – she is a beautiful woman Chief Inspector, very stylish too. So I concluded that you had been left here to look after your child.

"I took my chance to come and see you. I thought Madame Grondon would have warned you, but evidently she is still in shock at seeing me alive. Fair enough as millions of my fellow Jews did not survive the war," he said bitterly.

Lafarge was a little put out that he had been so wrapped up in his own business throughout the week that he had not noticed this frail looking dishevelled unshaven man watching from across the street, or perhaps he had hidden every time he saw him return.

That in any case was irrelevant now – just a matter of his pride being pricked –and also a warning for the future with regard to be more vigilant. He invited Rosenberg to sit which was a bit odd reflected Lafarge, as this was actually the man's own flat.

Lafarge poured them a generous dose each, though he was mindful of his responsibility of looking after Ancil and therefore would have to go easy on how much he imbibed.

"So Mr Rosenberg I really do not know where to start, for once I am at a loss as there is so much I want to ask you, you have been often in my thoughts these past few years," said Lafarge having settled in his armchair after checking on Ancil, who was fast asleep.

"I guess the first thing is I must explain why you find me in your apartment!

"It must look as if I took advantage of your disappearance and moved myself in from my rather decrepit flat but I can assure you I have not touched any of your things. As you can see all the paintings are hanging where they were when you had to leave."

Lafarge stopped – he had been on the point of somewhat tactlessly telling him his clothes were still in the wardrobe -- as Rosenberg had raised his hand with an empty glass in it, which he dutifully filled but left his as it was. Rosenberg used this pause to get a word in of his own.

"Firstly please call me Hal, hearing the sound of it makes me feel so good and almost reborn," said Rosenberg, his voice surprisingly strong given his physical appearance.

"I will tell you the details later as to why it feels so good but you can guess that with a name like mine I was obliged to change it when we went into hiding. However, before we go into that part of the story I also wanted to say I certainly bear no grudge against you for living here, if there is anyone I would have liked to see inhabit the place it is you Chief Inspector.

"You are one of the few who showed any kindness to us over the past few years, and you above all stand out as you saved our lives at a great risk to your own. So do not feel any guilt at all and I am here to talk to you not to repossess the apartment, as I do not intend to stay in Paris for long," said Rosenberg.

Lafarge felt a lump rise in his throat as he was not used to hearing such touching sentiments expressed about him. Indeed it was a remarkable thing that he and Aimee were together as he had once sacrificed her along with members of her family so he could spirit away a fugitive back to Paris, although he had ensured that she was saved by one of his colleagues. But it pleased him as he had been one of the few policemen to obstruct Bousquet's orders that infamous day.

What pleased him more was he had done it for altruistic reasons not because of his hatred for Bousquet and it was just about the only decent thing he had done throughout the Occupation.

Rosenberg had fallen silent all of a sudden, Lafarge would not have been surprised if this was due to exhaustion as the man sported dark shadows under his eyes.

"Forgive me Hal if you think I am being insensitive in not asking you about your wife and indeed how you spent the rest of the Occupation but your name came up the other day quite by chance," said Lafarge.

"I came across a man called Zilberstein and his business partner Meissner," said Lafarge leaving it at that so as to gauge Rosenberg's reaction.

A look of fury and then misery passed over Rosenberg's features, reassuring Lafarge his instinct about the two partners had been correct. He needed to know now how bad their treatment of Rosenberg had been.

"That man betrayed my wife and I, he is a murderer," said Rosenberg, his voice taking on a very different tone to the amiable one had had up till then.

"Who is, Zilberstein or Meissner?" asked Lafarge, upset for Rosenberg to have lost his wife with his money on the murderer being the ice cold Meissner .

"Zilberstein. Meissner has so much blood on his hands that my wife's is of little importance when you tot up the numbers on his account," hissed Rosenberg.

Lafarge was intrigued, this he had not expected. He had thought he might be looking at a case of fraud but murder, well that pleased him even more in view of his dislike for the two men. They had probably thought they were going to enjoy a fruitful life without anyone suspecting a thing and people accepting their response if they asked that Rosenberg had sold up and migrated to the States.

It amused him to think how uncomfortable they must be feeling now that purely by chance their gallery had been chosen for an attempt on a detective's life and thus drawn unwelcome attention on them – their discomfit would have been all the greater had they known Lafarge had saved Rosenberg's life.

"How did Zilberstein come to murder your wife?"

Rosenberg rubbed his hands nervously and looked to be on the verge of tears.

"I will come to that Chief Inspector, let me take you through the whole sordid story," he said, his voice calmness personified in comparison to the jerky movements he was making with his hands.

Lafarge refilled Rosenberg's glass and his own as he felt he might need it for what was to come. He stole a glance at the grandfather clock that stood by the entrance and saw it had gone midday which gave him an hour more – Ancil would have to be fed then and he doubted Aimee would return till late afternoon.

"That is interesting Hal, because they told me that you had sold Zilberstein the gallery. That you had known him before the War and had approached him following the Liberation," said Lafarge feeling it only fair to give him their version of events much as he knew it was total rubbish.

Rosenberg groaned.

"We met Zilberstein when we went underground in Paris. I certainly did not know him from before the war. From what I can ascertain the truth and him are not well known to each other, he was a dentist and operated out of a smart address near Avenue Foch," said Rosenberg.

"We had thought of going to our local doctor Dr Marcel Petiot and paying him to help us escape, but my wife had a sixth sense about him and said he made her feel uneasy. Indeed she had stopped going to see him well before the Nazis arrived."

Lafarge agreed that Rosenberg's wife had been spot on in her assessment of the good doctor, pity he had not been as wise. He had liked and trusted Petiot and had handed over Pierre-Yves de Chastelain, the fugitive lawyer he had brought back from Limoges, into his hands preferring him to Bousquet. Petiot had been uncovered subsequently to be a psychopath who had offered false promises of escape to all sorts of people from gangsters who had fallen out with the Bonny and Lafont gang, couples, families and individuals all united by one factor - they could afford his exorbitant fees.

Their escape route had been to end up as a pile of ashes in his cellar in his large house in Rue Sueur also near to Avenue Foch – he had since been guillotined although he had admitted to Lafarge he had spared de Chastelain, which should have been good news for the Chief Inspector save that the lawyer believed, correctly as it happened, he had murdered his ex-girlfriend.

Lafarge, though, pushed those uncomfortable memories to the back of his mind and gestured for Rosenberg to resume his story.

"We did have friends in common, even some who were now actively collaborating with the Nazis. People like Jean Luchaire, Sacha Guitry and Fernand de Brinon had been clients of both of us.

"Ironic when you think about it both Luchaire and de Brinon becoming virulent anti-Semites and yet they thought little about buying art from me and having their mouths prodded and poked at by a Jew. But that of course was before the Occupation," he smiled sourly.

"I did think of going to de Brinon and asking him for false papers but thought better of it. He was an arch hypocrite, married to a Jewish woman who of course he saved from the camps whilst whipping up anti-Semitic feelings and being an enthusiastic proponent of the Rafle."

"Zilberstein did have the chutzpah to approach de Brinon, who responded favourably because he said despite him being Jewish he was the only dentist who he had never felt any pain after paying a visit," said Rosenberg.

"Thus Zilberstein continued to practice, albeit discreetly with a smaller list of patients, all recommended to him by de Brinon so you can imagine the type, female and male.

"Abetz, Bousquet, Leguay, Lafont and Bonny hypocrites all came to see Zilberstein. Many a time I would implore Zilberstein to overdo the anaesthetic or inject them with some liquid that would induce a painful death but he would refuse," added Rosenberg bitterly.

Lafarge reluctantly conceded it was a wise decision on Zilberstein's part and would have been extremely foolish to sacrifice one's life for just one Nazi. He, however, whilst interested by Rosenberg's story wanted to hurry him along a bit as there would be time in the future to hear the detailed version but for the moment he was more interested in how Zilberstein had been responsible for his wife's murder and then stole the gallery.

"So both of you hid in Zilberstein's apartment? Or did he pass you on to a sympathetic family?"

"We stayed with him. He had a large house in Neuilly. Again I was surprised that he managed to carry on living there for despite de Brinon's protection, I do not think the others knew he was Jewish, his neighbours would have been aware of his religion."

Lafarge shrugged, he knew too well that some neighbours had behaved correctly during the Occupation. Some had simply carried on as before in never addressing their neighbours whilst yes there were those who had behaved abominably in denouncing not only those who lived next door but even people who they felt had made a disrespectful remark directed at them.

The Quai des Orfevres had a whole room piled high with such poisoned letters – like most police stations across the country -- those denounced fortunate if the missive was handled by a detective such as himself but many lucked out if the recipients were the zealots in the Brigades Speciales.

"Everything was fine to start with and we appreciated Zilberstein's courage in giving us safe haven. He was married at the time, perhaps he still is, to a charming lady called Liv. They did not have any children so we slept in a room that I guess had been set aside for them had they come along.

"Liv and my wife got on well and I with Zilberstein. I think from time to time, perhaps it was to gain my confidence forgive me if I sound cynical but later events give me grounds to believe he even passed on information to the Resistance that he gleaned from his patients. Of what value it was heaven knows given most of the time they would have had their mouths prised open and unable to speak!" he chuckled dryly.

"So what brought about the degeneration of your relationship?" Asked Lafarge, needing something concrete to take back to Pinault and demand a search warrant for the gallery and arrest both of them.

Rosenberg looked mildly hurt and then angered as he guessed correctly what Lafarge was trying to do, but having asked for a refill and received it he did acquiesce.

"Zilberstein said to me it was a bit of a waste leaving my gallery shut when the Nazis, especially Hermann Goering were voracious art collectors. Yes I see your look of scepticism, they were looters on an epic scale, but some did pay and when it came to galleries they would perhaps baulk at full price but they would pay a percentage," said Rosenberg.

"Even Goering?" asked Lafarge who could not believe the morphine-addicted obese former Reichsmarschall, who was on trial at Nuremberg, ever paid for anything having been notorious for his pillaging of art collections with the cuter curators such as Rose Valland at the Louvre packing up their artwork and sending it away to be hidden before the Nazis arrived.

Rosenberg smiled sourly.

"Well yes he did occasionally pay, though, no doubt, the money was stolen from somewhere else and it is here we get to the crucial part Chief Inspector.

"Zilberstein did not push the point about opening up the gallery and left it for a while but then one night he came back all excited and said he thought I should meet someone who was interested in being a front man."

"I take it this man was Meissner?" asked Lafarge.

"Yes indeed enter Mr Meissner. Although I did not meet him immediately, Zilberstein set about selling him to me that he had worked in the art world in Strasbourg before the war. I had not heard of him, which should have made me wary as I had paid several visits there to meet with fellow gallery owners and collectors and it was a small group in Strasbourg," said Rosenberg.

"He said Meissner was a trustworthy type whom he had met socially and did not appear to be an ardent Nazi. He said his knowledge of art and being bilingual had secured him a job with the Nazi section dedicated to 'collecting' artworks and sending it back to Germany.

"However, Zilberstein said Meissner had grown tired of this constant pillaging and he wanted to stand back a little and run a gallery.

"Zilberstein claimed he then struck upon the idea of re-opening my gallery with Meissner running it but on condition that were things to turn in the Allies favour and Germany was to lose the war I would return.

"This appeared an attractive option as it was after the Nazis had suffered the huge blow at Stalingrad and even though the Allies did not yet have a foothold in Europe it looked increasingly as if the Germans were on the back foot. "

Lafarge recalled how he had felt the same way, suddenly a surge of hope had swept through him and no doubt many of his compatriots – though one did not dare express such feelings in case one was denounced – that the Occupiers were not due for a permanent stay.

Zilberstein and Meissner he guessed had used this as bait for Rosenberg though, judging as to how the story had ended up they never had any intention of doing so whatever the outcome of the war.

Lafarge could understand how tempting it must have been for Rosenberg, who would have seen how many of his contemporaries and rivals had had their art works and galleries sequestered, not just by the Nazis but by people they had considered their friends before the War.

This gave him a chance of retaining an interest, albeit from a distance as the money they promised him would also come with two Ausweis passes—gold dust for even those French citizens who were not considered enemies of the state -- and false papers for him and his wife.

Lafarge poured them one more drink, telling Rosenberg that he would have to send him on his way after it as he had to feed Ancil and Aimee too would be back soon and keen to have a rest after her audition.

"We can continue this later if you like Hal. I can meet you in the café on the corner, even if you just want to talk about other matters and have some company," said Lafarge, who could sense the loneliness and sadness engulfing his guest and having been there himself he knew how despair could all but overwhelm one and he feared Rosenberg might go over the edge.

He could only do so much, but if he could at least offer him some hope – he could relate to losing one's wife but that was a void the widower alone had to cope with – of a brighter future in terms of at least getting the gallery back then they would have embarked on the right path.

"I appreciate that Chief Inspector. I realise you are rushed for time now and normally this sort of complaint would be conducted officially at Quai des Orfevres so I am grateful for your patience and understanding," said Rosenberg.

"If you will permit me I will apprise you of the details surrounding the betrayal before I go."

Lafarge, hearing nothing coming from Ancil's room rose and checked he was alright before nodding his assent to Rosenberg to continue.

"Well the offer appeared fair given I was optimistic it would be only temporary, plus with the other things promised which I mentioned before, and so after consulting with my wife I accepted," said Rosenberg.

"How much did they offer you?"

"100,000 francs, or 5,000 Reichsmarks according to the fixed rate at the time. More than enough to use as bribes if needs be and to live on once we got to Switzerland or Portugal.

"The money was good all we had to put up with was the replacing of 'Liberty, Equality and Fraternity' with the Teutonic influenced 'Work, Family and Fatherland' but we did not care."

"So did you sign any papers? Did you receive any of the money?" asked Lafarge.

Rosenberg nodded but at the same time his features hardened, and tears welled up in his eyes.

"Zilberstein even held a petit soiree as we say!" he said bitterly.

"Meissner came with someone he claimed to be his wife, she

was French, aristocratic nearing middle age but not a family I had heard of, Emmanuelle de Rougement. She was polite and distant. Her lack of warmth was equal to her husband's so they were ideally suited to each other.

"There was another French couple there too, introduced initially as being patients of Zilberstein's. I was curious as to why they had been invited, it was only later I discovered why.

"It was of course all bonhomie, plenty of champagne and even foie gras and caviar., unimaginable luxuries - what they would have cost on the black market! Although Meissner told us thanks to his contacts he had bought them at what the Occupiers called market price. That is from a leading traiteur.

"When one thinks that ordinary people were reduced to all but going through rubbish to salvage crusts, or queuing in the bitter cold with no assurances they would be able to obtain butter and bread once they got to the front. It made me feel pretty sick about the feast we were having, but then I thought how many of those queuing would have lifted a finger for us…not many I wager.

"Still less if they had known how much cash we were about to receive, 100,000 francs buys an awful lot of butter or eggs for that matter."

"Excuse me Hal but you are meandering again. I really need to know of what went wrong and how," said Lafarge, hoping he did not sound rude but desperate for the poor man to get to the point even if it was hard and painful for him to do so. After all it was he who had chosen to come to the flat, specifically to tell Lafarge so he had to fulfil that duty.

Rosenberg held his hands up and smiled.

"I have always had a habit of doing so. It drove my parents and teachers crazy!

"The evening progressed and after we had finished dessert Zilberstein and Meissner rose to their feet and in jocular fashion introduced the couple we did not know as actually being their accountant and his wife. They thought it was hilarious to have strung us along though we were rather non-plussed by their effort at humour, definitely Germanic not Jewish!

"The accountant smiled thinly and retired to the hallway

returning with an attaché case. From that he withdrew some papers, the ones I was to sign and I took it then be handed the case which I assumed contained the money."

Rosenberg said both he and his wife, who was his business partner, had signed the papers and had indeed been handed the case which contained their Ausweis's and part of the money owed. When he queried why there was money missing Zilberstein had smoothed things over by explaining it would be unsafe and attract attention if they were to be asked to open the bag whilst still in Nazi and Vichy territory.

They were to wire Zilberstein once they were in neutral territory and the rest of the payment would be arranged. Lafarge could see this was a persuasive argument.

"So what happened to the papers you signed? Did you keep a copy?" he asked.

Rosenberg looked even more doleful and shook his head.

"Again Zilberstein said the risk was too high, besides we would be travelling under assumed names so why would we be carrying papers with other people's names on it.

"He said the accountant would keep them as a neutral party. We argued that he was hardly neutral given he was Zilberstein's book-keeper but the accountant looked wounded by this and protested he would act in both our interests."

Lafarge sighed, this meant it would be even harder to prove any agreement about Rosenberg taking back his gallery had been struck, he had little doubt Zilberstein and Meissner would have amended the contract or even drawn up false papers with the aid of the accountant.

He did not need to tell Rosenberg this, for he had probably come to the same conclusion.

"So what happened when you and your wife tried to leave France?"

"All went well initially, Zilberstein saw us off at Gare d'Austerlitz two days later and our Ausweis's were legitimate as we passed through security and the ticket master.

"However, once we got to Limoges that is when it went badly for us."

Lafarge blew out his cheeks, the very name of the place, a

town in Vichy territory, made him uneasy after his experiences there on what was his first case back on the force after being released from a POW camp.

His colleagues had been fine but the Brigades Speciales had been odious and fanatical anti-Semites. He had seen how they dealt with Jews if they captured them so it took little imagination to work out how rough the Rosenbergs' treatment had been.

"The conductor on the train very courteously said that a Herr Meissner was waiting for us at the barrier. We were confused and said to the conductor but we have tickets through to Toulouse, and he replied that Herr Meissner was most insistent we disembark from the train as he wished to drive us the rest of the way, because he had something very important to discuss with us in regard to a business matter.

"Somewhat perplexed, though with a little hope that perhaps Zilberstein and Meissner had decided it would be safe to pass us the rest of the money in the relatively more relaxed Vichy Zone, we descended.

"We saw Meissner was at the barrier and went up to him having passed safely through a cursory security check of our papers.

"He was most amiable, well for someone so stiff and formal. He ushered us towards his smart Citroen and opened the doors for us to climb in.

"It was only then that we realised…" Rosenberg gulped and swallowed deeply unable to finish his sentence as he began sobbing uncontrollably, Lafarge felt uncomfortable at this outpouring of grief, though, he could understand his feelings, and the Chief Inspector also felt a surge of anger rise up inside him at the callousness and cruelty of the two men who had led this couple along. They were for his money – much as that was worth – as bad as Petiot. They had offered false hope whilst stealing the property of the desperate people who had thought they were in a safe haven.

They needed to be dealt with.

Chapter Five

Lafarge would deal with them through official channels, none of his summary justice, so long as Rosenberg stayed alive that is. He was after all relying on what he told him to be the truth, without any paper trail.

He knew who was the more likeable but that did not necessarily ensure crusty old judges would reach their decision based on that factor alone. Some of them had questionable records from their time serving during Vichy and might be known to either Zilberstein or Meissner leaving them open to blackmail or simply favouring them due to a shared tarnished back story.

Lafarge had withdrawn to Ancil's bedroom allowing Rosenberg to grieve on his own and then hopefully gather himself and tell the rest of that part of the story, although knowing the Brigade Speciale chief De Blaeckere's modus operandi, having seen it at first hand in Limoges, he could guess the gruesome outcome.

Having fed Ancil who then went straight back to sleep to his relief – having him leaning on his shoulder whilst Rosenberg told him about what happened would have appeared incongruous at best – he returned to the drawing room and made them both a cup of black market coffee.

Rosenberg added a dash of cognac to his but unusually for Lafarge the Chief Inspector eschewed this preferring to keep a clear head as he fancied he would have to go to the office and speak with Luizet about what steps to take.

As he had feared after Meissner had led them straight into the arms of De Blaeckere and his thugs. The couple had suffered appalling abuse, verbal at first and then physical.

"I was tied to a chair and then they raped her in front of me, it was appalling and I wished and prayed that she would die so the pain would end for both of us," said Rosenberg.

"De Blaeckere did not take part"- 'I will not sully my person by having a Jewess's fluids on my body, what would my wife think ... but you have a go' he would say and wave one more of his goons to have his way with her.

"My wife was as courageous as one can be in those circumstances, she bit one of their tongues and spat in his face when he yelped in agony which only served to earn her a dousing in the bath before they hung her by her wrists, stripped her naked and did unimaginable things to her body.

"De Blaeckere left her hanging there and said to me 'So voyeur enjoy the show did you? Bet this is the only satisfaction she has had for years … you should be thankful that real men are around. Tomorrow we will be back for more but in the meantime we will leave you together, I am sure you have a lot to discuss' and burning me with a cigarette which he then placed in my mouth he left us alone."

Lafarge felt nauseous and fury raged inside him, he hoped De Blaeckere had been caught and suffered after the Liberation. It was something he would have to check on because if he remained at liberty he would hunt him down personally.

"I am truly sorry for what happened to you Hal, I can only think it is of little consolation but De Blaeckere wet himself the only time I saw him in open combat, typical of that type attracted to the Brigades Speciales a thug to defenceless people and a yellow belly when someone dared to challenge them," said Lafarge softly.

Rosenberg smiled weakly.

"So tell me two things, how come you are here to tell me this and where was Meissner when this torture was going on, was he in the room?"

Rosenberg nodded.

"Meissner came in after they had left. His Teutonic civility had disappeared, he was very much back in 'we are the conquerors, you are the dirt on my shoe above all else as you are Jews' mode. He abused my wife, I won't go into the details but he smiled smugly and said "hmm French and Jewish juices a potent cocktail…must see if they will serve that more often".

"Then he turned his attention to me, he gave me a cigarette and unlocked the manacles which freed my hands, but my legs remained bound to the chair. He laughed in my face and chastised me for having been such a gullible fool, told me how amused he and Zilberstein had been at my naivete in signing everything to them so as to save myself and my wife.

"'You fool, you thought just because Zilberstein was of the same faith that you were in safe hands. He could not care less, human beings remain the same beasts regardless of their religion, survival above all else is their primal desire and if it came at the expense of you or anyone else so be it, and even better he gets to benefit financially from it. Far more in fact than Judas did, and Monsieur Zilberstein has no intention of hanging himself due to remorse.

"In fact it turns out Zilberstein and Meissner had been waiting for just such an opportunity, and the latter revealed that I had been the ideal victim because he acted for Reichsmarschall Hermann Goering and having sated his robber baron lust in pillaging the museums he had been seeking an 'investment' for post war Paris in the form of a gallery of his own."

"Hermann Goering is behind all this?" asked Lafarge his tone of surprise reflecting his feelings at this nugget of information.

"Yes Chief Inspector the fat jewel bedecked pig himself. Meissner was his 'agent' though there was precious little commission to be made as he stole most of it. His reward I guess was to be the front man for the gallery with Zilberstein also receiving a similar pay-off, not to mention life insurance in being protected from a train journey to a camp."

"Are you sure this is true and not another of Meissner's fantastical stories? I have met him and Zilberstein on two occasions now and I think I have yet to be told the truth by either of them," said Lafarge.

Rosenberg smiled sourly.

"Chief Inspector I would check your hand to ensure you still have it once you have shaken hands with them," he said with a dry chuckle.

"But yes I am certain Goering is the financier for the purchase, although of course I only received half and that was taken back once we were handed over in Limoges.

"I hope I am not being trite but you are a detective so you can double check such things by asking Meissner outright."

"You expect him to say yes? He may have done if Germany had won the war but with his alleged boss now in Nuremberg awaiting trial for having ordered and committed the most appalling crimes it is stretching the imagination to think he will be quite so accommodating," said Lafarge.

"You can but ask Chief Inspector. Even by doing so you may unnerve him, he will wonder how you have come by such information. That may bring me one step closer to recovering my gallery and to avenge the murder of my wife," said Rosenberg.

There were so many strands to Rosenberg's tragic story that his wife had literally been left hanging there whilst they digressed over Meissner, but judging by the state she was in there would have been little chance of her surviving.

Rosenberg saw the look on his face.

"I will tell you about that in a minute. But first to finish with Meissner, when I asked him why Goering should wish to have my gallery he replied because I possessed a jewel he desired above all else, the serpent bracelet Alponse Mucha designed for the Divine Sarah, Sarah Bernhardt," said Rosenberg.

Lafarge's jaw dropped that he had shared the same apartment building as the person who had owned or at least had been charged with exhibiting the extraordinary bracelet designed by the Czech artist responsible for many of the art deco posters portraying Bernhardt in her pomp in her various roles.

She had died in penury and minus a leg but in her heyday Divine Sara had enchanted audiences – his father normally a conservative when it came to theatre had purred when describing her Medea or her Cleopatra, the latter had drawn gasps from the audience as she appeared with two live non venomous snakes entwined round her wrist – and it had been appropriate for Mucha to design such a piece for her, although it had been made by the legendary Parisian jeweller Georges Fouquet.

"Goering usually just seized works of art, why did he behave differently over this?" asked Lafarge.

"Goering unlike many of that gang occasionally behaved correctly – this is what Meissner said and as I was presently tied to a chair who was I to argue -- and he believed that not only was he investing in one of the most famous privately-owned and well situated galleries in Paris but in the process acquiring one of the most sought after jewels in the world," said Rosenberg.

"So what do you really think?"

Rosenberg smiled, again one of his wistful sad ones.

"Perhaps there is a grain of truth in it, that a sociopath like him could think he is behaving properly but I do not think he cared what happened to me. In any case I doubt very much he was able to fit it on his thick arm and his investment in the gallery is not doing him much good now is it," said Rosenberg.

Lafarge nodded in agreement, it was unlikely Goering would ever get to visit his gallery let alone step outside Nuremberg prison as being the most senior surviving Nazi and with the death penalty on the table he would have to come up with quite some defence to escape that.

Lafarge did not care a jot for Goering's fate – large jocular uncle Hermann on the news reels and off them no doubt as bad and corrupt as the rest of the gangsters who initiated the genocide --but what did concern him was how could he present such a story and make it sound real to his bosses.

He could take Rosenberg along with him but this was not usually police procedure, indeed having him in his apartment and allowing him to tell his side of the story made Lafarge more like a private investigator than a Chief Inspector and ordinarily he should have told him to come in to the Qua and make a statement.

He wished he had made him do that as he had indeed first wanted to but little had he realised that it would be so complex. No now he would have to present the facts as coherently as possible and hope that they permitted him to take the investigation further.

"So you wanted to know about my wife and how I came to be sitting here today enjoying your excellent cognac," said Rosenberg lighting an umpteenth cigarette and trying at the same time to smooth a crease in his fatigued looking trousers.

"After Meissner had left I was moved from the cell and taken to another one by a detective. I could tell he was different to the others by the look in his eye, which was one of pity and to see at least a spark of a human feeling in your gaolers gives one hope and some solace," said Rosenberg.

"There was nothing he could do for my wife he said. He would try and get her some water and wash her but she was to remain hanging like that.

"I thanked him for his small gesture of kindness and then I do not know why I added it is the second time a French detective has acted humanely and he shrugged before asking who that had been and perhaps he knew him.

"I hesitated as I suddenly thought it might be a trap but then I thought better of it as this chap appeared genuine and so I said Inspector Gaston Lafarge. Well before you get angry Chief Inspector you should have seen his reaction, a great broad smile spread across his rather chubby face and he said he might have known."

Ah dear Chief Inspector Paul Broglie, that he should show some kindness came as no surprise to Lafarge, he and the head of what was grandly called the Bureau of Anti-National Activities Bertrand Guillemot had made life bearable in Limoges and the former had helped Aimee escape the clutches of De Blaeckere when he had raided her brother's property. It was not an episode that Lafarge looked back on with any great pride as he had fed De Blaeckere the information to serve his own purposes so he could get de Chastelain away and to Paris.

As it transpired Broglie helped by Guillemot – both loathed Bousquet from afar and despised De Blaeckere and were more than likely members of the Resistance – had engineered Rosenberg's escape, the hardest part had been persuading him to leave his wife.

Guillemot had used his higher rank to tell De Blaeckere he was going to have Rosenberg examined in hospital as he needed him fit for interrogation and not beaten to a pulp as his intuition as an intelligence officer told him he may be Jewish but he also possessed a hoard of useful information.

Meissner had evidently told De Blaeckere only the sketchiest of details about the couple – conveniently omitting his role in securing the Ausweis's – as Guillemot convinced him he could extract information on how Jews like themselves were managing to live undiscovered in Paris, who was helping them and so on.

Once in the hospital along with a doctor and a nurse who were in the Resistance they concocted a story that Rosenberg had suffered a fatal heart attack and armed with the signed and counter-signed death certificate handed it to De Blaeckere, guessing correctly that due to his virulent anti-Semitism he would not take the matter further as indeed he did not.

Rosenberg had then been handed on to endless different groups – "I took care of some of the Boche myself" he said with a joyful glint in his eye for perhaps the first time that day – before finally he was able to breathe free air as he put it and eventually make his way back to Paris.

"What have you been doing since?" asked Lafarge, who had quite lost the sense of time and having been keen for Rosenberg to be brief had become intoxicated by his story, whether it was because so many names from his past were involved or he could see a case evolving where he could truly redeem himself he did not know.

"I have been looking for my wife, hoping for a miracle. I met with some of the people who had welcomed Jews and other deportees seeking news of their loved ones at the Hotel Lutetia to see if they had any recollection of her.

"That was being overly optimistic, after all the thousands of people they had had to deal with, the endless tales of misery and the distraught relatives they were hardly likely to be able to recall a Mrs Rosenberg perhaps unrecognisable from the woman I left hanging in a dingy torture cell in Limoges," he said, his voice beginning to crack.

Rosenberg perhaps wishing to avoid an uncomfortable scene, like the one that had taken place earlier, pulled himself out of the chair and headed towards the door.

Lafarge went after him.

"Where will I find you, if I need you Hal?"

"I would rather keep that a secret, in case ... well I know I can trust you but were you to be subject to Meissner's torture technique should he outmanoeuvre you …well," he smiled his by now trademark wistful smile.

Lafarge moved to protest but Rosenberg intervened.

"Chief Inspector you have for sure come across many odious and evil types in your career but I warn you will never have come across one like Meissner. There is a reason Goering chose him as his agent, not just because he is cultured but because he is singularly twisted and perhaps the most sinister and dangerous man I have ever crossed paths with," said Rosenberg.

"I want revenge for sure Chief Inspector but I am too damaged from my experiences during The Occupation, I may have killed some of the enemy but I feel empty now. My hands were not made for fighting, they were made for handling beautiful creative things.

"You on the other hand are a man of action Chief Inspector, so if there is one way of paying me for this apartment then this is it.

"Bring that duo of unspeakable filth to justice and ensure they are guillotined. Then I will be at peace."

Lafarge gripped Rosenberg's hand tightly.

"You will have your peace," he whispered before closing the door as in perfect timing Ancil began to cry.

Chapter Six

Fernand de Brinon, former ambassador to the German Military High Command in Occupied France and subsequently elevated to Secretary of State by Petain before assuming the dubious honour of being the head of the Vichy government in exile, shuffled in on a walking stick to the visitors room at Fresnes Prison.

Lafarge had driven out to the prison, south of Paris.

De Brinon and the remaining Vichy paladins – Petain had been tried and imprisoned on the Ile d'Yeu off the Atlantic coast, Pierre Laval and Joseph Darnand executed – were better treated than the previous incumbents but regardless of this there were complaints aplenty from them.

De Brinon, though, could have some key information regarding Zilberstein, Meissner and the Rosenbergs. He had reluctantly left Aimee, whose morale had been boosted after securing the part in the film and which they had celebrated at Lafarge's favoured bistro 'Presque Mort' in the Pere Lachaise area leaving Ancil with Madame Grondon.

The outing had done both of them the world of good for Lafarge had needed a change of scenery after the draining intensity of Rosenberg's visit and Aimee too as she rarely went out apart from walking with Ancil. Now even that might become more limited with the threat hanging over them, and it was questionable how long the stretched resources of the Quai could allow for a man to be on duty round the clock watching over them.

It had not been a night for bad news so Lafarge had skated over the details of Rosenberg's story – especially the bit about de Blaeckere as not only had he tortured and killed her brother and sister-in-law, but then also tortured her when she was betrayed in 1944 as he had been moved to Paris.

Thus in an air of positivity and conviviality he filled their glasses on several occasions as had indeed the proprietor Jean-Luc Giraud and his wife Julie. The copious amounts of alcohol were balanced by excellent foie gras from the Perigord and oysters from Brittany. Lafarge had indulged in cervelles much to Aimee's disgust whilst she contented herself with foie de veau a la truffe.

The richness of the menu had never wavered even during the Occupation – questions that Lafarge never posed to Jean-Luc preferring not to know the answers – but had remained largely unknown to the occupiers it being in a relatively unfashionable neighbourhood and the name alone might have put them off even though it appealed to Lafarge's dark sense of humour.

His sense of humour was non-existent this morning as he watched de Brinon laboriously make his way to the oak table and a non-descript wooden chair, the type one came across in children's schoolrooms.

De Brinon unlike Bousquet was finding not just prison food but the place itself a tough challenge. Physically he had withered, his face was gaunt, his thin covering of hair lay matted across his scalp, and his finely-tailored suit was two sizes too big for him.

He did not look best pleased. Lafarge thought he looked a bit like an angry hawk with his beak like nose and narrowed eyes, though that might be a squint. Lafarge was not going to detain him for longer than he felt necessary, the only consolation was that for once he was not here to talk to Bousquet. He could have used the visit to probe the former police chief about the plot but he still was not ready for such a confrontation.

De Brinon's only chance of avoiding the death penalty lay in the courts deciding enough blood had been shed. He slammed his walking stick down on the table, narrowly missing Lafarge's hand which was holding a cigarette.

"Have you got a cigarette?" he said, Lafarge taken aback by his arrogance and similarly surprised by his reedy voice.

Lafarge hid the fury he felt and flipped open a folder.

"Monsieur de Brinon, what do you know about the betrayal of the Rosenberg's by your former dentist Zilberstein and Goering's art representative Meissner?" asked Lafarge lending a suitable amount of sarcasm to the job description of Meissner.

Lafarge did not look up from the folder, he pretended to leaf through the thick sheaf of papers, which had nothing to do with the case of course as he had not yet had time to note down all Rosenberg had said.

However, he had felt turning up empty-handed to interrogate de Brinon would not give the right impression. All that lay within the folder was the script for Aimee's film, but thankfully, de Brinon was in no position to demand to see the papers.

He could hear, though, a deep sigh and then silence.

"Monsieur de Brinon I asked you a question," he said sternly.

"Inspector you will address me according to my title which is Count de Brinon. My family title dates back to the Bourbons and as such whether you approve of my behaviour during the war or not, I would wager like many who served in the security forces and are still in a job you have switched sides and therefore are obliged to take against me, I deserve a modicum of respect," said de Brinon gathering all the self-respect that he could muster.

Lafarge eyed him and observed that de Brinon was struggling to keep his emotions in check, he looked almost as if he was about to break down. The title really was something he wanted to fight over for he had nothing else to hold on to, clearly he realised the race was run and the trial a formality.

It was pathetic but Lafarge felt no pity towards the man. With his aristocratic background, upbringing and education based on good manners and a clear moral compass of what was right and wrong, de Brinon had embraced Fascism and even if he objected to some of their methods had not raised his voice against them. He may have truly believed in Fascism whereas Bousquet was a hail fellow well met traveller, but that did not lessen his guilt.

Still he reasoned that to obtain something from de Brinon, to make him feel useful and perhaps feed him some false hope of salvation by helping the Chief Inspector, he would address him as Count and furthermore would give him as many cigarettes as he wished. He was sure de Brinon had plenty of cigarettes as his wife had been released and even if they had been shorn of power they had money aplenty.

De Brinon nodded his thanks as Lafarge lit his cigarette,

leaving the packet in the middle of the table, and leant back exhaling the smoke as if it was some nectar from the gods.

"I knew your father Chief Inspector, unlike some in here I respected him and liked him," said de Brinon shaking his head.

Lafarge was wrong-footed by this expression of sympathy which sounded genuine. He had addressed him by his proper title too, which he had not expected. However, he remained wary for de Brinon after years of experience was well-trained in flattering those in authority or who had power over him.

"A lot of people did Count. Thank you anyway," said Lafarge.

"Now to your question, I do not know a lot. I saved Zilberstein because he was useful, good teeth are an absolute must for your own health. My English nanny taught me that. Rotten teeth can have a detrimental impact on your heart...can you believe that Chief Inspector?" said de Brinon taking to his subject with gusto, though Lafarge prayed nanny anecdotes and teeth would be short-lived.

"Aside from that after I ensured he was immune from a trip to the east he was beholden to me and proved to be most effective in a different way. He provided me with information garnered from less than discreet German officers, as well as delivering into my hands French people who thought he was sympathetic to their cause," added de Brinon, who appeared to be energised by the memory and had drifted back to the time when he really had power.

Lafarge thought it best to leave him to it, the less interrupting the more insight he would learn and help build the case against Zilberstein and Meissner. Even if de Brinon had no direct evidence against them with regard to Rosenberg there would be enough he hoped to at the very least try Zilberstein as a traitor and collaborator.

To encourage de Brinon to continue Lafarge withdrew from his inside pocket a hip flask containing his favoured and best cognac Louis XIII, unscrewed the top and allowed the prison warder to take a nip – making the Chief Inspector feel almost imperial in having his own taster – before offering the prisoner some.

De Brinon shook his head and said he wished to drink from a

glass, the prisoners considered most high risk were forbidden from having them as there had been several suicides aided some suspected by the warders turning a blind eye.

"Prison routine and rules quickly teaches one how precious liberty is," said de Brinon smiling weakly.

Lafarge held his tongue, for what he wished to say to de Brinon would have probably ended the interview then and there. He did his best to hide the anger he felt but clearly that had not completely succeeded although pleasingly he observed de Brinon's expression was one of contrition.

Clearly de Brinon unlike Bousquet had decided to be as co-operative as possible with the authorities in the vain hope of saving his life. This served Lafarge's purposes. He wagered he could play on this and at the same time also have room to provoke him, for he did not wish to give the impression he sympathised with neither de Brinon's predicament nor that his appalling acts were due to patriotism.

"Well you saved Zilberstein from a significantly more barbaric incarceration, a favour you did not extend to thousands of other unfortunate souls," said Lafarge.

De Brinon winced, but did not protest and Lafarge left it at that. To his surprise, though, de Brinon did not let it lie.

"Well I did try to save another family. I wrote a note asking for the release of Moise de Caimondo's daughter, son-in-law and their children from Drancy," said de Brinon.

Lafarge would have dismissed this as so what one family among many, but the de Caimondo family were one of the most famous and prestigious Jewish families in France. He was astonished even to learn they had been rounded up, for even Bousquet had insisted to the Nazis only non-French Jews should be sent east.

Moise had died before the war but left as a legacy his art collection converting their enormous house in Paris into a museum dedicated to the name of his son Nissim who had been killed in the Great War.

Lafarge did not consider de Brinon's effort on their behalf particularly commendable, a piece of paper rather than fronting up to General Oberg or using his friendship with the

Ambassador Otto Abetz might have been more in order and shown a demonstrable willingness on his part to save them. However, again he held back and maintained a neutral tone.

"Was your recommendation successful?"

"From what I believe it was not. They were all sent to Auschwitz and I have had no news since of whether they survived," said de Brinon.

Lafarge made a note of asking those who had been in charge of the survivors, firstly at the Hotel Lutetia, , whether any of them had returned.

He doubted if he discovered any had indeed miraculously survived that he would pass it on to de Brinon or his lawyers, the man did not deserve any sympathy or salving of his conscience.

"Zilberstein might know because he was close to the family, he was their dentist as well," said de Brinon.

"Beatrice Moise's daughter still went to him during the Occupation, quite openly too, for though she wore the obligatory yellow star she would ride in the Bois de Boulogne and even competed in show jumping events in which the Germans took part.

"I even attended a cocktail party she and her daughter were at and she appeared confident that she was protected and the star was the only humiliation she would have to suffer."

Lafarge rather admired Beatrice's refusal to hide, whether borne out of her aristocratic roots and a belief in no one daring to harm a member of a family of such renown – though she should have been mindful of a previous generation of French aristocrats and similar complacency costing them their heads – or pride in being Jewish and refusing to allow the yellow star to be a mark of shame.

Nevertheless such defiance had not served her or her family well ultimately. His interest was in whether Zilberstein had played a role in the train of events that led to her and her family being sent to Auschwitz.

Lafarge replenished de Brinon's glass and took a swig himself, the sun might have been shining outside but the stone-walled room gave off little warmth and the breath from both of them could clearly be seen when they exhaled.

"Was Zilberstein apart from being her dentist especially close to Beatrice and her family?" asked Lafarge.

De Brinon took a while to answer. He scratched his nose several times and ran a finger along his thin lips. Lafarge could not tell whether this was a nervous habit, but such body language borne from experience of hundreds of interrogations set off alarm bells in him that the person was either lying or about to lie to his face.

"From what I can recall and please forgive me if I am not precise on the details, I was very busy so am bound to forget more mundane matters, he was something of a confidant to Beatrice….indeed sometimes I wondered whether he was more than just that to her," said de Brinon, a knowing smile creasing his features.

"I would hardly call a family who thanks to your accommodation with the enemy were arrested, held in appalling conditions and then transported to a place of unimaginable horror as being a mundane matter," shot back Lafarge, sickened by the faux respectability de Brinon used to hide his complicity in mass murder.

The smile disappeared as quickly as it had come from de Brinon's face, he took on a pained expression as if Lafarge's remarks had offended him, although he made no move to get up and leave which would be perfectly within his rights.

Lafarge had got his measure. De Brinon still thought the Chief Inspector could be a useful ally in his defence or at least to give a favourable character statement if he continued to help with his enquiry. More fool him mused Lafarge.

"I am sorry Chief Inspector, I put that across clumsily. All I meant …."

"I know perfectly well what you meant," Lafarge interjected sharply, he had little time to listen to de Brinon whining and trying to justify himself.

"Let us move on. Whether they were lovers is also immaterial to me, I want to know do you have any grounds to believe Zilberstein played a role in her arrest?"

This time de Brinon did not take his time answering, Lafarge was relieved as to him it was a sign the prisoner had accepted there was little room for procrastination. His brief moment of trying to extricate himself from a tricky situation had been unsuccessful and now Lafarge expected him to be more or less truthful.

In Lafarge's world no one not even the saintliest priest could be expected to tell the whole truth all the time, the Jesuits and many who had studied under them had had made a fine art of hiding lies under what they termed the quasi respectable cloak of the word equivocation. Apparently that dated back to some Jesuit priest who had been implicated in the Gunpowder Plot against the English King James I. It still said lie to Lafarge, however it was dressed up.

"Not directly as far as I am aware," said de Brinon.

"Spoken like a true Jesuit," said Lafarge, allowing himself a glimmer of a smile.

De Brinon laughed.

"I applaud you Chief Inspector, you are not just a student of French history," said de Brinon, whose expression revealed some of the warmth and charm that he had used to such devastating effect in gaining influence over Petain.

"When I say not directly, I mean I am pretty certain he is responsible for betraying the whereabouts of Beatrice's husband, Leon, and inadvertently their son, Bertrand" said de Brinon.

"You see you may have dismissed what I said earlier as mere gossip and irrelevant, at least I took it to be the case from your reaction, but I believe Zilberstein was madly in love with Beatrice and he would do anything to prevent Leon and Beatrice being reconciled as they had divorced in 1942 several months after she had converted to Catholicism.

"He learnt through Beatrice that Leon and Bertrand were hiding near Pau close to the border with Spain and that she was of a mind to either personally demand an Ausweis through one of her German contacts for her and Fanny or get Zilberstein to do so.

"Ordinarily Zilberstein due to his social standing as a dentist would never have stood a chance to be with Beatrice, Leon was a Reinach like the Caimondo's one of the most respected Jewish families, bankers, philanthropists, major players in the arts - Theodore his father had been a deputy but was more of an intellectual than a politician.

"However, war shakes up all sorts of things, social stature, marriages and personal relationships etcetera and presents chances to opportunists like a modest dentist such as Zilberstein. He saw his chance and he seized it.

"Under the pretence of agreeing to procure her and Fanny an Ausweis he obtained from her the station they would be travelling to and then went back to her for more information as to the residential address she wanted on the pass. Once she gave him that information Leon's fate was sealed. His son had the misfortune to be there at the moment they swooped."

Lafarge was revolted but delighted at the same time. De Brinon's evidence could bring a conviction of Zilberstein and it lent credence to Rosenberg's story too. It was not enough yet to give Rosenberg satisfaction, for that he needed to up the pressure on Meissner and Zilberstein in the hope of one turning on the other. He could arrest both of them and tempt them with more lenient treatment if they co-operated and gave him information on each other.

In effect he would play them off against each other, but he had no intention of allowing either to escape the guillotine just as he would not help de Brinon.

At the same time with both of them in custody he could pursue his investigation and try and uncover other evidence to help Rosenberg, his old friend Broglie if he had survived the Occupation could be one source. Memories of Broglie also conjured up a less palatable one of de Blaeckere, who cast his thuggish shadow over almost every case Lafarge investigated. Again he did not know what had happened to him at the end of the Occupation. He found it hard to believe that someone who had been so ardent a follower of Vichy could disappear even in the chaos that followed with hundreds of thousands of forced labourers and camp survivors returning.

Lafarge made a note to check on de Blaeckere. If he was still alive Lafarge would ensure he shared the same fate as his equally odious Brigades Speciales chiefs in Paris like Fernand David, who had been executed in May 1945.

His thoughts were interrupted as de Brinon returned having taken a bathroom break. De Brinon cast a different figure to the one he had met two or so hours previously. He appeared to be almost serene, not quite smug but pleased with himself, he was less stooped though one could hardly say he had an extra spring in his step as he made laborious progress on his walking stick to reach the chair.

Lafarge took this change aside from the delicious remedial qualities of the cognac to be down to de Brinon regaining the sensation he was of use to the authorities, that his diminished self-esteem had taken a sudden turn for the better and was on an upward curve.

His previous high rank in the administration would count for nothing in Fresnes, no extra favours just heightened vigilance that nothing untoward happened before he came to trial – Lafarge thought it ironic his father's murder had contributed to this – but a cold technocrat like de Brinon would have found that those of his fellow inmates who had either saluted him before or sought favours from him for advancement now had no need of him and that must have injured his aristocratic pride.

Lafarge reluctantly admitted Bousquet would have adjusted better to life inside. He had the ability to switch from talking about art and literature to more populist coarser subjects, he could hold an audience spellbound whether they were high born bourgeoisie or the blue collar worker .

Still from his perspective he preferred having de Brinon opposite him because he was at least co-operative. He did not, though, think there was much more to discuss. But again the former Vichy paladin had a surprise for the Chief Inspector.

"I do know that Zilberstein tried to save Beatrice when he learnt she had been arrested too with her daughter," said de Brinon.

"I was surprised that such an immoral man had a conscience," he added smiling thinly.

Lafarge wondered if de Brinon considered Zilberstein immoral would he be as harsh on himself. He doubted it, there seemed to be little contrition being expressed. De Brinon was extremely forthcoming about his one-time dentist but not even having perfect teeth appeared to be sufficient reason to spare him.

Personal distaste aside Lafarge knew de Brinon and his conscience was not his problem and it was for the prosecuting lawyers to put him right on how far his moral compass had slipped.

"I do not see why he thought he could succeed when you a high up apparatchik and collaborator had tried and failed," said Lafarge.

De Brinon blanched at that remark much to Lafarge's satisfaction, but true to form he refused to engage in a confrontational exchange and allowed it to pass. He still thought his strategy of co-operation and faux charm could work to his advantage further down the line.

"He had something that I could not provide and which he guessed would be a substantial bargaining chip. He offered Meissner ergo Goering a portrait of Irene, Beatrice's mother, titled La Petite Fille du Ruban Bleu by Renoir," said de Brinon.

"Irene had left the portrait – which was of her aged eight -- in the family's possession after she divorced Moise and remarried an Italian aristocrat."

Lafarge was delighted at this revelation – not obviously for the fate of the Reinach's – but because this showed a pattern from Zilberstein of offering art to Goering which gave Rosenberg's story total credibility and enough to charge him and Meissner.

"So what went wrong?"

De Brinon shrugged.

"I don't know. Zilberstein never spoke to me about it, but I can only surmise that by 1943 Goering's standing within Hitler's inner circle was not high due to the failure to supply the troops in Stalingrad, the latest in a long line of promises he failed to deliver on.

"If Goering's actions had matched his words I would not be sitting here," said de Brinon wistfully before swiftly switching back to the case in point.

"So even if he had spoken up on her behalf, his moods made him mercurial and unpredictable due to his reliance on morphine, it is far from certain he would have been listened to. I think Beatrice knew and approved of this approach by Zilberstein, for she had hunted with Goering before the war."

Lafarge shook his head in amazement at either how naïve Beatrice had been in putting her faith in her being saved by the greed of such a dissolute and capricious personality as Goering or that complacency had once again played a role as it had with her refusing to hide.

It made him feel incredibly sad and angry. Sad for the Reinachs and the de Caimondos of course and hearing such a story personalised the evil of the crimes perpetrated against the Jews, although of course there were many more such tales of horror being told across Europe to other detectives and security forces.

The anger Lafarge felt was the willingness with which his compatriots had aided and abetted the Nazis in pursuit of their annihilation of the Jews – hardly a new sentiment for him but it came easier to him when you knew some of the people involved.

De Brinon was fortunate that there was a guard in the room for otherwise Lafarge would have taken it out on him. He may not have been directly involved and no doubt would squeal he had tried to help them. However, he had been a willing enabler to the round-up of the Jews and without him and other paladins of the Vichy Government the Nazis would have found it more difficult to implement their plans.

Lafarge instead relaxed and pulled out a cigarette, pointedly he did not offer one to the prisoner – a rather pathetic gesture he reflected on afterwards but he did not think de Brinon deserved such little gestures of human generosity – and took a swig from his almost empty hip flask.

"What happened to the painting?" asked Lafarge, the cognac helping him maintain a relatively civil tone.

De Brinon shook his head.

"I do not know Chief Inspector. As I said I was not involved in the negotiations between Zilberstein and Goering. I did my little bit but I can see now that I had little hope of success if the painting did not buy her freedom," said de Brinon.

Lafarge exhaled and eyed de Brinon with a glacial expression.

"I only hope the painting is in better shape than is likely the case for the daughter of the owner of the painting and the rest of her family," said Lafarge.

De Brinon nodded solemnly.

"I hope they are all alive. Not just for their own sakes but selfishly for mine too as they could be useful character witnesses at my trial," said de Brinon.

Lafarge smirked at this causing de Brinon to look affronted.

"I think you may be needing much more than that," he said tersely.

De Brinon went to protest but realised it would be pointless.

Lafarge began to gather up his effects and motioned to the guard he could remove the prisoner.

De Brinon gulped and raised a shaking hand, suddenly looking older than his 61 years.

Lafarge glanced at him and raised an eyebrow in askance to what he wanted.

"I hope you are satisfied with the information I provided you with," said de Brinon.

Lafarge nodded.

"It saddens me to speak ill of Zilberstein, I rather liked him and he was a useful source of information for me," said de Brinon.

"Meissner is a far colder personality, and lethal too. There is plenty I could tell you about him but then I am sure you have enough, he did not hide his part in what are now considered crimes by the victors."

Lafarge held his hand up to stop him from saying more.

"You have done a fine job of condemning him, but I will be sure to soften the blow by telling him you were saddened in doing so," Lafarge said dryly.

"No doubt if he is still alive, for like you he will be charged with collaboration with the enemy as well as other capital crimes, he will wish to return the compliment at your trial."

De Brinon went deathly pale and struggled to rise from his chair, snatching at his walking stick which fell to the floor.

Lafarge held up his hand forbidding the guard to bend down and pick up the stick and forced de Brinon to get down on all fours.

"De Brinon selling out friends might have gained you currency with the Nazis but it is quite the opposite with me and I am fairly confident to say most of my colleagues, who are rather less compliant and brutal than their predecessors were," said Lafarge.

"You are not deserving of any special treatment de Brinon, to address you as Count would be a disservice to those who carry the title with dignity and distinction. You have been of help but do not believe for one moment this will be rewarded by me appearing in court to testify on your behalf.

"The sooner people like you are judged and disposed of the quicker we can move on and erase the stain you spread over France's reputation."

Lafarge stepped round de Brinon as he helped himself back to his feet and left without another word, although as he went to close the door he could hear the prisoner calling after him, his wheedling voice barely strong enough to carry.

"I am sorry Chief Inspector, I was being truthful when I said I liked your father and was upset by his death," he said.

"That is why to a certain extent I co-operated with you just now. But I have a feeling that you, Zilberstein and I are now locked into a race to see which one of us ends up in a coffin first."

Lafarge was minded to just walk on out but bearing in mind it was not just him at risk of harm but also Aimee and Ancil he turned and faced de Brinon.

"What do you know of a plot to murder me and harm my family? Is it simply common knowledge or are you involved?" asked Lafarge, trying to sound matter of fact but he knew his voice betrayed the nervousness he felt.

"I am not party to the plot Chief Inspector, I am not the type who is useful in hiring muscle or professional killers. I am a dreamer and a strategist.

"I wish them well though. I think France would be better off with one less sanctimonious bastard such as yourself," said de

Brinon.

Lafarge chuckled mirthlessly, said nothing in reply and walked out.

Chapter Seven

Lafarge took to the road an hour or so later after spending some time chatting to one of the prison guards Gerard Lavroux, who he had met when his father was murdered. He had impressed the Chief Inspector not least because he took the job seriously and appeared to be a man of integrity, which the majority of his colleagues were not.

Lavroux had furnished him with details of who had been to see de Brinon and Bousquet .There appeared to be a fair few shady characters who had plainly given false names or if they had given their real ones had not been obliged to sign in – a few notes to the guard on duty had been sufficient to buy their silence.

Lavroux, having fought for the Free French during the Occupation did not recognise any of the people and his fellow warders, some of whom were reticent about what they had done during the War, were not forthcoming about who they were.

Lafarge got no further with the Governor either. Jean Valentin had provided some crucial evidence in his investigation of the murder of his father and Lafarge's partner Hugo Levau but he clearly did not have the confidence of his staff and hence did not accrue any intelligence on his prisoners that was not already public knowledge.

Despite the scandal over two prison officers having murdered his father in rather typical Liberation style nothing had really been done to prevent a repeat. No, Lafarge remarked bitterly and openly to Valentin, the General wished that the public perception was that France was indeed free and only populated by courageous resistants, therefore anything that threatened to sully the image was an inconvenience and should be dealt with in house. All very well but the much needed reforms or clearing out of personnel in all areas – save ministers, chiefs of services and the most brutal proponents of Vichy and the collaboration – was out of the question.

Valentin did provide one consolation for Lafarge in offering him an excellent couple of glasses of cognac, the governor himself appeared in his look and slightly shabby appearance to be seeking solace in the bottle. Lafarge was tempted to ask him why he did not request a transfer, but then recalled Valentin was seen as a reliable supporter of the General and would not dare rock the boat by abandoning the most high profile prison in the country with its stellar cast of inmates.

Lafarge was content with the information he had obtained from de Brinon and mixed with the cognac he was in a good mood as he took the road to Villejuif from Fresnes which would then take him back to Paris. He was musing over how Villejuif had managed to neither have its name changed or been razed to the ground by the Nazis when he was jolted back to the present.

A black Citroen had drawn up alongside him – he had been paying scant attention to whether he was being followed apart from the occasional look in the mirror – with three men in it. A quick second glance reassured him they were police. A uniformed gendarme was driving with two plain clothes detectives in the back. He waved good-naturedly at the driver in a rare moment of camaraderie with colleagues he did not know, who waved back but indicated he should pull over.

Lafarge was surprised at this request but surmised they had no reason to know he was one of them given his car had no official markings. He acquiesced and pulled in by the grass verge which bordered thick woods, as the other car shot ahead and parked around 10 metres ahead of him.

He realised he had made a bad call when all three of the policemen got out of the car. He thought this must be a shakedown – post Liberation corruption was not limited to prison warders. It was commonplace for complaints to be made about either bogus policemen, wearing fake uniforms or ones that had been hastily discarded by local gendarmes who wanted to disappear and avoid retribution, or genuine ones who disgruntled at their pay favoured either verbal threats or beating the hell out of their prey to obtain 'bonuses'.

Lafarge would have to brazen it out. He was confident that once he flashed his ID badge it would be enough to warn the trio that any attempt to extort money would end badly for them.

The gendarme, a portly figure with a florid face and an impressive handlebar moustache reminding Lafarge more of a circus entertainer, approached on his own towards the driver's side whilst one of the plain clothes men, sporting quite a smart raincoat but with his fedora pulled down his features were hard to make out, was making for the passenger side. The third man – thin of build with a rodent like face and dressed in a well cut suit which Lafarge guessed had been paid for by this style of highway robbery – hung back, leaning in relaxed fashion on the boot of their car.

Lafarge felt sweat drip down over his eyes, and his stomach tightened as he acknowledged he was going to have to fight his way out of this, his gut instinct all of a sudden told him this was no shakedown. The furtive manner in which the man on the passenger side was approaching the car – not wishing to be recognised suggested to him he knew him – as the other two had made no effort to hide their identities and he knew neither of them.

They were still far enough away that he could drive off and try and reach Villejuif where at least he would be amongst people and the trio would not dare try anything. However, he did not fancy his car against theirs and reckoned they would catch him up before Villejuif.

He had never been especially fond of the countryside – his parents had had a beautiful house set in several acres of land near Tours but he had preferred to sit indoors or lie in a hammock reading, whilst his siblings frolicked on the grass or played hide and seek in the woods – but all of a sudden the dense forest had never looked more appealing.

He was not a bad shot but he preferred the semi-automatic pistols to the one he was holding in his hand now, which was an old-fashioned Lebel Revolver. He had both, but for what he considered a routine run to Fresnes and back he had not really thought he would encounter trouble. He cursed himself for his complacency and did not have the confidence that he would hit all three targets in the open, far better to drag them into the forest which would even up the odds somewhat.

Whatever he needed to bolt from the car, as the gendarme was almost up to his wing mirror and the detective – if indeed he was one – was slightly behind him on the passenger side. Lafarge waited for the gendarme to be within range of the door before opening it violently so it hit the officer in the stomach. He fell back groaning allowing Lafarge to dart into the undergrowth.

Lafarge battled his way through the low hanging branches of the trees and some bushes, thankfully without snagging his jacket on them or pricking his hand. Behind him he could hear cursing from the trio, though most of the abuse was being directed at the fallen gendarme.

That bought him more time to find a secure hiding place. He did not wish to venture too far in so as to lose his bearings. But first he had to overcome the rather significant obstacle of his pursuers.

He had one significant advantage in that having hidden behind a tree he could wait and he would hear them coming after him. He reckoned that only two of them would enter the forest leaving one to cover in case he managed to extricate himself from their pursuit. He cocked his pistol as silently as he could and he applauded himself on his timing for he heard a snap of a twig on the ground at precisely that moment.

The man could not have been 20 yards from him and he swivelled to his left round the tree and saw the gendarme, who thanks to his size presented a perfect target. Lafarge did not hesitate and fired, hitting the officer in the left arm, which aside from once again dumping the man on the ground also put his gun hand out of action.

The gendarme writhed on the ground, holding his arm and calling for help. Lafarge, though, knew he did not have time to run over and kick the gun away as the second assailant would now have worked out his position. Lafarge could only guess that he was approaching from the other side, and he did not fancy running from behind the tree to the next one.

Apart from the moans of the gendarme there was silence, no help was forthcoming from nature now and Lafarge began to tense up. He had not felt like this since he was in uniform and waiting for the Wehrmacht to attack back in 1940, when his unit was one of the few to stand and fight.

This time there was no question of putting his hands into the air and being marched off humiliatingly into captivity as had happened then. As if to re-enforce that a bullet hit the tree sending shrapnel from the bark flying, fortunately for Lafarge missing him. He knelt down and looked in the direction where the shot had come from but the bushes were too dense to make out a shape. He fired back nonetheless, hoping that would draw a reaction and he could zero in on his target.

His pursuer did not fall into the trap. Lafarge could feel the sweat pouring down, his hands were affected too. The finger clenching the trigger was soaked in moisture. He pulled it away and wiped it on his shirt and as he was doing so he heard a sound from behind him.

He spun round expecting to see one of the plainclothes detectives behind him. He almost laughed out loud when he saw it was a stag, eyeing him with suitable disdain for entering his kingdom and disturbing him from whatever business he had been about. What a regal creature Lafarge thought, far more dignified than most of the human race. At the same time he hoped the stag would not have taken such offence as to charge at him, and to his relief he did not. Instead it snorted as if to emphasise that it was his domain and then turned on its hooves and disappeared back into the trees.

In one of those surreal moments when Lafarge thought perhaps he was blessed with luck, the stag appeared to have collided with the detective, for he heard a scream emanating from the trees. He did not rush straight into them in case it was a ruse, but after the scream clearly became one of agony not of fear or surprise he went in its direction.

Brushing aside the branches he came upon the detective, who had had the fedora pushed down over his face. The hat now lay to the side of the wearer, who was desperately trying to hold his intestines inside his ripped stomach. The stag had disappeared, frightened off by Lafarge's arrival, but the detective was going nowhere, except to the mortuary. Lafarge recognised him immediately. He had been one of de Blaeckere's sidekicks in Limoges. He could not put a name to him but he recalled he had been especially keen to impress his boss with his viciousness in the torture cell and his lurid stories in the local brasserie.

His presence here confirmed that this was to do with the hit on Lafarge and not connected to Zilberstein or Meissner. To Lafarge though, it presented a huge problem as clearly the resources being devoted to killing him were both in human and financial terms seemingly bottomless, and suggested that his movements were being relayed to the group because he had been extremely careful on the way down to monitor the cars behind him.

He had not shared the information he was going to Fresnes with anyone, so it had to be someone inside the prison that had phoned the gang. He did not have the time to stand around working out who that might be, although he had a fair idea, as he still had one man to take care of. He bent over the wounded thug and rifled through his pockets, grateful to come across two packets of Lucky Strikes, which were an expensive commodity, and a tin hip flask. He unscrewed it and smelt its contents. To his disappointment it was not cognac but some sort of eau de vie.

He pulled out the man's identification card and saw there was a detective's badge as well. He was called or at least his present identity was Serge Simon, though, he thought that was unlikely to be his real name. Simon had temporarily forgotten his injuries and stretched out his right hand trying to reach his semi-automatic pistol.

Lafarge trod on his hand to prevent this happening, Simon's face going from a scowl to a painful grimace. His grimace transmogrified into an expression a gargoyle on Notre Dame cathedral would have been hard put to rival once Lafarge had poured the contents of the hip flask onto his open wound.

"I would have offered you a last sip if you had not made that stupid desperate move," said Lafarge before turning on his heel and walking off.

The gendarme had yet to rise to his feet. His enthusiasm for the job had evidently dissipated rapidly after taking two tumbles and a superficial flesh wound. No wonder he is so fat Lafarge mused, the man is a sloth. Well Lafarge thought he is going to perform one more act before he is literally out of the woods, thus he ordered him up and pressing his Lebel into the small of his back prodded him forward.

The gendarme was in serious need of breaking with a habit of a lifetime and having a wash but Lafarge would put up with smelling this malodorous man until he had secured him his goal.

They emerged from the forest not quite at the point at which he had entered but it worked to his advantage as the other detective had his back to them, positioned between the two cars.

By the time he heard them it was too late, Lafarge got off his shot faster hitting the man in the chest. He had managed to fire before he was hit but only succeeded in putting another bullet into the unfortunate gendarme.

Lafarge left the man lying on the ground to check on the detective, but he was not long for this world and incapable of speaking. He curled up in a foetal position but it was way too late for him to start all over again, no matter the prayers he was offering up. His race was run.

The gendarme too had had a day to forget and one which was not going to end with a bath in hospital but like his colleagues in the morgue. Blood poured out of his throat, Lafarge pressed down on it with a dirty handkerchief he extracted from the man's trouser pocket, but he knew it was hopeless.

Lafarge took their identification cards, pilfered their cigarettes and returned to his car which he was relieved to find had not suffered any damage and in fact even the tyres were untouched which surprised him. They had been so confident of murdering him that the thought had not entered their minds.

He got back in his car, lit a cigarette and took a swig from his own hip flask, though he had to use both hands as he was shaking so much, before driving off, not stopping in Villejuif in case the assassins had come from there.

Mixed with the relief from escaping with his life was a deep unease at how many more times he would have to watch his back and surely at some point his luck would run out.

There was little doubt in his mind that despite other foes he had had to run down including several plotters in a conspiracy against the General this was the toughest and most threatening group that he had ever had to confront.

He felt Aimee and Ancil would be better with him than if he sent them elsewhere where they would be more vulnerable. With the leak from Fresnes he could not rule out that members of his team were tainted as well – there was no question of him stopping what he was doing, things had gone too far for that .

This really was a fight to the end and if it resulted in his demise so be it, at least it would have been for a good cause and he rather enjoyed the thought of taking on the challenge of overcoming the seemingly insuperable odds stacked against him.

*

“We have few enough resources as it is and six dead policemen in a matter of weeks killed by one of their colleagues is not going to be a clarion call for recruitment,” said Pinault drily.

Lafarge grinned, though more from relief that he had reached the Quai without further disruption than amusement at his superior’s remark.

Pinault had listened to his account, and did not give much away in terms of what was going on behind his equally inexpressive features. He was already aware of the fact that three policemen lay dead just outside Villejuif and that a car resembling Lafarge’s had been witnessed speeding through the town.

“The local Chief Inspector rang me. You are bloody lucky they did not send out cars after you, for I imagine they would have shot you without asking any questions,” said Pinault without a trace of a smile.

“You need not look surprised at that Chief Inspector. What would you have done in their place? Three dead colleagues and a gunman on the loose, I would have given similar orders.”

“Well strictly speaking I only killed one of them sir. The gendarme was shot by one of the others, I was using him as a shield, and the third one was gored by a stag,” interjected Lafarge.

The stag part did provoke Pinault into raising his eyebrows.

“Yes, well I am sure the post-mortem will reveal all, although killed by stag is a new one for me in our line of work," said Pinault, his tone sounding unconvinced.

"Do we know much about the trio?, I only had brief and very unpleasant social exchanges with Simon in Limoges?" asked Lafarge.

Pinault nodded and pulled out a sheaf of paper from a folder making Lafarge wonder whether it was a dossier on him or about the plot itself. He would like to have had a look at it but he doubted Pinault would be so obliging.

"I had records look into them whilst you were on your way back speeding through the suburbs," said Pinault.

"You are right about the chap from Limoges, Simon. His real name was Amaury de Brissac, he is believed to have helped the Das Reich division in their massacre of the inhabitants of Oradour-sur-Glane and then disappeared only to engineer a post as a plainclothes detective in the 16th arrondissement.

"You did a service there, or the stag did …. the other two, the uniformed officer was Sergeant Louis Decruyere from what I have been told he was a non-descript layabout who rarely went out unless money was on offer. Again he will not be missed.

"The third man is more peculiar and makes me even more nervous on your and your family's behalf."

Lafarge looked askance at Pinault, being the subject of a hit was surely enough, why would the presence of this third man make him more anxious on their behalf and besides he was dead.

"You look confused Gaston and yes I can guess you are thinking how is it possible for things to get more serious than they are. Well the third man was the local Commissaire of police Henri de Genet, a decorated resistant with the full confidence of the General.

"By all accounts de Genet was due to be fast-tracked for promotion once things had settled down and the General had got the better of the Communists and exposed their ridiculous claim to be the party of 75,000 martyrs," said Pinault.

"Forgive me sir but why would de Genet's career depend on such a high level struggle?" asked Lafarge, getting ever more confused as to why de Genet would be involved in a plot to murder him and what this had to do with fights that were nothing to do with him.

"The Communists had accused de Genet of being a high level informer for the Gestapo and the Abwehr and would rather he be arrested and confined to Fresnes than be promoted to Prefect as the General had wished.

"It appears that from what took place today the Communists at least in this instance were correct but if the level of the plot against you includes people of such high rank as de Genet then I fear we are going to have a hell of a tough time not only in protecting you and your family but also in uncovering how deep it goes."

Lafarge swallowed long and hard, his mouth had gone dry, not just from the after effects of the cognac indeed he could murder one right now and Pinault usually kept a good stock, as he tried to assess what his superior had just told him.

De Blaeckere running things as he had suspected would have been manageable he felt as the man had many enemies, though if they were as numerous as his he was beginning to wonder, and could be gunned down or turned in just as easily if he showed his face.

However, Pinault had shone a whole different light on it and indeed the fact someone inside Fresnes – it had to be an official as prisoners could not have access to a telephone – had informed on his movements suggested the master puppeteer was very highly-placed.

Despite the General's edict all had to be presented as rosy and that aside from the main Vichy personalities the rest of France had been largely blameless – though the reprisals or the epuration had been brutal and undermined completely de Gaulle's policy – it did not go so far as to allow the bureaucrats and juniors of former Vichy paladins into entering the administration.

"Are you telling me in a roundabout fashion that where a commissaire is involved there is a minister pulling the strings?" asked Lafarge.

Pinault hesitated for a moment and looked at his well-manicured fingernails, leant back in his comfortable looking leather chair, and puffed out his cheeks. Lafarge realised that Pinault had more to consider in whether he should divulge more to his subordinate no matter that his and his family's lives were in play.

For Pinault aside from being the chief of detectives, which involved occasionally conducting interrogations as well as leading up high profile investigations, also answered to political masters, in this case Prefect Charles Luizet.

Luizet appeared an honourable enough man, although Lafarge had been present when Pinault had accepted an envelope filled with cash from a notorious collaborator Joseph Joanovici, a voracious businessman during the Occupation who had acquired the nickname 'Mr Metal' for the material he had made a fortune out of selling to the Nazis.

Whether this money had gone as far as Luizet, who was a Gaullist through and through, Lafarge did not know but he wagered that if it had done it would have not been used for personal gain but to fill the coffers of de Gaulle's party. They needed as much money as possible to combat what they saw as the new enemy and a far more dangerous one in the Communist Party, who would be financed healthily from Moscow.

That was fine by Lafarge, he had little time for politics in any case the events of the 1930's and then the War had cured him of any passion or interest in them, certain politicians had earned his respect but the parties themselves could go hang themselves as far as he was concerned.

It all depended whether Pinault could set aside political affiliations or loyalties and at the very least give him his opinion and perhaps even a hint as to who this person might be, though, to be fair to his boss that might not be possible at the moment given he had only known about de Genet for an hour or so.

Pinault evidently required more time to ponder his choice, for he rose up and wandered over to his drinks cabinet, an elegant double door walnut four legged piece which had been popular in the 1920's, pulling out a bottle of cognac and filling two glasses.

Once settled back in his chair and having taken a sip of his drink he appeared to have relaxed enough to speak at last.

"The Occupation as you know first-hand created some strange alliances, some have not endured beyond the Liberation, others have if anything been strengthened," said Pinault speaking in a neutral measured tone.

Lafarge nodded, and in his case there had been several odd unions none of which had lasted save with Aimee really.

"I think without having inside knowledge of any relationship in particular, that there is a group who through various different strands of friendship, some who were collaborators and others who were on the other side, have formed an alliance.

"Logically and this you and I as seasoned policemen would agree on, there is for want of a better word mastermind orchestrating or facilitating matters. I believe that with the country still in a mess, but I would add thanks to strong leadership from the General it is in the process of recovering, it gives such people the room to conduct their own vendettas without too much oversight.

"Thus yes I believe there is a Minister in charge. I cannot say which one though if I were investigating I would be looking at one who was close to de Genet. To have sent him on this mission indicates that they required a man of some ability and leadership. The fact he is dead will be a serious blow to them, but it could also hasten another attack on you although that may not be in the way you imagine it will come."

Lafarge reflected on the last part of what Pinault had said, if a high up Minister was involved then he had little room for manoeuvre as he had no close contacts in the higher echelons, politically his ones had been with Vichy through his father although he had rarely used them.

However, he did have currency with the General and his intimates due to having suppressed a proposed coup against him just after the Liberation.

That could be a counter-balance to whoever was trying to have him killed, for what reason he could not fathom but it could be anything as trivial as the Minister having been fed false information about him or a genuine grievance from the man. Again he was at a loss to understand how he could have aggrieved so a milieu that he had never mixed in and whose members of the present government were, apart from their names, unknown to him.

That made it even more sinister to him and Pinault was intimating that the next attack may be more in tune with a politician's natural weapons, wielding his influence and feeding stories to the media.

"So what would you suggest sir? If they use a gun I have mine to counter it but if they use other means, false stories furnished to the media or trying to have me posted to the equivalent of Devil's Island then I am powerless," said Lafarge, who was not too bothered about his own predicament but that it would also drag in Aimee and Ancil was too much to bear.

Pinault shrugged then rubbed his temple and squeezed the end of his nose, which was rather disconcerting for Lafarge but he hoped was a sign his boss was deep in thought.

"Well first things first Chief Inspector, I think France has had its fill with the Dreyfus story and only the insane would wish to revisit it and stir up all the divisions the protagonists did back in the day," said Pinault referring to the infamous prosecution of Captain Louis Dreyfus as a spy which had boiled down to anti-Semites in the military and political establishment being pitted against such literary heavyweights as Emile Zola, who eventually secured a pardon after a horrific spell of imprisonment on Devil's Island.

"With all due respect to you, you are hardly an ideal example to be another Dreyfus, aside from being a Catholic your record is shall we say colourful," added Pinault with a smile.

Lafarge nodded in agreement, he was hardly in a position to argue the toss over that point.

"However, on a more serious note if this does originate with a Minister, then I suggest you do what you do best and look into the Council of Ministers and perhaps you will come up with an answer. I will make some discreet enquiries which hopefully leads us to him. Failing those two options we must hope he shows his hand," said Pinault.

"I think with three more deaths that the latter possibility is quite a strong one. Whether he makes it obvious by exercising his political weight or through more nefarious means we shall see. However, I would watch your step which sounds obvious but be armed at all times and I will double the manpower keeping watch.

"Unfortunately, though, I would love to make this a long term possibility but due to budget restraints I can only probably allow this use of manpower for the next month. If there is an incident that requires extra men then again I will have to rethink your protection."

Lafarge thanked him and said he could look after himself, though, he had doubts he could fend off three more assassins, there were not many stags in Paris he drily remarked, but his priority was for Aimee and Ancil to be protected.

"Hopefully this matter will be resolved soon, but we really need one of them to be caught alive," said Pinault staring hard at Lafarge.

"I know sir. Next time, which I expect there will be another attempt, I will try and be less accurate with my shooting," said Lafarge smiling.

"I agree that is the only way we can hope to make any progress as aside from anything else I do not have the time to spare investigating it. Being the target should be enough to solve it, hopefully, I will survive to see it through to its conclusion and not be the phantom hanging over their trial!"

On that note Pinault asked him how the investigation into Zilberstein and Meissner was going and Lafarge recounted to him what de Brinon had told him. He also informed Pinault about de Brinon's demand to have a good word put in for him at his trial as a result of the information he had provided.

"I did not hear that," said Pinault abruptly.

That was that then thought Lafarge. He did at least mention it so his conscience is clear, even though he did it reluctantly. Clearly the only hope de Brinon now had was to either die in prison or have his trial postponed. This he hoped would not be the outcome in either the case of de Brinon or especially Bousquet.

"By the way Gaston," said Pinault.

Lafarge found Pinault's switching back and forth between addressing him as Chief Inspector and then using his first name as disconcerting as the commissaire's odd habits when he was thinking.

"I would tread carefully with ZIlberstein and Meissner. They do deserve to be fully investigated, and no doubt you will get to the bottom of the crimes they have committed, but they did not succeed during the Occupation through simply being brutish.

"De Brinon's account confirms that Zilberstein in particular is a formidable social climber, though only high ranking Nazis and Vichy could have welcomed a dentist into their version of high society! De Brinon as an aristocrat would have been cold shouldered by his family in the old days if he had invited his dentist to the house," sneered Pinault.

Lafarge laughed at his boss's snobbery, though, he conceded he had a point.

"However, it is an art and one would expect that he is putting to good use relationships he formed with people who have made their peace with the General and are still in the state apparatus.

"He will also have cultivated friendships with others who returned from exile, after all an art gallery is a rather higher social status symbol and easier to converse with ones clientele than when you have your hand or fingers probing the other's mouth!! Not to mention more appetising to talk about Renoir than a new tooth or filling!"

Again Lafarge laughed, Pinault had surprisingly proved a pleasant antidote to his afternoon spent scrabbling through the woods.

"Yes it sounds amusing Gaston but the serious note to it is that Zilberstein could call in his influential friends at any moment if he feels threatened, and I know you too well you are not one for flinching until you have got your prey," said Pinault.

"Just watch yourself. Zilberstein is a snake, Meissner is as well, and they will not hesitate to strike back at you if they think their backs are covered. What is more they know you are a target, so they could do themselves a favour in murdering you and gaining even more powerful friends."

Lafarge thanked Pinault for his sage advice and perceptive observations, they sat chatting for a few more minutes drinking a glass of the commissaire's fine cognac, before the Chief

Inspector took his leave as he was aching all over and hoped he could take a rare bath when he got home, if the water supply had not been switched off due to the unions.

He would use that time on his own in the bath to mull over how much he would tell Aimee, bad enough being a target for one gang but to be at risk from the subject of his own investigation made it a war on two fronts and everyone was aware of how catastrophically that had ended for the Nazis.

If a well-oiled highly disciplined war machine such as theirs had been incapable of prevailing the chances of a strong-headed unpredictable hard drinking dissolute policeman coming through unscathed were virtually nil.

Those were the type of odds Lafarge relished.

Chapter Eight

The odds were slightly redressed the next morning when Lafarge arrived at Zilberstein's gallery to discover Meissner lying dead on the floor by the door that connected the showroom to the back offices.

His mood was already a dark one, the aches form the previous day's adventures in the woods had not been assuaged by a bath, the Communist-dominated union had indeed switched the water supply off, though, the government press tried to spin it as due to shortages. They obviously had not been on the metro of late and been pressed against a mass of unwashed bodies, whose owners were just as foul-tempered due to the union action and knew full well it had nothing to do with an unexpected drought in mid-winter.

Aimee had been even more exercised by the lack of water as she began filming that morning on The Murderer is Not Guilty, and although she could cover her unwashed body with perfume, it was a very expensive way of making up for the lack of a wash. Even with his contacts on the black market Lafarge had to pay top dollar for the brand Aimee preferred, Jean Baptiste's Vol a Voile.

Still the expense was negligible if it kept her content and he made a note to stop by his contact later in the day to obtain a couple of bottles, for if the strikes continued they would be used up pretty quickly. Ancil benefited from what little water they had and now he was safely ensconced with Madame Grondon for the day.

The double man protection team had split up with one remaining at the apartment block, whilst the other escorted Aimee to the film studio. Lafarge had told her about what had happened outside Villejuif, reckoning that it was more than likely the story would appear in the newspapers despite the government's best efforts to prevent that happening.

He omitted to tell her, though, what Pinault had said. He comforted himself with the thought it was advice and not factual and there was no need to worry her any more than she was already.

Having survived Ravensbruck she would probably have brushed it aside nonchalantly, although she had been concerned about the latest attack she had been phlegmatic about it.. The fact that he had survived was the only thing that mattered, the assassins were dead and that was what counted. For her facts were relevant and not what ifs.

He still did not want to upset her recently found confidence and equilibrium least of all as she started on her first film since her incarceration. A lack of water was annoying but it would have been remiss of him to have added to it by telling her of Pinault's fears over a two-fronted attack, for that could have destabilised her.

That conundrum was of secondary importance now as he was confronted by Meissner's corpse. His neck had been broken, not by a fall although the murderer had tried to make it look like one by dragging his body over to the door which was ajar. Lafarge guessed the intention had been to give the impression that Meissner had fallen over and hit his head on the edge of the door.

The floor was finely polished but Lafarge was experienced enough to know when someone had broken their neck in an accident and when it had been done deliberately. He left the body lying where he had found it, tempting as it was to search for other bruises or signs of a struggle, and rang for the fingerprint man and an ambulance to ferry the victim to the morgue.

"Lafarge what are you doing here?"

Lafarge looked up and saw in the entrance the bulky figure of Chief Inspector Hugues Gilbert. He had been until recently a colleague of his at the Quai but due to shortages of experienced detectives in other arrondissements he had been posted to the 8th which was the station responsible for the gallery.

He rather liked Gilbert, who had retained his enthusiasm for the job even after 25 years on the force and working under Bousquet during the Occupation. He, like Lafarge had been at best equivocal towards Vichy and the Nazis, the rumour was he had saved a number of Jews the day of the Rafle and had ensured that they had remained undiscovered.

He was slightly older than Lafarge. Tinges of grey peppered his brown hair and finely-clipped moustache, but despite his thickset physique it was largely muscle rather than fat and his face was youthful, the most notable feature being his blue eyes. He was also sporting a well cut navy blue double-breasted suit, pink tie and blue shirt with well-polished black shoes and considerably better turned out than Lafarge..

Lafarge explained to Gilbert why he was there and that he had rung for help.

"No need to do that. Zilberstein called me when he discovered the body," said Gilbert, who sounded less anxious than when he had first arrived.

"I can take care of this as it is my patch. In any case this is hardly a case worthy of a Chief Inspector from the Quai. It looks pretty obvious he fell and broke his neck," added Gilbert.

Lafarge thought about pointing out to Gilbert that it was clearly murder, but then felt it was better to switch subject. In any case there was nothing Gilbert could do to stop the ambulance or forensics coming and they would make up their own minds as to what to do.

"I am going to see if I can find Zilberstein, a bit odd he rang you and there is no sign of him," said Lafarge.

"Suit yourself. You will probably find him in the back, I can understand it if he preferred to be in another room to the corpse of his partner," said Gilbert, in a dismissive tone Lafarge felt was unnecessary.

"How did he sound to you when you spoke to him?" asked Lafarge sharply betraying his rising anger at the attitude of Gilbert.

"He sounded naturally upset but not unduly anxious. I told him to ring for a doctor and an ambulance and they could deal with the matter if he felt it was an accident because it was not a police matter.

"He brushed my advice aside and insisted I come. He has influence so I bit my lip and came over. Not as if I have nothing else to do .... you should see the amount of unsolved cases and files to be read on my desk," said Gilbert, his tone markedly more friendly.

Lafarge smiled sympathising with Gilbert. However, despite the more amiable tone it was clear to Lafarge that his presence was a nuisance to Gilbert. Heaven knows why he was being so antagonistic but as Pinault had said rightly his subordinate was unflinching and he was not going to give his former colleague the pleasure of walking away tamely.

He left Gilbert to deal with the fingerprint man whilst he checked the other rooms and he did not have to look far for Zilberstein. He was sitting in the same office indeed in the same chair he had occupied when Meissner and he had talked with Lafarge the previous occasion.

He looked remarkably composed for someone who had discovered the corpse of his partner in crime for that was what they were to Lafarge. He would not be weeping over Meissner's death after what Hal Rosenberg had told him about their betrayal and treatment in Limoges.

He was almost tempted to go with Gilbert on this one and call it accidental, but there was something that prevented him from doing so. Maybe it was because if it was confirmed as murder by the pathologist then his main suspect would be Zilberstein.

Meissner's death complicated matters as far as Rosenberg's allegations went, for Zilberstein could disassociate himself from the events in Limoges and blame it on his partner. As for the theft of the gallery it would be one man's word against another's and Zilberstein could again claim he thought Meissner was going to Limoges to hand over the rest of the money.

No wonder he looked calm, though, his eyes darted nervously when he looked up and saw Lafarge as he had been expecting Gilbert.

"Surprised to see me Monsieur Zilberstein?" asked Lafarge.

Zilberstein swallowed hard before answering.

"I thought Chief Inspector Gilbert was coming. He said he was," said Zilberstein, his tone betraying his nervousness.

"Oh he is here, don't worry. He is with Meissner. He is waiting for the ambulance and the fingerprint man. I actually came here on another matter," said Lafarge.

Zilberstein did not register any emotion, at least outwardly, about the matter Lafarge had come to discuss

"Well can it not wait? My partner is lying dead in there and I am sure you can understand I am not really in the mood for talking at the moment," said Zilberstein, whose tone made it clear it was not up for debate.

Lafarge shrugged and thought Zilberstein could keep, he hoped the fact he had shown up would stir his curiosity as to why he had and also unnerve him. Lafarge could not believe that anyone could be so serene and that inside there was a maelstrom of emotions swirling around.

"Do you know if Meissner had any family in Paris?" asked Lafarge, who nevertheless had to go through formalities regarding the deceased and Zilberstein was the only member of the gallery who appeared to be present.

Zilberstein thought for a moment, too long in Lafarge's book, and shook his head.

"So he wasn't married or had been? No children? What about family outside of Paris, like in Strasbourg for instance?" asked Lafarge, rattling off as many questions as possible to upset Zilberstein's train of thought and give him less time to think of a lie.

"He was married but she died in a bombing raid. The children perished as well, I think there were two of them," said Zilberstein.

"As for other family members that I cannot tell you, Meissner was very discreet when it came to discussing his private life."

Lafarge thought this a lie as well. He doubted very much that two men who had been associates for at least four years had not spoken about family and other intimate matters. Lafarge kept a lid on his emotions and life too but over the years he would chat to his partners about such matters. It was a way of declaring trust in the other.

"Well if we cannot track down any family by the time the autopsy is done then you will have to come down to the morgue and formally identify the body," said Lafarge, taking some pleasure at seeing the discomfort suddenly flit across

Zilberstein's face.

"There has to be an autopsy? Surely it is obvious he broke his neck. And why do I have to identify the body, I just have done," protested Zilberstein.

"They are part of the formal procedure Monsieur Zilberstein. There is no burial otherwise," said Lafarge firmly.

Zilberstein muttered it was ridiculous and looked angry. Good some emotion at last thought Lafarge, useful ammunition for the future.

"So you found the body and then rang Chief Inspector Gilbert?" said Lafarge.

"He did indeed Chief Inspector as you well know for I told you so," said Gilbert in his crisp well educated voice from behind Lafarge.

Lafarge turned casting a quizzical glance at his colleague, who was leaning against the door frame.

"The fingerprint man and the ambulance have arrived. Why don't you go and join them whilst I take down the necessary statement from Monsieur Zilberstein," said Gilbert, his tone friendly but firm.

"After all it is I who will be handling the paperwork as it is my district and also he rang me."

Lafarge made sure Gilbert saw his displeasure although he had no room for manoeuvre as it was indisputably the latter's territory.

Meissner's corpse had been removed and the fingerprint man was going about his business so Lafarge left him to it and went outside to get some air. He walked aimlessly up and down the pavement, chain smoking, putting the time to use by observing that not even a prestigious address like this was exempt from the rubbish going uncollected.

Paris may be free of the Nazis with their daily round-ups and mass executions, the later largely out of earshot and eyesight of the populace unless the authorities had wanted to remind the Parisians of the penalties that came with upsetting their uninvited guests, but it was still a mess. The unions, thanks to their Communist masters, were firmly in charge of the city, able to close down transport – which happened regularly – turn off the water and shut off the electricity.

Quite rightly the people pondered why the General and the government, made up of people who had triumphed over the Nazis albeit with considerable help from the Soviets, the Americans and the British, were unable to clamp down on the unions and order the Communists politicians to be co-operative and cease their attempts at holding the city to ransom.

Those privations would be just about bearable if there was enough to eat, but rationing was still in place for even the basics such as bread and sugar, one needed the patience of Job and a lot of time on ones hands as queuing was the norm with no guarantee of success at the end of it. The baker and the butcher would do a typical Parisian shrug of the shoulders and say try tomorrow.

Some customers were so desperate they would plead with the baker to scrape up the crumbs and fill a bag with them, whilst butchers often did the same with the fat. Lafarge had ambivalent attitudes towards the Parisians, not just because of the criminals he had dealt with. They were the same anywhere though in the south they had a healthier bronzed look, but Parisians of any hue whether worker or boss had this arrogance about them that one only got in major cities.

However, whilst he hoped the shortages and rationing would teach them a bit of humility he did feel sorry for them that they had to contend with those and terrible housing conditions – at least for a huge percentage of the inhabitants – which had a knock on effect on their health with diseases such as tuberculosis prevalent.

All in all an atmosphere ripe for revolution but the people were worn down, all they could wish for was that things would turn the corner and that a compromise would be found, even if it meant the General departing the scene, ungrateful as it might appear.

If the bigger picture was dark his own smaller one was as gloomy with the myriad of problems he was confronting. He reached for his hip flask but then realised it was empty, he had forgotten to fill it in the morning, distracted by the lack of water, Aimee's first day on set and getting Ancil ready for Madame

Grondon.

He looked around to see if there was a café nearby but instead of seeing one he saw Rosenberg instead. Rosenberg clearly did not wish to be seen, he was staring into the window of an haute couture designer diagonally across from the gallery, but there was no mistaking it was him.

Lafarge went to cross the street but Rosenberg must have seen him and went scarpering down the pavement. Lafarge could not summon up the energy to chase after him and watched as he disappeared round the corner.

Lafarge wondered how long Rosenberg had been there. Indeed it set him thinking about Meissner's murder and could Rosenberg have seen something or worse was it him who had been the perpetrator?. He sincerely hoped it was not the case. After all the man had been through he could understand the desire for revenge but sympathy would not stand in his way if he had to arrest him.

He tried to shrug the thought aside, but it was impossible to ignore the possibility especially after Gilbert re-emerged from his talk with Zilberstein and asked him if he would like a drink.

Lafarge said he would have preferred to talk to Zilberstein about another matter. He acquiesced after Gilbert, striking a more co-operative note than earlier, said it would be possible but he would have plenty of time as he was remaining in the gallery for the rest of the day.

They stood at the zinc bar in a café that was on the street that Rosenberg had turned into. Lafarge hoped he might have taken refuge in there to wait until he had left the gallery, but there was no sign of him.

"So what do you want to talk to me about? Something that came up from your discussion with Zilberstein I hope," said Lafarge, who wondered whether Gilbert had taken him away out of sight of the gallery so Zilberstein could leave.

Gilbert took a sip of his glass of red wine, Lafarge of course had ordered a cognac, and nodded.

"He says he thinks he knows who murdered Meissner if it does turn out you are correct," said Gilbert.

Lafarge's interest level went up a few notches, as did his

suspicions. Interesting that following their chat Zilberstein's opinion had changed and that he also had an idea as to who had murdered his partner, it all sounded wonderfully neat and tidy.

He set that aside for the moment and waited patiently for Gilbert to go on.

"He believes the man who used to own the gallery and then sold it to him and Meissner could be the murderer," said Gilbert.

"Hal Rosenberg," said Lafarge.

Gilbert shot him a surprised look and nodded. Lafarge remained silent not wishing to give him any inkling that he knew him.

"He says Rosenberg has been hanging around the gallery and had accosted Meissner outside on a number of occasions, on one of those shoving him against the door and grabbing him by the throat," said Gilbert.

Lafarge thought that was the least he deserved, but on the other hand this did not look good for Rosenberg. He was interested that Zilberstein had seemingly escaped similar attention from Rosenberg when he was as implicated in the swindle and the betrayal.

That could be being saved for later, to twist the knife further into Rosenberg thought Lafarge. Suddenly the light bulb went on fully inside Lafarge's head, this was the reason Gilbert had taken him away from the gallery, to give Zilberstein more time to think.

Unfortunately Lafarge had bought the drinks and Gilbert had now done the honourable thing as he put it and ordered his round. The smug smile on his face as he said it told Lafarge his colleague was enjoying himself at his expense.

That he did not appreciate but he took solace in the fact he had been far from fooled, but he was willing to play along for the moment. In any case whatever little game they were up to it did not mean Rosenberg was in the clear. Lafarge did not want to believe it but the evidence in the hands of a less partisan detective would result in his being arrested and charged.

"Did Meissner lodge a complaint for harassment?" asked Lafarge.

Gilbert shook his head.

"Zilberstein says he and Meissner did not want to report Rosenberg because they knew he had had a tough time during the Occupation and lost his wife," said Gilbert.

Lafarge chuckled mirthlessly.

"I don't think it is a laughing matter Chief Inspector," said Gilbert sternly.

You would be laughing too if you knew what I know about their involvement in Rosenberg's 'tough time' thought Lafarge. However, he did not trust Gilbert enough to impart any of that part of the story although he was relieved that his colleague did appear totally unaware of their crimes during the Occupation.

He could perhaps use this to his advantage later on. He suspected Gilbert was on the payroll of Zilberstein. The way he had behaved in the gallery and now acting as his messenger boy was evidence enough.

Lafarge conceded he could be being paranoid but then six fellow policemen had tried to murder him.

"Zilberstein and certainly Meissner must regret that generosity of spirit now," said Lafarge, his sarcasm missed by Gilbert.

"I think Meissner is past caring now. Anyway more to the point Zilberstein says he saw Rosenberg in the area this morning when he was on his way to the gallery.

"He says he looked shifty and was walking furtively along the street. However, he did not come into the gallery although now Zilberstein thinks perhaps he had already been in and this time he had gone too far with Meissner. Even Zilberstein admits that his former partner was lacking in charm and could be brusque," said Gilbert.

Brusque indeed Lafarge mused. Sadistic cheating bastard more like. That he kept to himself and asked Gilbert what his next move was.

"I will wait for the outcome of the autopsy. If it is murder then I will see if Rosenberg's fingerprints are on file and compare them to what the fingerprint man comes up with. If they are not on file I will try and run him down and arrest him," said Gilbert.

"What are you going to do about this other matter you wanted to talk to Zilberstein about?" he asked Lafarge.

"That is a very good question," smiled Lafarge.

"I will mull it over. I too will wait for the outcome of the autopsy. I think you should tell Zilberstein to be extra wary of his own security. If it was Rosenberg then there is every chance he will try and confront Zilberstein," said Lafarge.

Gilbert nodded said thanks for the drink and made his way back to the gallery.

Lafarge downed another cognac and thought he had bought himself some time if Gilbert stuck to what he had said he would do. The autopsy would take a while, Rosenberg's prints might well be on file if there had been any break ins before the War or lodged in Limoges if they had gone through the protocols down there when he was arrested with his wife.

All that would take time which would be crucial breathing space if Lafarge was to track down Rosenberg before Gilbert did and either warn him or get his side of the story. Either way he was determined to help him and if necessary ensure he escaped.

Zilberstein was the one who deserved the guillotine, not Rosenberg and Lafarge would do all he could to ensure that was the outcome.

His superiors might frown upon this type of justice but if Lafarge had learnt one thing from the Occupation it was time for the cheated little man to be treated better than the cheater who wielded influence.

Chapter Nine

Lafarge found Rosenberg quite by chance having searched fruitlessly when he returned home after drinking with Gilbert. He was not in the best of humour by the time he had walked back from Montaigne to Pere Lachaise, the metro having stopped operating due to the union responsible for the electrical supply having gone on a wildcat strike.

Aimee had come back soon afterwards in high spirits after her first day of filming – she told Lafarge that her nerves had disappeared as soon as she stepped in front of the camera thanks largely to the star Prejean putting her at her ease and being a delight to work with.

Lafarge smiled content for her that she had not frozen under the pressure, impressed by her strength of character in being able to set to one side her experience of Ravensbruck and now the added threat of the people who wanted to kill him but who would also not hesitate to hurt her and Ancil.

He was not so sure about Prejean, though, and it had nothing to do with Lafarge not appreciating his portrayal of Georges Simenon's legendary detective Inspector Maigret. He was pleased that he had been pleasant to Aimee but he had a distinctly chequered record during the Occupation. A hero from the Great War, the dapper good looking Prejean had failed to display similar heroism once the Nazis had assumed power.

It was not so much he had carried on acting, many of his profession had, although some stars like Jean Gabin had left and joined the Free French Army whilst others had been active in The Resistance. Prejean had not gone as far as Robert Le Vigan who had collaborated openly with the Occupiers, but he had gone on an infamous propaganda trip with several prominent silver screen personalities, including Danielle Darrieux, to Berlin and posed smiling in front of the Brandenburg Gate.

In a way this film represented as much as a chance for him as for Aimee, his way back after being incarcerated post the Liberation. No wonder Prejean had played the gentleman,

Lafarge thought wryly.

In any case Lafarge had thought to raise his own spirits and to celebrate Aimee's first complete day of filming he had taken her out for dinner to his preferred bistro 'Presque Mort'. The owners Jean-Luc and Julie Giraud always managed somehow to have fresh quality produce – they had been closed down once during the Occupation when an abusive customer they had thrown out informed on them to the authorities -- and Lafarge never posed any questions. Indeed occasionally through his black market contacts he furnished them with some products which earned him both their friendship and a substantial discount on his bills.

It had been on the way back from a long and enjoyable dinner – confit de canard with foie gras melting on top and tarte tatin washed down with copious amounts of good wine and a couple of cognacs at the end -- he had espied Rosenberg sitting in a café.

He escorted Aimee back home – the plain clothes detective kept a respectful distance so as not to be picked up by anyone who might be following the couple – and collected a very sleepy Ancil from Madame Grondon and then returned to the café hoping Rosenberg was still there.

To his relief he had not left, indeed he had a full glass of red wine sitting in front of him. Lafarge knocked on the window and waved, Rosenberg looked up startled and seeing it was Lafarge he relaxed and smiled, pointing to the seat opposite his.

Lafarge ordered a cognac from the barman, who contrary to the popular image of his profession possessed a winning smile and looked happy to have some business despite the late hour. Lafarge surmised it was probably because he was young that he had yet to take on the grumpy what are you doing in my bar attitude and drink had not become a respite for him either judging by his healthy complexion.

"Monsieur Rosenberg will be happy for the company, Chief Inspector," said the barman.

Lafarge was taken aback by the young man's observation, not least because he knew who he was. He was certain that he had never been in the bar – even though it was in easy walking distance of his apartment but if he drank it was usually at home or a café closer by than this one – and guessed the barman had seen him walking in the neighbourhood on a regular basis.

However, given recent events he was immediately on his guard but played it as if he had not noticed and simply flashed a friendly smile.

"Monsieur Rosenberg is a regular here?" asked Lafarge.

The young man – his clean-shaven appearance with well-looked after teeth yet to be stained either by tobacco or coffee was again not the norm for a Parisian barman – nodded.

"He comes in usually around 10 every night, sits at the same table, orders three glasses of red wine at most, and sits there sometimes reading a newspaper or a book, but most of the time stares out the window," said the barman, his tone suggesting he felt sadness but also liked Rosenberg.

"You are the first person I have seen come in here specifically to speak with him, whether it augurs well that you are a policeman is another matter!" he said grinning.

"So Monsieur ...," Lafarge decided the exchange had gone on long enough that he would like to know who he was talking to.

"Alain Concarneau, you can just call me Alain," he replied, without adding any other background information.

That was fine by Lafarge as he had done this for two reasons. Firstly he would run Concarneau's name round the Quai among different departments and see if he was known to any of them, and then they could filter it out to the different arrondissements in case they had information on him. Secondly if he came up clean then he would use him as someone to provide information or look over Rosenberg.

Judging from what he had said Rosenberg had no one, though, obviously he had chatted to Concarneau.

"Does he talk to you much?"

"Yes, he does every so often. He is perfectly pleasant, never gives any trouble or gets drunk. I think he is just happy to be somewhere he can feel at ease and not be stared at for always being on his own," said Concarneau.

"I have a fair few clients like that and I dare say other bars too, many more since the Occupation came to an end."

Lafarge grunted and nodded, though, he was not sure the young barman's observation was true. He did not frequent bars that often – despite his consumption of cognac he could resist the urge to dive into the closest cafe to a crime scene or after interviewing a witness or suspect – but he queried whether the Parisian male had been so traumatised or left guilt-ridden by the Occupation that the found the best way of dealing with their demons was by drinking on their own.

He found it an odd remark and wanted to find out more about Alain Concarneau, if that was indeed his real name. For the moment, though, Concarneau could relax because Lafarge had to deal with Rosenberg.

He had taken so long in getting to Rosenberg's table that the latter's glass was almost empty, so by way of apology he ordered him another.

Rosenberg did not look in a good way, dark bags under his eyes, unshaven and gaunt. His clothes, though, were well pressed and clean, although the navy blue suit hung off him. He had lost more weight even since their meeting only a few nights ago.

Lafarge looked round to see if there was a bar menu of some sort as he was going to order something for Rosenberg, whether he wished to eat or not. This time of night a sandwich was probably the best they could hope for.

He ordered a cheese sandwich for Rosenberg and settled back into the chair.

Rosenberg actually looked happy when the sandwich arrived, so it set Lafarge thinking that perhaps the reason he was so thin was due to lack of funds. He asked him straight out but Rosenberg shook his head and replied he found little time for the basic comforts these days, his sole goal was to get proper restitution for himself and bring those who were responsible for his wife's death to justice.

Lafarge sympathised with him but he still needed to know the truth about Meissner, so he could either rule him out or get him away from Paris.

"I saw you today Hal, but I think you saw me too and that is why you fled," said Lafarge.

"What were you doing round Avenue Montaigne, and don't reply window shopping," added Lafarge.

Rosenberg smiled.

"Yes I saw you and I am sorry for not coming over but I was worried that Zilberstein or Meissner had called you as well as that other guy who looked like a policeman," said Rosenberg.

Lafarge was relieved that Rosenberg appeared to believe Meissner was alive, he did not think the man was a liar, although he had had time to think up a story.

"Why would they have had to call the police? You are right the other guy is also a detective but he is responsible for that arrondissement not me. I was there on your behalf to ask them more questions, not directly concerning your matter but something that lends weight to your claims," said Lafarge, who was unprepared yet to divulge what de Brinon had told him.

Rosenberg's eyes light up but he was intelligent enough to realise Lafarge wanted an answer before he received any extra information.

"Well I had been in there prior to your arrival. I know it was a stupid thing to do but I could not resist as I thought the more I show my face the more nervous they will become, what with you also making enquiries," said Rosenberg.

Lafarge sighed, Rosenberg despite all that he knew first-hand about the duo's ruthlessness was either being naïve in thinking by making them nervous they would surrender meekly or preparing the ground for a self-defence plea. However, as he had clearly said he feared Meissner and Zilberstein had called the police Lafarge had to opt for Rosenberg being naïve which was probably the greater crime.

"That Hal is a damn stupid tactic. Meissner may not have the forces at his disposal as he did during the Occupation but that does not mean they lack the means to get rid of you and this time make it permanent," said Lafarge, making clear his annoyance.

Rosenberg looked hurt but Lafarge was not going to pat his hand and tell him he understood.

"So what happened between the three of you? Were there any other clients or staff members present?"

"We had a lively discussion. I said I would not stop coming back and threatened to make a scene at their next opening unless they paid me the rest of the money they owed me and gave me back the gallery," said Rosenberg, his voice rising as he finished.

"I said in return I would not reveal Zilberstein's duplicitousness nor Meissner's role in what happened to me and my wife during the Occupation."

"How did they react to that threat?" asked Lafarge, who regretted not keeping a closer eye on Rosenberg but had believed the reason he had come to him in the first place was so he would pursue his own enquiries.

Rosenberg grimaced at Lafarge's use of the word threat, but it could be perceived as that especially as he had none of the paperwork to prove the deal had taken place.

"What other currency did I have apart from that? Besides blackmailers and conmen like them only understand such language," said Rosenberg defensively.

Lafarge cursed under his breath, for were Gilbert to get Rosenberg into an interrogation room he would be able to twist his words into a convincing case against him. Rosenberg could not help himself, he was too emotional and whilst that was understandable it made him vulnerable to clever and manipulative detectives such as Gilbert and subsequently prosecutors.

"That does not answer my question Hal. How did they react?" asked Lafarge, his tone indicating his impatience.

"Zilberstein just laughed but Meissner was more placatory," said Rosenberg.

That surprised Lafarge, not so much Zilberstein's dismissive response but that the outwardly aggressive Meissner had been more positive about coming to an arrangement.

"In what way was Meissner placatory? He was willing to come to an agreement or at least come up with some form of compromise?"

"He indicated that while I was a pain it was one he wanted to be rid of and if the only solution was to come to an arrangement then he would consider it. He insisted, though, that they should remain silent partners in the gallery," replied Rosenberg.

"He said without apologising of course that they deserved to remain linked to the gallery because they had kept it going as a business concern through tough times. I retorted 'what through the Liberation when you lost your employer and best client, Goering'," said Rosenberg, a grin for once lighting up his face.

"He did not appreciate that at all. However, he admitted he wanted to withdraw from being in the front of the house and live a quiet life. I bet he does because if Goering is ever asked about his pillaging of art his name is bound to crop up," added Rosenberg.

Lafarge concurred with that, though, whether prosecutors at Nuremberg would have the time to interrogate Goering about his ravaging of the finest art works throughout Europe given the list of his other alleged crimes was a moot point.

In any case Meissner's desire for a quiet life had come true but not in the way he envisaged. For now Meissner was residing in the morgue, having his body poked and prodded by Lafarge's friend Frederic Durand the pathologist. Meissner had been taking a calculated gamble in trusting Rosenberg to keep to his part of the agreement, but it sounded like he would have more of a problem with getting Zilberstein to yield.

"So how did Zilberstein react to Meissner giving in?"

"He was not happy. He looked surprised at first and then his usually sunny disposition, all a facade in any case, disappeared and he ushered Meissner into the back.

"They were definitely arguing, raised voices and all that. Meissner kept on repeating how tired he was and they had had a good run and perhaps the time had come to take a back seat but with the bonus they still had shares in the gallery so the money would not run out.

"Zilberstein simply would not give ground. He argued that they had come through worse situations, they had rebuilt a client list since the Liberation without being asked tough questions about provenance of the paintings or how had they survived as a business during the Occupation.

"He said my threat was an empty one, no one who had been clients of the gallery before the Occupation had even asked what had happened to Hal Rosenberg. No one would listen if I did make a fuss. Zilberstein even had the nerve to say he a dentist had managed to make a proper business out of the gallery which did not speak volumes for my financial acumen!" snorted Rosenberg.

"You managed to overhear most of their conversation, I wonder why Zilberstein even bothered in taking Meissner into the back office," said Lafarge.

Rosenberg smiled slyly.

"I saw the door to the office was shut and listened in," he said with a triumphant look on his face.

"Aha. How did it end between them and you once they came out to the front of the house?" asked Lafarge.

"They tried to cover up the differences between them and said I should come back in an hour when I would have an answer. That is why you saw me across the street, and I fled as I said because I did not want you to know I had gone behind your back," he said.

"I just wanted to give my plan a chance and if they refused then you had a free run. I am sorry.

"I will go back there tomorrow morning instead. I did not bother hanging around waiting for you to leave but at least I can return with this burden off my back, that you at least know now," said Rosenberg.

Lafarge felt he was genuinely apologetic. He also clearly had not got anything to do with Meissner's murder, for to have made up such a detailed story in the few hours since would have been well-nigh impossible, especially someone as nervous and highly-strung as Rosenberg.

However, Meissner's death had complicated things even more for Rosenberg, not only had he lost any chance of his recovering the gallery but Zilberstein had fingered him for the murder. Gilbert clearly believed Rosenberg was the culprit, but Lafarge had his suspicions about his colleague and why he held that opinion.

Lafarge ordered them two more drinks, the bar was not empty by any means with some of Concarneau's lonely drinkers standing by the bar, and several couples occupied the more comfortable booths. When he asked Concarneau what time he closed, the young barman smiled and replied when he decided it was time to go.

Rosenberg said this would be his last drink as he had to get back to where he was living by one at the latest. Lafarge asked him where that was and he responded by saying it was an apartment owned by friends but he did not have a key. Lafarge thought the friends were understanding hosts waiting up almost every night for their guest to let him in.

However, that was not his concern but with time pressing he needed to warn him he was the prime suspect in Meissner's murder.

"Hal I am sorry to tell you this but Meissner is dead," said Lafarge, not bothering to sugar coat the truth.

"I am not sorry he is dead obviously after what he did to you and your wife, and probably many others. However, I am sorry because it is a blow to you and in more ways than one."

Rosenberg's face clouded over, his hopes of his horrific story finally coming to a satisfactory conclusion dashed. He put his head in his hands and ran them down his face, if it was possible he looked even more fatigued.

"So that is why the other detective turned up. How did he die? It must be Zilberstein … have you or your colleague arrested him?" asked Rosenberg, but his tone did not carry any optimism for being a clever man he had registered why Lafarge had taken his time to tell him.

Lafarge went through the motions of shaking his head.

"If it is any consolation Hal I believe you, that is why I let you tell your story first. It rings true to me and already knowing what they did to you it is clear to me that Zilberstein killed Meissner. I would say he did it in a fit of pique, he does not come across as a man of physical courage and certainly not capable of confronting Meissner if he thought about it too much.

"Nope he lashed out and lucky for him Meissner died, for I do not see his partner taking being assaulted lightly.

"However, now we have to focus on you. My colleague Gilbert is convinced you are guilty. He is ambitious and bright and will not waste time in chasing you down."

Rosenberg clasped his hands together, not in prayer but to stop them shaking. He did not speak so Lafarge pressed on.

"As far as I can see you have two options. One is to stay put and await arrest, you can then fight your corner while I use the time to try and build up the case against Zilberstein. I will break him I assure you if I have to, he is scum and I have a particular dislike of this one.

"This feeling has been from the moment I met him, being shot at in his gallery did not help any either even if he may not have been responsible for that," said Lafarge drily.

Rosenberg smiled briefly and took a sip of his drink, accepting Lafarge's offer of a cigarette.

"So there is that possibility, although, I would try and persuade Gilbert to press the prosecutor to send you to Cherche Midi prison which is marginally better than Fresnes and has the advantage that no Vichy thugs and apparatchiks are housed there," said Lafarge.

"It is normally for German military personnel but a few special cases are allowed to be imprisoned there. I know this is not ideal especially for you being Jewish but there are no SS or Gestapo prisoners, solely Wehrmacht, who are considered to have less blood on their hands with regard to the round-ups.

"The other one is simple. You pack your bags and flee and wait for me to contact you when I have finally succeeded in arresting Zilbertin. Do you have friends you can go and stay with?"

Rosenberg thought for a minute and shook his head.

"I am not certain if any of my friends or clients are still alive or living where they used to. It is not as if I can phone them given the problems with the unions and many lines still being down. I would not risk just turning up either," said Rosenberg.

"But do not worry about me Chief Inspector. I am used to running and hiding. If there is one thing I am good at due to the past few years it is lying and going to ground," he added with a bitter smile.

Lafarge smiled too, pleased that Rosenberg had chosen this course of action. For regardless of Cherche Midi being a better option to Fresnes, he would still be vulnerable and it would be almost impossible to keep him separate from the German prisoners.

"I suggest you go back to the apartment, pack your bags and leave first thing in the morning. If you wish I could come and pick you up and get you out of Paris to a train station that will not have people looking for you," said Lafarge.

"It is a bit late and I have had a little bit too much to drink, even for me, so driving you now would not be in our best interests."

Lafarge could see Rosenberg was genuinely moved, tears streamed down his face and he held both his hands out and clasped Lafarge's which were wrapped round his cognac glass. Lafarge never one for shows of emotion – part of his father's legacy – was moved too but he fought back the tears welling up and managed to extricate his hands so he could drain his glass.

Rosenberg laughed at Lafarge's discomfit. Ordinarily the Chief Inspector would not have appreciated being the source of ridicule but because it was the first time Rosenberg had laughed he let it pass.

*

Only a few hours later as dawn was breaking Lafarge pulled up outside the café, Rosenberg having explained he did not want even the Chief Inspector to know where he was living.

The café had not yet re-opened, there was no sign of activity within, and so Lafarge waited patiently for Rosenberg, occasionally stepping out of the car to stretch his legs and smoke. He had emphasised to Rosenberg he needed to be back in Paris at Meissner's autopsy at midday, which meant that every minute he was kept waiting reduced the distance they could travel outside Paris.

Half an hour went by and Lafarge was getting progressively anxious about Rosenberg's whereabouts. It set him wondering as to what nearby meant in the fugitive's vocabulary for if he was walking to meet Lafarge then he observed drily he must be traversing Paris.

Rosenberg finally emerged out of the gloom a few minutes later, not offering an apology but saying he had been watching Lafarge for all that time to check there was no one else with him or anyone suspicious hanging around close by.

Lafarge was not best pleased but accepted that Rosenberg's caution was understandable. He asked him if he had thought about where he might like to go, while warning him their options were limited with the time constraints.

"I was thinking Tours would be good for me," said Rosenberg.

"Tours are you sure?" asked Lafarge in a surprised tone.

"What is there for you in Tours? Apart from the chateaux I cannot think of any reason to visit the place and you are not going as a tourist," added Lafarge attempting to inject some humour into the situation.

Rosenberg smiled.

"My friends gave me a contact there. It may not add up to much but a quiet provincial town is a perfect place to go to ground. There is something to be said for being bland and innocuous," said Rosenberg.

Lafarge nodded and wondered what his life might have been like if he had grown up in a place like Tours. Would he have become a tourist guide, a daily routine of visiting Chenonceaux, Azay Le Rideau and the other chateaux, content in his safe little life nestled in the self-satisfied bourgeois comfort of the Loire valley. Or would he have rebelled and gone to Paris for the unpredictable excitement that engendered.

He hoped it would have been the latter but in any case that was all irrelevant as he had ended up with it as it was and he rather envied Rosenberg heading off to the dullness that was Tours. He glanced at his watch and saw that it was coming up to 8 o'clock which meant they were going to have to hurry if he was to be back in time.

He doubted traffic would be a problem with petrol rationed and few people which meant people only ventured out on the roads in emergencies or if they had jobs that required them to travel, and there were not many of those at the moment aside from salesmen and the military.

With over 200 kilometres of Route Nationale 10 to cover it was going to be a tall order. Nevertheless he had promised Rosenberg and he was not going to go back on it now.

Rosenberg travelled light Lafarge observed, as he loaded a battered brown leather suitcase into the boot of the car. Either he did not expect to be away for long, which was assuming rather a lot in that Lafarge would be able to build enough of a case against Zilberstein quickly, or it was a habit he had acquired when he had gone into hiding after Limoges.

"You left plenty of clothes when you disappeared. I stored them in the cellar, we could go and get some of them if you like," said Lafarge.

Rosenberg shook his head and said they better get going.

They made good headway and Lafarge stopped off for petrol at Versailles.

As he pulled out he noticed another Citroen also exit the petrol station. He did not mention it to Rosenberg in case he was worrying him for nothing, but he had seen it follow them into the station and unless he was mistaken with just one pump the driver had not had time to fill it up and exit so quickly.

He slowed down deliberately and glanced in the mirror. There were at least three people in the car behind, by their head apparel all men. Lafarge patted his pocket to reassure himself that his gun was indeed there. He had spare ammunition in the glove compartment but he doubted he would have time to reload.

The driver made no effort to overtake Lafarge on the 10 kilometres stretch of road from Versailles to Trappes. Lafarge eventually pulled off down a side road allowing the other Citroen no time to follow them. He then turned round down the narrow lane, hindered by a herd of cows which was just exiting from its field.

Rosenberg did not ask any questions, he had been dozing fitfully anyway, and Lafarge offered no explanation. They settled in behind a truck, Lafarge content to lose a bit more time so long as the lorry offered protection from the other Citroen and its occupants.

They lost their buffer when the truck pulled in at Le-Perray-en-Yvelines but there was no sign of the other Citroen much to Lafarge's relief. He lit a cigarette and put his foot down to try and make up some time but he made up his mind to stop in

Rambouillet which was the next big town, and phone Durand to ask him if he could delay the autopsy till mid-afternoon and inform Gilbert.

Lafarge pulled in outside a brasserie on the main street of the town most renowned for having a rarely-used royal chateau – though probably best known for Francis I dying there. There were a few workers in blue overalls standing at the zinc-topped bar but no sign of the three men. He had not seen the car on the street either, so he ordered two coffees and asked the barman for tokens for the telephone.

Durand was fine about the delay. He said he had enough customers to divert his attention, and promised he would ring Gilbert to tell him, adding he would give a better excuse than Lafarge's 'due to technical reasons'…."You were never very good at covering your tracks Gaston," the pathologist chided his friend. Lafarge chuckled, thinking if only Durand knew how good a liar he could be.

Lafarge walked back from the booth to the bar in good spirits but stopped in his tracks when he saw no sign of Rosenberg. The barman, more the standard type than Concarneau, broad shouldered slightly overweight and with a florid face because of broken blood vessels, beckoned him over.

"Two men took your friend outside about five minutes ago," he whispered.

The work men eyed Lafarge suspiciously as he pulled out his service revolver, until he flashed his badge. The barman told him they had turned right out of the door, Lafarge thanked him and pulled the door towards him looking carefully to his right.

There was no sign of them but Lafarge saw there was a street diagonally across from the brasserie and guessed that is where they had gone. He crossed over and peered round the corner and saw Rosenberg being dragged along by the two men. They were about 100 metres ahead of him. He crossed over to the other side of the street and shadowed them.

He knew he needed to act before they got him into their car which meant he might have to fire his gun. This risked alerting the local gendarmes but he could not afford to let Rosenberg be taken away, for the chances were he would be lost forever.

He saw their car was parked another 100 metres down the street – it had a clear run to exit the town in that direction -- so his time was limited.

He picked up speed while creeping along between the cars and the houses. Just as they reached the car, Lafarge rose up and yelled police.

The two men froze, dropping Rosenberg to the pavement. Lafarge reckoned this was a pretext for going for their guns, so he levelled his at them and with his other hand he flashed his badge to confirm he was indeed police.

They surprised Lafarge by raising their arms, and after looking around to see if the third man was anywhere to be seen he crossed the street. As he did so the front passenger door swung open catching him in the open.

Instinctively he threw himself to the ground, though, it offered little better cover than if he had remained standing. He pressed his face to the asphalt surface, screwed up his eyes as he heard the passenger walk towards him and even more so when he heard the man cock his pistol.

He waited for the moment to come, but instead to his consternation he heard the man laugh.

"Alright Chief Inspector you can get up."

Lafarge sighed, rose unsteadily to his feet, dusted down his suit trousers and met the eyes of Gilbert.

"Jesus Gilbert," gasped Lafarge.

Gilbert laughed but stopped abruptly.

"Chief Inspector what did you think you were doing?" asked Gilbert, his tone harsh.

"How did you know where I was? Who informed on me," asked Lafarge.

"You take me for a fool? I could tell you were going to do your best to help Rosenberg escape so I placed a man outside your building last night. I hear you have someone else watching it too, but that is your problem," said Gilbert.

Lafarge felt a certain sense of relief as it meant his man had not informed on him and also Gilbert had no idea that the man watching the apartment was a policeman. Gilbert was one of those seemingly rare birds these days, a policeman who was not out to kill him.

"I thought I had lost you when you pulled off that smart manoeuvre on the road to Trappes. Fortunately we got lucky in that one of my men had to go to the bathroom and as he stepped out he saw you going into the brasserie," said Gilbert.

"What are you going to do?" asked Lafarge wearily.

Gilbert smiled.

"Well my men and I are going to take him back to Paris and process him. I will then join you as planned at the autopsy," said Gilbert.

Lafarge was stunned.

"Why should I arrest you Chief Inspector? What good would that do? I have what I want and no good will be served by arresting a top class colleague," said Gilbert clapping Lafarge on his shoulder.

"However, I am warning you Lafarge do not try and interfere any further in this case. There are influential people who do not wish the due process of the law to be disturbed. We have had far too much disturbance to that in the past few years and now is the time for the reputation of the police and the legal establishment to be restored so it is respected once again," added Gilbert.

Lafarge groaned.

"So you are telling me the reputation of the police and the law will be best served by condemning an innocent man, one who was betrayed by the killer during the Occupation? Jesus Christ Gilbert I thought you were a clean policeman but even you have been bought off," snarled Lafarge, disregarding the fact Gilbert still had the gun in his hands.

"I am not one to desist, I never have been and will not change just because the regime is more democratic and is not rounding up thousands of innocents. Sending knowingly just one innocent man to the guillotine is as bad. Zilberstein has to be brought to account not only for the murder of Meissner but also for what he did during the Occupation. Jesus if he is to be given a clean slate for betraying his fellow Jews then what hope of a new start do we have!!!"

Gilbert smiled sympathetically at Lafarge, put away his pistol, and breathed in deeply.

"Listen Lafarge, you are a good man and I respect what you are saying. However, my hands are tied on this. Do you think I want to waste a whole day chasing after you to bring back an allegedly innocent man? No but there are those higher up who want it so.

"Now you can go and argue the toss with them but I doubt you will be heard. The best you can hope for is that Rosenberg gets a long prison sentence. There is nothing you or I can do to alleviate his situation, indeed you are lucky that it was me who volunteered to come after you, from what I hear you have had a fair share of our esteemed colleagues try and eliminate you altogether.

"There is a time when even the boldest and most honourable of us must cede that one fight too many could be fatal. Lafarge I advise you this is the day. You have a contract out on you, the last thing you need is to have the whole of the establishment against you.

"Please listen to me on this."

Lafarge smiled sadly and shrugged his shoulders but at the same time thanked Gilbert, then looked at the crest-fallen Rosenberg, who was being placed in the back of the car.

He went round and knocked on the window. Rosenberg had not been handcuffed so he was able to wind down the window.

"Thank you Chief Inspector for trying," he said, his words not coming easily.

"I am sorry I failed you this time Hal. However, don't think this is the end of it. We will nail the bastard," said Lafarge patting his arm before walking off down the street.

Chapter Ten

"So you want to arrest Zilberstein, despite the warning Gilbert gave you?" asked Pinault wearily.

Lafarge nodded. His drive back had only hardened his resolve, not because he felt humiliated by having been bested by Gilbert, in fact he appreciated the heartfelt warning from his colleague and also he actually believed that it was better for Rosenberg he was in a cell than wandering aimlessly again around France.

At least Lafarge knew where he was. Rosenberg's enemies – or rather the influential friends of Zilberstein's – too would have had their fears assuaged in knowing their scapegoat was now a step closer to fulfilling the role they wanted him to fill – be executed for a crime he had not committed.

Lafarge wondered what it was that granted Zilberstein such a protected status. Surely the regime would want rid of such an odious personality, who shamefully now owned one of the prime art galleries in Paris. It only made Lafarge more determined to hound Zilberstein and procure a confession out of him, to see him shamed and judged, no matter the consequences for himself.

Lafarge did not know whether at last his guilt from what he had done during the Occupation had won the battle of his conscience – he had thought when he gave Hal and his wife safe haven that that was enough to salve it but evidently not.

Even the return of Aimee and her desire to be with him after what he had done to her, by sacrificing her and her family to de Blaeckere and his goons so he could whisk de Chastelain away, should have been enough evidence that he was being too hard on himself and he was not a bad man.

However, Lafarge felt a gnawing discontent over the whole situation. Yes he was pig-headed – he did not want to see his one good deed during the Occupation go to waste with the man executed for a crime he clearly did not commit -- but he also felt he owed it to Rosenberg to see him right.

Pinault had received him cordially, joking if he had come across any more stags as allies on his way to see him. However, once he brought up the topic of Zilberstein and Rosenberg as well as told him about Gilbert's warning Pinault's expression took on a resigned and pained look.

It was clear whilst Pinault was in no way involved in the cover-up he wanted no trouble and what Lafarge was suggesting could only end in provoking that. Times were febrile enough that Pinault's own position was not regarded as safe.

There had been murmurings from both the right wing and the Communists dissatisfied with his handling of the murder of successful publisher Robert Denoel, who had collaborated with the Nazis but before the War had been more even-handed and published both anti-German and anti-Semitic publications including by the twisted but brilliant Louis-Ferdinand Celine.

These murmurs eagerly reproduced by the newspapers had also begun to attract reactions from the likes of ministry of Interior technocrats, quoted anonymously of course, criticising Pinault. One report had even asked why he had not put his best detective Lafarge on it. Ordinarily Lafarge should have been flattered, but as he did not agree with the tenet of the argument that Pinault was incompetent he did not feel the compliment was being used in a constructive manner.

In any case Lafarge knew that such a delicate political murder as Denoel's was – he had been carrying a dossier with explosive revelations pertaining to the publishing world under the Nazis which involved many who were now heading up publishers as well as probably information of those same technocrats now attacking Pinault – not one the powers that be would wish handed to someone with a reputation like his.

Which made it all the more ironic that his case appeared to be even more sensitive than Denoel's. It also made it doubly hard for Pinault to give him the green light. He feared it might prove to be the spark that caused his removal from his job. The only thing Lafarge hoped for was that Pinault might turn a blind eye, but out of courtesy he wanted to at least broach the topic before he went ahead with his strategy of shadowing Zilberstein and then arresting him, or at least trying to destabilise him by putting him in an interview room.

Pinault poured them both a generous serving of cognac before settling down behind his desk.

"Gaston this is a delicate matter," said Pinault.

Lafarge smiled thinly for he knew Pinault was being diplomatic in his use of language and what he meant was do not even think about pestering Zilberstein, he is protected and his protectors will ensure he is not harmed.

Lafarge remained silent forcing Pinault to expand on what he had said.

"I do not know whether Rosenberg really murdered Zilberstein's partner but I can assure you there are more powerful forces than me who will ensure it is resolved," said Pinault.

"You more than most in this building know how complex things were during the Occupation, relationships formed through necessity, learning things about people which were stored away for a day when they might come in handy should the Nazis leave.

"Undoubtedly Zilberstein is one of these types. Now he allegedly did things that are unbelievably callous and criminal. However, despite being a highly unattractive individual he is evidently a very resourceful man, for whatever he learned about some of the people who are in power now is sufficient for him to be immune from prosecution."

Lafarge sighed and rose from his chair, walking over to the large window that gave out onto the Seine.

He looked down on the Parisians taking an early evening stroll, young and old, some dressed smartly, others doing their best to look presentable, but were clearly wearing clothes that before the Occupation would have cut a dash but were now faded and threadbare.

He pondered whether the smartly-dressed ones were profiteers from the Occupation, the shabbily-dressed ones those who had suffered but still had pride in going out and breathing in free air showing their persecutors they had survived despite all the pressures and forces that had been levelled against them.

Was this how he saw Zilberstein and Rosenberg, it was

perhaps too neat an analogy and for all he knew the couples could be the reverse, the persecuted now dressed smartly and the oppressors or profiteers down at heel. He doubted it somehow and he cursed a system where the majority of those who had laughed, drank with and eaten with let alone done the Germans bidding had not suffered any fall out for their cowardly acquiescence with such an evil entity.

Well if he could put at least one of those bastards away then there was no one more suitable than Zilberstein both on a personal and professional level. Rosenberg did not deserve to lose his life having lost his business and wife thanks to the French State, but whilst he would refrain from putting them in the dock – even Lafarge accepted that was beyond him and foolhardy – he would not let it protect the man who had been the perpetrator of this calumny.

He liked and respected Pinault but he felt his advice was influenced by the problems he was encountering with Denoel.

"You will not like this sir but I cannot desist. You talk about the complexities of the Occupation and yes you are right I know too full well how complicated things were not only with relationships but in all areas, from watching what one said in case it was misinterpreted to the way one looked at 'our masters'," he said.

"I did some things I regret enormously, and there are other moments where I was a passive observer. Which was worse I do not know, but all I do acknowledge is that they lie equally on my conscience.

"The one decent thing I did do was save Hal Rosenberg and his wife and I will be damned if I am now going to see him go to the guillotine at the expense of a man like Zilberstein simply because he has a dossier on someone who would prefer it not to surface.

"You and I walk past people every day, whether it be in our apartment blocks or on the street or occasionally in here, who should be incarcerated or have been executed for the crimes they committed. They were given free licence to do so by a Vichy regime that claimed to be saving France but instead plunged it into being an accomplice and ultimately a perpetrator of unspeakable crimes.

"I will not be party to another murder committed in the name of the French State for that is what it will be if Hal Rosenberg is found guilty.

"I would like you to pass that message on to whomever it is that is protecting Zilberstein. Tell him that I will come up with incontrovertible proof that Zilberstein is not only guilty of the murder but also of condemning several Jews to death through his actions during the Occupation.

"I would add that the French State owes me a huge favour which I have not called in or felt the urge to do so, but I will do now. If it had not been for me, thanks to the support of you and the prefect, we would once again be living under a dictatorship though sugar-coated as a monarchy."

Lafarge halted there and waited for Pinault's response. He had done his bit, perhaps gone too far, but he had drawn on his last card in spite of his dislike of politicking.

However, he hoped his actions in preventing a coup d'etat in the early days of the Liberation – which would have seen the restoration of the monarchy in the form of the Comte de Paris who would largely have been a pawn in the hands of the far right Catholics who had opportunistically followed de Gaulle only because they disliked the Nazis more than the General – would have its desired impact on the man protecting Zilberstein.

Pinault shifted uncomfortably in his chair and fiddled with a couple of files on his desk.

"De Gaulle is no longer in power Gaston," said Pinault.

"That sir is irrelevant. The people who have replaced him owe me just as much as he does and do not for a moment think that if you refuse to pass the message on I will stop there," said Lafarge, his temper rising as he realised Pinault was attempting to keep the debate to a minimum.

Pinault glanced angrily at Lafarge but the Chief Inspector had had enough.

"I know you are under pressure due to another case and any trouble from another quarter will be unhelpful. But hell are we going to repeat the errors of the Occupation and cave in to political pressure, just be their thugs and accomplices in cracking down on the unions and other dissident forces?

"Of course we have to remain loyal but we also need to demonstrate that we are independent when it comes to cases we believe are worth pursuing and that those who are genuinely guilty have to be brought to justice, not simply acquiesce and replace them with a scapegoat.

"I am not asking you to devote several men and resources you require for other cases, we are short enough in manpower as it is to the extent we have had to keep on some old types whose idea of an energetic investigation is to wander over to the coffee pot to see if it is full.

"All I want is to be given a few weeks to see if I can nail Zilberstein. If I fail then fine go ahead with your railroading Rosenberg and you can throw in the extra bonus to the man protecting him that I will hand in my badge."

Pinault looked even more uncomfortable at this passionate outburst from his subordinate, Lafarge, though, felt exhilarated in finally letting go of his frustrations. He had had to fight to join the police force in the first place, over-riding the objections of his father and step-mother.

He found it ironic now that his father had allowed himself to be influenced by his step-mother, an inveterate snob who thought Lafarge would be damaging the family's standing by becoming a policeman instead of the legal profession as he held a law degree.

She must really have regretted that in the end his father had relented and helped through his contacts for Lafarge to go straight into plain clothes and the Crime Squad. It had been him who had arrested her and his step-brother Lucien for the murder of his father the previous year.

Lafarge, though, was counting on Pinault the man of action rather than the politician, the side of him that had impressed de Gaulle or at least those who advised the General and recommended he replace his highly-regarded predecessor Georges-Victor Mass when spurious charges were brought against the latter.

Pinault drummed his fingers on the desk, twiddled the end of his pencil thin moustache, sighed and then rose and to Lafarge's relief did not show him the door but poured them both another glass of cognac.

"You are as stubborn as a damn mule Gaston when it comes to situations like this," said Pinault, whose tone was amicable not adversarial or angry.

"It is clear you understand what I am contending with here, problems are mounting daily for me and it is not exactly a vibrant employment market out there for former policemen, especially the sort of well-paid jobs that one can get if one leaves with an approving reference.

"I think neither of us fit that category, or at least I won't if Denoel remains unsolved, although at times I feel that the powers that be would prefer I fail and use me as a scapegoat.

"However, he is not your concern. In fact you are damn lucky you are not involved, it is a no win case. Truth be told the Zilberstein/Rosenberg case is not seen as sensitive by the government as a whole, but there is definitely someone who would prefer it left alone.

"Rather that the case is now closed and Zilberstein is allowed to carry on his grubby little life, hopefully battling with his conscience which will end with him slipping a rope round his neck one night.

"As we both know very few criminals have such tussles and from what you have apprised me Zilberstein is the type who will sleep easily at night.

"That thought irks me a great deal Gaston as it would with any criminal being able to decide when they turn the light on or off or having the liberty to choose what they will eat next. I also take on board what you said about us being free thinkers when it comes to cases and not repeating the errors that led shall we generously say to the sins of the past.

"You are my best detective Gaston, your judgement sometimes is questionable and I would say your political antennae are zero as in this case. However, I can ill afford to lose you through you resigning, whether I lose you to a bullet is beyond my control," he said with a smile which Lafarge had trouble reciprocating. Pinault's humour was an acquired taste.

"Thus whilst I am fully focussed on Denoel's murder and spending all my waking hours and those of most of my men on it I have no time to wonder as to what my Chief Inspector is up to.

"That is the leeway I will give you Gaston. Now if Zilberstein comes after you as in making a complaint to the man protecting him or demands Gilbert has a stern word with you then we will have to bring the curtain down on it.

"The chances are of course that Zilberstein will complain, I cannot imagine he would dare go further than that, so I think it best Gaston if you go about this discreetly. That makes your task even harder and with his partner dead the list of people you can speak to ever smaller.

"However, that is your problem not mine and one I am sure with your ability to think outside the norm you will surmount. I will stand by you in that there is no question of you being drummed out of the force on my watch. I will of course have to instruct you to desist from your investigation if I receive such an order.

"Is that satisfactory enough for you?"

Lafarge exhaled and felt his heart pounding proud with himself for having fought hard but equally so of Pinault for having the courage to give him permission to pursue the case. He shook hands warmly with Pinault after agreeing to his conditions and moved to leave only to stop at the door when his boss called out.

"I am glad you are my son of a bitch Gaston, for I would hate to be your enemy, you scare the hell out of me," said Pinault smiling once again before looking wistfully out the window.

Lafarge grinned and thought what a perceptive man Pinault was.

Chapter Eleven

"Our stern-looking friend here died from being struck on the back of the head with a blunt instrument," said Durand.

Lafarge had joined Durand and Gilbert for the much-delayed autopsy on Meissner, his colleague greeting him with a wry smile but left it at that for which the Chief Inspector was grateful. Durand and he were longstanding friends – one of the few still standing – and did not ask if his 'technical reasons' for being late had been satisfactorily resolved.

Lafarge felt nothing as he stared at Meissner's corpse. It was not always the case even with those who were suspects or the culprit, but given the dynamics of a blackmailing couple Lafarge knew it could just as easily have been Zilberstein lying on the slab being picked apart expertly by Durand. Blackmailers were only connected by greed and it was only logical that one would eventually become surplus to requirements.

Lafarge also was keen to get the autopsy over as quickly as possible, the room in the basement was sinister enough – badly light and smelling of formaldehyde and other chemicals which at least overrode the sickly smell of death – but it had been here that his partner Levau had been murdered the year before and he had only been saved from joining him by Durand intervening and disabling the assassin.

Lafarge had even deliberated whether it served any purpose to come to the autopsy given that in Gilbert's eyes anyway they were going through the motions – protocol had to be observed and the blanks in the case had to be filled in so the judges trying Rosenberg could feel their consciences had been salved when they returned the already prepared guilty verdict.

However, he accepted reluctantly that he had to play his role in this charade for quite aside from keeping Gilbert on side in believing he had learned his lesson he needed to know as much about the death of Meissner as possible so as to turn up the pressure on Zilberstein.

Durand did not know he was being used in this manner,

although his findings were always factual and dispassionate – he had withdrawn to his basement and his ghoulish work after losing too many comrades and friends in the Great War preferring as he remarked to Lafarge to see the dead not befriend those who were to die – he would be furious that his work was being used to pervert the course of justice.

"Are you sure Durand? I was led to believe he had hit his head on the edge of a door," said Gilbert, his tone deeply sceptical.

Durand glanced up at Gilbert not looking pleased.

"Well Chief Inspector Gilbert I would say you have been led up the garden path to that particular door. No it is quite clear a blunt instrument put an end to this man's life," said Durand so emphatically that there was little point Gilbert continuing with his theory.

This pleased Lafarge enormously as Durand had destroyed Zilberstein's version of events which was why Gilbert now looked flustered. It did pose a question though as to why Gilbert had allowed the autopsy to go ahead without reassuring himself beforehand that the pathologist would prove accommodating.

This presented Lafarge with an opportunity for perhaps Gilbert had not been bought off and had just been instructed to find and arrest Rosenberg and the rest of the case would run its course. He would chat to him afterwards and see if the outcome of the autopsy had changed his mind or that he was indeed acting for the protectors of Zilberstein and would adjust the evidence accordingly as the enquiry went along.

"Any ideas as to what the blunt instrument might be Durand?" asked Lafarge.

"I would say something with a broad base, like a blotter or an ashtray," Durand replied.

"What about a sculpture?"

"Yes, that could be a possibility," said Durand looking quizzically at both Gilbert and Lafarge.

"The murder took place in an art gallery, hence why I asked," said Lafarge.

"You are on your game Gaston," said Durand drily glancing up at him.

Lafarge smiled.

"I had one of your other customers in the other day, the one who ran into an angry stag," said Durand.

"You really do send me the most interesting clients Chief Inspector Lafarge. In that respect you are way ahead of your colleagues," added Durand.

"A stag? How on earth did that happen?" asked Gilbert after he and Lafarge had retired to a café following their visit to Durand.

Lafarge laughed and told Gilbert, whose expression went from concern to amusement.

"That is crazy! Some chiefs would not have believed you, you are fortunate to have Pinault as your boss."

"Well Durand let me into a secret, Pinault insisted on seeing the corpse which is not something he usually does. I don't blame him mind you on both counts," said Lafarge.

"I agree with you on that, I thought I would become desensitised to staring at corpses, but some of them what they have had done to them is inhuman and beyond one's comprehension," said Gilbert.

Lafarge nodded and wondered why people like himself and Gilbert spent days trudging down to Durand and observing the worst excesses that man or woman could inflict on another. Did one ever become immune to such sights and did one's mind ever become dulled to imagining the agony some of the victims endured? Blessed were those who died instantly.

"I agree sometimes I feel real anger or upset when I have to sit in on an autopsy with Durand. He does a wonderful job and is very conscientious. His humour is relatively respectful of the victim unlike many others in his profession.

"However, it also makes me nervous too when I then realise, if one has not already got the suspect in custody, the mind of the criminal you are going after and what if you fall into his or her hands. Are you in effect looking at yourself on that slab?

"With Meissner, though, I did not feel a thing. To me he is as bad as the man who more than likely put him there," said Lafarge, surprised at himself. He rarely expressed his feelings unless it was with Aimee or a close friend.

Perhaps it was because there were so few of the latter left that he had felt the need to do so. However, he also felt at ease with Gilbert, again a rare experience with a colleague. It had not been the case during the Occupation, although prior to that there had been several he had been good friends with.

Most of them had like him joined up and many had not returned, killed as the Germans wept through France. Those that had were like him appalled at the politicisation of the police, both gendarmes and plain clothes, and the brutality of the Brigades Speciales.

Several had been executed during the Occupation for feeding information to the Resistance or for aiding Jews to escape – Lafarge had escaped such a fate by blocking a fellow detective from entering his apartment where the Rosenberg's were hiding – whilst others had thrown their lot in with Bousquet and become willing participants in the worst excesses of the regime.

Gilbert was one of the few that remained although he had not been as friendly with him as he had been with others. Gilbert had always kept himself apart when it came to finishing a tough shift and going to relax in a café afterwards.

Nobody appeared to know what he did in out of office hours, there were precious few of those and nobody joined the police for fixed hours or at least on the plain clothes side. Those who joined inspired by films about Chief Inspector Maigret soon realised there was little clean about the criminal world, that those one dealt with were far from accommodating or willing to break bread with one like some in Simenon's books, or indeed a patient wife awaiting at home to cook, iron and advise one on what to listen to on the radio.

Even if one possessed the great qualities of Maigret, urbanity and compassion, those were soon extinguished unless you had the strongest of characters.

Lafarge was not conjecturing that Gilbert compared to Maigret – for a start he smoked unfiltered Gitanes not a pipe – but he could see him as a rare example of a detective returning to a long-suffering wife in a nice apartment and being well looked after.

"I know often I wonder how much longer I can do this job for," said Gilbert leaning back in his chair and stretching his arms.

"Each time I catch a criminal and he is sent down or guillotined I should be satisfied and pleased with myself for taking another danger to society off the streets.

"However, instead I feel like Sisyphus pushing the rock up the hill, I have to start all over again because there are endless bad people out there. Not even two World Wars could rid us of all of them.

"Christ some of the worst ones actually flourished and have come out of the Occupation stronger than they were before it."

Lafarge nodded, signalled to the waiter for another round – he was as usual drinking cognac but Gilbert had opted for a Biere de Garde.

"Which neatly brings me round to Meissner and Zilberstein," said Lafarge.

"Ah yes I thought we might end up talking about them," grinned Gilbert.

"Well quite apart from the fact one of us needs to go back to Durand in half an hour when Zilberstein is due to identify the body, I think we need to revisit what happened in the gallery given what we learned from the autopsy," said Lafarge.

"I'm listening," said Gilbert.

"Well it is inconvenient to say the least for Zilberstein that his version of events does not concur with the official autopsy. I think on that alone Rosenberg should be released pending further investigation by the two of us," said Lafarge.

"Now I am going to be bold here and suggest that you may have been sold a false line regarding Zilberstein and Meissner that you were under no circumstances to let them come to any harm. I would wager that it was part of your remit when you were transferred to the eighth.

"I think they are high maintenance protection, lord knows why. Perhaps they had some sensitive information on the person who is using his influence to protect them. You must have had a hard time explaining Meissner's death. No doubt it was impressed on you how important it is for you to keep Zilberstein alive and out of prison."

Gilbert looked thoughtful, to Lafarge's relief he did not look either angry or hurt by what he had implied. However, there was a world of difference between how he looked and what his answer might be. Lafarge realised he may have Pinault's tacit backing but more than anything ne required an ally on the ground and Gilbert was the logical answer because he knew the case and more than likely was aware who was looking out for Zilberstein.

Gilbert took a sip of his drink, plucked at his tongue to extract a stray bit of tobacco which had stuck to his tongue and dropped it in the ash tray.

"Given your reputation for frank talking you have been remarkably diplomatic in your language Gaston," said Gilbert, his tone neutral.

"Let us deal with the one fact in your analysis stroke theory. Yes, the autopsy findings present serious problems in view of the initial description of events by Zilberstein. However, he has yet to give an official statement so that can be amended."

Lafarge breathed in deeply, he did not like the way this was going nor how brazen Gilbert was in saying it straight out.

"Nevertheless and this is where we address your allegations about where my loyalty lies, and indeed questions about my probity, I am not going to tell Zilberstein about the autopsy findings. He will sign a statement but it will be no different to what he first told me.

"I am willing at times to let things pass, or to help someone because I have been asked by a person who I respect or a superior has ordered me to do so. However, if the person I have been asked to look after lies to me then I consider that as a breaking of the contract of trust between us.

"No one makes a fool out of me or thinks they have carte blanche to take advantage of me. I will explain this to his protector of course. Now that does not mean Rosenberg will be released and Zilberstein charged instead, don't get your hopes up.

"The nature of the beast has not changed much from the days of the Occupation. If one detective is unwilling to bend to his master's demands then they will find another one and that will not be too hard.

"What I am going to do is to give Zilberstein one more chance to explain what happened. He has given two different versions so far, so my guess is that he is an intelligent man and unless he is overly confident he will give the same testimony as the second account.

"I will say, though, Gaston that you should not push too hard on this one. My superior leant gently on me for sure but he gave me the impression the protector is someone extremely powerful and ready to do anything to see that Rosenberg is guillotined. You do not want to be accompanying him, for he will find a pretext to do just that even if you are a Chief Inspector.

"Is it worth risking your life for? Even if you escape that I am sure they will demand you resign."

Lafarge felt a chill travel down his spine. He wondered who this seemingly omnipotent figure is, that cast such a spell of fear over so many usually solid and courageous types like Gilbert.

The is it worth risking your life for seemed to come up relentlessly in this investigation and whilst touched by so many people's sudden concern for his welfare he was not going to be dissuaded from his pursuit of the guilty man. If that also meant he had to take down the person protecting Zilberstein then so be it he would do so.

He did not of course divulge this to Gilbert, for he really would have thought him mad. However, he knew of a way he could get the protector and if he could bring him to heel publicly then that might serve as a warning to others that the days of wielding one's power in a criminal way – even if those doing so were democratically elected – were over.

"Yes, Gilbert I believe it is," said Lafarge.

"Shall we go and see Zilberstein and reunite him with his former partner?"

"You are not suggesting we kill him?" said Gilbert briefly looking alarmed.

Lafarge laughed.

"If only Gilbert if only. It would resolve a lot of problems would it not!"

Zilberstein was waiting for them in the lobby, dressed as he always seemed to be in a black tailcoat, silk blue tie and a winged collar white shirt. Lafarge thought he looked like an undertaker and his lugubrious expression only added to the impression.

"I see you have come suitably dressed," remarked Lafarge dryly.

Lafarge was delighted as Zilberstein flashed him an angry look, before they ushered him down the stairs to Durand's 'office'.

Durand was waiting -- although he had switched on his radio which was playing Edith Piaf's La Vie En Rose which made Lafarge chuckle given where they were -- and drew back the sheet covering Meissner's body. The advantage for Lafarge and Gilbert was that having attended the autopsy they could pay attention to Zilberstein's reaction.

A flicker of emotion crossed Zilberstein's face and to Lafarge's astonishment there was even a hint of a smile. Lafarge looked at Gilbert, who nodded back to say he had seen the smile too. Zilberstein mopped his brow, mouthed just loudly enough it was Meissner and stepped back.

Gilbert indicated to Lafarge that he would accompany Zilberstein to the exit. Lafarge acquiesced realising that if he were to go as well Zilberstein might sense something had altered. It also gave Gilbert the chance to ask him one more time for his version of events.

"He's an odd fellow that," said Durand.

"Who?" Lafarge asked.

"Not your colleague you fool, the fellow who just identified the corpse," said Durand.

Lafarge grunted and shrugged his shoulders.

"I know he is. I suspect him of having murdered Meissner. A falling out amongst thieves and blackmailers," said Lafarge.

"So I take it he is involved in the art gallery? Hence why you asked if it could be a sculpture," said Durand.

"My my you are alert Durand. Playing and fiddling with dead has not dulled your mind," said Lafarge lighting up and offering one to Durand.

"Yes and you might raise that an octave higher when I tell you the reason I say he is an odd fellow. I am certain he has been here before, and I think it may be more than once. I was surprised he did not acknowledge that he had met me before," said Durand.

Lafarge's fatigue -- which had just taken hold of him after his rather long and eventful day – disappeared within seconds. His thoughts of wishing Gilbert would hurry back and they could go home thrown to the wind.

"Good lord Durand. Are you absolutely certain?"

Durand nodded vigorously.

"Yes, although I get many people coming here, dead and alive, it is the latter funnily enough I remember best. Maybe because of their differing emotions, my clients obviously are rather lacking in them save those whose faces are transfixed in terror at the moment of their death and …."

"Yes, yes Durand sorry to cut you off but when was he here and for whom? It does not matter if you cannot recall if he was here twice, that can come later," said Lafarge.

Durand scratched his head and shuffled off towards a small office where he kept his records and normally a couple of bottles. Lafarge hoped he returned both with the paperwork and a bottle.

He duly delivered on both fronts, although, Lafarge could tell why he had brought the bottle as the folder he was carrying was extremely bulky.

Lafarge looked askance at Durand when he saw the bottle contained eau de vie de vin.

"We can't all afford cognac Gaston. Lord if I had served you cognac all these times you have been here I would be reduced to penury and have to sleep in my office," grinned Durand.

"I am amazed you can tell the difference between this and the chemicals you use," Lafarge joked.

Durand smiled and indicated for Lafarge to pour which he did, over generously truth be told which provoked a mischievous glance from his friend. Gilbert then returned and Lafarge having informed him why they needed to stay he also poured himself a glass.

"So Zilberstein stuck to his version of events, he says he saw Rosenberg push Meissner and his partner fell back and struck his head on the edge of the door. I noted it all down and in as much as it is official it will at least appear in my verbatim notes should he alter his testimony when he comes to draw up his formal statement," said Gilbert.

"The smile sealed it for me. He is so arrogant and sure of himself that he felt he could do that, effectively laugh at us and say well I did it but I am not going to pay for it," said Lafarge bitterly.

"I know ordinarily we would have him. You can take him if you want but you know what that is going to bring down on you," said Gilbert.

"I will take him down Gilbert. If anything my resolve is stronger now than even when I said that to you in the café. I have had enough of the French police being taken for granted, the awful years just passed we deserve a hostile press and even more so from the people," said Lafarge.

"However, we should show we learned from it and nobody is above the law, neither are the less well- off to be used as scapegoats."

Gilbert smiled sympathetically.

"Look why don't we go about this in the manner in which the Chicago police -- or at least those that were clean – did with Al Capone?" suggested Gilbert.

"What do you mean?"

"All the murders he ordered, the beatings, the thefts etcetera they never got him on that. But they did finally trap him on failure to pay taxes and off he went to jail," said Gilbert looking pleased with himself.

Lafarge stared at his glass and thought well might Gilbert look content, for that was an inspired idea, though with one big question mark over it.

"That is brilliant Gilbert. However, one point why would finding another thing to charge Zilberstein with have any more chance of succeeding in ridding ourselves of his protector? I would have thought he is immune from anything through his hold over whoever it is wants him spared prison or any harassment," said Lafarge.

"I think a lesser charge might be permissible. We can but try and I am with you on this, I do not want to see that smug smile on his face when he walks past me in the street," said Gilbert.

"That is something for us to get with tomorrow morning. However, before I waste my time I need you to clear this with your superior," said Lafarge.

Gilbert nodded and clapped him on the back.

"I've found it," said Durand, waving a piece of paper in his hand his eyes ablaze with satisfaction.

"Very good Durand, your mind was not playing tricks on you," said Lafarge smiling.

Both Lafarge and Gilbert gathered round Durand and read the form, which was written out in Durand's clear handwriting of an autopsy carried out in September 1944. The piece of paper he was holding was the form with the signature attesting to the identification of the victim.

"My God!" both Lafarge and Gilbert cried in unison.

Durand looked at them both searching for one of them to answer.

"That man is called Zilberstein," sad Lafarge.

Durand shook his head but Gilbert confirmed Lafarge was correct.

"Believe me Durand I know Hal Rosenberg and the man who has just identified Meissner is not him," said Lafarge, his voice trembling with emotion.

"Gaston I am very sorry. However, I am sure he presented identification documents confirming who he was. He was here with a detective, who unlike you told him he had to sign the form" said Durand.

Many thoughts were running through Lafarge's head, according to the form it was Rosenberg identifying his wife. This meant she had survived the torture at the hands of de Blaeckere and his thugs which surprised him enormously having seen their handiwork on a woman when he was in Limoges.

Had Meissner suddenly rediscovered a conscience and intervened with Rosenberg having escaped. Perhaps he thought if he were to return they could use her as a bargaining chip in keeping him quiet. Heaven knows what went through their minds.

Another possibility of course was it really Mrs Rosenberg. But then that would have been pointless unless by proving her death it released some funds into their hands as executors. If the real Mrs Rosenberg had died at the hands of de Blaeckere it was not something they should be aware of as it would have gone unreported like so many did under Vichy and the Nazis.

"How sure are you that it was Mrs Rosenberg?"

Durand looked confused. As well he might, thought Lafarge. He knew his friend prided himself on an orderly process and good bookkeeping which usually avoided any embarrassing errors.

"Let me have a look at the other papers," said Durand.

He took a long slug of the eau de vie and plunged into the folder again, withdrawing a thick pile of papers.

"Right it says identification papers were not found on her, hence I imagine why the husband was asked to sign a paper attesting that it was indeed her. If you are going to harangue me about laxity and not demanding they be produced I think you will give me the leeway that it was chaos after the Liberation," said Durand.

"So many people wanted to disappear, thus papers galore were either ripped up or lost conveniently and forgers made a pretty fortune. That is not a bad occupation actually, they will always thrive," mused Durand.

Lafarge grunted, not in the least bit interested in Durand's observations on the prospects within the criminal profession. He wondered how potent the eau de vie was. Whilst it had barely had an effect on him it appeared it had an adverse one on Durand.

"I take your point and I think Gilbert does too. We are not holding you responsible for this but we do need to know what the cause of death was," sad Lafarge gently.

Durand peered down the page.

"Strangulation," he said.

Lafarge glanced at Gilbert, who raised his eyebrows.

"One last thing if you don't mind Durand. Are there any

observations you have noted down regarding marks on the body? I ask because I know Mrs Rosenberg was tortured when she fled during the Occupation."

Durand scanned the papers and shook his head.

"No, there are no such indications," he said.

"I take it that physical torture leaves traces, even two years after it took place?" asked Lafarge.

"That depends but judging by cadavers I have performed autopsies on of torture victims of the Nazis and regrettably our own police, they did their work so enthusiastically that yes it would leave traces even that long after the event," said Durand.

"Well then it was not Mrs Rosenberg. I have seen the torture techniques of the Limoges Brigades Speciales and I can tell you their brutality and enthusiasm as you put it Durand were on another level to even the Gestapo," said Lafarge.

Durand sighed and handed the papers on the autopsy to Lafarge.

"I imagine you will need these then," he said.

Lafarge nodded and thanked him, reassuring Durand that no blame could be or would be attached to him.

"One more thing Durand before we leave you be. I don't expect you to remember his name but did the detective sign anything? It prays he did as it would be more than helpful if we had his name," said Gilbert.

Durand shook his head.

"These are the only papers I have and none were signed or counter-signed by him as you can see. I was expecting him to counter-sign the identification paper but he said I could be just as good as him as a witness and besides it was my 'home'."

They took their leave of him, Durand had cheered up a bit thanks to the reassurances of both Lafarge and Gilbert.

Once outside in the dark – the electrically-light streetlamps were extinguished due to another strike by the unions -- both exhaled deep breaths.

"Christ Gaston what have we got ourselves into?" said Gilbert, his voice lacking its normal confident tone.

Lafarge chewed his lip and thought for a moment. He agreed

with Gilbert that what had looked relatively rosy a few minutes before in going after Zilberstein on fiscal issues and obtaining permission for that now looked a very remote chance.

Zilberstein looked likely to have been involved in two murders. The question was could they do anything about it?. One thing that consoled him was Gilbert was now on his side as he clearly did not like being taken for a fool by Zilberstein. Whilst Meissner's murder might have to be classified, but not if Lafarge had anything to do with it laid at Rosenberg's door, a previous offence surely was fair game for Zilberstein to be pursued over.

They walked together in silence, both mulling over what they could do next. For Gilbert it was a big leap if he took it as he had sworn to protect Zilberstein. Lafarge felt for him over his dichotomy, he had no such qualms but he would feel stronger if his colleague became a fully-fledged ally and not someone he felt was keeping an eye on him.

They were so caught up in their own thoughts that they passed several cafes without even thinking of easing their feet and their minds not to mention warming them up against the bitter cold with a drink.

Time enough for that mused Lafarge. His mind was on how to ease Rosenberg's plight and he saw little chance of having him released so his best route was to find cast iron evidence against Zilberstein or someone else having committed Meissner's murder.

"Ok Gaston I will approach my superior and demand that the strings protecting Zilberstein if not cut altogether at least be loosened," said Gilbert when they finally did stop for a quick drink.

"I think then we will bring him face to face with Durand in a confrontation so at least we can obtain an official identification of him having been present at Madame Rosenberg's post-mortem and from there we have an opening into his deal with them over the gallery and from there into Meissner's murder."

Lafarge smiled and shook Gilbert's hand.

"It is just as well to have one clear-headed man amongst us. That is sublime Gilbert," said Lafarge.

Gilbert too smiled.

"Well one that wants to keep his when this is all over at least," he said.

"Although there is one thing that intrigues me which is what happened to Madame Rosenberg. Despite you saying that they must have disposed of her body in either a mass grave or unnamed one, who then was the corpse that turned up on Durand's slab?

"Also who was the detective that refused to sign the form....there are several things here that fail to make sense," added Gilbert.

Lafarge scratched the back of his neck and thought about it for a second or two. Gilbert had a point.

Rather than get nearer to the truth they had only served up more questions to be answered but if anything it actually fired him up even more to overcome all the political obstacles and solve the murders.

"Well my dear Gilbert I recommend you do everything in your power to keep Zilberstein alive until he is confronted face to face in our de-luxe room at the Quai. After all it is your duty to do so as your part of the partnership," said Lafarge with a grin and bid him farewell.

Lafarge was in a cheerful state of mind when he made his way to the metro which appeared to be back on track with the government patching together an agreement with the unions, though likely to last on previous history only at best a couple of days.

He would have been markedly less so if he had noticed the sharply-dressed couple who rose from the table of the café he and Gilbert had stopped at and trailed after him into the station.

Chapter Twelve

The metro might have been running again but the trains were intermittent and Lafarge, exposed to the elements on the platform of Jaures station, stamped his feet to try and keep warm.

He reflected on the irony of his present investigation and the station where he was at the moment marooned. It recalled a previous conflict between France and Germany when a hasty name change had taken place, switching it from Allemagne at the outbreak of the Great War to Jaures in honour of Jean Jaures, the renowned editor of left wing journal L'Humanite. An anti-militarist he had been assassinated by a French nationalist, the suitably named Raoul Villain. Extraordinarily Villain had been acquitted post War – whilst he had never tempered his hatred of all things left wing and been killed in the Spanish Civil War by the Republican forces – and the sense of injustice had simmered ever since but on a political front.

Now Lafarge too faced a conflict, but bizarrely he was taking on a member of a government containing the Communists, who were protecting Zilberstein. They had clearly placed business above oral scruples in dealing with the Nazis . Lafarge wished there was a newspaper editor as fearless as Jaures that he could go to. However, the editors of the newspapers that were available played the political game and were as subservient to the new administration as the likes of Jean Luchaire had been to the Nazis.

Luchaire's collaboration had cost him his life – he had been executed in February though it perplexed Lafarge that a newspaper publisher should be judged before a high level former minster such as Bousquet who had actively ordered the round-up of Jews – and whilst there was no fear of similar punishment for his successors they too had fallen into line with transmitting the message of reconciliation and the myth that a minority of French people had collaborated.

His thoughts were interrupted as the lights of the train

signalled he could stop stamping his feet, though whether the carriage would be any warmer was a moot point. However, his attention was diverted by a woman who was perilously close to the edge of the platform and looked as if she was going to jump.

Such tragic events were a sadly regular feature post the Liberation – a mix of survivors of the camps unfairly feeling guilty for having lived whilst family and friends had perished or disillusioned former Vichy camp followers whose loss was less keenly felt – but Lafarge moved quick as a flash to prevent another pointless loss of life.

He swooped to pluck the woman away from the edge and pushed her back against the crowd of people who were preparing to step forward and board the train. One of them, a good looking middle-aged man grabbed her.

He nodded at Lafarge whilst he placed a coat round the woman, who was Lafarge observed in the light shone by the train striking looking and would have been beautiful but for a scar that ran down the right side of her face from below the eye to her chin.

The three of them boarded the train, better to be in the relative warmth of a crowded carriage than out in the cold awaiting for god knows how long for the next train to come along.

The woman sobbed and buried her head in the man's shoulder, her arms round his neck. He looked sheepishly at Lafarge, who smiled back sympathetically. The rest of the passengers who had boarded at Jaures either eyed the floor nervously, or tut-tutted in that peculiarly austere puritanical Catholic fashion for they regarded such acts as a sin.

Lafarge flashed his badge at those who did. One who particularly attracted his distaste was an elderly woman with a fur stole and a rat like dog pressed close to her ample bosom.

"You will of course be reporting her detective," said the woman.

"It is none of your business madame, and it is Chief Inspector," replied Lafarge coolly.

"It is your duty to do so. And for your information I am a Baroness," said the woman.

Lafarge shrugged dismissively, wondering why a smartly-dressed Baroness was slumming it in the Metro and in an arrondissement not renowned for having aristocratic residents. That was usually the 6th and 7th on the Left Bank or the 16th or Neuilly.

He turned his back on her, restraining himself from making further comment as she seemed to be the type who warmed to a confrontation.

"Thank you Chief Inspector. I apologise for my wife's moment of madness. I am Jerome Beauregard and this is Maria," said the husband, who Lafarge noticed spoke with an accent tinged with a foreign lilt.

"Will you be taking her to hospital? She obviously needs attention," said Lafarge, his tone clearly indicating that Beauregard should do as such.

Beauregard smiled, but it was not a warm one.

"Let me be the judge of that Chief Inspector. We have confronted many difficult occasions in our lives, as I imagine many in this carriage have," Beauregard said elliptically but clearly did not favour more discussion on the subject.

Maria continued to hide her face in Beauregard's shoulder, and Lafarge studied his face. For a man who had almost lost his wife minutes ago he had remained icily calm – was it because she had tried it before wondered Lafarge – his piercing blue eyes yielded little save a coldness which suggested a streak of callousness or cruelty within.

Lafarge told himself to stop being so judgemental, if this was a commonplace event no wonder there was a certain weariness and so what attitude from Beauregard.

An awkward silence descended on the trio, broken only by Maria's sobs

All of them alighted at Pere Lachaise and Beauregard gave a Lafarge a cursory nod of the head as if to say thank you again but good night whilst the buxom Baroness and her yapping dog loitered for no apparent reason behind them.

Lafarge wandered down Rue du Chemin Vert before taking a left – a shortcut he habitually took – and coming to the crossroads with Rue de La Roquette he bumped into the Beauregards again.

In the dim light which shone down from a first floor apartment he could see both feigned surprise at seeing him.

"You look lost," said Lafarge, resisting the urge to add for people who appeared to live in the area.

Beauregard smiled. However, Lafarge could see again the eyes lacked the warmth to go with the smile which put him on his guard.

"Oh no Chief Inspector we are just getting some fresh air. I thought that was a better remedy for Maria's stupidity earlier," said Beauregard.

Lafarge thought it a tasteless remark but if he expected Maria to agree he was disappointed, for she chuckled inanely. He had no idea what games the couple were up to, he wondered even if they were perhaps a psychiatrist and his patient testing out some new experiment in seeing how she behaved amongst people when out of the asylum.

It had also crossed his mind that Beauregard either as husband or doctor had been extremely negligent in allowing Maria to get so close to the edge of the platform. Perhaps that was why he was reluctant to take her to hospital, the accusatory looks he would get for being a careless husband or the risk he could be taken to task by his colleagues for lack of duty of care to a patient.

Lafarge again bid them good night and trooped down Rue de La Roquette eager to get home, see Aimee and hear about her day filming and peer in on Ancil.

He got to the front door that opened into the courtyard but his ears pricked up when he heard a click behind him.

He wheeled round to find Beauregard and his wife – or patient -- emerging out of the darkness. He made to go inside relieved that it was just the mildly irritating couple but for the first time it was Maria who called out.

"Chief Inspector I wanted to apologise for not thanking you myself. You were very courageous in coming to my aid, risking your life for a silly selfish fool," she said with a smile, hers carrying a lot more warmth than that of Beauregard.

Lafarge let the door shut on him and moved towards Maria.

"Please think nothing of it Madame Beauregard. I only did my duty and saved you and your husband a lot of trouble and misery," he said.

"By the way where is your husband?" he asked.

"If you turn round you will see," she said flashing her sweet warm smile.

Lafarge a little confused turned around and saw Beauregard blocking his path to the door. There was no smile on his lips this time that had been replaced by a gun in his left hand.

Lafarge raised his left hand to the side of his head and scratched it, buying himself some time before the detective across the street would be alert enough to notice something was up.

"Who are you really?" asked Lafarge.

Beauregard shrugged his shoulders as Lafarge felt Maria's breath on his neck and at the same time a sharp jab in his back.

"Chief Inspector all will be revealed once you have taken us upstairs and introduced us to Aimee and Ancil," said Maria.

Lafarge shook his head in astonishment at the depth of intelligence they had on him and his family. Someone had briefed them well or they had been watching the building for days.

"I refuse to take you up there," said Lafarge, unwilling to visit any more danger onto his close family.

Maria sighed and it was clear to Lafarge now that the reason Beauregard was short on conversation was that it was she who was the chief of this operation.

"Listen Chief Inspector," she whispered digging the sharp object hard enough that he could feel the skin on his lower back coming loose.

"I really do not want to leave you dying out here on your own. I would much rather you look into the eyes of your beloved wife and child as you and they bid farewell to the world.

"We were told to ensure that was the case. All three of you and we do not want to disappoint the person who sent us. He is a perfectionist and demands that quality of those he entrusts tasks to.

"So I say again Chief Inspector, move and open the door!" she hissed.

Lafarge glanced quickly across to the plane tree that lay opposite the entrance vainly searching for the detective who was on watch.

Beauregard looked in the same direction and laughed. To Lafarge's surprise unlike his smile his laugh was a genuine one.

"No cavalry coming for you Chief Inspector. Your colleague has gone to the place that you saved Maria from going to earlier … or thought you had. Your Good Samaritan Act was a delight to watch and even better that it was successful," said Beauregard laughing so heartily that it racked his whole body.

Lafarge groaned and wondered who of his colleagues now lay dead across the way. Aside from hoping he did not know him too well, he prayed the man did not have a wife and children, in these poverty-stricken days the police were not generous in granting death money to the bereaved families.

"So you gambled that I would intervene? You were prepared to die if I had failed to save you or ignored you completely? What would you have done Beauregard in that instance?" asked Lafarge.

Beauregard shrugged.

"That is irrelevant Chief Inspector. We are where we are and please no more delaying, open the damn door," said Beauregard,

Lafarge nodded resignedly and pushed open the door.

Madame Grondin's light was out and Lafarge made his way towards the staircase with Beauregard to his side and Maria behind him.

"That is far enough!" rang out a female voice from an alcove to the left of the stairwell.

Lafarge stopped but Beauregard raised his gun and moved to fire it. Lafarge not giving a damn about Maria and her sharp object, dived at Beauregard and knocked him to the ground which sent the gun skittling back across the courtyard.

Beauregard would not be answering for the murder of the detective as in the collision he had hit his head on the wall of the stairwell and judging by the way he was lying he had broken his neck.

Maria tried to take advantage of Lafarge being on the ground by bending over him and stabbing him with the sharp object. Lafarge saw it was a stiletto and vainly tried to wriggle free, but Maria succeeded in piercing his left shoulder. He screamed in agony but did manage to fight her off, landing a punch in her stomach with his one good hand. Maria reeled backwards but came for him again.

This time, though, Lafarge had got to his feet but did not have time to reach for his pistol in his holster. Maria caught him again, this time scraping his left side and as he reached instinctively to touch where the wound was she brought her other hand round with full force and slapped him across the face with the back of her hand.

He collapsed to the ground, only saved from another stabbing by the report of a gun and Maria clutching her leg and staggering in vain towards the door before she too fell to the ground.

She lay there moaning and trying to stem the flow of blood from her leg, before a large figure emerged from the darkness to bend over her and tie a tourniquet round the limb.

The person the turned to approach Lafarge and to his utter amazement he stared up at the face of the haughty Baroness, who smiled benignly down at him adding a "Tut tut I told you so".

"I am only sorry I did not arrive later and was able to save your colleague," said the 'Baroness' as Lafarge lay on his sofa and Aimee cleaned and bandaged his two wounds.

Both were relatively superficial, the blade had not penetrated very deep into his shoulder and a rib had been responsible for Maria only being able to scrape his side with the second attempt. It was more his face that was smarting, he could feel a bruise growing on his cheekbone, as well as his ego at being saved by an elderly woman.

Whilst he was being tended in relatively comfortable surroundings -- aided by a fine bottle of cognac -- Maria had been taken under armed guard to hospital and Beauregard's corpse was on its way to Durand's morgue.

Aimee hid her anxiety well when she saw a strange elderly

lady helping Lafarge through the door and dumping him on the sofa, after all she had seen far worse in Ravensbruck. She struck a business like tone, her only concern that Ancil not see his father in this state.

However, the attack had made her face reality. Prior to this she had felt secure and that the contract on Lafarge pertained to him only and Pinault had been covering himself in putting a detective on duty to follow her to the studio and back again.

This incident brought sharply into focus how wrong she had been and now her and Ancil's safety were genuinely under threat her priority had to be to keep them out of harm's way. Lafarge knew the risks and had a gun to protect him, they had nothing and the murder of the detective showed the assassins' determination and ability to circumvent the security around them.

Still that discussion could be postponed till this curious character purporting to be a Baroness and her dog had departed. She knew too that in Lafarge she would have a sympathetic ear and it would not surprise her if he had already reached the same conclusion. There was no question of her abandoning the film, for this was her big chance to make something of her career and shrug off the label of being one of Sacha Guitry's 'girls' only there on stage or film due to his patronage.

The dressing was done and Lafarge, whose pallor had improved considerably from when he had first stumbled in, gave her a warm kiss of gratitude and pulled himself up a little so he could lean against the end of the sofa and light a cigarette.

"All is well with the world now Chief Inspector," said the Baroness dryly.

Lafarge chuckled and then grimaced as it triggered pain in his rib that had probably saved his life.

"So tell us about yourself Baroness. How on earth did you come to be in the courtyard, why were you following them and I guess less important are you really a Baroness?" asked Lafarge.

The Baroness, who retained some of the beauty she must have had in her youth with a remarkably unlined face, and rich silver hair contrasting sharply with brown eyes and a firm mouth, smiled.

"I am Baroness de Chavanel and late of the Resistance," she said proudly before pointing at her dog, who was lying at her feet.

"I always found having this little mutt a most useful aide when I worked with the Resistance during the Occupation.

"Whether it was taking him for walks which allowed me to do drops, or picking up information left by fellow Resistants, or in provoking German officers to initiate conversations as they recalled the dogs they had left in Germany.

"The Germans can be incredibly sentimental. Mention Schubert and it can have the most extraordinary effect on some of them. Misty-eyed nostalgia, tears and so on.

"But it does not change my point of view of them. They were and remain the enemy," she added with such vehemence that it made Lafarge thankful she was on his side.

The 'mutt' – who went by the name Nats – was remarkably well behaved lying obediently at his mistress's feet having been fed some scraps by Aimee. She did not risk the water due to its unreliability which had made many sick due to the dirt in it.

"I know your boss Pinault from those times and even before. He approached me both because he has so few spare bodies and also an elderly haughty woman with a dog clutched to her bosom is a perfect cover. No one would consider me a threat unless they knew me from my years in the Resistance. They would just dismiss me as an old busybody," she said with a wistful smile.

Lafarge looked at the Baroness with admiration and thought what a smart little devil Pinault was. Sometimes he took him for granted at his peril which should also make him wary of how he proceeded with his investigation. He could not cross certain lines -- which he sometimes liked doing – as Pinault would have no qualms in bringing him to book.

"I followed you from the morgue to the café and then to the metro. Chief Inspector Gilbert was not my concern and with all due respect to you he looks as if he can look after himself, but that couple immediately caught my eye," she said.

"For a start they had no chemistry between them, when they

were at the café barely a word exchanged and clearly it was a hierarchical relationship. We may be in a more liberal enlightened age but women rarely have the upper hand in relationships and this Maria was obviously Beauregard's boss, not companion.

"When they followed you without finishing their drinks it was evident to me that they were following you. Leaving your drinks is a luxury few can afford these days, and I see this is not a problem you have Chief Inspector.

"Anyway after that piece de theatre at Jaures and seeing them alight with you at Pere Lachaise I decided to beat you and them to your place. I thought it unlikely they would hit on you on the street but I regret I did not take into account the detective across the street.

"The consolation is three lives saved. I would caution you though Chief Inspector to be extra vigilant and to perhaps think of somewhere your wife and child can stay until this is sorted out. They may have failed but they are professionals and had certainly done their research on you and your habits.

"So beware I am not infallible nor are you."

"I find that hard to believe of you Baroness," said Lafarge.

She flashed a smile revealing pearly white teeth, picked up Nats and bent down to shake Lafarge's hand who also got an appreciative lick from the dog and having bid Aimee goodnight she left.

The Baroness had not only saved their lives but also due to her age and unlikely back story had lightened the atmosphere despite the serious nature of the incident. It did not change the overall picture that Aimee and Ancil would have to find alternative living arrangements but for that night at least it could be put off. All chance of discussing it was put off when Gilbert phoned.

It was not a courtesy call, aside from a brief how are you typical of Gilbert's style and a quick dig about being saved by a grandmother. Lafarge groaned at the thought that this will spread like wildfire round the Quai and other police stations in Paris.

"Are you fit enough to come to the Quai now Gaston?"

Lafarge ached all over and he thought Aimee might object if he got up to go. He said as much to Gilbert ensuring Aimee heard. True to form Aimee raised her eyes to the ceiling in fury and pointed at his bandaged torso and shoulder.

"What is so important in any case Gilbert?" he asked.

"I have fast-tracked the confrontation between Durand and Zilberstein. I am nervous that Zilberstein might be shaken after the visit to the morgue, what if he recognised Durand and thought he would say something after he left?. That might prompt him to flee."

"I doubt Zilberstein would run away without the money, the thing he values most in the world," said Lafarge interrupting Gilbert.

"In any case Durand will be busy with this hitman who ended up dead at the bottom of my stairwell."

Gilbert swept his objections aside.

"Durand said he can deal with the corpse in the morning and wants to get this over with. I agree with him and so I am going to fetch Zilberstein now. I can swing by and pick you up first if you prefer.

"I feel more reassured if there are two of us there when we meet and besides you are Durand's friend. You are certainly the man who supplies him with the most business," he added laughing.

Lafarge did not feel like laughing and he was not best pleased at Gilbert pressurising him. He was more than capable of handling a confrontation on his own. There had to be something else and he asked Gilbert straight out.

"You are a clever bastard Gaston. It is about your landlord," said Gilbert.

Lafarge clicked as to why Gilbert had been so insistent, the real reason was to do with Rosenberg and he feared the phones were tapped hence his reference to landlord.

"Is it serious?"

Gilbert sighed.

"It is very serious. It could change the whole nature of your rental agreement. A third party has laid claim to certain parts of the contract and that his ownership of the apartment is false."

Lafarge groaned and realised he had no option but to go to the Quai – he did not like being made a fool of and Hal Rosenberg obviously had questions to answer.

Chapter Thirteen

"Madame you claim that Hal Rosenberg asked you to kill me and my family? I find that totally preposterous," said Lafarge.

Gilbert had first taken Lafarge to the Salpetriere Hospital across the way from Notre Dame to see Maria who was under guard in a private room. The surgeon had said she could not be moved for several days but was well enough to be questioned.

The hospital that once housed largely prostitutes and mad women – their welfare largely ignored and rats looked on them more often than the doctors and nursing staff -- was now open to all and convenient for the police as it was close to the Quai.

Maria – as she would be until her fingerprints were analysed – lay in bed her leg slightly raised and heavily bandaged. Lafarge was once again struck by her beauty despite the scar, although the scowl that clouded her face did not augur well for the interrogation.

However, her opening gambit took Lafarge by surprise in dryly observing how they had both been fooled by the old lady. He had smiled sheepishly and agreed but added he owed her more than Maria did. This provoked a sneer prompting Lafarge to quickly re-adjust to the fact he was dealing with a professional killer and she had let the mask slip slightly before putting it back on quickly.

He now sat at a safe distance from her bed with Gilbert on the other side absorbing what he felt was a fantastical accusation that she and her husband Beauregard had been hired by Rosenberg to murder him and his family.

A smug smile crossed her lips.

"You can find it as preposterous as you like Chief Inspector, but I swear to you that is the truth," she said.

"He came to you looking for help did he not with regard to his gallery and taking it back from Zilberstein?"

Lafarge nodded. He was not going to lie as it would get him nowhere and he guessed she would clam up if she felt he was.

"Do you have your hip flask on you? I would love a nip of

Cognac and a cigarette," she said taking Lafarge again by surprise at how much she knew about his personal habits.

What alarmed him was that these were the sort of things Zilberstein could not know but Rosenberg would.

"Do you think that is wise after your operation?"

She laughed though it sounded hollow.

"Chief Inspector if I am to die, I would rather it was with the taste of cognac and tobacco on my lips than the after taste of coffee and cheap tobacco waiting for the blade to fall," she said.

Lafarge could not but agree with her for she would be condemned to death as an accessory to the murder of Inspector Darnell, one of the new intake who had served under General Leclerc and had been engaged to be married to a niece of the great warrior.

He did not inform her of this it would have dashed any hopes she had of clemency and he needed her to be as garrulous as possible.

Duly furnished with a cognac and a cigarette, both Lafarge and Gilbert joined her, she sat up in bed and smoothed back her black hair, pointing at her scar.

"You know how I got this? A Gestapo thug in Limoges told me to look in the mirror they had erected in one of their torture chambers. He proceeded to rape me with my head pressed against it so I could not only feel the brute inside me but also see his disgusting face pleasuring himself," she said.

"The others including I am ashamed to say some French brutes stood around and laughed and drank as he raped me. Not one man raised a voice of protest, I may sound naïve but I prayed that one might find an ounce of humanity in him to say enough.

"Once this bastard Ernst had soiled me others bayed to have me too. But he became all proprietorial as if we were a couple, he was as you can tell either schizophrenic or a sociopath – truly emblematic of the master race -- and to prove his point he smashed the mirror and with a shard of it he cut me.

"The pain was dulled by the shock I felt. I collapsed to the floor trying to stem the blood. I was fortunate that he did not touch my eye. All the men crowded around and spat on me saying I was now untouchable and began to kick me and punch me.

"I thought that this was the end and wondered why I deserved such a fate when I was neither a resistant nor a Jew. My crime was to have worked in the smart women's clothes shop and to have accidentally dropped a cup of coffee on a dress bought by Ernst for his French whore.

"She demanded I be suitably punished and watched the whole disgusting humiliation. I survived because before I lapsed into unconsciousness two men barged into the room with a couple of gendarmes and courageously pulled me out of there…"

"Broglie," said Lafarge interrupting her.

She threw him a surprised glance and nodded.

"He is a good man," said Lafarge without offering any further explanation.

She swallowed deeply and put her hand balled in a fist to her nostrils, and looked on the verge of tears. Lafarge looked at Gilbert, who like him was clearly uncomfortable and similarly moved by her story.

Lafarge was not sure what this had to do with the pathway that led her and Beauregard to trying to murder him but for the moment he – clearly with the tacit agreement of Gilbert – would give Maria the leeway to continue with her story.

"Broglie got me medical attention and pleaded successfully with Ernst's superior to have me liberated. He argued that whilst the Limoge inhabitants might swallow Jews and Resistants being rounded-up a well-respected and pure Aryan girl was a step too far," she said.

"I received no apology and Ernst remained in his post. I was made to pay for a new dress for the whore and sacked from my job but I was free. Though of course I was not free mentally, the shattering memories of those hours in the room will never leave me.

"However, Broglie stayed in touch and he promised me one day there would be a chance of revenge. He said there was a resistance cell nearby and there was a man amongst them who would gladly help to kill Ernst. That he had perpetrated the most appalling humiliations on his wife and that Broglie had helped him escape."

Lafarge took a sip from his hip flask and now saw where this was leading, which was not good news for Rosenberg.

"That man was Hal Rosenberg," he said.

She nodded and he told her to continue.

"Rosenberg and I met when Broglie took me for a drive into the countryside, to the grounds of a house that he said had lain abandoned since the couple living in it had been arrested and executed for being Resistants," she said.

Lafarge broke out into a cold sweat at this revelation, he stood up and turned his back and walked to the window feigning a sudden pain in the shoulder she had stabbed.

For the house she had described was the one where he had first slept with Aimee.

.

He had not only betrayed his wife Isabella in doing so but also let down Aimee by leaving without a word thinking he would never see her again.

Maria's story was bringing back so many memories it was becoming unnerving, but he took a deep breath and hoped that when he turned round his face gave little away of the impact it was having on him.

At the same time he was able to think outside the box and reflect on whether she had been coached. The person who had ordered Maria to murder him, Aimee and Ancil would have briefed her on every detail of his background and obviously knew him very well.

For the moment, though, he would postpone judgment till she had finished and then it would be Rosenberg's turn.

"Are you alright Chief Inspector Lafarge?" Gilbert asked, his tone reflecting a genuine concern.

Lafarge did a good impression of a grimace as he turned round to face them again.

"Nothing that cannot be solved by a good tug on the hip flask," he said forcing a grin.

Gilbert laughed and waved his empty glass. Lafarge lobbed the flask to him and he gratefully re-filled his vessel.

"Please continue Madame. What took place in this discussion between you and Rosenberg? Was Broglie party to it or did he prefer to keep his distance so he would not know what was discussed if the plan was to fail?" asked Lafarge.

Maria shifted in the bed and reached to scratch the bandage round her wound.

"Sorry it is itching. I wonder could you fetch the nurse and see if she can unwrap it so it is less tight?" she asked Gilbert.

Gilbert nodded at a uniformed officer, who left the room.

"Broglie as you suggested kept away from our chat. Hal confirmed all that Broglie had said and he would provide the arms and the people to kill Ernst. He offered me the chance to be one of them by joining his cell," she said.

"I said I would love to but I had no weapons training. I had never lived in the countryside and shot guns were alien to me. He reassured me that only a few hours were needed for me to learn how to fire a gun accurately and my hatred for Ernst would take care of the rest.

"He was convincing and Broglie travelled back alone to Limoges," she said smiling for the first time which light up her whole face and made the scar seem insignificant.

"In fact learning to shoot over the next few days became an enjoyable process as the image of Ernst filled my mind. I was ready soon enough and became increasingly impatient to go after him. However, Hal and his commander Richard Levallois, a former law professor in Lyon but who had adapted to a vagrant's life in rural France very well, told me to bide my time that their contacts in Limoges would alert them when it was time.

"Finally the opportunity arose on the back of another horrific crime by the Nazis, the massacre at Oradour-sur-Glanc…" shc said her voice lowercd to a whispcr and rcsorting to taking a large gulp of the Cognac.

Lafarge and Gilbert looked at each other, the massacre of over 600 people by an elite Nazi SS division, some of whom were Frenchmen born in Alsace, had caused widespread revulsion. Some were locals and others refugees who had sought sanctuary in the pretty but non-descript village close to

Limoges.

"The massacre had been sparked by us capturing one of their officers - a highly-decorated Sturmbannfuhrer Helmut Kampfe," said Maria, stubbing a cigarette out with some force onto her bedside table.

"Regrettably some of our hotter-headed colleagues took justice into their own hands and burned him alive with some other prisoners we had. This had nothing to do with anyone in Oradour but it mattered little to the SS soldiers, they were never ones to pose questions about whether their actions were justified.

"Anyway it meant that all the personnel, both Milice and Gestapo were required to go to Oradour and carry out what was laughably called an investigation so as to satisfy the protests from Petain and his Ministers. They were on their last legs in any case with D Day having taken place days previously, but the Francophile ambassador Otto Abetz still insisted on an investigation.

"This of course I heard afterwards, it was not as if we had a source within Abetz's inner circle and others claim it was ordered by another officer in Das Reich.

"Whoever did they offered us the golden chance we needed, as Ernst being the sloth he was, used his senior rank to stay behind claiming someone needed to remain and ensure there was no uprising by an increasingly emboldened populace."

She was interrupted by the arrival of the nurse. Lafarge always thought they looked like white clothed nuns with their high tricorn like hats. She looked especially lacking in a bedside manner, harsh-faced and seemed like she had never allowed a trace of a smile to crease her features.

Her expression scarcely softened as she sniffed the air and smelt the heady mix of Cognac and French tobacco, and looked appalled when she saw the burn marks on the bedside table where Maria had stubbed them out.

No doubt all this was going in her report later but for the moment she attended to her professional duties. She took Maria's temperature and then without her expression changing felt her leg. Maria grimaced and the nurse obliged her by easing the pressure on the limb and loosened it.

"Is that better Madame?" asked the sister, her voice as harsh as her features.

"I would recommend that Madame refrain from either smoking or drinking as this will do nothing for the blood flow and could cause complications. Furthermore I would ask you Chief Inspector to call a halt to your visit within the hour and come back tomorrow," she added.

Lafarge felt it was not a request but a statement of fact and was about to protest only to see Maria nod like an obedient schoolgirl, unrecognisable from the fearless resistant and contract killer from moments before.

Lafarge, though, was not going to let the nurse dictate to him.

"We take note of your advice Sister but we are hard-pressed for time. We are of course understanding of Madame Beauregard's status but I will add she brought it upon herself and but for the intervention of Baroness de Chavanel my family and I would be in the morgue," he said.

"So you will excuse me if I am resistant to your advice," he added firmly.

The Sister looked clearly annoyed by being challenged but said nothing and sashayed out of the room. Lafarge did not think it was the end of the matter and no doubt she would be seeking out a doctor to support her.

Thus he wanted to hurry things along to where they became relevant to the events of this evening. It was just about still the same day though the clock was ticking close to midnight. Besides he too probably required some sleep in order to be fresh enough for a busy session with Rosenberg and then the confrontation between Durand and Zilberstein.

That might have less significance if Maria's allegations about Rosenberg were true. Zilberstein would of course have to explain why he had sworn a corpse was Mrs Rosenberg when it was not, but Meissner's murder would be harder to pin on him.

For if Rosenberg was capable of ordering the murder of Lafarge and his family then he genuinely was a prime suspect for Meissner's death.

"You have a way with women of a certain type I see Chief Inspector," she said tartly.

Lafarge flashed a look which clearly indicated his anger at the remark, but it was undermined by Gilbert softly chuckling.

"I think you should recall Madame that you are under arrest for accessory to murder of a detective and attempted murder of a Chief Inspector and his family," he said unable to suppress the fury in his voice.

She laughed which did not improve his humour.

"Yes, one that you have plied with Cognac, which I am sure will meet with disapproval from your superiors not to say the investigating judge," she said with a smug look.

"Madame if you please return to the attack on Ernst," Gilbert said.

That seemed to focus her mind once again, much to Lafarge's relief. She was right, though, he doubted Pinault would be best pleased he had supplied her with Cognac but he would smooth that over. It was not going to save her from a guilty verdict.

However, she might avoid the guillotine if her lawyer was permitted to introduce the story she had just told them.

"We found Ernst thanks to Broglie. He was doing his bit for Franco-German relations, not in securing the town but in screwing his whore at headquarters. He had deployed the men he had left to do the hard work of course," she said.

"Broglie left but not before he gave us the keys to the room that Ernst was in, saying we should lock up afterwards. He left three of his most reliable men to keep up an appearance of normality in the station as he ensured that the other men on deployment stayed away.

"We left a few men outside as insurance and just Hal and I entered the station. We burst in on Ernst and Helene Briand. That was her name. Ernst looked punch drunk, shocked to see us and naked he was not a pretty sight. She ran towards us pleading that she had used her affair to provide information to the Resistance.

"She was sobbing, her make-up was running down her face, a very unattractive sight. Her pathetic pleas, though, allowed Ernst to go for his uniform and reach for his gun. Broglie had managed to remove the magazine at some point in the morning.

"So you can imagine the look on Ernst's face when he pulled the trigger and nothing happened except a dead click. He looked distraught, his lips quivered and he peed involuntarily on the floor.

"I laughed and Hal went over and slapped him around a bit before pushing him to the floor so he knelt in his own urine.

"He cocked his pistol and said this is for my wife and your other victims. Ernst mumbled something like 'you do not understand it is not what you think' but I am not certain what his words were exactly and in any case it made no difference as Hal either did not hear him or ignored him and shot him."

Lafarge breathed in deeply and looked across to Gilbert, who was rubbing his temple and staring at the floor. Ernst may have been a psychopath – Lafarge had not had the pleasure of meeting him he had either been on leave or had not yet taken up his post – but the description of his final moments were grotesque.

Lafarge cleared his throat.

"What happened to the woman?"

Maria smiled with a satisfied look on her face.

"I took care of the whore. I stroked her hair and told her to dry her tears. She grabbed me round the hips and thanked me for showing mercy. She said her unborn child would also be grateful.

"That made me even madder. I was not going to spare her in any case. How could I forget how she had urged on Ernst to punish me, all over a bloody dress, and then sat and watched as I was raped and almost beaten to death."

"So what did you do?" asked Lafarge.

"Why I drew her up to me. I stood back and then put a bullet apiece in her breasts and said, 'these were not created to be suckled by bastards born of Nazi seed'.

"She did not die instantly, so Hal stepped in and put a bullet between her eyes."

"My God," cried out Lafarge, transferring those brutal images to what she and Beauregard would have done to him, Ancil and Aimee had they succeeded in gaining access to their apartment.

Maria eyed Lafarge with a look approaching disdain.

"Yes Chief Inspector Hal Rosenberg is a very different personality to the one you thought you knew. Both he and I are two more victims of the war, the wounds are internal but they are just as fatal," she said in such a glacial tone it probably had the desired effect in sending chills up Lafarge's spine.

"Not so fatal that it turned you into a murderess," said Gilbert.

Maria ignored Gilbert's remark and looked into Lafarge's eyes.

"What would you have done in my place Chief Inspector?"

Lafarge swallowed and tried to look away but he failed. He knew she knew that he would have done the same thing. What frightened him was he and Maria Beauregard were cut from the same cloth and the only difference was that he had succeeded where she had failed – murdering someone.

Chapter Fourteen

"So Madame we would like you to explain how and why Hal Rosenberg asked you to murder me and my family?"

Lafarge and Gilbert were back by Maria's bedside, they had terminated their interrogation shortly after her gory account of the end of Ernst and Helene. Both of them were drained and in equal measure horrified by the brutality of the couple's executions. Whilst both could understand the motives for revenge, it was another thing to hear the graphic details and the enjoyment it still gave Maria.

She had seemed disappointed that they were leaving, the stern-faced Sister was delighted and as Lafarge had suspected had returned accompanied by a none too happy looking pale-faced doctor, who looked as if he had been roused from a deep slumber to deal with them.

Lafarge had had a troubled sleep, disturbed both by Maria's account, the similarities between them and that there was indeed a link between her and Rosenberg. However, before he confronted Rosenberg he wanted to hear Maria's account because he was deeply sceptical of her claims.

The logic that Rosenberg wanted him and his family wiped out did not wash with him. He would have to have a perverted mind to have set up Lafarge through the intricate story surrounding Zilberstein and Meissner, although that part now seemed cast iron in veracity hence his despatching Ernst, and then manipulating him to even resorting to taking him out of Paris.

Clearly he possessed the make-up now of a man capable of killing but he had not taken the perfect opportunity when the two of them were alone in the car. There were plenty of holes for Maria to fill in if she were to convince both him and Gilbert that Rosenberg was some sort of criminal mastermind in manipulation.

Whilst professionally matters were far from simple, domestically things were in a better state. Aimee had put on a brave face when she left for the studio – a trusted neighbour had agreed to step in for the absent Madame Grondin and look after Ancil. She said to Lafarge they could talk about where they could move to when both were back that night.

She too was perplexed by the possibility of Rosenberg being fingered for organising the hit but looking on the bright side she added, if it was indeed him then there would be no need to move out after all.

Lafarge had tempered her optimism – without revealing Maria's alarming testimony about Rosenberg and his aptitude for meting out justice -- by saying he would postpone judgment on that till he had spoken both to the patient and the accused.

Maria too looked refreshed and her pallor was much improved. However, this time there was to be no offer of Cognac or cigarettes despite sporting a newly-replenished hip flask and a couple of packets of his black marketer's Gitanes.

Unlike the American tobacco which was largely filtered Lafarge stuck loyally to the French brand which was not filter-tipped, he did not resort to the mais version that he left to the factory workers, as even if some tobacco became encrusted on his lips he found the Cognac washed it down very well and indeed tasted better with the pure French tobacco mix.

If patriotism was judged on that alone then he ranked among the truest. This thought made him grin which provoked a surprised look from both Gilbert and Maria.

"Apologies both I was thinking of something not pertinent to this investigation. Please madame you are free to answer but once again caution you that Chief Inspector Gilbert is taking down a verbatim account. This can be and will be used in interrogating Hal Rosenberg, and in anticipating he will deny a lot of this will be assessed by us and could result in further charges of false testimony against yourself," said Lafarge.

Maria grinned darkly.

"Chief Inspector Lafarge as I am potentially facing the guillotine I think a charge of false testimony would be the least of my troubles. In fact given that what I am about to tell you confirms my guilt I think you would be even more cynical than you already are to doubt my sincerity," she said.

Lafarge gave a cursory nod and puffed out his cheeks. He held his tongue as he wanted this over and done with sharpish as a very long day of interrogations and a confrontation lay ahead. However, he would remain circumspect over her insistence that her evidence was unimpeachable as she had been caught in the act in any case so dragging Rosenberg into it did not necessarily confirm his guilt, for it could be for any number of reasons.

"Hal and I lost touch after the Liberation. We moved south to the Marseille region after the Ernst assassination. It was felt by the rest of the cell that we had lost our enthusiasm and zealousness for the fight and that we were of no use to them anymore," she said with a tone of bitterness.

"We were not best pleased at being cut adrift like that. However, whilst I accepted that we had a reaction to avenging our respective traumas I was still up for the fight."

"Was that the case for Rosenberg too?"

"Yes absolutely he was keen to continue sabotaging the Nazis efforts to retain a hold in France. That is why we went to the Marseille region and we did our fair share of killing I can tell you. From Vercors to the Var we racked up a long list of Nazis and collaborators," she said proudly.

"Hal, though, was always anxious to return to Paris and claim back what he said he had been tricked out of. So once Paris was liberated he left, but I stayed to mop up what was left of the Milice

"When they were dealt with I turned my attention to the ones who had given up and incredibly thought they could resume their lives as they had been.

"Unfortunately we made some errors, got their identities wrong or they had moved addresses. However, we judged that a greater good was done in saving the justice system from being overloaded and many of those we killed had not bothered with such niceties as court cases, so why should they be given a chance to plead for their lives.

"At the end of it all, though, even I had had enough of bloodlust but accepted to do one more job. This took me to Paris as the target was a former Milice commander, Paul Touvier. They hoped he had been amongst the 70-odd Miliciens executed in the prison in Haute Savoie but soon discovered otherwise.

"He was tracked to Paris and I was selected to kill him. Anyway it was a failure. Touvier either had been informed by one of our circle, or just by good timing his fairy godmother spirited him away. Whatever happened he was gone."

Lafarge was beginning to get increasingly impatient. He did not need to know all about her past history, this was something for her lawyer, and he could tell Gilbert was of the same mind.

He was also concerned that as she took a long winded route to telling them about her and Rosenberg she would at the same time be buying time and making it up as she went along. Lafarge was not taking her lightly, she had proved she was a resourceful woman and if even part of what she had told them about her story was true she was strong character and not one to be easily broken.

"Madame please can we move onto what we are here for. The events that led up to last night," said Lafarge.

She did not look best pleased, the glacial expression she had worn when she made to stab him the night before returned. However, she had little choice.

"I rented an apartment with my lover … yes Chief Inspector the man you killed last night," she said shooting him a glance that was loaded with contempt.

Lafarge held her gaze, refusing to give ground. He shrugged and said nothing.

"You killed a decent man Chief Inspector. Bernd was a good German, he was from a Communist family and had fought the Fascists in Spain and then with the Resistance here. He was courageous and devoted to me," she said her voice breaking for the first time that morning.

She wiped a tear from her eye. She was genuinely upset, and Lafarge felt it was the first time as she had sounded almost disengaged when she described the rape and subsequent revenge. He made a mental note of that.

"So you and Bernd were lovers but you were not married?" asked Lafarge.

She shook her head.

"So we can take it that Beauregard is not your real name," said Lafarge.

"You can find that out for yourselves Chief Inspector. Is that not part of what you are paid to do," she said haughtily.

Lafarge remained impassive.

"Very well Madame please tell us how you came across Hal Rosenberg in Paris. I am intrigued, after all it is a big city in chaos still and with tens of thousands of displaced people, a very limited postal and phone service and yet you just happen to get back in contact with your old comrade-in-arms," said Lafarge.

Maria did not appreciate his sarcasm, her lips curled into a look full of disdain.

"Purely by chance actually Chief Inspector, these things can happen. One day I was walking in the neighbourhood and I bumped into Hal. He did not look like the Hal I had known in Limoges, he looked properly down on his luck. He told me his bid to reclaim the gallery had failed and he was at his wits end as to how to reclaim it.

"I asked him if I could help and he said he could do with a bed. We were never lovers if that is what you think he implied but we were incredibly close of course."

This now made sense to Lafarge, Rosenberg's secrecy of where he was living and telling him he would prefer to meet him outside the café when he offered to help him flee. Hearing her version it also cast doubt on Rosenberg's innocence as he had been living with the couple who had tried to kill him. He had never met either of them before so Rosenberg was the only connection.

"You generously offered him a bed ... where is your apartment by the way?" asked Lafarge.

"If you are thinking of replying in the same smart fashion you did about your names, I am sure Rosenberg will give it to us straight away."

Maria looked at him menacingly but ignored his dig.

"Well you can ask Monsieur Rosenberg then," she replied clearly enjoying the small bit of power she wielded over the detectives.

"Bernd and I had enough money. Our cell had shared in good Communist fashion the funds we took from the Milice and collaborators we killed. You don't need to look at me like that Chief Inspector. Broglie told me detectives are dab hands at pilfering the dead's wallets. Even he admitted to it and he was one of the good people.

"It worked out fine with Hal. He was a model guest and managed to make ends meet through his ration card. He also had some money he said he had been given by this man Zilberstein."

Lafarge held up his hand to stop her. Dealing with her firmly was the only way of keeping her in her place.

"Did he say why Zilberstein had given him money? Did you not find it odd that he would so such a thing when he had rejected his claim on the gallery?" asked Lafarge, his tone sceptical.

"Chief Inspector I had enough respect for Hal that I was not going to start pestering him about being weak and giving up so easily. As far as I was concerned it was his affair and he dealt with it," she said.

"Well if you are as fond of him as you say you are and you certainly are opinionated I find it hard to believe that you restrained yourself from making a comment," said Lafarge enjoying the look of irritation it provoked in Maria.

"Can I go on Chief Inspector? You did say how hard-pressed for time you were and sarcastic remarks are not helpful," she said.

"So how did I come to be the target? Was the money Zilberstein paid him part of the deal?" asked Lafarge deciding to please both of them and get the rest of the interrogation over and done with.

She shook her head.

"I would not accept money from Hal. As I said our bond was strong and I would do anything for him," she said.

"He told me that if he was to have any chance of regaining the gallery he needed an irritating detective out of the way. He said that this detective was protecting Zilberstein and his partner but if he were to disappear then the message to those two would be clear that they would be next unless they gave him back his gallery.

"He said you and him got along. He had further ingratiated himself with you by allowing you to stay on in the apartment he and his wife had lived in before you saved them on the day of the Rafle. However, he saw no alternative but to get rid of you as you were barring his way to re-establishing his life to some extent as it had been before the Occupation.

"He left the planning to us after he told us to follow him the morning you offered to help him leave Paris so we would recognise you. The plan was for him to stay in hiding until you were disposed of and then to return and make another offer to Zilberstein."

"Despite him being arrested for Meissner's murder you still went ahead with the plan to murder me and my family, that part I am sure he did not demand. From what I have ascertained of you over the past 24 hours that extra touch has your stamp on it," said Lafarge.

"As an intelligent woman I am amazed you did not pose yourself questions as to why he would wish me dead when he had allegedly murdered Zilberstein's partner. Surely that was enough of a message to send the gallery owner," added Lafarge coldly.

She smiled. Alarmingly it was one of her glacial ones.

"Chief Inspector he is alleged to have murdered Meissner. For all we knew it could have been you, not the first time a policeman has covered his tracks by implicating an innocent party.

"During the Occupation of course it was a free for all but now well there is at the very least a cursory investigation so you have to be inventive or creative in hiding your guilt," she said.

Lafarge laughed, but it was a brittle one which carried no humour behind it.

"You accuse me of setting up Rosenberg when you have 100 percent implicated him in the attempted murders of my family and I as well as the murder of my colleague. That is remarkably careless for an intelligent and calculating woman," he said.

"If I were a cynic I would almost think you have done so

deliberately."

He heard Gilbert clear his throat and looked at him to see a trace of a smile on his lips.

If he had hoped that his remarks would provoke her into an angry outburst he was to be disappointed.

"That was indiscreet I admit but then I thought I was talking to a soon to be dead man. It is regrettable the way things have turned out not least for Hal," she said.

Lafarge grunted his disapproval at her.

"Well Madame you will have every opportunity to clear things up with him when you meet for a confrontation once you are well enough to leave hospital," said Lafarge.

"Oh yes Madame do not look so surprised. This is the routine, we are not going to simply take your account and then compare it to Rosenberg's and see which one we believe or the person who charmed us the most wins the lottery.

"This is the part of the job Gilbert and I get to enjoy the most. Two possible criminals, one who has implicated the other, having a good old he said she said.

"Why you look as if you have gone all pale all of a sudden Madame. We will tell the nurse when we leave. Come on Gilbert, Madame needs some rest."

With that Lafarge swept out, a surprised Gilbert trailing in his wake leaving an even more stunned Maria sitting up with her mouth hanging open.

"That was a bit sudden Gaston," said Gilbert once he caught up with Lafarge after telling the Sister to attend to the patient.

"It was time to wipe the smug look off her face and I thought the mention of confrontation would have the desired effect. It is a very useful weapon. Turn up the pace all of a sudden and bewilder the suspect, who has thought they are in control of the interrogation.

"Besides which Gilbert, she was beginning to get on my nerves and I need some fresh air and a drink!" said Lafarge savouring the taste of his Gitanes.

*

"Some of what she told you is true, but the claim I ordered your murder is vile and total rubbish," said Rosenberg.

After a couple of drinks with Gilbert, Lafarge had come to the Quai and whilst waiting for Durand and Zilberstein to arrive had sequestered Rosenberg for interrogation.

Gilbert was on his way to the apartment in which Rosenberg had co-habited with Maria Prevot and Bernd Schneider. Rosenberg had quickly resolved the matter of her name and the address of the flat, which was in Rue Merlin, a small street not far from Lafarge's apartment in Rue de la Roquette.

Lafarge hoped Gilbert would turn up more information about Prevot and Schneider from the search. Her refusal to reveal the address and her real name he put down more to being bloody-minded more than anything else. Rosenberg certainly could not have helped as he was already incarcerated.

Lafarge had also sent two men – Duvilliers and Grandhomme – to search Meissner's address which he kicked himself for not doing already. He had been too fixated on Zilberstein being responsible and not taken enough care to think about other possibilities or indeed to have the flat in Rue Oudinot in the chic Seventh Arrondissement searched in case other things turned up that could point him in another direction.

In any case he needed the whole investigation to be unimpeachable otherwise the defence would highlight gaps in it and play on his being obsessed with Zilberstein from the outset. Regardless of Rosenberg also being Jewish he could see the lawyer trying to accuse him a former Vichy detective, whose late father had been high up in the hierarchy, being motivated by anti-Semitic feelings.

Rosenberg, who looked haggard and tired, had been very upset by the accusations made by Prevot.

Lafarge had his doubts about them as well but he could not just dismiss them due to a natural antipathy towards the woman. That also would not go well in court and he was already on dodgy ground having conducted the interrogation of her given that he had been the target. Pinault had given his assent on condition Gilbert had been present and taken the notes himself.

Lafarge was not only grateful to his boss's seemingly boundless belief in him but also he had refrained from jokey remarks about being saved by the Baroness. That would doubtless come.

"So Hal tell me why did you not want me to come and pick you up that morning? I mean if your relationship with Prevot and Schneider was that innocent then there was no need to hide where you lived," said Lafarge.

"It was hardly as if I was going to climb the stairs and demand entry to your flat so I could have a good look around."

Rosenberg nodded and held his hands up.

"I was worried that you might be followed and I did not want any harm to come to her and Bernd. They had been very good to me and being a fugitive they risked a lot," he said.

"She claims the reason was you wanted them to see what I looked like," said Lafarge.

"They could have looked out the window if that was the truth and saved them a walk on a cold morning," replied Rosenberg.

"It was dark Hal so they would have had a fair bit of trouble in seeing what I looked like if they had to look out the window. Knowing what it is like in Paris at the moment even if there was a streetlamp beside your entrance it was probably not working," said Lafarge.

"I take your point Chief Inspector. However, they may have followed me but I certainly did not ask them to for the purpose she claims," said Rosenberg.

Lafarge offered Rosenberg a cigarette and asked the uniformed officer to fetch a coffee for both of them. He acknowledged that Rosenberg appeared sincere, but it still gnawed at him as to why else two complete strangers – they were obviously unaware of the contract out on his life – would attempt to murder him and his wife and son. They were doing it as a favour for a friend and not for money, so it was someone who knew him pretty well.

"She says she came back into contact with you by seeing you in the street one day," said Lafarge.

Rosenberg nodded, though, he did not look very happy. Mind you Lafarge reflected Rosenberg made him seem like a positive fount of joy, he could not recall a single smile or laugh yet although admittedly he corrected himself there had not been many occasions for Rosenberg to do so.

"It was as much a surprise to me as apparently to her," said Rosenberg.

"Truth be told if I had not been so desperate I would have preferred that meeting to be our last one.

"I know you look surprised at that Chief Inspector but bear with me. Do not worry I am going to be brief and skate over details that she probably gave you already about the time round Limoges.

"However, my overriding reason for deserting her eventually was not simply to return to Paris but she frightened me. I don't mean that I felt endangered by her, we were very close and one had to be to fight alongside each other like we did, but her brutality and interminable desire for revenge made me fear I could become like her.

"I had sated my revenge on Ernst, his mistress I could not have cared less about whether she lived or died. Plenty of mistresses' of the Nazis did survive, but once Maria had shot her in her breasts I put her out of her misery.

"I returned and just wanted to move on but I have the impression that for many like Maria it is proving very difficult."

Lafarge admired Rosenberg's ability to empathise with someone who had put him in close proximity to a death sentence and he told him as such.

"I am sure you have been with people in dangerous situations which has created a bond. That tends to give one some understanding of their behaviour subsequently and fortunately you survived. Not only would I have regretted your death but also I would have lost the only person capable of clearing me," he said with a warm smile.

Lafarge smiled back. He was prepared to take Rosenberg's word against Maria's but he was still perplexed as to where this desire to accept someone's request to murder him had stemmed from.

"When you stayed with them, did you get any inkling from people they saw or mentioned who might have directed them to murder me?" asked Lafarge.

Rosenberg shook his head.

"They had very few people to the apartment, and as you are

aware I spent large parts of my time going to the gallery so what they got up to I do not know," he said.

"Maria had barely been to Paris before the Occupation, her whole life she had lived in Limoges, and Bernd was German and had aside from Spain lived in the Pyrenees before becoming a member of the Resistance.

"I was quite surprised they had settled here. During our time together Maria had remarked how she would love to one day live in the south of France on the coast and when she and Bernd became lovers that desire to fulfil her dream became even stronger.

"Although she came here to kill this guy Touvier I would have bet against her staying afterwards.

"When I said I was returning to Paris she became rather aggressive and made sarcastic comments, that I would not find happiness or love like I had had with my wife, only sad memories awaited me.

"She said that my wife had told her she would never go back there unless it was as a couple, it was pointless to try and recreate something without both of us being there."

Lafarge was suddenly alert – he had been thinking ahead to the impending confrontation with Durand and Zilberstein – and he leaned forward looking intently into Rosenberg's eyes.

"Maria knew your wife? How is that possible? She worked in a shop in Limoges and the only thing your wife saw of the town was the police station and the cells," said Lafarge.

Rosenberg looked blankly at Lafarge as if the Chief Inspector was playing with him or trying to trick him.

"You have got a great poker face Chief Inspector. You could make a killing at the game," said Rosenberg.

"My wife and Maria were cellmates for two to three days. It is through Maria I know my wife was murdered by those pigs Ernst and De Blaeckere."

Lafarge maintained his poker face but inside his head the wheels were turning and a very nasty thought was forming. It was one he would rather not contemplate giving credence to but it had legs on it.

For the moment, though, his focus was on Rosenberg and

trying to help him extricate himself as much as he could. His instincts borne from several years of detective work and dealing with murderers told him Rosenberg was not guilty.

Rosenberg was innocent, not because he seemed calm and respectable but because, as Lafarge had discovered, there is not an identikit marked murderer.

Man or woman they came in every form -- any detective who claimed they were born of the same character but some hid it better than others was plain lazy and probably guilty themselves of pinning the crime on the wrong person.

Murder came about through many different reasons and motives hence why Rosenberg to a conscientious detective like Gilbert would have marked him as the likeliest suspect. Lafarge conceded that but for knowing Rosenberg, albeit through very different circumstances, he might well have come to the same conclusion.

He did not believe that he was siding with Rosenberg because he felt sorry for him. Empathy and Lafarge were not common bedfellows. Working for opportunists like Bousquet had weaned him away from such feelings. It was very hard to empathise with the human race once one had been tainted by working for or alongside callous, brutal, racist and in many cases sociopathic colleagues.

One could sympathise with the victims, he clung to that as a means of knowing he still had some form of human feeling with regard to his job, but when it came to suspects he eschewed the humanity shown by Maigret.

He was dealing with people whose crimes had gone unpunished during the darkest period of French history. Royalists would probably argue the toss that peremptory trials and executions to sate the fervour of the people during The Terror were as bad. He was of the opinion the aristocracy had brought a lot of that upon themselves through ignorance and bad governance.

The Jews were totally innocent and victim of sheer blinding hatred and jealousy whilst the Resistants had taken up arms as anyone would do if their country was invaded and their army humiliated.

Zilberstein filled him with loathing but Rosenberg was a good man, who had survived but at a great cost and was now in danger of losing everything.

"I am on your side Hal. However, I am going to be frank with you," said Lafarge.

Rosenberg looked relieved but also apprehensive.

"Conveniently and I say this with the sarcasm it is due several unfavourable factors have been brought to our attention which point at you being guilty of murder and my attempted murder.

"Add to that conspiracy to murder my family and the fact the claims are from one of the perpetrators and you can see why my superior and my colleague might be tempted to tell me to stop looking elsewhere and prepare the case against you for the magistrate and an eventual trial.

"Now I can only gain more time if you are able to provide me with something concrete or a lead.

"So I need you to think hard and not just over the past few days events but going back to when you still had the gallery and they were pressuring you to hand it over.

"Even that is contested as if Zilberstein was to admit to that then a case against him might look stronger and ergo lend yours more credibility.

"So please reflect. I am going to sit here for a few minutes. I have another engagement which is due soon so I cannot spend the rest of the day incarcerated here with you. Once I am gone they will take you back to your cell and it may very well be that by the end of the afternoon I will have no option but to charge you for these capital offences."

Lafarge glanced at his watch and registered that the confrontation between Durand and Zilberstein was due in half an hour, so he had more time than he had thought. However, he was going to let Rosenberg remain ignorant of that as in Lafarge's opinion short sharp prods generally worked to focus minds.

He got up and stretched his legs, paced round the square room, remarking on the peeling cream paint, the stains on the floor and the walls, which were a mix as he well knew of tobacco, coffee and blood, largely innocent people's blood during the

Occupation when the Brigades Speciales thugs had beaten the 'truth' out of their prisoners.

Some of the Brigades Speciales detectives had been pretty good at their job, tracing resistance lines with good old-fashioned methods and tracking down the right people. However, it was once they were inside the rooms like this that their baser instincts had come to the fore.

He had witnessed a few of them – sickening assaults simply because they did not receive the answers they wanted or they were affronted because the prisoner was not in the least bit intimidated by them and their devotion to their cause surmounted the needs of the interrogator.

Most of the Brigades members had gone to ground once the Germans had deserted Paris and those who had tried to make a fight of it had been rounded up. Some had fought vainly to maintain the status quo – they were different to the Lafont-Bonny gang in that they were diehard devotees to the Nazi/Vichy line not opportunistic gangsters – and had died with their boots on.

Others had been arrested and faced a firing squad pretty quickly and the rest it was only a matter of time, Lafarge hoped, would face the same fate. He had suspicions several of them had willingly signed up to fulfil the contract on him and if successful take the bounty and use that to escape.

He stopped his pacing and looked down at Rosenberg, asking him if he wanted a coffee. He nodded and Lafarge left him to his thoughts. On his return and having given Rosenberg a tot of cognac in his coffee he sat back down again.

Rosenberg sipped his coffee, thanking Lafarge for the sweetener. Lafarge took both of his neat although the coffee was so revolting he added a drop of Cognac to it.

"So Chief Inspector, forgive me for the formality but in here and given my situation I prefer to use your official title, I believe I can give you that lead you require," said Rosenberg.

Lafarge leaned forward expectantly.

"However, if you believe me I feel you are going to need all your powers of persuasion to extend the investigation," said

Rosenberg.

"I say this because it is going to entail you travelling a long distance and incur expenses which knowing how bad things are economically may cause your superior to deny your request and for him to conclude I am doing this simply to buy time."

Lafarge looked pensive but then shrugged.

"I have heard many fanciful stories in this room before Hal. There is always time for another one. Let me hear what you have to say and I will judge whether it is worthy of pursuing," said Lafarge gently.

Rosenberg relaxed visibly, took a sip of his coffee and lit a cigarette Lafarge had offered him.

"When we struck the deal, such as it was their silent partner wanted something extra," said Rosenberg.

"Hermann Goering never settled for a price, he always wanted more. This time he desired an artefact that perhaps was not the most valuable piece in the gallery but it was definitely the one with the most sentimental value.

"The piece was the snake bracelet designed by Alphonse Mucha and executed by Georges Fouquet for 'The Divine Sarah' Sarah Bernhardt.

"You are seemingly a cultured man Chief Inspector – I observed you had kept all my paintings on the walls of the apartment whereas others might have taken them down and replaced them with their own -- but in case you are not aware of the links, Bernhardt and Mucha were very close.

"She had adored his work since he created the poster for her role as Grismonda and he many years later knowing her fondness for snakes came up with this as an idea for repaying her for her faithful custom and in effect making his name and fortune."

Lafarge appreciated Rosenberg thinking he was cultured but truth be told whilst he considered himself well-read and he was fond of the cinema but art was not his forte. Although he would not admit it he had precious few paintings to put up on the walls and that was why Rosenberg's still adorned them.

He knew enough about art to acknowledge Rosenberg's paintings were valuable but the thought of a visit to an art gallery did not inspire much enthusiasm in him.

Thus Rosenberg had educated him on the relationship between Bernhardt and Mucha, although he was aware the Czech-born artist had been responsible for the famous posters promoting the actress and her characters.

"Bernhardt died in 1923 so how did you come to own the bracelet? You must have been at university when she died and not in charge of the gallery," said Lafarge.

"Chief Inspector the gallery has been in my family's possession since 1892," said Rosenberg rather testily, obviously unimpressed by Lafarge's lack of research.

"Bernhardt and my father were intimate at one time, which was not something that my mother appreciated as few women could compete with 'Divine Sarah' and she felt threatened.

"My father, though, would never have left my mother and so those storm clouds gradually blew over, even though I believe it hastened an early death for my mother," he said sadly.

Lafarge chided himself for failing to look into the history of the gallery, another thing he had let slide due to his obsession with Zilberstein.

" She died in 1921 and my father and Bernhardt became close friends again, although this time it was no more than a friendship.

"Proof of this is in her will as she left the bracelet to my father. I would have thought Mucha would have been a more apposite recipient but he never challenged the will.

"My father never displayed it at the gallery but on his death bed in 1937 he said to me that I was free to show it in the gallery and if one day financially things were not bright I could sell it.

"I never felt the need to sell it but I did use it unashamedly as a selling point for people to visit the gallery and I believe it has or had a galvanising impact on the clientele as far as other sales went.

"Sadly little did I know that one day I would be placed in a position in which I would have to forcibly hand it over to a sociopathic kleptomaniac in the form of Goering," he said all but spitting the former number two in the Nazi hierarchy's name out.

Lafarge breathed in deeply and rubbed his eyes, he felt tired and he did not feel in the mood to take this story to Pinault and probably Luizet. He could see where this was headed and in his present frame of mind he would be incapable of arguing in favour of where Rosenberg wanted him to go.

Zilberstein would deny this allegation flat out, Meissner was dead leaving just Goering to admit the deal took place and he received the snake bracelet as part of the agreement.

Lafarge took a large gulp of cognac, rubbed his chin somewhat hesitantly before clearing his throat and asking for confirmation from Rosenberg. Just so he actually had it in black and white even if it again made him sound rather dumb.

"So Hal you are telling me that the answer to this whole confounded conspiracy and murder lies not here in Avenue Montaigne nor in the Quai but hundreds of miles away in another country and the man who holds the key to all of this is presently on trial for unimaginable war crimes," said Lafarge trying to make light of the whole scenario.

He even thought that it was ludicrous and he believed Rosenberg's story. He could only imagine how Luizet and Pinault would respond.

"You want me to ask my superiors to sign off on me going to Nuremberg to obtain an interview with Goering when our government and those of our allies are focussing on obtaining a condemnation of him for mass murder," said Lafarge with a suitably sceptical edge to his tone.

Rosenberg did not look affronted or surprised by Lafarge's response he simply smiled and nodded.

"He may be responsible for murdering millions Chief Inspector but my only interest is in my life and staying alive," said Rosenberg.

"Forgive me for sounding selfish but I think each and every victim of the War would concur that was what was most important to them even if they were murdered alongside others and buried in mass graves.

"I would also suggest that the French justice system is interested in turning a new page and not following the same route as the judges or police during the Occupation who delivered thousands of questionable judgements following equally dubious arrests and confessions obtained under duress during interrogation.

"There those are arguments you can use when you see your superiors," he added with what for Rosenberg amounted to a self-satisfied grin.

*

Lafarge had no time to pass by and see Pinault and for that he was grateful as he would have to have a good long think about how he would couch the request to go to Nuremberg.

That might even be the easy part then he would have to prepare to question Goering and that was something for the moment he did not wish to contemplate. The thought of being opposite one of the originators of the machine that engineered mass murder and other appalling crimes would mean a hard enough battle with his own emotions, which he had found hard enough to suppress at the best of times. He could cope with the likes of de Brinon and Bousquet for they shared a common language to start with and he had either worked for them or knew enough about them from common acquaintances to feel at an advantage when he entered the interview room.

Goering would be quite another challenge. Lafarge's German was cursory at best. He had learned it at school but had preferred English and had paid for that by emerging from school speaking both languages poorly. He had had an unforeseen chance to resume German when he ended up in a POW camp and picked up the odd phrase by conversing with the guards. However, do you have a cigarette or a tin of fruit – when he wanted to trade on the black market which flourished there -- was hardly likely to be useful when questioning Goering.

He was grateful to be able to push those problems aside and find that Durand was waiting for him in his office. He looked out of place not only because he was in an office with natural light but also the traditional white coat was nowhere to be seen and instead he was dressed in a smart navy blue suit, with a well-pressed white shirt and red silk tie. Lafarge whistled his appreciation not least because his friend had taken this confrontation so seriously that he had a Croix de Guerre – France's highest military decoration -- to his lapel.

"Don't get carried away Gaston it is only a bronze star," said Durand dryly, referring to the bronze star being the lowest level of the award.

Lafarge chided him for his false modesty.

"It is still a croix de guerre. I did not see too many in the POW camp," said Lafarge.

Durand smiled before tapping his watch indicating that he was on time but Zilberstein was not.

"I know, I thought it was me who would be late. He is not aware of the significance of the appointment so I don't think he is going to try and skip it. In any case I have Gilbert picking him up. If another 10 minutes goes by without any sign I will ring the gallery," said Lafarge.

He had decided to hold the confrontation in his office,as it was less claustrophobic than the rooms downstairs and he thought a slightly more convivial atmosphere might provoke Zilberstein to let slip something they could at last pin on him, or at the very least a lead.

The detectives had yet to return from the apartments of Meissner or Prevot and Schneider's. He would have loved to obtain a warrant for Zilberstein's but he knew that he would need to have a very good reason, so much depended on the confrontation and if anything of material value showed up in their other searches.

He offered Durand a coffee and a cognac, the pathologist accepting both, and just as he had poured them both generous doses of both Gilbert knocked and came in immediately without waiting for an answer.

Lafarge tried to look past Gilbert to see if Zilberstein was with him. Gilbert indicated he was waiting in the corridor to which Lafarge gestured somewhat impatiently for him to bring him in.

He motioned to Durand to stay where he was seated, his back to the door.

Zilberstein, formally dressed as always, bustled through the door his air of self-importance and annoyance at being summonsed plastered over his florid pudgy face.

Lafarge rose from his desk, lifting his hands which Durand correctly interpreted to mean he should get up as well and turned slowly around to face Zilberstein.

Zilberstein almost dropped his silver-topped cane as he recognised Durand from the day before.

Lafarge wondered whether the recognition was solely to do with their most recent meeting or had the wily Zilberstein realised Durand was there due to the first time they had crossed paths. Lafarge knew Zilberstein had a capacity to think quickly and play the stone-faced I know nothing role.

He hoped to unsettle him further by not giving him any time to think of an explanation.

"Take a seat Monsieur Zilberstein. You recall Professor Durand from yesterday, probing your old partner Meissner's corpse," said Lafarge laconically.

Zilberstein nodded and passed a red and white spotted handkerchief across his lips. Good sign thought Lafarge he is already nervous. Gilbert took up position to the right of Zilberstein, leaning back against a desk with his legs stretched out so they almost touched the dentist turned gallery owner's chair.

"Now the reason I have called you here is not due to that, we are still holding Monsieur Rosenberg for his murder whilst we pursue other avenues of enquiry," said Lafarge noting with satisfaction that a look of disappointment flitted across Zilberstein's face.

"The reason is that Professor Durand says you and he have met before."

Zilberstein glanced at Durand and turned back towards Lafarge shaking his head.

Lafarge did not say anything instead he nodded his head vigorously at Zilberstein. The latter narrowed his eyes, more a look of confusion than anger. He turned to Gilbert, thinking he still had an ally in the room, but the Chief Inspector looked down to the floor and shrugged.

Lafarge indicated to Durand to take the floor.

"We have indeed met before Monsieur Zilberstein," said

Durand his tone clipped but courteous.

"You visited my theatre of operations with a man claiming to be a detective on the occasion of identifying the corpse of a Madame Rosenberg. The woman whose husband Chief Inspector Lafarge is presently holding for the murder of your former partner.

"Before you protest that I am mistaken I have your signature on both forms and they match."

"So Monsieur Zilberstein can you explain why you first of all forgot to mention this yesterday and secondly more importantly what were you doing with the corpse of Madame Rosenberg?" asked Lafarge, who had stepped in straight away without letting Zilberstein obfuscate.

Zilberstein once again wiped his lips with the handkerchief but did not venture an explanation.

"It is strange indeed you would be aware of Madame Rosenberg's death given you said that she and her husband had left with Meissner after you struck a deal. An agreement very much loaded in your favour I might add.

"Now you claim that as far as you were concerned they encountered no trouble in reaching safety. This is something that has been flatly contradicted by Rosenberg and by another credible witness, who saw them both after they had been arrested in Limoges.

"So it is something of a miracle that Madame Rosenberg ended up back in Paris and far from being the life and soul of the party a corpse on a slab in Professor Durand's morgue."

Lafarge gave Zilberstein a hard stare which this time he was pleased to observe the man did not return but looked genuinely flustered.

His handkerchief was no longer sufficient to mask his nervousness. He allowed his tongue to dart from between his lips and licked them, his bottom lip moving up to hide his top lip.

"So what do you want Chief Inspector?" asked Zilberstein, a note of defiance in his voice although whether it was the last line of defence Lafarge could not tell.

"Well if you could start to tell the truth Monsieur Zilberstein that would be a good start," said Gilbert sharply.

This prompted Zilberstein to jerk his head towards Gilbert, his expression one of incredulity and then transforming into one of anger at what he obviously viewed as betrayal.

Get used to it thought Lafarge. You after all have made a fortune out of it and littered the way with corpses.

"You will tell us who this Madame Rosenberg was, for at the time you presented yourself at Professor Durand's she had been dead for some time. I believe the corpse you identified as Madame Rosenberg was too fresh for it to be her and she showed no signs of torture which also proves it was not her for the Gestapo had gone to work on her in Limoges," said Lafarge.

Zilberstein resumed his impassive look, his brief flash of emotion banished. However, Lafarge thought behind the mask he was in turmoil for he knew that in this moment he was on his own. His protector or protectors could not help him here as Gilbert had flipped to the other side.

All he could try and do was buy time with some explanation that would ensure he left the Quai at the end of the session.

"I admit yes I did indeed attend the identification of Madame Rosenberg's corpse at Professor Durand's morgue," he said.

"I regret that I failed to mention this yesterday. I banked on Professor Durand's memory not being as sharp as it is evidently. I also admit that the woman was not Madame Rosenberg but my avarice got the better of me.

"When I heard from Meissner that she had died in Limoges I panicked. We were the sole beneficiaries through the agreement and if one of them died could claim their half of the gallery permanently.

"However, we needed a corpse as proof, especially as that fool Meissner had totally messed things up by first of all betraying them, then Rosenberg escaping and to round it all off Madame Rosenberg had died."

Lafarge was delighted that at last there was progress but he was struck too that there was not an iota of sympathy or regret for the fate of the Rosenbergs. Zilberstein had recounted it all in a monotone, devoid of emotion save again a glimmer of anger when he spoke of Meissner's incompetence. Conveniently he was blaming the dead partner for betraying them.

That did not matter for even if he could not prove Zilberstein had acted in collusion with Meissner over the betrayal the consequences were as much Zilberstein's fault as Meissner's for he had entrusted their security to him.

"So how did you obtain a corpse then? Also who was the detective you brought along for the fraudulent identification?" asked Lafarge.

Zilberstein smiled.

"My dental skills are not what they were Chief Inspector. Once I took over the gallery I very rarely practised except on important clients. One of them was Alois Brunner, commandant of the Drancy internment camp. He sent me his mistress, a French woman called Mireille Jeanjean who he employed as a nurse at Drancy so he could keep her close.

"She was a thoroughly nasty person, a failed actress who blamed the Jewish dominance of the film world for her career not being a success. Total bloody rubbish of course! I had seen a film she had been in and she was patently out of her depth, indeed rumour had it that she had slept with the producer to get the part and he was of course Jewish!

"Anyways she boasted to me how she had avenged the slight to her ego by giving a lethal injection to Max Jacob in the infirmary at Drancy. She said he had pneumonia and would not have lived much longer in any case, and it was pointless to put him on a train to the east when a healthy individual could take his place," said Zilberstein smiling sourly.

Lafarge shook his head and poured another drink for himself, Durand and Gilbert, purposefully not offering one to Zilberstein. So this was how the great man of literature and the arts Jacob had died, a man who had been close friends with the likes of Pablo Picasso, Jean Cocteau and Georges Braque.

He had been unaware at the time of his arrest in February 1944 as he was in Spain with his family trying successfully to get passage on a ship for Argentina. That had all ended unhappily the ship carrying his wife and daughter sent to the bottom of the sea so Jacob's fate would have understandably passed him by.

"The truth is always new," said Gilbert breaking his Trappist monk silence for the first time since he had brought Zlberstein into the room.

Lafarge, Durand and Zilberstein all stared at Gilbert. Lafarge credited Gilbert with a lot but he had not reckoned on him being a philosopher. Indeed he was annoyed that his colleague had interrupted Zilberstein's statement, for Lafarge did not want him to revert to type as he had been very informative once he found his tongue.

"Sorry, it is just something Jacob said once. He was a friend of my parents-in-law. It was part of the reason I decided to become a policeman, a means of testing whether it carried weight or not and who better to test it out on than suspects or witnesses," said Gilbert apologetically.

Lafarge was duly impressed and surprised in equal measure. He could tell Gilbert was a cultured man but he had not wagered he mixed with or was linked to the circles of such intellectuals and artists, the demi monde one might say.

"And Chief Inspector, has Jacob been proved right?" asked Durand, perhaps the most intrigued of the trio given he could never ask the truth of his clients.

"I would say you see the truth as you want it to be, but it does not necessarily mean it is. Lafarge and I seek to obtain the real truth for without it we would never be able to take a case to court. So I guess we present what we perceive to be the absolute truth to the judges and it is for them to acccpt it as such or not.

"If they do not then I have to accept that they believe the truth of the case lay elsewhere, which I suggest proves Jacob is right."

Durand nodded whilst Lafarge thought thcrc wcrc some grounds to agree with that, but was keener to get back on track with Zilberstein's account.

"Monsieur Zilberstein thank you for inadvertently sparking this fascinating philosophical digression but let us please return to terra firma and your version of the truth," said Lafarge drily, pleased to see it provoked all of them to laugh quietly, including Zilberstein.

"I can see where this is leading to but you need to tell us yourself."

Zilberstein looking visibly more relaxed nodded. Lafarge acknowledged reluctantly Gilbert had played a good hand there.

"Madame Jeanjean who was married to an officer who was with General Juin fighting the Nazis in Italy, had an infected gum. To be truthful she had clearly not looked after her teeth properly for some time and they required a lot of work," said Zilberstein with some disgust.

"I told her as such and said she would require several visits if she was not to start losing her teeth. She looked horrified at the thought and pondered aloud what 'sweet Alois' would think of her if that happened and demanded I rescue as many of them as I could."

"Please Monsieur Zilberstein, you can spare us the intimate details of her dental problems. Please proceed to what happened once you had her settled in your dentist's chair," interrupted Lafarge.

"Don't worry Zilberstein the Chief Inspector is like that with me too when I conduct a post-mortem. He is an impatient man. He does not understand that we medical professionals are as proud of our work as he and Gilbert are of theirs," said Durand smoothly.

Zilberstein smiled and Lafarge was forced once again to admit it was helpful to have Durand and Gilbert present for whether by accident or design they were smoothing things over when they threatened to become tense.

"Very well Chief Inspector I gave Madame Jeanjean an anaesthetic so as to attend to her gum infection and she had an adverse reaction to it," said Zilberstein glumly.

Lafarge stared at him and gestured with his hands for Zilberstein to carry on. Zilberstein looked hesitant but receiving no encouragement from either Durand or Gilbert he had no option.

"She was convulsing and foam was coming out of her mouth, I held her down to try and at least reduce the convulsions but to little effect. I had no one with me so I had to leave her writhing on the chair and fetch some phenobarbital which I injected her with.

"However, it was not sufficient and I had to watch her die. It was not a pleasant sight. To witness one of your patients breathe their last before your own eyes is a sign of ultimate failure!!" said Zilberstein.

Lafarge shook his head in disbelief at Zilberstein's total lack of empathy. Although the woman had enjoyed living in the misery of Drancy, murdered Jacob and been the mistress of a mass murderer in Brunner. She would not be missed.

Her husband too had been spared a miserable return to see his wife tarred and feathered as so many mistresses of the Nazis had been – even the celebrated ones such as Coco Chanel and Arletty had fled into exile in Switzerland or like the actress been imprisoned,and in the case of Jeanjean more likely executed.

Lefarge had killed too but he had at least felt remorse, albeit belatedly and only after he had paid a sacrifice in the loss of his wife and daughter. Seemingly it had not been sufficient for he had lost family member after family member since, some dying and others like his sister and son incarcerated.

He certainly did not consider it hypocritical to castigate Zilberstein for being so unsympathetic.

"Your upset for Madame Jeanjean's violent death is duly noted," said Lafarge acidly.

Zilberstein flinched briefly before puffing out his cheeks dismissively.

"You appear to care for the murderous bitch more than Brunner did," he said contemptuously.

"I doubt Alois Brunner had a human sentiment in his body mind you. The only person he cared for was himself and it probably saved my life.

"I obviously had to tell him she had died. It was my mistake because I injected her with out of date local anaesthetic which I should have checked but as I say apart from the odd patient like Brunner I was not really practising anymore and so having not bought medication some of it was no longer safe to use. Stupidly I did not check.

"Anyway when I told Brunner of my plan to use Jeanjean's corpse in place of Madame Rosenberg's as I needed it to secure half the gallery permanently he loved it. He may have sworn undying loyalty to Hitler but like anyone he had a price and he could tell that his time at Drancy was coming to an end.

"He needed money he said so he would overlook the death of Jeanjean and that I was Jewish if I would pay him blood money."

Lafarge was appalled and impressed at the same time. The chutzpah of Zilberstein to think of such a devious plan and propose it to a brute and avid anti-Semite like Brunner was astonishing. Or it took one avaricious sociopath to know another.

"So it was Brunner who came with you to Durand's morgue?" asked Gilbert.

Zilberstein shook his head.

"He was afraid of being set up. He had become paranoid like a lot of the Nazis in Paris at that stage of being assassinated. Also he felt a French detective would be more appropriate for such a procedure. So he asked Rene Henoque, head of the second Paris Brigade Speciale, to accompany me to the identification," he said.

"Why did Henoque refuse to sign the forms then? He had the authority to do so and one thing Vichy had in common with pre-war French administrations was an obsession with bureaucracy," said Durand.

"He like Brunner was nervous about what was coming and wanted as little on paper as possible because he was already preparing to flee, he did not wish to leave a paper trail to indicate to de Gaulle and his forces that he was still in Paris by this stage," replied Zilberstein.

Lafarge could see why Henoque had good reason to belatedly try to cover his tracks. He knew Henoque and loathed him having had several run-ins with him for his torturing of suspected Jews, resistants and communists.

He had been one of the more sadistic members of the Brigade Speciales, and owed his position to his uncle Lucien Rottee, the highly effective head of police intelligence. There was no way of confirming this part of Zilberstein's account as Henoque had disappeared and Rottee had been executed in May 1945.

"Once I had obtained the cash from the bank – for there was also money which was liberated on proof of her death – I had to go to see Brunner personally at Drancy," said Zilberstein swallowing deeply.

"Were you not nervous he was luring you there to secure the money and then hold you with the rest of the Jews?" asked Lafarge.

"I made sure I had a letter from Ambassador Abetz guaranteeing my safe passage," he said.

"However, of course I was nervous as Brunner was a man of no morals whatsoever. Otto Abetz possessed a few, well enough that I could trust him," he added with a tired smile.

Lafarge had met Abetz and had found him a slippery character, he had been close friends with Bousquet which said a lot, but he had at least been cultured and a Francophile. Brunner he had never met and he thanked his lucky stars for that.

"Did it not make you feel ashamed that you were going to the centre of Vichy and the Nazis operations for sending your fellow Jews to the east and the death camps?" asked Gilbert sharply.

Zilberstein rubbed his hands nervously and again dabbed the handkerchief on his lips.

"Yes as you have seen Messieurs I am not a man given to showing much emotion, you may see it as a fault but I cannot do anything about it. However, that day yes my stomach was in turmoil as I entered Drancy and saw thc misery all round me," he said, though, Lafarge noted his voice remained a monotone.

"It did not seem overly crowded but this was July 1944 and I think even the wheels of Vichy and Nazi bureaucracy and order were screeching to a halt. So the round ups of thc Jews, communists and the Roma had stopped. I imagine you and Gilbert would know more about that than me," remarked Zilberstein.

"If you are hoping to provoke us Zilberstein you have chosen the wrong targets," said Gilbert testily.

"Lafarge was abroad and I was orchestrating a resistance cell in the city, preparing them for when the Allies finally got close enough."

Lafarge and Durand looked at each other, both pleasantly

taken aback by Gilbert's revelation.

Zilberstein did not look in the least bit chastened by his telling off.

"The only solace I found was that the guards looked frightened, they realised that the end was coming. However, at the same time it did not appear to ease the problems for those left in the camp as this fear increased their brutality towards the prisoners.

"I saw several beatings whilst I made my way to Brunner's office, and a dog was set upon a woman, who had dared approach the wire fence and ask me if I had any food on me. I will pass over the details of what her state was after the attack," he said, again dabbing his lips and this time mopping his brow.

"If I had hoped Brunner's office would at least be a sanctuary of sorts from the violence I was quickly disabused of that notion. There was fresh blood on the floor, bullet holes and what I took to be human flesh splattered on the walls.

"Brunner behaved as if it was all normal. He offered me a drink, which I accepted more to steady my nerves than a wish to stay there any longer than I had to, and at the same time held out his hand for the envelope which held the money.

"I made sure I first gave him the letter from Otto just to make it clear that there would be consequences if he tried to prevent me leaving. He just laughed, in a deeply unpleasant way and ripped up the letter. He again gestured for the envelope.

"He was drunk, his eyes were bleary and bloodshot and he mouthed some veiled threat to me, indicating the wall and waved his pistol in front of my nose. He pulled at my hand which was holding the envelope but I refused to allow him to take it by force. I possessed some dignity still.

"I handed it to him, drank my drink in one and left.

"Every step I took I thought I would hear him order me to stop. Instead all he said or at least what I understood as he was slurring his words as I departed was if only all Jews were like me and business was as easy. He wished he could send me more patients it would save space on the trains.

"I did not react I just made the narrow gateway exit my goal, although I cast a glance or two into the camp, there was a roll call of kinds taking place in the courtyard. Shadows from the U shaped living quarters crowded over it but I could see several men and women being led to a gallows with the others being forced to watch them being executed.

"This was when Brunner tugged me back. I had not heard him coming up from behind. He and two guards forcibly turned me towards the fence and he hissed in my ear that I was obliged to look as I appeared to be someone in need of a reality check.

"He said that the tide of war would change again. He would be back and this was the fate that awaited me and other Jews who had slipped through the net this time round."

Lafarge sensed Zilberstein had said all he was going to about that day as he had come to an abrupt stop. There was little point in pressing him as it was not pertinent to their case. At any rate the sight of several people being hanged would remain with anyone no matter how insensitive they were and Zilberstein could be left to deal with it as best he could.

Zilberstein asked to be excused to go to the bathroom which proved perfect timing as it allowed Lafarge and Gilbert to confer. They permitted Durand to stay as he could provide wise counsel and Lafarge valued his judgment.

He possessed a cooler temperament than his hot-headed friend and whilst all three of them had little sympathy for Zilberstein, they could not judge him just on his immorality in dealing with Brunner. Lafarge had certainly made compromises during the Occupation and he had little doubt Gilbert had as well. Had Durand turned a blind eye here and there to causes of death of people brought to his morgue? Yes thought Lafarge, even someone as upright and decent as Durand probably did.

The truth of the matter was there was not much to discuss but instead it was a chance for a breather from what had been a pretty harrowing session.

Zilberstein returned and asked how much longer he would be required, adding he had an appointment back at the gallery at seven that evening. Lafarge looked at the clock and saw it was five fifteen but it was more for his own information, not to work out how much longer they would have the pleasure of

Zilberstein's company.

"I should warn you Monsieur Zilberstein that at the moment at the very least you are facing charges of falsely identifying a corpse for the purposes of defrauding the Rosenberg estate and theft," said Lafarge.

Zilberstein's eyes darted to the left and the right.

"Does that mean I am facing jail?" he asked his voice steady, although Lafarge reckoned he was struggling to sound calm.

"Yes," replied Lafarge coldly.

"How long am I looking at?"

Lafarge shrugged.

"It is not up to me, it will be the prosecutor's recommendation and the judges will decide. I would imagine if you want my opinion that you are looking at between five and 10 years," said Lafarge, trying to suppress the enjoyment he got out of saying it.

Zilberstein stole another glance towards Gilbert.

"I am not sure that will please certain people," he said.

"I would suggest you are taxing their patience Zilberstein. These type of people are willing to protect so long as they themselves do not feel threatened or the person they are looking after does not become too much of a problem," said Gilbert.

"I would say that you are becoming a major pain for them and they might well cut you loose.

"Still you are the only one who will be able to weigh up how much of a hold you have over them and if you have used up all your currency with them."

Zilberstein began to look ever more uncomfortable, shifting in his chair and bringing the handkerchief to his lips.

"Of course this is just the start. We have to ask you about Meissner's murder and the attempted murder of me and my family," said Lafarge, twisting the knife ever further into the cold fish sitting opposite him.

"Now, just hold on a minute Chief Inspector! Rosenberg murdered Meissner, I saw him do it. As for the attempt on your life I have no idea what you are talking about. If you recall I left you in the morgue and I cannot see how I could have organised a hit on you," said Zilberstein.

"Besides Chief Inspector from what I hear you are being targeted. I can categorically guarantee you that I am not behind that."

Lafarge rubbed his chin and thought he is sticking tight to his story about Meissner and Rosenberg and his protestation regarding the hit on him rang true. He was not, though, going to let him off the hook so easily regarding Meissner.

"You have just as good a reason for killing Meissner as Rosenberg. Relations between the two of you were not good following the deadly fiasco in Limoges, you told us how angry you were with him.

"I think the unexpected return of Rosenberg and then my becoming involved, which was also not figured into the scenario, completely threw Meissner.

"I believe he began to panic and advised you that it would be best to sell to Rosenberg, or to allow him to take back the gallery. Meissner argued that you had enough money stored away from participating in blackmail and extortion during the Occupation.

"Your row degenerated and Meissner demanded you pay him half for the gallery in cash. You are a coward Monsieur Zilberstein, and the thought of being left on your own filled you with terror. Meissner was the strongman of your couple and without him you faced a very uncertain future, for I am sure Rosenberg is not the only person who was seeking redress.

"Meissner was right of course, look at what you are facing aside from financial ruin you have jail time coming. If I were you I would accept it."

Lafarge sat back, feeling exhausted but hoping that Zilberstein was even more so and would concede. Gilbert sensing his colleague's fatigue stepped forward and poured a glass of cognac for all of them except Zilberstein. It was not so much out of discourtesy but mindful of the disapproval awaiting them for giving Maria Prevot cognac the night before.

"Chief Inspector you have a devilish mind and a vivid imagination," said Zilberstein.

"I insist I did not murder Meissner, my conscience is clear on that. I also resent you labelling me a coward. Like I said I find it hard to show my emotions.

"It stems from my childhood, cold unloving parents who distanced themselves further from me when I chose to be a dentist and not follow my father into the legal profession.

"I funded myself. I worked as a garbage collector and then a waiter. That is how I know the value of money, maybe my avaricious nature. I know how to survive Chief Inspector. I make no apology for my behaviour during the Occupation.

You may find this abhorrent but I cannot change my nature. I am not alone in having compromised nor profited from the Occupation. Unlike Doctor Petiot the majority of the people I helped did escape and were not gassed and burned in a charnel house in the 16th arrondissement of Paris."

Lafarge stopped him there. Unfortunately he knew full well about Petiot. He had been his family doctor and he had entrusted the fugitive lawyer Pierre-Yves de Chastelain into his care rather than deliver him to Bosuquet. He had disobeyed his orders despite Bousquet telling him to fetch him from Limoges as he regarded him as the main suspect in the murder of actress Marguerite Suchet.

Petiot had been guillotined but had set Lafarge's mind at peace at least over de Chastelain that he had been a rare bird in having successfully made his way to safety. "You always paid your bills," was how the eccentric mass killer had explained it to an astonished Lafarge.

"We shall check on that claim Zilberstein. If true it will I am sure be taken into account but equally what happened to the Rosenbergs will also be held against you even if you did not intend harm to come to them," said Lafarge.

"Of course we only have your account now as Meissner is dead. Rosenberg is adamant Meissner would not have acted unilaterally so ultimately it is your word against his and that may have to be decided in the courts.

"Fortunately for you your morals will not be on trial, although of course your acts stem from them.

"Right back to Meissner please," added Lafarge coldly.

Zilberstein did not look very happy but then his future did not exactly look rosy. He had arrived believing it was a formality indeed to help finalise pinning the blame on Rosenberg but due to his arrogance in thinking an elderly pathologist would not have a reliable memory one error had cost him dearly.

Now he was engaged in a salvage operation.

"You are right Meissner did want to end the partnership," said Zilberstein.

"He thought that we were attracting too much attention. Even with the protection we have as Gilbert said earlier Meissner was worried they would become nervous they would become embroiled in a scandal they can ill-afford to be dragged into.

"I was unhappy about this and did not agree with him, but we had arranged to talk it over one last time. However, when I arrived for the meeting I found him lying dead in the gallery."

"So you did not see Rosenberg kill him as you stated originally?" asked Lafarge, barely able to contain his surprise.

Zilberstein shook his head.

"I thought it must have been him as I saw him running away from the gallery," said Zilberstein.

Lafarge groaned and rose to his feet, coming round the desk to stand over Zilberstein. He did not flinch. Instead he stared up defiantly at Lafarge.

"The fact I did not see him actually do it is irrelevant. Who else could have done it? Certainly none of our staff were capable of murdering him. Meissner always treated them well and they knew nothing about our business during the Occupation," said Zilberstein.

Lafarge greeted his explanation with a grunt. Zilberstein was working off his own logic but Lafarge had his own opinion and he pressed on with it.

"Was Meissner married?"

Zilberstein looked confused at the abrupt change of tack.

"Yes it is hard to imagine such a cruel man having loving thoughts for anyone, but now I recall there was a whiff of scent in the gallery that day. I thought perhaps it was eau de cologne but it was too feminine for that," Lafarge mused.

"Fortunately the fingerprint man put me right and said he recognised it as it was his wife's favourite, Guerlain's Vol de

Nuit. Not perhaps the most in vogue being over 10 years old but a very pleasant aroma would you not say Zilberstein?," said Lafarge staring hard at him.

"Now unless either of you had a preference for women's scent, you were very close after all, I would suggest that a female acquaintance or client was in the gallery shortly before Meissner died."

Zilberstein grimaced and held his hands up in the air.

"Yes, alright, neither of us are married, I only ever had the one unrequited love, but Meissner had a girlfriend. They had been together for two years," said Zilberstein beginning to sound as weary as he looked.

"How did they meet?" asked Lafarge.

Zilberstein shrugged.

"Come on Zilberstein, answer the question. How did they meet?" Lafarge asked again his tone bordering on aggressive.

Gilbert cleared his throat and Durand looked questioningly at Lafarge.

He carried on as if he had not registered their warnings.

"Okay Zilberstein I am going to add another question to the one you should have answered by now, where did they meet?" asked Lafarge, who had now moved to stand directly over Zilberstein.

Zilberstein swallowed deeply but had little room to manoeuvre his hand with the handkerchief up to his mouth.

"You are not leaving here till you tell us," said Lafarge.

Zilberstein looked furious at being badgered like this.

He had apparently conveniently forgotten that he had already admitted to two crimes and could count himself fortunate Lafarge was going to permit him to walk out of the Quai that evening, although he would have to surrender his papers. All this was to come but Lafarge was counting on him, the arch-survivalist, snatching the fig leaf he had offered him.

"They met in Paris and at a party in January 1943," he said with a resigned tone.

Lafarge sighed in relief rather than satisfaction.

"Thank you Monsieur Zilberstein. You can go now, one of my men will deal with taking your papers and if you have some we need and they are at the gallery or your flat then he will go with you. We will also be conducting a search of your apartment, indeed I think they have been there for quite some time now. It could be a bit of a mess," said Lafarge smiling smugly.

Zilberstein's face clouded over but he made no protest, he appeared to be indeed tired and beaten. No doubt though he would be calling on his protectors to see what they could do. He gathered his coat and made for the door where an inspector was waiting, before he turned to face Lafarge.

"Chief Inspector have you not forgotten the most important question? What her name is?"

Lafarge glanced up from a folder he was pretending to study and smiled at Zilberstein. It was not a warm one.

"Oh I already know her name Zilberstein. Your answers confirmed it," he said.

"It is Madame Rosenberg," he added firmly.

Zilberstein looked genuinely impressed and at the same time alarmed, whilst both Gilbert and Durand gasped in surprise.

"Do you know where she is Zilberstein?" asked Lafarge hoping the shock of his revelation would catch Zilberstein off guard.

Zilberstein remained standing but leant against the frame of the door, whether to steady himself or through tiredness Lafarge did not know nor really care.

"Logically Chief Inspector she should be in Meissner's apartment," he replied.

Lafarge took him at his word for Zilberstein's tone was sincere not sarcastic. The fight had gone out of him for now.

"When was the last time you saw her?"

Zilberstein scratched his head and took his time answering.

"I think I saw her a fortnight ago perhaps. She did not come to the gallery very often. We did not get along particularly well. I did not socialise with Meissner as we saw enough of each other during the day," said Zilberstein.

Lafarge showed little sign of allowing Zilberstein to leave or of letting him sit down. The inspector he had asked to accompany Zilberstein stood in the doorway blocking the crooked gallery owner's way.

"So tell us Zilberstein when exactly did Madame Rosenberg become part of the fraud?" asked Lafarge.

"I deny there is any fraud regarding Rosenberg's part of the gallery Chief Inspector. As to the fake identification of Madame Rosenberg's corpse she knew from the start. Meissner came back from Limoges with her," said Zilberstein.

"She was grateful to us for rescuing her and for pointing out to her the huge error of judgement she had made in marrying Rosenberg. Meissner had told the French Gestapo thugs she was an Aryan who had made an error long before the war to marry a Jew. She confirmed this to them" added Zilberstein.

Lafarge felt revulsion towards Zilberstein but restrained himself.

"So you three collaborated to deprive Rosenberg of what is rightfully his? That is until Meissner panicked and you and Madame Rosenberg then conspired to murder him and at the same time implicate her husband as the murderer," said Lafarge.

Zilberstein laughed.

"Chief Inspector you are obsessed with me murdering Meissner. I once again insist I did not. I told you I arrived to see Rosenberg fleeing and Meissner dead," he said.

"You may not have been there Zilberstein, but it is my belief you hatched the plan with Madame Rosenberg. She confronted Meissner at the gallery in your place. You had poisoned her mind against him just as he had done with her about her husband," said Lafarge.

"Yes Zilberstein you told her Meissner was going to desert her and leave Paris taking the money with him and that you could do nothing. She was facing penury and at risk of being charged with fraud. I imagine you had ample evidence to prevent her from coming forward to say she was the apparently dead Madame Rosenberg miraculously brought back to life.

"So I think she lost control and when Meissner admitted he wanted to leave she realised once again she was being betrayed and lashed out. You arrive and being nice understanding Zilberstein recommend that another problem can be dealt with by accusing her husband of the murder, made easier that you had seen him running away.

“She gets Meissner’s share and can disappear and you have sole control of the gallery,” said Lafarge.

Zilberstein rubbed his eyes.

“Like I said Chief Inspector you have a devilish mind and vivid imagination,” said Zilberstein.

“However, much as I was transfixed by your story I think it is a wonderful work of fiction.

“Now if you don’t mind I will go to the gallery and then home to see what a mess as you put it your men have left both places in.”

“You better collect what you require from the gallery because as of tomorrow morning it is closed till further notice,” said Lafarge.

Zilberstein halted and turned with a look of fury on his face. Evidently Lafarge had misjudged him and he still had a spark of fight left in him.

“You have no right to do that Chief Inspector!” he yelled.

Lafarge was delighted to have finally provoked Zilberstein into losing control.

“I have all the rights a Chief Inspector possesses especially when it has been a crime scene twice in several days. It is also being contested as to who is the rightful owner. Your business account if it is separate from your personal bank account will also be frozen so no funds can be moved,” said Lafarge crisply.

“I hope you have sufficient money to maintain some sort of lifestyle Zilberstein,” added Lafarge, though his tone lacked any semblance of sincerity.

“This is outrageous Chief Inspector! I have been as open as I could be with you. I have admitted to two crimes, I am willing to take the consequences. Closing the gallery and freezing my business account is totally out of order,” hissed Zilberstein.

Lafarge shrugged and gestured towards Gilbert.

Gilbert turned to Zilberstein.

“Chief Inspector Lafarge is acting within his rights Monsieur Zilberstein. Indeed he is being generous towards you. For if it had been me I would have not let you leave the Quai this evening. You disgust me, a sentiment no doubt shared by my colleague," said Gilbert disdainfully.

"However, he is giving you some time to enjoy a bit of liberty so I would make the most of it. Go to the cinema, eat lavishly and whore around if you wish to," he added.

Zilberstein shot a look of disgust at Gilbert.

"You were paid well to keep an eye out for me and now you turn on me. You are pathetic," he said.

"We shall see if either of you are in a job or at the least still based in Paris once I have spoken to my influential friends. You have over-stepped the mark," he added angrily before storming out.

"Just as well for me that my clients cannot complain," said Durand.

Lafarge and Gilbert laughed. However, both knew come the morning despite Lafarge breaking with historic practice and allowing Zilberstein a few days grace as well as limiting himself in the seriousness of the charges he had brought, they could face a backlash.

Chapter Fifteen

"The Minister will see you now Monsieur Le Prefet, Comissaire. Chief Inspector please if you can wait,"

Lafarge could hardly argue and sat smoking whilst the Minister of the Interior's senior aide – dressed like Zilberstein favoured he noted sourly in tailcoat and stiff winged collar – accompanied Luizet and Pinault into his chief Andre Le Troquer's office.

Lafarge had been rung very early in the morning by Pinault to be told to go straight to the magnificent Hotel de Beauvau. The Ministry of Interior headquarters had been there for nearly a century ever since the time of Napoleon III when the then Minister had thought it more practical to be opposite the Elysée Palace, rather than situated in the fashionable seventh arrondissement on the opposite side of the Seine.

To Lafarge it cast a rather sinister reflection of who held power, was it the head of state or the person responsible for domestic security?

One had to be very trusting of the person put in charge of such a ministry for they had a wealth of dossiers on every minister no doubt. One had to pray they were of a more benevolent disposition than the cunning and thoroughly disreputable but highly effective Minister of Police Joseph Fouche, under Napoleon I he had wielded more power than the Minister of Interior.

Bousquet had exercised power when he was in charge of the police but times had changed and the present Minister of Interior, the one-armed Le Troquer, being a close friend of Gouin's, was making sure Paris's finest and those outside the capital knew who was in charge.

Lafarge knew from the look on Luizet and Pinault's faces as he greeted them on a chilly slate-grey-skied morning that he was about to face the consequences of his treatment of Zilberstein. He would not have been surprised had Zilberstein walked to Hotel Beauvau from his gallery to protest – their proximity to each other rather convenient mused Lafarge.

Luizet and Pinault had been civil with him and he could tell they were sympathetic to his circumstances. Pinault going so far as to say he found he had handled the affair well and unusual for Lafarge with restraint. He had taken that as a compliment … of sorts. It was not their heads about to roll in any case, although they were probably being castigated for allowing the investigation to get out of control.

Lafarge took some consolation that at least he now knew who Zilberstein's protector was. As to why Le Troquer was protecting him he probably would never know.

There had been no mention of Gilbert so he had to surmise that he was going to be the sacrificial lamb. That was fine by him – Gilbert was a decent man and had been courageous in supporting him so he did not begrudge him if he escaped punishment – as he was weary.

It was not just this case which for him represented so much of the moral crisis that had enveloped the country from even before the Occupation, but had reached its apogee in the open collaboration of the French Government.

The compromises one had had to make throughout it if you were a half decent human being as opposed to the thoroughly nasty types or types like Bosquet who had sacrificed morals for ambition had been exhausting. He could see it on other people's faces, not just colleagues, some would barely look you in the face when the question arose of so what or where were you during the Occupation.

This did not excuse Zilberstein.

His desire to survive and not suffer the fate of millions of his fellow Jews was understandable – heck Lafarge could hardly judge him on that given he had murdered three people so as to save his own life and compounded it by stealing jewels worth hundreds of thousands of francs – but that he should prey on them to make his fortune was beyond the pale.

Lafarge contented himself with probably twisted logic that his quartet of victims had been three collaborators and an Abwehr colonel.

He laughed to himself that legally speaking he probably

merited the guillotine more than Zilberstein, the jury of the public may judge him less harshly but that did not carry weight in a court of law.

No he was ready for premature retirement, besides he still had the jewels and so he and his family's future was financially secure. Whether they were safe from further attacks was less certain. Zilberstein would be content to be left alone but Madame Rosenberg for whatever misguided reason she had targeted him would not stop. He hoped he could reach out to her somehow and dissuade her from further attempts, and detoxify her mind against him.

There was little hope now for her husband and he chided himself for his lack of thought for him. All he could aspire to would be clemency, Lafarge prayed the French State did not wish to knowingly execute the wrong person for the crime. He would serve time and then be released discreetly, with one hoped sizeable compensation.

As he was finally ushered into Le Troquer's even more ornately decorated office he was ready to concede. Indeed he wanted to have the pleasure of telling the Minister he had had enough, he disagreed with the privileged treatment of a common criminal and collaborator such as Zilberstein and therefore would be resigning with immediate effect.

Le Troquer greeted him courteously but formally. Bald with a neatly-clipped grey beard, the right sleeve of his well-cut navy blue suit hung loose where his arm had been amputated during the Great War for which he had been decorated with the Croix de Guerre.

Both Luizet and Pinault had remained and were seated in Louis XV chairs opposite Le Troquer, who sat behind a large oak desk. He gestured with his left hand for Lafarge to take a chair between his two direct bosses.

"I prefer to remain standing Monsieur Le Ministre," said Lafarge politely.

Pinault and Luizet both turned round with worried looks on their faces. Lafarge tried to assuage their fears by smiling and hoping his posture reflected a look of a man relaxed and at ease with himself.

"What I have to say will not take very long Monsieur Le Ministre and I am sure it will meet with your approval," he added.

Le Troquer raised his eyebrows but again gestured with his left hand for Lafarge to proceed. The Chief Inspector did keep to his word, at least restricting himself to 10 minutes which he thought was sufficiently short to make his points and offer his resignation.

He could not see the reactions of Pinault or Luizet, as they had both turned towards Le Troquer when he came to a close. After all they were answerable to him and if he gauged Lafarge's comments as being disrespectful or exaggerated they would be held responsible regardless of the fact he was speaking on his own behalf and offering his resignation.

Le Troquer sat back in his chair, twiddling a letter opener in his one hand, before dispensing with it and instead lit himself a cigarette from a gold-plated cigarette box. Lafarge noted he did not offer one to any of the other men in the room, nor had he asked if they would like a coffee judging by the lack of cups save on Le Troquer's side of the desk.

Lafarge could have done with a cognac right at that moment, his mouth and gone quite dry. No matter how much he swallowed or tried to summon up some saliva it just would not come. Le Troquer despite his lack of a right arm had an aura about him, not just because he had power over them but he sensed it came from within.

A man who had overcome the loss of a limb and carved out a successful career post war was one to be respected. He had shown he had moral courage too as along with Gouin had defended their mentor and former Prime Minister Leon Blum at a show trial in 1942. Their defence had been so good that the trial had ended with Vichy more being in the dock than Blum.

However, never ones to take defeat graciously Vichy and the Nazis had imprisoned him and he had ended up in a compound neighbouring Buchenwald Concentration camp. The elderly Socialist had survived the War and even came out of it plus one as had been allowed to marry whilst a prisoner.

The perversity of the Nazis knew no bounds Lafarge mused.

Thus to many people Le Troquer, who had moved to Algeria after the trial, was seen as a rare beast and a hero in both Wars. This rightly-earned status made Lafarge wonder even more why a creep such as Zilberstein would have Le Troquer in his thrall.

However, he would have to ponder that conundrum in retirement.

"Thank you Chief Inspector for your selfless offer, and for your observations about the case," said Le Troquer, his tone neutral.

"You may be pleasantly surprised that your superiors have spoken very highly of you. They say you are a contrary character, and this case certainly supports them on that. However, they also claim you have become more of a team player since the Liberation.

"I can understand you being an individualist under Bousquet mind you! It must have been nerve-wracking having to play a double game even if your father could watch your back to an extent.

"Anyway I have listened to what Luizet and Pinault have said and now your account. I am minded to accept your resignation but to suspend it for a few months longer. I have a special mission for someone of your talents and who is now at liberty due to having no case to investigate here in Paris," said Le Troquer evenly.

Lafarge was uncertain of how to react. He was surprised for sure and curious to know what this mission could be so he felt it best to remain silent until Le Troquer had elucidated on it.

So he simply nodded which he thought appropriate both to acknowledge his gratitude and for Le Troquer to continue. He also regretted he had not taken the seat offered to him and hoped the Minister would be brief.

"You are married with a baby boy I believe Chief Inspector. I say this because if you accept the offer you will have to tell them that you will be away for some time," said Le Troquer, who kept his gaze on Lafarge which the Chief Inspector could not shake.

He was not going to reward Le Troquer with an answer until he knew what the mission was so he kept his counsel.

"We have had to recall one of your colleagues from

Nuremberg. We have lost a fair few of our most talented legal minds to the war crimes trials. Aside from the two judges there are another 10 or so lawyers on the prosecution team," said Le Troquer.

"They are all above reproach, which was not an easy task given the disgraceful comportment of many judges and lawyers during the Occupation.

"They do, though, require protection. As you can imagine the Allies wanted somewhere symbolic to try the leading Nazis and Nuremberg was a logical venue with the Nuremberg Laws and the huge rallies there. Well I need not go on Chief Inspector. You being a man of culture and interested in the news will have seen the Leni Riefenstahl films, the eulogies to Hitler.

"However, the court room may be fit for purpose, after a lot of work preparing it, but the city itself is devastated. Finding housing for the team was devilishly difficult, but again was accomplished. However, in the ruins and on the streets, or what passes for them as piles of rubble run for miles, there is danger aplenty.

"During the day there is little sign of it as the Trummerfrauen are everywhere clearing rubble, aided by their children if they are still alive. However, at night despite a curfew for the locals – apart from those few who have jobs in the hotels and what pass for cafes – you are best advised to travel in groups as there are gangs roaming looking for rich foreigners to accost and take their money, watches, jewellery, even their lives if necessary.

"The gangs are on the whole made up of the kinds you see helping their mothers during the day, but there are also veterans too, still not willing to acknowledge hostilities are over and bitter at the defeat. Weapons are not in short supply.

"There are no taxis, buses are a rarity, and cars to ferry the legal teams and other allied personnel are few and far between. So a lot is done on foot. Whilst there are soldiers aplenty in Nuremberg we have assigned a man of your rank and several detectives, largely of retirement age due to lack of resources here, to act as a security detail for the legal team.

"So I return to the point I started at. The Chief Inspector has had to be regrettably recalled. The reason for it should serve as a warning to you Chief Inspector. The only consolation is that it was not due to him being recognised by a survivor as a former thug or torturer.

"However, he was caught in a honey trap by the wife of a former SS officer. Fraternising in the French Zone is frowned upon but a bit more relaxed in the American one which is where Nuremberg is. Nevertheless even the Americans have their limits and they were right to recommend his return home.

"The woman had some sort of recording device and he made indiscreet remarks. She then threatened to go with the recording to the Americans unless he gained access to the defence documents concerning the former head of the SS Ernst Kaltenbrunner.

"He had to look to see firstly if her husband featured and the strength of the evidence they had against Kaltenbrunner. The scar-faced fool believes he stands a chance of being acquitted. He should be lucky to escape from the hangman.

"Happily the Chief Inspector in question caved in quickly and accepted the offer of no stain on his record so long as he led us to the woman – for we feel it is best she is held in custody till the trial is over and also reveals where her husband Otto Frank is -- and also agreed to return to France.

"So this is how a vacancy has come up which I would very much like you to fill as it appears to suit your strengths and you are also of a suitable rank," said Le Troquer.

Lafarge succeeded in suppressing a smile, though, it took a lot of effort. He could not believe his luck. He was going to Nuremberg after all. Hal Rosenberg may at last have someone smiling down on him.

"Monsieur Le Ministre I appreciate you listening to my superiors and to them for speaking on my behalf," said Lafarge.

"I accept your offer on condition that my wife is not against my going. As you are aware there is a contract out on me and only a couple of nights ago there was an attempt on my life but with the intention of also harming my wife and child.

"So I have to take into account that by going away I am leaving them exposed and in danger."

"Absolutely, I understand the predicament you are in. The

only thing I can give you is a reassurance that your wife and child will be under constant watch. I know that sadly one of our brave officers has already paid with his life in doing so but hopefully there will be no repetition of that," said Le Troquer.

Lafarge thanked him and his superiors and made to leave.

"One more thing Chief Inspector," said Le Troquer.

Lafarge turned to face the Minister, who he was surprised to find was only a few yards from him.

"This Zilberstein business is most unfortunate and I admit frustrating. I cannot go into the details as to why he is 'special' but judging from what your superiors have said about you I think it would be a crying shame if you were to leave the force.

"We have few talented, hardened detectives remaining since the purge following the Occupation, and crime is hardly going to stop is it! Death and taxes they always say are the two fixed things in life, well I would add crime to that list … a lot of the time it is a critical ingredient of both those anyway!"

He held out his hand and Lafarge accepted it, although he was a long way from accepting what he had just said about Zilberstein. The Minister did not realise how much of a golden opportunity he had just offered him in sealing both Zilberstein and Rosenberg's fates.

*

"Of course you must go Gaston. A ministerial order has to be obeyed. Besides you going away for a while will probably take the heat off here and you never know in six months when you return they might have given up and found some other poor soul to target," said Aimee.

Lafarge did not know whether to be happy or disgruntled that she had taken it all in her stride and had been extremely positive about the opportunity being presented to him.

He had not burdened her with too much of the detail as to why he was being offered this unexpected trip to all but destroyed Nuremberg, as that would only confuse her. Also he could sense that she was delighted because he was going to be able to return and tell her what the monsters looked like, the ones who had been responsible for the camps like Ravensbruck where she had been sent and for which Ancil provided a permanent reminder.

For once he was spot on.

"You know life is very weird," she said.

Lafarge nodded, he could hardly disagree with that notion.

"I received a note at the studio from a friend of mine, Marie-Claude Vaillant-Couturier. I was in the Resistance with her and then by coincidence we ended up in Ravensbruck together. Indeed she was allocated to my delight to the infirmary," said Aimee, the passion that Lafarge adored in her and which he so rarely displayed himself reflected in her eyes.

"It was she who told me, discreetly of course, about the gassing of the Jews, Roma, homosexuals and lord knows sundry others at Auschwitz because she had been deported there first. She was probably bloody lucky to leave Auschwitz alive.

"Anyway she has given evidence at Nuremberg, you may have heard about it? It was powerful, I saw it on a Pathe newsreel and it was pretty damning. As if they really need a trial those pigs to determine their guilt," she added all but spitting the last part of her sentence out.

Lafarge recalled only too well her testimony as it had appalled him and his colleagues. For it highlighted the criminal acquiescence of the French state. She had recounted that from a trainload of 1200 Jewish women she had known at Romainville internment camp in France none had survived more than a month in Auschwitz, all of them sent to the gas chambers.

She had served as an excellent eye witness to what life was like on a daily basis, she added personal detail of the cruelty, the privations and the executions to the paperwork the Nazis had so efficiently compiled in their obsession with bureaucracy for this organ of death.

"However, it will feel good for me to have someone who I am so close to present when their sentences are delivered," she said.

"I hope you return to me telling me the fear you saw in their eyes, that they trembled and had to be helped out of the court room. If you come back with such accounts it will be like ending a chapter, although the book will never be closed for all that I saw and heard there. I say this and I was one of the fortunate ones being in the infirmary!"

Lafarge held her close as she began to sob. This was often the case on the rare occasions they spoke about the camps. He would never broach the subject feeling it was insensitive on his part, and it was best to let her have time or select the moment when she wished to talk.

She had too much class to ever say she regretted being with him although he was surprised given that he had betrayed her once before -- although the faithful and courageous Broglie had acted on his instructions and whisked her away – and he had worked for the state apparatus that had been responsible for sending her to Ravensbruck.

He had been worried initially about how she would behave towards Ancil, but in a way he was the glue that stuck them together. She was an impeccable mother and a loving wife. He was with her because he loved her, not through a guilt trip which he had feared at first not only through his actions down in Limoges but also due to the death of his first wife Isabella and his daughter.

True to form Aimee quickly recovered and dried her tears, wiped the mascara off and attended to Ancil.

Lafarge thought it best to talk of lighter fare. After Ancil had been bedded down for the night and he had poured them both a drink he asked her how the filming was going.

She wiggled her hand up and down suggesting good and bad.

"I am enjoying working again, and the camera holds no fear for me. Playing a role suits me. It was after all what I did when I was in the Resistance," she said smiling.

"However, there are problems with Albert."

"Prejean? Why because of his behaviour during the Occupation?" asked Lafarge.

Aimee nodded.

"He is a charming man and a talented actor. However, some of the crew and a few of the actors are openly hostile towards him. The say it is a bad omen for the film and a disgrace he is in it," said Aimee.

"It is only because the director Rene Delacroix is so desperate to make a mark on French cinema that he is resisting letting Prejean go. He thinks that this film can not only launch his career but also remind people that Albert is a strong leading man and he is not responsible for the worst excesses of Vichy."

Lafarge wished him luck on both scores, but whilst he could not foretell the future for Delacroix in French cinema his instinct told him that Prejean would struggle.

It was one thing to have acted in films during the Occupation -- people had to live after all -- quite another for actors like himself and Danielle Darrieux to have gone to Berlin on a promotional tour and to visit German film studios.

"Albert regularly finds white feathers in his dressing room, which is a bit rich as he was awarded the Croix de Guerre in the Great War. A lighting engineer even spat in his face, saying his cousin had been executed by the Nazis for allegedly sabotaging a propaganda film."

"Lots of people who won the Croix de Guerre ended up on the wrong side this time round Aimee. What happened to the lighting engineer?" asked Lafarge feeling rather sympathetic towards the man and feeling Prejean was quite fortunate to have just been spat at.

"He was fired of course," said Aimee, who to Lafarge's surprise did not sound at all upset about it.

"I would have thought the union would have reacted very angrily to that," said Lafarge.

Aimee shrugged her shoulders.

"Delacroix has been quite selective in his hiring, the lighting engineer apart. He is one of those devout Roman Catholics and has trawled the film world here to track down those of a similar mind.

"Also those working on the film are desperate for work, so whilst many were sympathetic to him there was little solidarity with the lighting engineer," she said.

"Sounds to me like Delacroix is doing his own version of religious profiling," said Lafarge, who the more he heard about the film the less he liked its chances of succeeding which made him concerned for Aimee and her future.

"Are you worried this is going to harm your prospects afterwards?" he asked as diplomatically as he could.

He thought he saw a flash of doubt cross her face, but if it had been it disappeared in an instant.

"I am convinced that this will help me find other parts," she said.

"There is a lot of enthusiasm for the French cinema to develop, huge amounts of talent in all areas are returning, some of whom employed me before they escaped, and for sure there will be others to come through.

"I think that I can succeed. Even if this film is a turnip I am pleased with my performance so far and I think both for me and Albert it can be a useful vehicle.

"I mean Jules Berry being in it has to be a recommendation in itself. He would not endorse a film unless he thought it worthy of his name being associated with it," she added proudly.

Berry was indeed a fine actor – his performance as the Devil in Les Visiteurs du Soir which came out in 1942 was spellbinding -- but Lafarge also knew he was an inveterate gambler and that he would sign on to any film so long as the money flowed into his coffers and then disappear as quickly into the hands of the casino owners.

Thinking of Berry and his diabolic performance also regrettably reminded Lafarge that if there was one good thing about the Occupation it was the cinema and several of the films produced had been quite remarkable.

Henri-Georges Clouzot's Le Corbeau and Marcel Carne's Les Enfants du Paradis would stand as classics in his mind for decades to come even if at present the director of the Corbeau was banned for life from even walking on to a film set due to some misconceived notion he was a collaborator.

That was totally hypocritical when one considered Prejean was back on a set and then more sinister still the likes of Zilberstein could get away with fraud and probably murder.

Just as he was getting into one of his brooding moods and how life was so unfair the phone came to Aimee's rescue.

The phone did not operate on a regular basis -- the unions at fault once again for striking -- and whilst guest sometimes looked longingly at the device, for it was by far from a permanent fixture in many homes in France, he had need of it for his job.

"Gaston it is Gilbert."

Lafarge tensed immediately at Gilbert's tone of voice which suggested bad news was on the way.

"Yes what is it?

He could hear Gilbert clear his throat, which was never a good sign from anybody.

"It is Hal Rosenberg. He is in a bad way, appears there was poison in his food. He has been taken to Pitie Salpetriere and they are working on him now. It does not look good," said Gilbert sounding almost tearful.

Lafarge swore under his breath and noted his breathing was becoming rather rapid.

"Where are you ringing from?"

"The Quai, I sent Grandhomme and a trusted uniformed officer to the hospital with him," said Gilbert,

Lafarge was pleased about that, Grandhomme was a decent detective and a reliable character.

"I think we should lock down the Quai, as whoever did this might still be in the building," said Gilbert.

Lafarge thought furiously, not least was he still alright to deal even with Rosenberg. No reason why not was his response.

"You are probably right. You better inform Pinault. He can tell Luizet. However, I think the authorisation to shut it down will have to come from one of them. At the same time I think I should go straight to the hospital," said Lafarge.

"I will see you there, after I deal with Pinault. I just hope he is on our side," replied Gilbert, before hanging up.

Lafarge had exactly the same thought running through his head as he hurriedly kissed a confused looking Aimee and left the door open on exiting.

Chapter Sixteen

"Who do you think poisoned him?" Lafarge asked Gilbert once the latter had joined him at the hospital.

Gilbert shrugged his shoulders in a manner perfected by the French.

"Thanks for your insight," said Lafarge dryly.

Gilbert smiled and informed him that they might learn more once a thorough search of the Quai had been completed. Luizet had been none too pleased to be told that their most high profile suspect had been poisoned. He immediately ordered a lock-down and for a select group of detectives and uniformed officers, hand-picked by Gilbert and Pinault go floor to floor to see if they could find the phial of arsenic.

Rosenberg had undergone bowel irrigation once the medical staff had diagnosed it as being arsenic poisoning, in an effort to flush out the poison. It sounded particularly unattractive to Lafarge, but needs must.

Rosenberg had now been taken back to a private room and was resting, although the nurse – thankfully not the harridan they had had dealt with before – said talking to him would be impossible this evening as he was hovering between life and death. She said with rather more cheer in her voice than Lafarge thought it warranted that the likelihood of him dying had come down from 90 per cent to 60 per cent.

He wondered whether this same rosy outlook had been delivered in similar fashion to the patient.

In any case he had little need to speak to Rosenberg as he doubted he had paid someone to poison him. He had little reason to commit suicide because as far as he was concerned things were looking more positive for him. That is at least what Lafarge had conveyed to him and he had told Gilbert to avoid telling him about the betrayal of his wife.

Lafarge had little doubt that Madame Rosenberg had turned against her husband, but he wanted it confirmed by her. Zilberstein's word on anything had to be treated with caution, not least because he needed to cast himself in as good a light as possible so he did not finally lose Le Troquer as his protector.

Whether they ever caught Madame Rosenberg was a matter he preferred not to contemplate at this moment. In any case that would be Gilbert's problem not his.

"Who do you think is behind it, though, Gaston?" asked Gilbert.

Lafarge felt like responding in kind with a shrug, but thought better of it. After all being flippant was alright occasionally but this was serious, even more so that a detective or a uniformed officer had aided the person.

The question also was had they done it for money – not impossible as their pay was basic and goods which one really wanted were expensive on the black market – or because of some belief as in there were still Vichy ideologues within the force.

That too was possible. If that was the case it made him even more thankful he was taking off for Nuremberg. He felt really uncomfortable because with a contract out on him and the ease that they had got to Rosenberg suggested he was vulnerable even inside the Quai.

"I think there are only two suspects. Zilberstein and sorry to say Madame Rosenberg has to be a possibility," said Lafarge sadly.

Gilbert let out a loud whistle which startled both the nursing staff and the patients they were attending to inside a ward. He held up his hands to apologise.

"Good lord you really think she would try and murder her husband? She is some piece of work," said Gilbert.

"A very beautiful piece of work my friend," retorted Lafarge.

"I am trying to work out when exactly she turned against Rosenberg. Logically it was Meissner who did that when they were in Limoges but it all appears a bit sudden. Maybe they worked on her in Paris, but she had to go to Limoges otherwise Rosenberg would have pulled out.

"Anyway much as it intrigues me, they looked very much a loving couple when I helped them, I my friend am being sent to Nuremberg. Perhaps, though, you were already aware of that," said Lafarge.

"Yes it has done the rounds of the Quai," smiled Gilbert.

"So where are they going to send you? Tahiti, Algeria....Indochina?" asked Lafarge, half-joking.

"Amazingly they have kept the faith with me and told me I can stay on the case. Albeit I will have to conduct further enquiries on my own and refer everything directly back to Pinault," he said.

"All roads lead back to Pinault..." said Lafarge allowing his pause to signify his doubts about their immediate boss.

Gilbert tapped his thigh as if he was playing the piano.

"I know they do. However, I think it is more a management thing than anything more sinister. I think he is a straight up guy. I do not see him facilitating the poisoning of Rosenberg.

"In any case he has enough pressure on him at the moment with the murder of Denoel. I believe there is a lot of pressure on him to get it resolved quickly and in a suitably uncomplicated fashion," said Gilbert.

Lafarge grinned. It was not just them then who were being coerced into coming to a conclusion that was politically convenient and despite the evidence pointing clearly to others.

"Yes, I am sorry I should not be so suspicious of Pinault. After all I probably owe him for still having a career in the force. He has helped me twice over in fact. Firstly he cleared me after the Liberation and then with Le Troquer he and Luizet gave me a glowing reference.

"Imagine that!"

They both laughed. Lafarge had something in the back of his mind, it was the reason he could not totally discount Pinault being involved; the time he and Luizet had gone to the Ritz to arrest 'Mr Metals' (the collaborator Joseph Joanovici) over a failed coup against de Gaulle and instead had left with a large envelope stuffed with cash.

No doubt in his mind Pinault knew about such an arrangement and so if he was ready to make compromises, the question was, were there any limits?. To them the priority was the new state continued on its way unhindered and if anything threatened that then action had to be taken.

"Well Gilbert I wish you luck with that. It was hard enough when there were the two of us and I do not imagine they are going to give you much leeway. All I ask is that you take your time too, but for a different reason.

"I have no idea how long I will be away but I have been given a chance which I did not think would come my way of resolving Rosenberg's innocence. I won't go into the details as well even I found the story a bit far-fetched and it would have been a hard sell to Luizet and Pinault.

"However, now that I am actually going there I can devote my energies towards that and at the same time protect our finest legal minds!! Just make sure my efforts are not wasted and that Rosenberg is still alive when I return. That is to say he has not been tried and executed.

"Your priority must be to catch Madame Rosenberg. That is likely to be a tough task, although I think she may well be still in Paris. Zilberstein gave us the impression he had yet to do so. Banks are obliged to report large foreign transfers and I doubt his influence extends to having such things suppressed.

"On your own it will be exhausting and I will not blame you if you give up on Madame Rosenberg. However, string it out as long as you can for her husband's sake.

"Zilberstein can live his life out as he wishes, if they want him to remain alive so be it. However, I will be damned if Rosenberg has to pay a price for him again."

Lafarge halted there realising his nerves had got the better of him and he was addressing Gilbert as if he was a new recruit.

Gilbert, though, did not take offence and yet again Lafarge regretted he would be missing his equable temperament in Nuremberg.

Lafarge's euphoria and mild amusement at being sent to Nuremberg had worn off and he felt uneasy about his trip not only leaving Aimee and Ancil, who could still be in danger regardless of his leaving, but also he too would lack the protection he had in Paris.

"You have enough to worry about where you are going Gaston," said Gilbert.

"Have you thought about why they are sending you there? Just be extra careful, you are out of your comfort zone and I would not put anything past any of our politicians, regardless of whether they were with de Gaulle.

"Now that peace has been restored those old loyalties no longer exist and it is very much a buyer's market as we have seen with Zilberstein. His reach could stretch as far as Nuremberg.

"It won't be the Germans you will have to be most concerned about but your compatriots," added Gilbert giving him a consoling pat on the shoulder.

*

Lafarge had expected Nuremberg to be damaged but nothing had prepared him for how bad it was. The once beautiful mediaeval city was all but destroyed. He shuddered at what a dreadful fate Paris had escaped thanks to the intervention of the Swedish diplomat Raoul Nordling in persuading the military governor of the city Dietrich von Choltitz to disobey Hitler and not detonate the explosives.

No such good fortune had befallen Nuremberg as a fierce battle between diehard Nazis and the US Army had wreaked its destruction. It was astonishing to Lafarge that they were even able to hold the trial and house the hundreds of lawyers, judges, journalists and others and he pondered what delightful abode awaited him.

The prisoners at least had dedicated living quarters, he reflected drily. He had no idea how the damage compared to other cities in Germany as when it had not been dark the blinds on his carriage and the rest of the train had been pulled down on the orders of the Military Government, who did not wish for it to be seen.

Lafarge thought it a ridiculous rule given those reaching journey's end would see the extent of the destruction and only set them wondering what it was like in the rest of Germany. One thing he was certain of was that he hoped business would be wrapped up quickly for living in this rubble was not going to be fun. Besides he had travelled relatively light – three bottles of cognac were his most treasured possession in his case although he hoped the French delegation would have access to some should he run out – and it turned out to be a wise decision as nobody was at the station to welcome him.

So it was not in the best of moods he trudged into the lobby of the Grand Hotel, which itself had had some hasty work carried out on it to lodge as many of the leading lawyers and judges as possible. Several had decided to take rooms elsewhere, as it was a long way from being its old de luxe self, but the man he was to meet Edgar Faure, the deputy French Prosecutor had stayed put.

A receptionist directed him to wait for Faure in the bar and registering that it was just after two in the afternoon he availed himself of a cognac hoping the lawyer would pay the bill as he had no Reichsmarks on him.

The waiter was not strong on conversation but then Lafarge could understand that he like all the foreigners in the city was an uninvited guest. Like the receptionist he was of military age but did not carry any noticeable physical legacy of the war, so he was one of the lucky ones.

"Chief Inspector Lafarge?" Lafarge looked up and saw a well-dressed slightly rotund moustachioed balding man of average height.

He got to his feet and stuck out his hand which the other man took readily. Lafarge liked the warm twinkle in his eyes and thought this is a man I will get along with.

"Edgar Faure. I am glad you have ordered a drink. I think I will have one myself. Don't worry I am not performing in court today," he said smiling.

"I would not tell a soul even if you were, sir. I would quite understand if you drank during court days in any case. Seeing the news reels is shocking enough but I imagine they are the sanitised version," said Lafarge sympathetically.

Faure sighed and shook his head.

"The prisoners have had access to a psychiatrist here. It is mostly so we can have assessments of them but lord myself and my colleagues except perhaps the Soviets could do with a session with him.

"The horror of the cruelty inflicted on the concentration camp inmates has been beyond even what I thought. It is hard to turn my head to the left in the court room and look at the defendants. Some are in theory less culpable than others but they share a collective guilt for being in the know about what was going on.

"Some of the witnesses have been as chilling. Otto Ohlendorf, a 38-year-old economist turned mass murderer headed up one of their killing squads and yet in court he showed no contrition and all but sought pity for the mental strains carrying out such orders had on him and his men!

"The only positive thing to emerge from his testimony is that he placed the noose firmly round Kaltenbrunner's neck. Kaltenbrunner had been working on extricating himself by claiming he acted as a brake to Himmler's genocidal desire and had been effective when he replaced Heydrich once he left for Czechoslovakia.

"Well Ohlendorf displayed as much mercy for him as he did for the thousands of unarmed women and children he executed during the war."

Faure smiled sadly and took a gulp of his cognac. Lafarge noticed a slight tremor in his hand but again that was understandable, the man probably had dealt with murder cases before but these were on such a scale and of such ferocity that it would shake anybody.

"Anyway Chief Inspector I hope you do not have to sit in court on too many occasions whilst you are here. Kaltenbrunner of course is the reason you are here, although he will be unaware of that," said Faure whilst also raising his hand with an empty glass in it and signalling to the morose waiter for another two cognacs.

"I trust you will be more careful than your predecessor. From what I have read you are married and have a son. Your wife was also a camp inmate so even less reason for you to sit in on the testimony.

"However, whilst the work may seem unexciting I can assure you it is anything but. There is danger everywhere from the unexploded ordinance to bitter former German combatants to the boy gangs that are motivated either by thoughts of avenging the deaths or imprisonment of their fathers to simple desire to obtain some easy money so as to buy some goods on the black market ... their first step on the criminal enterprise ladder.

"However, a short-lived one too for some as several have been murdered or ended up in prison. Thus you have to be permanently alert, for your sake as much as ours."

The drinks had arrived and Lafarge held his tongue till the waiter had left.

Faure smiled.

"You can speak freely in front of him Chief Inspector. He is one of the Soviets who fought on the wrong side. He sided with General Andrey Vlasov and joined his Russian Liberation Army. Nikolay was fortunate to make it to the western front, Vlasov did not and is in Soviet hands," said Faure.

"From what I have learned Nikolay is hoping he is not sent back to the motherland. Thus for the moment he is alright and who knows the Military Government may find a use for him in our growing tensions with our Soviet allies," he added sarcastically.

"But surely he is at risk working here?" asked Lafarge glancing over to Nikolay, who was chatting to the barman.

Faure shook his head.

"The Soviets are under strict instructions to fraternise with us as little as possible so here is definitely off limits. Just as well for the staff I might add, the behaviour of the Soviets when they are drunk is not palatable," said Faure.

"Rudenko the Soviet prosecutor is a dreadful character, ascetic and lacking any empathy whatsoever. He dismisses the losses of others and says he is only interested in Soviet ones.

"They did suffer terribly I concede that but they began the war as the Nazis allies and were not shy in taking a part of Poland.

"Indeed Rudenko prosecuted the 16 Polish Underground leaders at the show trial in Moscow last year. So his idea of justice runs contrary to mine or my western colleagues. However, realpolitik and all that dictates they should play a role here.

"Whatever our reservations about that we will not be volunteering up the likes of Nikolay even if he fought on the Nazi side. He is fluent in English and now German as are the other members of staff. They have been carefully hand-picked and are indebted to us as the majority of their former comrades have been returned home or will be.

"Shame really Vlasov was quite a hero in the early days of the Nazi onslaught in the Soviet Union. However, you pay for your poor choices and he did. He was captured by his former compatriots along with most of his men.

"Nikolay and the ones here had disobeyed their direct commander General Bunyachenko and surrendered to the US Army. They made the right choice."

Lafarge thought Nikolay and his fellow former turncoats were fortunate indeed.

However, he still felt they were taking a gamble by being quite so up front in where they were working and it would not take too much for a loose phrase or indeed done deliberately for the Soviet authorities to demand their repatriation or simply kill them on the spot.

After all Faure had said how dangerous Nuremberg was.

Lafarge thought Faure was being a bit hard on the Soviets and not least because the French had if anything been more enthusiastic allies of the Nazis.

From supplying hundreds of thousands of people for STO or Compulsory Work Service in Germany – he had gained his freedom as a result of Vichy sending them as the Nazis had agreed to send back a certain number of POWs – and rounding up the Jews to suppressing Resistance cells in the Vichy run areas they had proved themselves reliable partners.

Lafarge did not think it wise to debate it with Faure at this precise moment, especially as he wanted to create a good impression and cultivate him so he could gain access to Goering.

"So sir where will I be living and what hours do you want me to be on duty?" asked Lafarge wishing to bring matters back to himself.

"You have a room reserved here. Since your colleague's indiscretion we prefer that you are under our roof. It means also that if there is an emergency here you are on site. Your three juniors are in a house on the outskirts of the city, although, one is always on duty here.

"The walk to the courthouse is not far it is less than three kilometres but as I said before you will be kept busy! Not that there is a lot to do outside of your duties. It could be a lonely few months for you Chief Inspector but at least in this hotel the food is good and as you know by now the cognac is excellent quality," he said smiling and his eyes twinkling.

"Right I will let you settle in. I am off to see a couple of witnesses to go through their testimony once your colleague turns up.

"Speak of the devil here he is now. Louis Bonville is rather a stern fellow but reliable and I would entrust him with my life," added Faure, who got to his feet and picked up his overcoat and homburg hat.

Lafarge also rose and shook Faure's hand warmly before turning round to accompany him out of the bar. However, on seeing his colleague he stopped in his tracks. For staring at him was not Louis Bonville but the former collaborator and avowed enemy Louis de Blaeckere.

Faure did not appear to notice the evident hostility as he introduced them. Lafarge, though, wondered whether Gilbert had been correct and he had been set up.

One thing was for sure was that only one of them would be leaving Nuremberg alive and Lafarge counted on it being him.

Lafarge downed a third cognac to steady himself after Faure had left with 'Bonville' and debated whether to simply expose his colleague. In theory he should do as quite apart from his past de Blaeckere might well be feeding the defence information.

On the flip side he was uneasy that he may have been lured into a trap and was unsure who to trust. Faure appeared genuine but he would require more time to get the measure of him. Another thought occurred to him too was that the other two members of the protection team might be former acolytes of de Blaeckere's. If they were then he really had a serious problem.

It set him pondering whether his predecessor had really been guilty of what he had been accused of or had been victim of a ruse so he could be forced home and Lafarge brought out.

He took the stairs to his room, which was on the third floor, as the lift was out of order. He passed several men in uniform, largely Americans, which gave him some comfort.

His room was not big but the bed was comfortable and the curtains -- a rather vulgar gold with matching tassels – closed which also reassured him as it meant he would not be disturbed by any outside light.

That is if they worked of course.

He opened the window and smoked a cigarette whilst observing the view. If he craned his neck to the left he could make out the courthouse, otherwise all he surveyed were ruins.

He lay dispirited on his bed and contemplated what sort of strategy he should deploy. One thing was certain he would not go to his colleagues billet at risk of being caught in a trap. He would, though, need to meet the other two members of the team to have a clearer picture of what they were like.

He would also make de Blaeckere's life as tough as possible and avoid having him posted too often on night duty at the hotel. He would also have to factor in how de Blaeckere might target him. He must have known he was coming – either through official channels although sometimes they were not efficient or because it was indeed a trap. In that case de Blaeckere would have his plan already well in place.

Failing to get to sleep he thought there was nothing for it but to take advantage of de Blaeckere being with Faure and to have a walk round the city whilst there was still a bit of daylight. He would also go back on what he had earlier sworn not to do and pay a visit on the billet and see if the other two detectives were there.

They would not be expecting him to drop by and he could size them up.

Maps were obviously in short supply so Lafarge asked the receptionist for directions. He looked surprised that Lafarge wanted to walk saying it was quite a distance and he would be returning after dark.

"Well I don't have a car? I would not imagine bus and tram services are up and running. So unless you have a carriage hidden away with a live horse I am compelled to use my feet," said Lafarge sardonically.

The receptionist, a tall and muscular dark-haired man, did not look happy at his remark and replied he was only offering advice.

He added in fluent German – albeit with a thick Russian accent – the streets such as they were were best not walked at night on one's own and he was trying to be helpful to someone who had just arrived.

Lafarge apologised but insisted he was going regardless.

The receptionist shot him a look of be it on your own head but I warned you. It made Lafarge wonder whether the Americans would have been better served by retaining the old staff – those that had survived the war – even if they would have been diehard Nazi followers.

Some of their best clients from the past 15 years now sat in less sumptuous surroundings a couple of kilometres down the road whilst their conquerors slept in the rooms they had occupied previously in the old building that had been fused together from a farmhouse and a hop barn.

Where the staff had scattered to heaven knows but he doubted the Americans move to throw them out had done wonders for their already low popularity.

He thanked the receptionist, taking a note of his name which was Vladimir, to which he got a gruff have a good evening.

He exited the Grand and wandered through the streets. There were not many people around. A few women, middle-aged to elderly though the rigours of rationing and the war could have aged them, were struggling to clear the rubble, their expressions determined but when they saw he was not there to help turned to anger.

He quickened up his pace in case one of them vented their ire by hurling a rock at him. The only men he saw were either disabled – some still wearing their tattered uniforms with the lucky ones still in possession of their great coats which at least would keep out the worst of the chill not that it had offered the poor bastards much protection in Nikolay and Vladimir's former homeland – or frail and old.

Very rarely did they meet his eye, even when one

inadvertently moved out of his way but Lafarge also went the same way. A mumbled apology emanated from his lips but it was hard to discern as he kept his head bowed to the ground and the brim of his hat covered his face.

Lafarge passed by the station and made for the Fleisch Bridge which traversed the River Pegnitz . He was heading for the north of the city, fortunately not to the north east of the city which he had been informed by Vladimir had borne the brunt of the Allied artillery and bombing. His destination was the heart of the medieval city Sebalder Alstadt.

The bridge was not damaged at all but this was a false dawn for Sebalder Alstadt itself was a mixture of rubble and empty spaces where once houses had been for many had burnt to the ground as they had been made of timber. A massive air raid in January 1945 had all but destroyed the beautiful neighbourhood, killing thousands.

Lafarge feared what the north east part of the city looked like if this did not rate according to Vladimir as being destroyed.

De Blaeckere's billet was beyond Sebalder Alstadt. The burnt out ruins would have suited vermin like de Blaeckere – there were plenty of them scuttling around – and incredibly he saw signs of human habitation in some of the former residences he passed. Washing had been hung out to dry and battered pots and pans littered the exterior of cellars which is where he surmised the inhabitants lived. He shivered at the thought. The chill wind was biting even with his overcoat on he felt it so lord knows how the residents kept warm.

Eventually he alighted on the house. It was not difficult to find as it stood on its own, all the other houses had been flattened. It was a wonder how it had survived. However, for the three men who lived there it was ideal as it gave them space and a clear view of anyone approaching the house.

It was a grey stone three-storey building. He could tell someone was at home as there was music playing inside. A tall slim man of around 30 opened the door to him. He looked the worse for wear for drink, his brown eyes were bleary and his gait unsteady as he wandered back down a hallway.

Lafarge gave him a black mark straight away for his lack of security. He had not even asked him his name thus allowing a perfect stranger into the house. Lafarge followed the man down the hallway and turned right into the large room from where the piano music was playing.

The man had collapsed into a brown leather armchair, which looked in pretty decent condition. He raised a glass to his lips and knocked back the clear liquid in one.

He looked to his right and saw that what he had taken for a record was actually another man seated at the piano playing. Once the pianist realised they had company he finished his tune and turned round. He was definitely clear-headed unlike his house mate. He was of a similar age to the drunk but much better presented, his blond hair was brushed. He had shaved and was smartly dressed.

"Who are you?" he asked warily.

"Chief Inspector Lafarge."

With that the pianist got to his feet, whilst the other one tried unsuccessfully to stand before falling back into the chair.

"I am Inspector Hugo Devries and he is Inspector Sebastien Guillemot. We are both from Lyon," said the blond detective, putting out his hand to shake Lafarge's.

Lafarge obliged although he was unused to shaking the hands of subordinates. He did not bother doing so with Guillemot, who appeared to be finding it hard to focus on anything.

Devries looked uncomfortable at the state of his colleague and in an effort to lighten the atmosphere offered Lafarge a drink.

Lafarge accepted and Devries poured him a cognac.

He offered him a seat by the piano as he began to play again.

Lafarge sat there patiently smoking and sipping at the cognac. He did not recognise either of them from his time in Limoges, but that was not to say de Blaeckere might have been acquainted with them. Lyon was where de Gaulle's emissary Jean Moulin had been captured, undoubtedly betrayed by one of the leading resistants who he was meeting with. He had been tortured but that had been by the Germans and eventually was executed.

He waited till Devries had finished Franz Liszt sonata. Lafarge was not an aficionado but he had stolen a peep over his colleague's shoulder and he had to confess he rather liked it. Whether it was due to the playing of Devries or the tune itself he did not know.

"So call this just a courtesy visit. I arrived today and I wanted to come over and meet you," said Lafarge smoothly.

Devries smiled.

"Well here we are Chief Inspector. Welcome to our humble lodgings. It cannot compare to the Grand but it is more habitable than what many poor buggers have to put up with," said Devries.

"I must excuse Guillemot's state. However, he has been doing double shifts recently as Bonville has been away on leave and we were not counting on your predecessor being recalled.

"Guillemot also made the mistake of sitting in on several sessions at the courthouse. No doubt you were briefed to avoid doing that?"

Lafarge nodded.

"The trouble is there is nothing else to do when you are waiting around there. There is neither a convivial bar nor a park to sit in. So Guillemot who I would venture is the most sensitive of us and dare say inquisitive to find out the gruesome details of what those beasts did decided to ignore the health warning. That was a week ago and he has barely drawn a sober breath since, apart from when he has been on duty," Devries said with a sympathetic sigh.

Lafarge's attitude to Guillemot softened. However, though, he understood his reaction he would have to shape up now. Especially as he could not count on de Blaeckere and was going to take care of that problem as soon as he feasibly could.

He briefly reeled off what he required of them, which was slightly different to his predecessor's demands. However, he met with no objections. Indeed Devries appeared delighted that the shifts especially the night time ones were to be more fairly allocated with Lafarge assuming most of them which appeared to him logical and fair given he was staying at the hotel.

Lafarge was also interested to learn that de Blaeckere rarely worked nights. He had taken the day time shift which Lafarge assumed meant he had not discarded his criminal past and was probably dealing in the black market. Lafarge may have only been in Nuremberg for the best part of a day but from what he had heard and seen it was hardly be the night life that had de Blaeckere skiving off doing night-time guard duty.

He was more intrigued by de Blaeckere having taken leave. He did not wish to press Devries on that as it might appear odd him asking about a detective he had apparently just met. Devries seemed sharp too and might raise his suspicions. Also he did not want him informing de Blaeckere that their superior had been enquiring about his movements.

He also had yet to resolve in his mind whether Devries was above suspicion himself. Guillemot might have been suffering from a guilty conscience having watched the reels of where the Nazi and Vichy victims had ended up but he doubted it.

His reaction was genuine if Devries was to be believed and whilst it was well known now that many of the executioners on the Eastern Front had resorted to drinking copious amounts some to ease their nerves before the killings, other times it was offered as a reward for a good day's work and for very few it brought them peace for their guilty consciences.

"So where do you get your food, cigarettes and alcohol from? There is rationing but I imagine you are not subject to those rules," said Lafarge hoping Devries would let slip that de Blaeckere was a furnisher of the goods.

He was to be disappointed.

"There is a French Army delivery once a month for those of us who are not in hotel accommodation. However, that is unreliable but we have friends within the US Army who sign off on supplies and we get our alcohol from the Post Exchange. It is cheap too," Devries said.

"That is good to know if I ever feel the need to just sit in my room and drink," said Lafarge with a grin and glancing at Guillemot.

Devries laughed politely.

"Do you ever have trouble from the locals?" asked Lafarge.

Devries looked surprised at the question.

"Well you know sir that fraternisation is not permitted," he replied somewhat defensively.

"I am aware of that but that is not the reason I asked the question. I mean you are quite exposed out here and I heard that it is a hostile environment for a whole host of reasons," said Lafarge.

"Whether you fraternise with the women of Nuremberg is not my concern and I would fully understand if you did.

"However, the black market, whilst tempting given the lack of shops and reliable deliveries, would be another matter."

Devries smiled sheepishly.

"Yes, we are rather a lonely outpost here," he said sighing.

"However, that is an advantage as not too many street urchins or the gangs that prowl the neighbourhoods venture out here.

"If we do go out occasionally at night it is usually to US Army friends places. There are some bars but you are taking a risk, both in terms of the company that you share in them and the quality of the alcohol.

"The local brew is not bad Rotbier, or red beer, but we, myself and Guillemot that is as Bonville largely keeps himself to himself, prefer usually to stay in and have friends round. That is if they wish to make the trek and we are not too exhausted after night shifts," he added with a well-timed yawn, which Lafarge could not make out whether it was genuine or a piece of dramatic license.

Lafarge slapped his knees and stood up, he had the impression this pleased Devries. As for Guillemot he was now snoozing in the chair.

"Can I use your bathroom please? I know I could go on the way back to the hotel as there is no lack of choice but it feels rather cheap to pee over the ruins of what was someone's home," said Lafarge.

Devries smiled and pointed towards the stairs which was down the hallway adding it was on the first floor to his left.

*

Lafarge did not need to go at all but was using it as a ruse to be able to see a bit more of the house and also if de Blaekcere's room was on the first floor to have a look inside it.

There were four rooms on the first floor including the bathroom, which was a decent size and relatively clean too.

Either one of the trio were quite conscientious when it came to keeping things clean or they had been provided with a housekeeper.

Lafarge made sure he had not been followed up the stairs by Devries before taking a peek inside the other three rooms.

Two were locked but the third one was open. It appeared to be Guillemot's as there were a couple of dirty glasses on the bedside table, the bed was unmade and there was an empty bottle of bourbon on the floor.

He was just about to step back outside into the corridor when he noticed a box poking out from under the bed. He walked over bent down and saw there were several photographs. His inquisitive nature forbade him from walking away, so he picked up the dozen or so and leafed through them.

Most of them were of banal situations like family sittings or parties but one demonstrated why Guillemot was so emotional and it was not to do with the evidence he heard or the reels of the camps he watched in court. In fact it explained why Guillemot ignored the advice and went into the sessions.

Guillemot was staring up at him frowning but that was not what gripped Lafarge's interest. It was the fact that he had a pale star on his jacket. Guillemot was a Jewish survivor of the camps.

*

Work proved to be pretty mundane -- escorting the group back and forth from the courthouse was not very demanding although Lafarge did not permit himself to become complacent. Truth be told, though, he kept a closer eye on de Blaeckere than on any potential external threat to himself in any case. He also kept tabs on Guillemot, but more like an elder brother and ensuring he did not fall completely into a drunken rut which for the most part he did not.

However, he used most of his time to become close to Faure. He was a convivial character, free of pretension, with a brilliant mind. He had been a child prodigy academically gaining a degree aged just 15 and a law degree before he was 20. He was very humble about that and was big on self-deprecatory humour. Aside from that he had been an active resistant before escaping to Algeria.

He was not judgmental, well at least towards Lafarge. Others who had opted to remain and not join de Gaulle invited scorn, whilst those who had played an active role in Vichy were beneath contempt especially Bousquet. That pleased Lafarge no end.

Faure and he had a mutual friend in Henri Gerland, also a lawyer but one who had stayed in France. However, he had helped Lafarge on more than one occasion even when he had been on opposing sides and had housed de Chastelain in Limoges.

Faure said he had met de Chastelain on a couple of occasions and had jousted with him as well in court. Lafarge was relieved that they were not better acquainted as he did not wish to go too deeply into setting him up with Petiot. Even if Petiot had been telling the truth and he had escaped – one of the rare ones – his involvement in the doctor's fantasy world might alarm Faure.

He did not wish anything to disrupt their burgeoning relationship as aside from genuinely liking Faure he also saw him as being the conduit to gaining access to Goering. Lafarge had never been one to be patient and once he heard from Faure that the trial was nearing its end he decided to act.

He decided not to try and be clever with Faure, but to be straight with him. Well as straight as he wished to be. He would not mention Zilberstein or Rosenberg by name in case Faure was aware of the reason he had been effectively exiled from Paris.

"How easy is it Edgar to have access to the prisoners," asked Lafarge after they had finished dinner and retired to the bar where Nikolay had brought them without asking two large cognacs.

Nikolay was well used to their habits by now and he had become friendly in his gruff way. Vladimir on the front desk had retained a rather superior air certainly towards Lafarge, as if he had yet to forgive him for setting off on foot despite his advice to the contrary. Even though nothing untoward had happened to Lafarge evidently that still rankled with the turncoat.

Faure played with his moustache and exhaled a cloud of cigar smoke.

"Almost impossible, only their lawyers and very occasional family visits are permitted. Otherwise there would be queues of people lining up and not just Germans. You have seen how notoriety attracts all sorts either in court or even writing letters to defendants and those awaiting the guillotine," said Faure.

"You look disappointed Gaston. Can you tell me who and the reason why? Perhaps then I can weigh up if I can obtain a special pass for you."

"I need to see Goering on behalf of a friend of mine. It is not for someone who dared me to or for a bet. It is because my friend is in dire straits and incredibly his life depends on fat Hermann," said Lafarge.

"Good grief! I am sure Goering will be flattered. The only life he is interested in saving is his and despite an initially strong performance in the witness box -- he crucified Robert Jackson the lead US Prosecutor – he was exposed for what he is by the English counsel David Maxwell-Fyfe," said Faure.

"The trial is far from over as several defendants are still to testify and be cross-examined but for Goering there is simply a hiatus between this and his certain death by hanging. He still dominates the others but only really because they are more broken than him.

"I would venture that he has little interest in helping anyone, especially someone from the prosecuting quartet of nations which I imagine your friend is from."

Lafarge nodded.

"I am willing to pass your request to his lawyer, a curious but able fellow called Otto Stahmer. He has performed very well in impossible circumstances.

"I don't know him very well but he has been civil on the occasions I have had to confer with him. Ultimately it is up to Stahmer if anyone can have access to Goering. However, don't get your hopes up too much if he says okay as it is conditional on the final word of the defendant.

"You will have to tell Stahmer what you wish to speak to

Goering about. I would encourage you to be open about what you are going to broach with him. For if you are not you risk having the conversation brought to a speedy end."

"Why will Stahmer be present at the meeting?" asked Lafarge.

"No he will withdraw once you have been introduced. Goering, though, can close it down when he wishes to. However, there will be a Military Policeman present at all times. He is not always a German speaker but you will not know that.

"This is to keep the defendants on their toes and I would recommend you keep off politics. Not that you are going there to discuss it but it serves little purpose to try and win him over by sympathising with him. He is highly intelligent and will know you are lying.

"Be straight with him. How is your German or English?"

"Both are passable, though, I would feel more comfortable speaking German. I fine-tuned it in the POW camp," he said grinning.

Faure laughed.

"I had no such ahem good fortune so my German is poor. I would speak German then that should gain you some credit with him and obviously he is a rare audience these days where your Vichy past will help you," said Faure.

Lafarge did not take to that at all.

"It is something I would prefer not to talk about. I have tried to put it behind me like many others have. Anyway you said politics should be off limits," said Lafarge.

"I am not saying you go into the good old days or anything of that nature. Of course not that could get you into trouble with the guard. All I am saying is you can drop it into the conversation how you were a POW but returned to resume being a detective during the Occupation," said Faure.

"That is all. This friend what is his charge? Treason, collaboration, murder?" asked Faure.

Lafarge had been waiting for this. He had been surprised how speedily Faure had passed onto the detail of obtaining a meeting with Goering. They had become close but he was also wary of imparting much of the true nature of his reason for seeing Goering.

This stemmed from having served Vichy or like many who had lived through the Occupation had learned that sensitive information was best not shared with too many people – not even one's family or closest friends -- for one did not know who was reliable and who was an informer.

Also even if Faure was trustworthy there was a chance he might tell de Blaeckere about it and that was something he did not want. De Blaeckere might be ignorant of the Zilberstein case and solely interested in fulfilling the contract on him.

However, there was a strong chance he was an active partner with Zilberstein and Meissner. For he had been in Limoges and it was hard to believe Meissner had had the power to spirit away Madame Rosenberg without the express permission of de Blaeckere.

Of course de Blaeckere would have expected to receive a financial reward. There was nothing philanthropic about de Blaeckere.

Lafarge could of course have been totally straight with Faure now that he knew him better and told him about Bonville's true identity However, Lafarge had set his sights on finally settling matters with the torturer of Limoges.

Nevertheless he gave Faure a fairly honest account of the story and the various characters involved, with a few alterations here and there like their jobs and religion. He hoped that this would sate Faure's interest and he would not seek to make any enquiries about the case back in Paris.

"I have one other request Edgar. I would prefer that this stays between us. I know you get on with the other three of my colleagues and for the most part they are decent people. However, I like my personal business to remain that," said Lafarge.

Faure looked uncomfortable and shifted in his chair.

"I can assure you I will be discreet. However, you have been here long enough now and know that everything gets around. It begins at the raucous parties of Jackson's staff and filters down and then spreads," said Faure.

"Anyone requesting an appointment with Goering is bound to arouse both suspicion and interest.

"So I would prepare for that. Don't look so surprised Gaston obviously people are going to ask questions as to why a French Chief Inspector wants to talk to Goering and what it is about. I would prepare a good cover story for their questions. They are unlikely to come in a formal setting.

"The interested parties may hope to catch you off your guard, at a party or here in the bar. Also do not make them think it is about stolen art for God's sake otherwise they may get ideas and think they can use you to get rich.

"Plenty of people are not here to see justice done. They are here because they believe they can learn information that will lead them a step closer to a hidden treasure trove and assure them of never having to wear a uniform or work again in their lives.

"You have seen those westerns surely, usually Errol Flynn stars in them, of the man who rides into town and has come from another one where gold has reportedly been discovered. The seedy profiteering types get him drunk or charm their way into his company in the belief that he will get them rich.

"Of course the rumour is wrong but he is ignorant of this and in order to put them off the scent of what he is really after he talks up the gold story. When they discover that he has been telling lies or equivocating they kill him…and of course at that moment Flynn the hero arrives ...," Faure allowed his voice to trail off as he felt the message was clear enough.

"Well that was a colourful way of telling me to watch my step! Except in my case there will be no Flynn is what you are implying," said Lafarge with a broad grin.

Faure smiled.

"I have always been a bit partial for the western genre. I can tell you in confidence that de Gaulle is quite the opposite and indeed questioned my bona fides after our first meeting!" he said with a wink.

"However, Gaston you could be in for a long wait. It is possible you will not get to see him but also that you might have to wait for a couple of months till the verdicts and as it is likely that he will be sentenced to hang he may not wish to see anyone aside from his intimates."

"So in the meantime heed my warning. I will help by delaying the request to Stahmer till I feel it is appropriate. However, I can also at least prepare the way by organising for you two to meet.

"It may save you a lot of trouble in the long run.

"Also Stahmer is going to be rather pre-occupied for the moment as Goering like all the other defendants are preparing their final statements to the court. Going through the motions for most of them I would venture but at least they get to plead for their lives in front of a proper court unlike those that plotted to assassinate Hitler.

"The Soviets are the exception of course. Indeed they rather admire the manner in which Hitler's beast of a judge Freisler dealt with the conspirators but the defendants will get a fair hearing from the other judges.

"You should attend this session. I notice you have resisted it so far which I understand but this one will be worth it to see how very ordinary and defeated are the men who thought they would set the flame burning for 1000 years.

"I think you would find it rather instructive in how rather dreary and grey the majority are. Colourless bureaucrats and ideologues who condemned millions to death either through fiery intemperate racist language or a signature on a piece of paper."

"You might add we had many like-minded people in France. I may sit in but I saw Laval shortly before his execution and that was a shocking experience. No gold-topped cane and puffed up peacock pleased with himself look but a broken man shuffling along with his feet chained," said Lafarge.

"Poor him," interjected Faure sarcastically.

"Your father though was a decent man," he added rather too quickly for Lafarge's taste.

Lafarge let it pass. He was all for moving on.

*

In the end Lafarge did attend. The alternative was to spend time with de Blaeckere – thus far he had succeeded in avoiding him as he tried to work out the best moment to strike. He did not, though, want to attract attention from the French entourage by highlighting the hostility between the two of them.

He also enjoyed the company of Devries but he had opted to partner up with Guillemot for the most part so he could take him under his wing and keep an eye out on his drinking in particular. Not that Lafarge held back when there was a whiff of cognac in the air but he showed restraint whenever the two of them were off duty and they went to a beer garden.

After hearing the 21 final statements he was in need of something stronger than a beer. However, his compunction was to drink a bottle of cognac in his room. The lack of contrition or taking responsibility when they had a last opportunity to do so had been astonishing.

Kaltenbrunner had even bemoaned the fact that Hitler had not sought closer co-operation with the church – Lafarge doubted the late German Chancellor was the type to listen to priests sermonising as he loved to give his own at great length whether the listener liked it or not.

Julius Streicher the publisher of the disgusting weekly newspaper Der Sturmer, which fed anti-Semitism with tirades of base and hate-filled abuse of Jews, although Roman Catholics and other groups were not immune from verbal assaults either, had claimed never advocating the extermination of the Jews just the creation of another state.

Literary -- if one could term the journalism in the paper as that -- evidence indicated otherwise and the man who had millions out of hatred was likely to never get to spend it.

Others such as Hess and von Ribbentrop had been deeply unimpressive, the former appeared mad whilst the latter's appearance really shocked Lafarge as the arrogant puffed-up peacock who had strutted around Europe smartly-dressed but looking ever so pleased with himself had been reduced to a shabby broken figure with his face resembling that of a shrunken peanut.

His arrogant demeanour of pre-War and the early years of victory had evaporated and 'My Bismarck' as Hitler had ludicrously termed him offered a pathetic defence and there was little chance of him returning to his former career as a champagne salesman.

As for Goering, he was too old in any case to resume his flying career where he had been a hero but like Petain he had sacrificed any principles and morals to become a murderer on a scale barely credible to an average human mind.

Lafarge grudgingly conceded Goering may have lost weight but he retained an aura and charisma that the majority of the others lacked. Now the leading Nazi with his rasping voice he assumed some of the responsibility but stopped far short of a full mea culpa.

All this he mulled over on the way to join Guillemot at the Hexenhaeusle or 'Witches Hut' a historic beer garden situated a 10 minute walk from the courthouse and at the foot of Nuremberg Castle. It had re-opened since the cessation of hostilities despite the Castle having been heavily damaged.

Guillemot had persuaded him to come but he had still returned to the hotel to freshen up and down a couple of cognacs.

"An appropriate place to have a drink after that disgraceful and cowardly spectacle," Guillemot sneered.

Lafarge nodded.

"We should have had a similar trial in France. Rather than judging them one by one it would have been far better to have all of them lined up in the same box," said Guillemot.

"De Gaulle did not wish it that way," said Lafarge.

Guillemot made a face.

"Indeed what the General says is what God demands!" said Guillemot spitting the words out.

*

"Careful what you say Guillemot. There are some of our compatriots over there and they may not be as amenable to what you are saying," Lafarge whispered.

Guillemot turned and saw several French army officers carousing openly with local women. He turned back to Lafarge and raised his eyebrows.

Lafarge laughed.

"Come now Guillemot the war is over and this non-fraternisation rule is impossible to enforce. There are precious few secrets in any case that can be kept and the court is better for nothing being held in camera. Otherwise no end of conspiracy theories would be concocted. Heaven knows there are enough already but all of which can be shot down," said Lafarge.

"Come on drink your beer and let's talk about something else."

If Lafarge had hoped to calm Guillemot he was to be disabused of that very quickly.

"I don't feel like changing the topic," he said with his tone now downright surly.

He rose and walked over to the French officers table, bending down to whisper something in the ear of the one closest to them, a colonel. Whatever he said clearly provoked the colonel as he launched himself out of his chair, dumping the middle-aged German woman on the ground, and slapped him on both cheeks.

The garden which was bursting to the seams went silent and the pianist – who was slightly better than Devries – brought his tune to an abrupt climax.

Lafarge went to intervene as he feared Guillemot would retaliate and then the man would be in serious trouble. The colonel had clearly been drinking for a long time and the false courage engendered by the alcohol had dissipated as he saw the bigger Guillemot weighing up whether to hit him back or not.

It did not take too many words from Lafarge to convince him to sit down and the Chief Inspector -- much against his own will as he had little respect for many in the French military – apologised on behalf of his colleague.

The apology was accepted with relatively good grace by the officers but glancing at the woman, who had picked herself up and was making a scene about her dress being torn, Lafarge thought he could sense she knew why Guillemot had reacted the way he had. Her expression was not one of sympathy but of hate.

Lafarge was shocked at this but then there were many accounts emerging of the women concentration camp warders being as brutal if not worse than their male counterparts.

"That was very stupid Guillemot. I could send you back to Lyon for that," said Lafarge angrily.

Guillemot did not look in the least bit afraid of the threat.

"But you won't will you Chief Inspector?," he said with a

smile.

"You are correct. However, what did you say to him?"

"I told him the French Army had not improved since the Dreyfus Affair. Keener to consort with the enemy that had murdered millions of my fellow Jews than to see justice done," said Guillemot, his anger clear.

That explained to Lafarge the look on the German woman's face. Clearly she had a good understanding of French.

"That woman reminds me of the one who got your predecessor into trouble. These German women are nothing but provocateurs and mean trouble," said Guillemot.

Lafarge laughed.

"Come now Guillemot did my predecessor really cross a line? He just made a mistake with the woman he fell for," said Lafarge.

Now it was Guillemot's turn to laugh, though, caustically not with genuine humour.

"She fell into his lap because Bonville directed her to," said Guillemot.

Lafarge felt his heart up a beat. His instinct had been right, he had been set up. That was fine for he had suspected it but it was good to have it confirmed.

"How do you know he did? Furthermore why have you left it till now to tell me?" asked Lafarge.

"I heard him talking to her. I speak fluent German having learned it at school and studied it at university," said Guillemot.

"The two of them had never got on and Bonville showed little respect for Duchamp. Bonville was close to being dismissed on several occasions but Devries acted as peacemaker.

"However, there was nothing he could do when Duchamp was discovered with her. I am certain Bonville is the one who brought the affair to the French legal team's attention. Duchamp being an honourable man did not deny it although he realised it would mean a black mark on his record and being sent home.

"I did not inform you because firstly I sensed you are an intelligent man with good antennae and would not fall into the same trap as Duchamp and was it worth my while bad mouthing a colleague."

Lafarge wondered how soon it would be before de Blaeckere acted against him. He had been surprised that nothing sinister had happened to him since he arrived – a rarity for him in recent years – but then he had largely lived in the cocoon of the hotel, the trips back and forth to the courthouse and occasional evenings out with Guillemot and more rarely with Devries.

"It sounds to me that you are not overly fond of Bonville," said Lafarge.

"I must say he is a cold character. He is not very sociable.

"I would like to know how he spent the Occupation," Lafarge added dangling the carrot in front of Guillemot's face hoping he would consume it readily and make him ponder the question.

Guillemot's features softened.

"I find him abhorrent. He is uncultured, makes tasteless remarks, especially when he has drunk a bit, and quite frankly I am surprised he was brought here," said Guillemot.

Lafarge was encouraged to hear de Blaeckere was loose with his tongue. A night spent with Faure could have placed him in all sorts of trouble. However, Lafarge still wanted him on his own and to deal with him once and for all. The way justice worked in France was still too arbitrary and de Blaeckere may have contacts like Zilberstein who could get him out of trouble.

They had already succeeded in placing him in Nuremberg, far away from where he might be recognised. Lafarge wagered that the deal was if de Blaeckere took care of him then he would have carte blanche as to where he could flee to.

He was pretty sure that Guillemot was ignorant of de Blaeckere's war record but his dislike of him was clear and that could only work in Lafarge's favour.

Lafarge had an ally and if he needed to fully engage him all he needed to do was tell him about his own personal experiences of de Blaeckere's 'justice' and then sit back and let Guillemot do the killing.

After all he had earned the right to have someone else do it for him.

Chapter Seventeen

"I will have the soup and then the lamb plus a bottle of Grand Cru Classee St Emilion Bordeaux please," said Lafarge as he settled back in the dining car of the train taking him back to Paris.

Lafarge had been delighted on returning to the Grand Hotel to be handed an envelope by Nikolay which had inside a letter from Faure, informing him he had leave starting on the morrow as the court had adjourned to consider the verdicts.

Faure had also included a return travel pass first class to Paris giving him a two week break there. Faure had said he more than merited it as it was a job well beneath his talents which he had borne with good grace and with some of the French delegation also due to take a mini break they could afford to let one of the detectives to also go on leave.

Lafarge could not have been happier for aside from agreeing with Faure about the job's limitations he was finding Nuremberg depressing.

This was due to the disgusting details from the trial and the inhumanity of the defendants.

Their very greyness and ordinariness also appalled him, men who not so long ago due to Leni Riefenstahl and the evil genius of the propaganda chief Josef Goebbels had appeared like superior beings, even the most inconsequential like the former minister of the interior Wilhelm Frick and Nazi philosopher Alfred Rosenberg.

However, reluctant as he was to admit it he was also depressed by the destruction wrought on the city and the people. He could only imagine that what he saw in Nuremberg reflected cities across Germany. It would take money and plenty of it to rebuild the cities and the destroyed factories but that could be found from somewhere.

The biggest challenge facing the Allies – discounting the Soviets who were already showing clear signs of having their own agenda – would be winning the battle in building a relationship with the populace. The enmity in the eyes of the Trummerfrauen and often reflected also in the looks their children gave him suggested they were in for a long tussle.

He had been fortunate to secure a first class compartment to himself and for the first time in several months felt genuinely relaxed. He had fired off a telegram to Aimee at the studio to warn her of his return but neglected to do the same to Gilbert. He did not envisage troubling his colleague whilst back in Paris as strictly speaking he was still on re-assignment.

The dining car was surprisingly empty, only 10 or so fellow passengers availing themselves of the well-stocked cellar and astonishingly, given the serious rationing prevalent all over the continent, copious menu.

Four of them were American Army officers, three colonels and a general, there was a couple and four men, all in smart civilian clothes, eating on their own.

Lafarge sized them up and discounted the quartet as potential hit men due to age, weight and disability, as one had lost an arm. Thus reassured on that account and having eaten and drunk well, including two cognacs, he retired extremely content for the night even leaving a generous tip for the taciturn German waiter.

He awoke in the middle of the night desperate for a pee and cursing himself for drinking the whole bottle of wine -- the cognac never being the guilty party in Lafarge's lexicon – so stumbled down the darkened corridor to the loo at the end of it.

Returning to his compartment he lit a cigarette and poured himself a glass of cognac -- Faure had kindly handed him a bottle before his departure -- and he settled back to read Andre Gide's The Counterfeiters.

However, his reading was interrupted by a knock on the door. He put the chain across the door and opened it seeing in the dim light the guard. He thought this a bit intrusive and odd but then perhaps it was what happened when one travelled first class.

"I am just checking to see everything is alright sir," said the guard.

Lafarge relaxed.

"Yes thank you. Why do you ask?"

The guard passed him a rolled up note which a somewhat surprised Lafarge pulled open to read. He was even more surprised to read the contents. "I have been alerted that there is someone on the train who wishes you harm and I would like to enter your cabin to reassure myself that this person is not holding a gun or a knife to your back. It will take only a minute."

Lafarge thought about it for a minute and decided why not if the guard wants to be reassured then he can come in. He is only doing his job and I can then return to my reading and at least he has fore-warned me so I will be on my guard for the rest of the journey. Obviously one of those civilians was not as innocent looking as they appeared. His money was on the one-armed diner, a well-crafted disguise bound to elicit sympathy and also be discounted quickly as a suspect.

He smiled at the guard and undid the chain, opening the door at the same time.

"I thank you for your diligence but really as you can see there is no one here. You can check the bathroom too," said Lafarge.

The guard grunted and opened the door to the tiny bathroom, peering inside. Lafarge had moved to look over his shoulder and was on the point of making a remark when the Guard turned swiftly round with his forearm swinging and caught Lafarge full on the mouth with his elbow.

Lafarge was flung back by the impact against the wall and whilst shocked he thought it had been an accidental coming together, the guard not realising he was so close behind him. He was rapidly disabused of that notion.

For as he struggled back to his feet he saw the guard was holding a serrated knife, and to add to his astonishment when he finally managed to stand again he saw he was looking at de Blaeckere.

His bête noire was gloating at finally netting his prey. Lafarge on the other hand was brimming with fury at himself for being so lax in letting him into the compartment, the fact the uniform had distracted him was simply not good enough for a man of his experience. The lights having been dimmed for the night time had not allowed him a proper look at the man's face but again he should have been more wary.

However, he had to grudgingly give de Blaeckere praise for his ruse. His opponent deserved a slap on the back in congratulations although Lafarge desired more to punch him in the face. The fact he was holding a knife in his hand made that an unenviable challenge.

Lafarge expected it to all be over very quickly – he did not believe de Blaeckere would be sympathetic to his writing a final note to Aimee and Ancil – but instead his erstwhile colleague gestured for him to move further inside the compartment and sit on the bed.

Lafarge thought this was a win for him and a definite loss to de Blaeckere, who had allowed his gloating in his moment of triumph to get the better of him and instead of finishing the job neatly and quickly he wanted to savour a few more minutes of his enemy's discomfit.

Lafarge felt bold enough to reach for his glass and down the remnants of it and light another cigarette. De Blaeckere appeared content for his victim to enjoy those last few moments, standing with his legs apart between Lafarge and the door, whose chain had been replaced.

"How the hell did you manage to get on the train?" asked Lafarge.

"You will be in trouble for deserting your post," he added, though, he realised his protestation sounded pathetic.

De Blaeckere grinned, revealing his misshapen tobacco-stained teeth.

"Oh Lafarge you are such a prig amongst many other things," he sneered.

"Faure and his Gaullist leeches can wish what they want against me, but I am not returning. I have more than enough money made from the black market in Limoges and Nuremberg. I will be even richer once I am paid for killing you.

"Indeed I doubt I will have to work for many years to come."

De Blaeckere had confirmed what he had thought. This was his farewell job before settling abroad.

"I do not understand why you waited for a train rather than murder me in Nuremberg. You must have had plenty of chances and there would have been numerous suspects amongst the locals," said Lafarge.

"Yes I could have done but this guarantees me a trip back to Paris and payment on arrival rather than fearing someone has seen me in the ruins. Here you cannot escape. The windows are locked tight and I am between you and the door," said de Blaeckere.

"Also being close to you like this it gives me even more personal pleasure. I need not waste words either as well frankly you are not worthy of them."

Lafarge laughed which provoked a look of surprise from de Blaeckere.

"Words come hard to you anyway de Blaeckere, you are a man of action especially when the victims are suspended from the ceiling or chained to a chair," said Lafarge supressing his fear by acting brazen.

That earned him a slap across the face. It stung like hell but he managed to hide how much it hurt by forcing a smile.

"So now that we are at the end of our road how much is Madame Rosenberg paying you so handsomely to get rid of me?"

"I am not going to give you that satisfaction Lafarge. Also who is to say it is her?" said de Blaeckere.

"There is, though, one thing I can thank you for and that is by taking care of the other assassins you reduced my competition and increased the bounty for me."

"I am delighted to help your retirement fund. No doubt Zilberstein and Madame Rosenberg or Meissner as she became have also been generous in their donations to it," said Lafarge.

De Blaeckere smiled thinly.

"They have played their roles, yes. This part of it I can tell you so your final case at least is wrapped up for you before you close your eyes for the final time. I connived with Meissner to facilitate his leaving Limoges with Madame Rosenberg whilst having my way with her before she left," said de Blaeckere.

"She was most willing and I was jealous of Meissner for she was quite something. Anyways where I am going there will be plenty of her kind. Meissner, though, was the type of man I admire, strong-willed and determined.

"Zilberstein is even stronger than him, devoid of any tender human emotion like me I suppose, and hence was why he accompanied me to identify Madame Rosenberg's corpse. Of course he and Meissner were emboldened by the political protection they had and it also provided me with reassurance."

Lafarge was left unmoved by de Blaeckere's remarks, he already held him in such low esteem that what he had or had not done to Madame Rosenberg barely mattered. The man was a lowlife and his acts defied the term baseness but he was also not blessed with brains as within seconds he had all but admitted Madame Rosenberg was the person who ordered the hit.

He realised that time was running out. De Blaeckere as he had already remarked never much of a conversationalist, except when impressing his goons in the cafes of Limoges, was clearly beginning to think of the life of luxury that awaited him.

"What makes you so sure that Madame Rosenberg will pay you? She killed Meissner without the slightest hesitation when he threatened to leave. He might have meant considerably more to her than a thug with a weakness for wetting his pants when he is threatened," said Lafarge recalling with pleasure the time they had come under fire in Limoges when attacking a resistant's house.

De Blaeckere swung the knife at Lafarge's face. He raised his arm quickly enough to escape with just a knick on his limb. He could feel the blood trickling down the inside of his pyjama top but it was he who had touched a raw nerve as he had wanted to.

"I will enjoy dealing with your whore of a wife when you are gone Lafarge!" he hissed.

Lafarge laughed.

"Your lack of appreciation and value of women will be your undoing de Blaeckere," he said.

"I would go prepared for a nasty surprise."

Lafarge moved to pour himself one more drink and pulled a cigarette from his packet. Instead, though, of pouring the liquid into the glass he got a grip of the neck of the bottle and withdrawing his arm as far as he could against the window brought it round with full force catching de Blaeckere on the cheekbone.

De Blaeckere stumbled back towards the door, managing still to hold onto the knife. He bounced back off the door but was unsteady on his feet. Lafarge jumped on top of him, making sure he avoided the knife but pinning the arm holding it against the wall. He kneed de Blaeckere in the groin who shot a look of alarm mixed with hatred at his assailant.

De Blaeckere did not put up much of a fight as Lafarge had suspected knowing him for the bully and the coward he was.

Lafarge had only come across a few of the Brigades Speciales who were courageous, the majority crumbled when cornered.

De Blaeckere was no different.

"Please spare me Lafarge. I will disappear. I have the money I need like I said and perhaps now I have learned my lesson. I promise you I will never return to France whilst you are alive," he said in between sobs.

Lafarge stared down at him and now in possession of the knife dragged it along de Blaeckere's throat. He looked wild-eyed with panic but he barely struggled. He appeared resigned to his fate.

Lafarge got to his feet and lifted de Blaeckere up as well.

"What is your compartment number?" Lafarge asked.

De Blaeckere began to sob again but this time they were tears of relief.

"I am in 34 in the next door carriage," he stammered.

"Is that where you stowed the guard?"

De Blaeckere nodded.

"I take it he is alive?"

De Blaeckere took his time before nodding. Lafarge had his doubts he was telling the truth.

"Okay I am going to return you to your compartment. I will free the guard and will tell him what has happened and you will be kept under watch until we reach Paris. Then I will turn you over to my colleagues and it is up to you how much you tell them.

"As you are facing almost certainly a death sentence I recommend you tell them everything including your post Liberation activities. You can expect little salvation from

Zilberstein or Madame Rosenberg. There are only so many places on their lifeboat and you have no reservation," added Lafarge.

De Blaeckere nodded and wiped some of the drool from his chin. Lafarge forced some cognac down his throat, unwilling to risk handing him a potential weapon.

He accompanied him down the corridor but as they turned the corner at the end of it Lafarge stopped suddenly. De Blaeckere looked at him and reflecting on it later Lafarge thought the thug knew what was coming.

Lafarge pinned de Blaeckere against the door of the lavatory-- looked left and right to make sure there was no one around -- and with his free arm he opened the carriage door before hurling him out into the dark empty space of the night.

If de Blaeckere shrieked with terror – which Lafarge hoped he did – then it was conveniently drowned out by the shrill whistling of the steam engine.

Lafarge closed the door, checked belatedly the lavatory was unoccupied which it was, and decided against checking on the guard. He regretted if the guard was dying and could have been saved but he did not want to draw unnecessary attention to himself.

Miraculously there was no trail of blood either. His cut had been a superficial one and he had purposefully not cut de Blaeckere to prevent him bleeding all over the corridor. Also he had wanted him to think he was not going to die after all and needed him as calm as possible.

Lafarge took a final gulp of cognac, smoked a cigarette and lay back on the bed with his heart racing and thoughts aplenty. However, once he had run through them all he turned on his side content that like the ones before him he would not be accused of the murder of de Blaeckere.

For he had to admit despite having initially acted in self-defence in the eyes of the law he had murdered de Blaeckere. His war record would not be taken into account and in any case questions would be asked as to why Lafarge had not exposed him when he was in Nuremberg.

None of this of course was known by anybody else so Lafarge

was free from being blackmailed over that unless the person who had set up his Nuremberg trip felt bold enough to deal that card. He doubted somehow they would dare.

It was game over for his worries. Now only Rosenberg's remained to be resolved.

Chapter Eighteen

"Stahmer has agreed for you to meet with Goering," said Faure.

Lafarge felt elated at the news. He had returned in late September, a few days before the verdicts were delivered, well rested from his stay in Paris, which he had spent largely with Aimee and Ancil.

Aimee had still been filming and he had spent those days taking Ancil out, walking around Butte Chaumont. The film had finally wrapped days before his return with Aimee pleased with the end result, of her performance at least. The film was due to be released in mid-November and he expected to be back for the premiere, although it was due to be a low key one given the director was largely unknown and Prejean being damaged goods.

He had not set foot inside the Quai. He judged it in a rare moment of wise political judgment that it was best not to be seen in the place even if Le Troquer had been replaced by Edouard Depreux, who was a former resistant and had edited the illegal Socialist newspaper Le Populaire.

As far as he was concerned he was still on a leave of absence and he wanted to avoid an uncomfortable encounter with either Pinault or Luizet. Whilst both had spoken up for him he did not think of them as people he would socialise with outside.

Gilbert on the other hand he had seen on a couple of occasions. The reasons were both social and business. He had missed his company in Nuremberg, Guillemot was a decent man but he was too maudlin at times, understandable given his war-time experiences.

There had been as Lafarge had expected little progress in the investigation. This was not Gilbert's fault, but without the manpower he had only so much he could do. Effectively whilst Lafarge had been side-lined in Nuremberg the same thing had happened with Gilbert, only he had avoided exile from his family.

Gilbert being a stubborn sort had persisted and on several occasions refused offers of being placed on another case. Lafarge had thanked him for sticking to it but advised him to move on. Gilbert declined his counsel and said he felt he could bring it to a successful conclusion with Zilberstein in prison at least. Their main suspect had continued as if nothing had transpired, the gallery was doing very well by all accounts.

However, the departure of LeTroquer had heartened Gilbert as although he remained influential he and his successor Depreux were not on good terms according to those the Chief Inspector spoke to.

Gilbert could find little trace of the phantom-like Madame Rosenberg and it was made harder in that officially she was still dead despite Zilberstein's admission to him, Lafarge and Durand. Such were the frustrations of French bureaucracy. However, Gilbert believed that if they could ensnare Zilberstein then he would deliver Madame Rosenberg for he would as always wish to strike a deal.

When that time came Gilbert would not disabuse him of that possibility, for his desire to capture Madame Rosenberg was as great almost as that of Lafarge's. His disgust at her actions drove him on.

Thus the news Lafarge had on his return that he had been granted the meeting with Goering was good cause for elation. It potentially was a major step closer to perhaps sealing the case against Zilberstein and then securing the arrest of Madame Rosenberg.

Lafarge thought he knew why Goering had given his assent – Colonel Burton Andrus the commandant of Nuremberg Prison had allowed the request so clearing the final barrier.

The days when the former World War I fighting ace and one-time heir to Hitler enjoyed being centre stage and held court to the media or to sycophants were coming to an end. He had been found guilty on all four counts of the indictment and condemned to death along with 10 other defendants – 11 if Bormann was included but that was in absentia as no one had seen him since he left the Bunker as the Soviets closed in.

Faure, who was justifiably pleased with the outcome even if

three of the defendants were acquitted, said they would be hanged within weeks.

Lafarge's meeting was set for the next day and he required little preparation in terms of what he wanted but he knew that he would have to get to the point quickly for he was allocated 15 minutes.

That was asking a lot when one was meeting for the first time an intimidating figure like Goering. Although Lafarge hoped Goering might be more compliant now he faced death.

Lafarge thanked Faure for playing such an influential role in obtaining the meeting and made to leave the bar to go upstairs and rest before it.

"Did you see Bonville on your train?" asked Faure.

The question stopped Lafarge in his tracks. He stared at Faure, whose expression did not reveal anything.

He was the master of the opaque look. Lafarge knew he would have to tread carefully. He had no idea whether Faure might be involved, if he had told de Blaeckere to follow him and kill him or if the question was a perfectly innocent one.

"Why do you ask?" Lafarge asked.

Faure smiled and gestured for Lafarge to resume sitting. He raised two fingers to indicate to Nikolay to bring them their usual cognacs.

"Well I did not care very much for the chap but he disappeared the day you left on leave," said Faure, his tone like his look neutral.

"We or rather Devries and Guillemot scoured as much of Nuremberg as they could. The US Military were not minded to help, although, they subsequently became interested when Devries discovered two GI's bodies in the ruins near their billet."

This sounded a very interesting turn of events and Lafarge was all ears.

"It turns out the two men were well known in the black market trade. Their local connection in Nuremberg a fellow by the name of Karl Dollberg was also found dead a few weeks later," said Faure.

"What has this got to do with Bonville?"

Faure eyed him carefully. Lafarge began to have an uneasy feeling that he may have been implicated in something which for once he was innocent of.

"Dollberg like all good black marketers had left a note in case something untoward happened to him," he said.

"In it he listed his American contacts and other Allied citizens. The two GIs and that of Bonville were on it. Along with several other names of course, but they have been accounted for and are presently facing charges of varying degrees of seriousness."

"I take it they are to be tried elsewhere. They don't fit the profile of those being tried there at the moment," said Lafarge trying to make light of the situation.

Faure smiled and nodded.

"Well they would have to wait their turn as it has been decided that other war crimes trials are to take place following this one," said Faure.

"Don't worry Gaston you will be going home. I am not staying on either. This has been a very traumatic and upsetting experience. Listening to that testimony of the survivors, and of those who were directly involved executing the orders handed down by the likes of Goering, Kaltenbrunner and Speer.

"Frankly I am astonished that Speer is condemned to 20 years and his deputy Sauckel is to hang. The latter is a brute, no doubt about that but Speer was the orchestrator and the brains behind the usage of slave labour."

"Sounds to me you would have liked all of them to hang," said Lafarge.

Faure shook his head without elaborating further.

"Anyway we got side-tracked," said Faure, who had removed his glasses and was trying to stem the flow of tears coursing down his cheeks with his red and white spotted handkerchief.

Lafarge did not make a remark. He just waited for Faure to regain his sang-froid. He could understand why his compatriot had broken down and indeed wondered if it had been the first time. Perhaps there had been many moments in private, but this was the first time had shown any in front of him.

His upset contrasted sharply to the 20-odd defendants, whose remorse had been limited and far from universal.

Fine they could live in denial of their responsibility thought Lafarge, that is their right, but to not express remorse or show emotion having been found guilty and condemned to death that he found extraordinary. Neither Laval nor, de Brinon or Bousquet had either. Their crimes were so huge perhaps it was impossible to accept first of responsibility and secondly that they had been wrong.

To do so would crack the façade of self-belief and from there oh dear thought Lafarge that would be a rocky descent for them into all sorts of nightmares. They would be the better for it after coming through it but then it was easy for him to say. He was at peace with his list of victims. Besides he did not have a day of reckoning and nor would he face one.

However, for the moment he had to appear concerned about the fate of the most recent one, war criminal, rapist, murderer, and to round it all off post war black marketer de Blaeckere and much to no doubt the French state's chagrin employed by them.

"The Americans think that regrettably Bonville murdered the three of them and realising it was only a matter of time before he was arrested fled. We prefer to believe in the lesser of two evils and Bonville was worried he might be the next victim and did a runner," said Faure.

Lafarge was relieved for the turn the story had taken was in the end not to implicate him.

"Don't worry Gaston you were not under suspicion," said Faure laughing, clearly having observed the relief that had enveloped Lafarge's features.

"Indeed Edgar it is perceptive of you. I was beginning to be concerned that I was a suspect. In any case it is bad enough that Bonville is involved. In answer to your original question I did not see him on the train. I too found him a far from genial character and I think Guillemot was of the same opinion," said Lafarge.

"I would wager he would have kept his distance from me if he had been on that train," added Lafarge, who was warmed by the memory of putting distance between himself and de Blaeckere when he hurled him from the train.

"Yes, quite I can see the logic in that," said Faure.

"So what will happen about Bonville? Have you informed Paris to look for him and arrest him?" asked Lafarge trying to sound genuinely interested.

"Yes, I told them. It should only be a matter of time if he is in Paris that he is found. Meanwhile they are doing background checks on him and trying to ascertain how someone of such dubious character was hired by the police. They are also looking into how he was assigned almost immediately a highly-sensitive post."

Lafarge ears pricked up at this information.

"What is this not being handled by the police?"

"Well the matter of finding him is of course but the intelligence service is handling the background checks as patently the police failed. We want to avoid such an embarrassment in the future. Well you and I might be heading home but there will be others replacing us," said Faure.

Lafarge laughed to himself that he had escaped lightly when he had been interrogated by Pinault after the Liberation. The intelligence service had not been required. Still he would love to know the identity of the person who had permitted de Blaeckere to be passed fit for service and then sent to Nuremberg.

However, he felt it politic to not make such a suggestion as it could arouse suspicion as to why he was interested. He would see with Gilbert if he had a contact in the intelligence service in Paris who he could ask.

For the moment, though, that was not his priority.

De Blaeckere was an irrelevance, even more so now that Lafarge was not implicated either in the black market ring or in his disappearance, and Goering loomed large.

*

Large, though, was not the adjective to describe the Reich Marshal's physique anymore. Lafarge had been taken aback on seeing him from afar in court. His waistline which had been grotesquely obese during the War had as if in direct linkage to the decline in his power shrunk dramatically.

He was even more struck when Goering was escorted into the

prisoner's box by the white helmeted Military Policeman. He was not especially tall. He was officially five feet eight inches and his pre-trial weight of 260 pounds had withered away.

However, what had not eroded was neither his authority nor charisma even if his dove grey uniform, which hung loosely off him, was shorn of the multiple medals he had ludicrously sported at the height of his power.

He stood and appeared to appreciate the fact that Lafarge had risen to his feet when he entered. He smiled, and to Lafarge's surprise it was a reflected in his eyes also twinkling. However, he stood for a whole minute – down to 14 and counting thought Lafarge – and ran his eyes over his visitor.

Goering was sizing him up, and to Lafarge's relief he had passed a test for the condemned prisoner sat down and in an indication of his desperate desire to be in charge still he indicated the Chief Inspector should sit too.

They were separated by a wire mesh which came down halfway on a desk although there was an opening which allowed Lafarge and Goering to see each other clearly. The guard sat to Goering's right, slightly hidden to Lafarge's eyesight by the mesh. Rather incongruously Lafarge noted the number 17 was imprinted on the mesh.

He directed Goering's gaze to the number.

"I would have thought you would have accepted to see me only on condition it was cell number one," sad Lafarge speaking in German.

Goering looked at him poker-faced and Lafarge thought he had made a strategic error by playing on his ego. Perhaps he had achieved the opposite in pricking his pride.

All of a sudden, though, Goering's face creased up and he let out a loud laugh. It did him no favours as his good looking face took on a more sinister look of a gargoyle.

"Well if they leave me to number 17 on the night of the executions then I will be a happy man," said Goering chortling.

Lafarge smiled. He was surprised Goering could make light of his dire situation but put it down to bravura or that he held out some unlikely hope he would have his sentence commuted to life imprisonment which would condemn him to having to live out the rest of his days with Hess, the former head of the Navy Erich Raeder and former minister of economics Walther Funk .

Lafarge would rather death than sharing that fate with one lunatic and two dour elderly men. Others had received lighter sentences, the sanctimonious and smooth Speer getting only 20 years.

However, he thought making a joke out of that would be going too far. Besides as he nervously observed the clock was ticking.

"So Chief Inspector you too have had your trials in France I hear. Laval and Darnand executed, Petain a life sentence. A heavy price indeed for a fellow Great War hero to pay," said Goering ruefully.

"However, I envy Laval and Darnand."

"How so Reich Marshal?" asked Lafarge purposefully using his rank even though he had been under strict instructions from Andrus to desist from doing so.

Quite apart from Lafarge finding it a pathetic rule he also wanted to pander as much as possible to Goering's ego. He had to tread a fine line between that and sounding overly sycophantic but he was betting on taking a respectful attitude – with regard to his rank not to his outrageous crimes – would sit well with Goering.

He was after all there to save a man's life.

"They got to die a soldier's death by firing squad. I on the other hand, a real soldier unlike them, will be hanged as a common criminal," he fumed.

"I have appealed against that of course along with Keitel and Jodl. The very least the Allies can do having dispensed victor's justice is allow us to choose how we exit this world."

His anger appeared genuine but Lafarge was singularly unmoved. His millions of victims were given no choice either in their fate, had had no recourse to lawyers as courts were dispensed with, or the mode of despatch. A sociopath's charm can only go so far, their self-pity is unedifying.

"Reich Marshal you will excuse me but I am pressed for time. I have questions of an official nature which would not have been directly pertinent to your case examined here in court," said

Lafarge adopting a firm tone.

Goering's eyes flickered and lost their warmth. It was chilling to Lafarge to see how easily the mask of bonhomie slipped from Goering's face. It was as if he had ordered a child to do something and the youngster not liking the demand reacted in a spoilt fashion. That mood swing encapsulated in one moment how lethal Goering must have been for his rivals and those whose fates rested on his decisions.

He may have been successfully weaned off the morphine which had made him a more formidable foe in the witness box – certainly for the United States prosecutor Robert Jackson -- but it showed his temperament was not dictated uniquely by the drug.

"I am tired of answering questions Chief Inspector. I have answered questions from a psychiatrist, several interrogators before the trial, my lawyer and then the trial itself. If someone was to ask me what I wanted for breakfast, though that is not going to happen in this godforsaken place, I am not sure I would be bothered to answer," he said.

"I am exhausted. There is unlikely to be anything in this for me, you are incapable of threatening me with a worse fate than I already face, and frankly aside from the company you provide I have no use for you.

"So I suggest you either leave now or for the remaining what 10 minutes you find a topic that we can talk about which will please us both."

Lafarge nodded. He had been prepared for this in as much he had expected Goering to be difficult. He just had to hope the subject he had chosen would not be met with the same truculent response from Goering.

"Well the only thing we have in common Reich Marshal is Paris," said Lafarge.

At that Goering's eyes to Lafarge's relief gleamed. Not only did it bring back memories for him of Nazi Germany at its apogee but also all the rich pickings the avaricious thief had had of the art and antiques, not to mention the jewels which he had bedecked himself with. In his often morphine-addled state he had failed to notice the ridicule he had attracted for doing so.

The Luftwaffe's young pilots and air crews had not joined in the ridicule for they had paid with their lives.

"Yes Paris such a beautiful city. I for one was delighted von Choltitz did not obey the Fuhrer and destroy it," said Goering referring to the commandant of Paris who had when the war was still going well for the Nazis bombed Sevastopol to ruins but had lost his enthusiasm when with the Allies closing in he had been instructed to do the same thing to the French capital.

"I spent many a happy moment there although I tried to avoid too many rendezvous with Laval, Bousquet and the other Vichy leaders. Especially de Brinon, he was so pompous and his flattery odious."

"Well we agree on that then," said Lafarge.

The gargoyle grinned.

"They had their uses but I left the others to deal with them. Heydrich enjoyed his classical music and would mix that with talking about the Jewish Question with Bousquet and Laval. Bousquet and Heydrich suited each other, untested on the battlefield and as a result desperate to prove themselves to their respective leaders," said Goering.

Lafarge held his tongue. There was little wrong in what Goering had said about the zealous enthusiasm and ambition shown by the younger generation but the indolence of the Reich Marshal could not excuse him from the genocide. For it was he who had passed the Nuremberg Laws, it was he who had created the Gestapo and it was he who had signed off on the Final Solution.

"Indeed Reich Marshal you preferred to visit galleries and museums," said Lafarge.

"You are believed to have taken some of the finest art works not for the German state but for your own pleasure," said Lafarge.

Goering glowered at the accusation.

"I paid for them. I deny that I stole these artworks you are claiming I did. I will concede that I was given a generous discount. My agent Bruno Lohse was very effective at securing these discounts.

"He of course is in denial and to save his own neck has

testified against me here. A remarkable lack of gratitude given the paintings he was allowed by me to keep as a payment.

"However, as the late Count Ciano remarked in 1942: 'victory has 100 fathers, defeat has none'. He got little right but on that note he was correct.

"Tell me Chief Inspector is that your area of expertise, art theft?" asked Goering in a menacing tone.

The spoilt child persona had returned, evidently the Reich Marshal was nervous his booty would be discovered and taken away from him. Not that he would have much use for it but his wife Emmy and their daughter Edda could benefit from the proceeds.

"It is of little importance what my area of expertise is Reich Marshal. I worked under Bousquet during the Occupation. I think that should tell you enough," said Lafarge, who felt perhaps he had said it a tad too aggressively.

Goering looked both relieved and pleasantly surprised that his trove was not under threat and he was talking to a fellow traveller. One who had managed to survive the cull. Lafarge would not disabuse him of that.

"I am not here to obtain answers regarding your art collection. I only want to know about one piece and if it is still in your possession as I have been told that you obtained it when you bought a gallery in Paris," said Lafarge.

Goering rubbed his chin thoughtfully. After a few moments he leaned forwards. The guard did not move to prevent him from doing so. Lafarge leant towards him.

"You are talking about Lohse's deputy Meissner and that Jewish partner of his Zilberstein," said Goering.

Lafarge nodded, his heart beginning to pick up a pace.

"Yes at the time it seemed like a worthwhile investment. I wanted to have a permanent gallery in Paris where I could exhibit the paintings and show up my philistine colleagues," said Goering, whose voice was quite different to before as he warmed to the subject.

"However, because my stock was slipping with the Fuhrer due to the inadequacies of others I preferred that my part in it remained secret.

"I imagine it will be the case forever now. My dreams of retiring and then running a gallery are unlikely to be realised," he said sadly.

Lafarge smiled at the unlikely thought of Goering giving up his titles and power to run a gallery in Paris. It was too far-fetched to even contemplate.

"You could have exhibited Hitler's art there," said Lafarge in jest.

He thought he had gone too far with that but he had been unable to resist.

Goering showed little reaction.

"The Fuhrer had many qualities but painting was not among them. However, you will find art of mine in the gallery. All far superior to that of Hitler's," said Goering.

Lafarge noted that. There would be some pleasure in seeing Zilberstein's face when they showed him the warrant to do a complete inventory of the artwork. Indeed it could cause such a scandal that even if Zilberstein escaped prosecution for murder he would be ruined.

Lafarge's heart was now racing as he moved in for the decisive question. Zilberstein being out on the street would not clear Rosenberg.

"Zilberstein told me that as part of the deal you received the snake bracelet that was made for Sarah Bernhardt," he said.

Goering nodded, his eyes gleaming with pleasure.

"What a beautiful jewel it is. Fit for such a great actress, although I never saw her perform," he said.

"Is it still in your possession Reich Marshal?" asked Lafarge unable to suppress his excitement.

"What is it to you Chief Inspector? It seems odd that you should travel so far to ask for one particular piece of jewellery even if it did belong to your greatest actress," said Goering.

"Has Zilberstein sent you? Another of the vultures circling before I am even a corpse," Goering sneered with disgust.

Lafarge shook his head and took a calculated gamble.

"Far from it Reich Marshal, I am presently investigating the murder of Meissner and Zilberstein is my prime suspect," said Lafarge.

Goering looked shocked at the news.

"Meissner is dead? Zilberstein is the chief suspect? Ha I never thought he could be trusted. Ghastly man, who betrayed his fellow Jews at the drop of a feather or the rustle of a note," said Goering.

It sounded to Lafarge that Zilberstein was a fortunate man in Goering being locked up, for whilst his former enemies were now protecting him his business partner clearly would have wrung his neck if he had been a free man.

Goering went silent. Lafarge allowed him time to think. He could not imagine why Goering would need time to recall if he still had such a memorable piece of jewellery. It made him wonder whether he was playing games.

"I am sorry Chief Inspector but I am unable to help you. I either lost that piece of jewellery in my departure from Carinhall or it was stolen by one of the SS guards who arrested me on Hitler's orders," he said.

"Goodbye Chief Inspector. I hope you secure a conviction of Zilberstein for Meissner's murder. Meissner was a good man and if I believed in God I would be looking forward to seeing him again," added Goering.

Lafarge felt crestfallen. He had thought he was on the brink of salving his conscience and saving Rosenberg but his hopes had been dashed.

A tap on his shoulder told him that his time was up and to all intents and purposes he was so disappointed he felt for him it really was the case.

*

Lafarge sat at his desk in his room writing down what Goering had told him about Zilberstein and the deal to buy the gallery. It was not enough to clear Rosenberg but it was insurmountable proof against Zilberstein.

The fact it would also be sufficient to restore the gallery to Rosenberg also meant precious little as he would remain incarcerated.

It did little to raise Lafarge's morale. He consoled himself with one of his last bottles of cognac which he had brought back from Paris.

A knock on the door interrupted his work. He thought it might be Faure, who would be wondering how his meeting had gone even though Lafarge had not told him what the matter he wished to discuss with Goering was about.

He was not in the mood to talk but he opened the door and to his surprise saw it was an American Military Policeman. It was not the one who had escorted Goering to the meeting. This one was taller, more muscular and would have pleased the Nazi defendants as he conformed to their lunatic theory of the master race, as he had blond hair and blue eyes. The only minor problem for them was he was the enemy.

"I think you have got the wrong room," Lafarge said.

"You are Chief Inspector Lafarge are you not, sir?" the policeman asked in English.

Lafarge nodded.

"I am staff sergeant Hank Malinowski," he said holding out his hand which Lafarge shook.

"I have a very important message for you regarding a delicate matter. I would prefer if we could discuss this in your room," he whispered.

Intrigued, Lafarge ushered him in.

He offered him a glass of cognac and to take the chair at the desk. He stood by the door, cradling his glass of cognac in one hand and placed his service revolver on the side table. He had become too used to bad surprises and he was taking no chances.

Lafarge remained silent inviting Malinowski to break the silence as it was he who had something to say.

"The Reich Marshal appreciated your visit this morning," said Malinowski.

Lafarge was taken aback.

He had not expected this, if anything he had thought perhaps the MP was here to pose questions about de Blaeckere and his black market activities. Faure might have been satisfied with notifying Paris about keeping an eye out for de Blaeckere but with two GIs murdered that was not going to be enough for the Americans.

"You look relieved Chief Inspector," observed Malinowski.

Lafarge smiled.

"I am pleased he found it to his liking. However, he did not need to send an emissary to tell me this. Although the courtesy is noted," said Lafarge drily.

Malinowski grunted, clearly not appreciating the sarcasm.

"I apologise sergeant. What is your connection with Goering?"

Malinowski withdrew a packet of cigarettes -- Lucky Strikes as obligatory an accompaniment for an American soldier as his weapon and Lafarge thought having smoked them on the odd occasion when his Gitanes had run out as deadly -- and light one.

"I am in charge of one of the watches of the prisoners. In the course of my duties I have had several occasions to talk with the Reich Marshal," said Malinowski putting his fingers to his lips to pull some errant tobacco from them.

Lafarge thought Malinowski could not be anything but a military man with his leaden delivery and clunking vernacular.

"I infer from that you have formed a relationship with Goering," said Lafarge, dispensing with the prisoner's title now that he was free of his company and did not require his help.

"Yes, I have. He is a very interesting man, of course his crimes are appalling, but so long as we do not discuss his Nazi past he is good company. Compared to the majority of the other prisoners he is by far the most personable," said Malinowski.

Lafarge raised his eyebrows. From his brief audience with Goering Lafarge knew he possessed charm but describing a mass murderer as personable perhaps reflected why Malinowski was a staff sergeant and not an officer. For Lafarge it dishonoured the millions of Nazi victims and the destroyed cities across Europe from Coventry to Rotterdam to Leningrad.

"You asked me about our relationship Chief Inspector so it is only fair that I reply honestly," said Malinowski.

"I believe you come from Paris so you are used to meeting colourful well-travelled characters. Being a policeman you have also come across all types of evil personalities.

"I on the other hand come from the tiny town of Chadron in Nebraska. They are decent, hardworking folk but nothing too flashy about their characters. Everyone appears content with their lot as even the young stay and take over the farms or shops from their parents.

"However, I wanted a bit more than that. My father is still fit enough to manage the cattle on our farm and so he did not stand in my way when I volunteered. I would have preferred a combat unit but I had some law enforcement experience and so they sent me to the 793rd Battalion.

"Pretty run of the mill duties but I got my move away and actually saw some frontline action at Remagen under First Lieutenant John Hyde. Despite our reputation for being bone crunchers and skull crackers we showed there that we could fight as well and as bravely as the regular forces.

"Now we have responsibility for the most notorious criminals in the world.

"After almost a year of peering in through the peep holes looking at the men who we had jeered and booed at on the news reels when they rolled over most of Europe there is bound to be some connection with the prisoners.

"For the most part they are now pathetic, broken men and I have no sympathy for them and indeed I and the other guards enjoy those moments when some of them have nightmares. I hope it is about their victims, though, some are so self-absorbed I fear it is to do with their impending deaths or the long years of imprisonment that awaits them.

"However, Goering is different to the others. He is a colourful character who uses his charm to get what he wants."

Lafarge was glad that Malinowski had not been completely hypnotised by Goering. However, it was clear whatever Goering wanted lay in Lafarge's power for him to deliver. This could mean only one thing that the Reich Marshal had sent Malinowski to strike a deal.

"So what does he want from me?"

Malinowski waved the bottle at Lafarge and the Chief Inspector nodded his assent whilst also holding out his glass so the MP could pour him a drink.

"He accepts the verdict and the sentence of the court but he rejects the manner in which it is to be carried out," said Malinowski.

"I know that sergeant. He told me this morning," said Lafarge.

"Well he refuses to be hanged as do Keitel and Jodl. However, the other two are hoping the court will allow their appeal and permit them to be executed by firing squad. Goering, though, does not believe that will be successful so he wants to make other arrangements," said Malinowski.

The Staff Sergeant cleared his throat before he went on.

"He would like you to procure for him a cyanide capsule. He prefers to die by his own hand than the hands of a hangman.

"In return you will receive the bracelet you asked him for."

Lafarge rubbed his temple. He had to digest what was on offer and what he had to deliver. The ramifications of the latter were enormous.

If he agreed and obtained it he would be not only be defying the court in aiding a war criminal by frustrating the judicial procedure but he would also effectively be committing murder by supplying the poison. There was also another significant factor which would provoke fury.

With Hitler, Himmler and Goebbels having escaped justice -- Bormann was really a nonentity rarely featuring in the news reels but having been Hitler's gatekeeper his value in the defendant's box would have been the nearest thing to the Fuhrer they would get – Goering was the highest profile of the defendants.

The Americans may have eased off over the murders of two of their own, best perhaps to not delve too deeply into the black market as all sorts of embarrassments might emerge, but were Goering to escape the hangman then they would spare no effort to discover who facilitated his death.

Humiliating the Americans was not a very intelligent move and carried high risks.

Lafarge had taken risks aplenty but this one was in a different league entirely. However, the upside was for him also an enormous one as the bracelet would definitively clear Rosenberg.

"Goering told me he no longer had the bracelet," said Lafarge.

Malinowski smiled. Lafarge did not like it very much as it was a smug one. However, he appreciated it more when Malinowski withdrew from his pocket the bracelet.

He had to admit that even to a cynical soul like himself the bracelet was stunning, both in design and the jewels that made it up. A snake coiled round the wrist and onto the hand with another shaped in the form of a ring and its head turned round to face the head of the other serpent.

However, Lafarge did not believe that the kleptomaniac that was Goering - the trifles he left as payment maybe salved his conscience that he was not stealing but to those outside his circle it was clearly theft – appreciated the piece for its design but more for the rubies, diamonds and opals that adorned it.

The bracelet would never have fitted round his fat wrists, even in his slimmed down state. Malinowski appeared to read Lafarge's thoughts.

"He says this was the last thing he would look at before he went to bed every night. He gave it to his wife but rarely permitted her to wear it. I can see why," said Malinowski.

Lafarge nodded in agreement. He could see why one might kill for it and why it had been Goering's price for being a partner in the gallery.

He could still say no and let justice run its course – why should Goering escape the noose when the military men Keitel and Jodl would also hang and had accepted they would if their appeal failed. However, the positive side of the argument amused him in that the irony would be Goering's last act would, unknown to him, save a Jewish man's life.

"Okay I am reassured he has it. However, what he is asking places me in a very difficult position. If I am discovered I will face the death penalty so he must understand I am reluctant to agree to this," said Lafarge.

"The practical side too presents problems. Not least where do I find the cyanide capsule and without attracting attention either now or once Goering is dead. It is hardly as if they are much in demand these days now that the fighting is over.

"He will not be around to face the consequences unlike you or me," added Lafarge.

He hoped this would focus Malinowski's mind and perhaps he could point him in the direction of someone who could furnish the capsule. Lafarge was gently letting him know that he would not spare him if he was arrested.

Malinowski looked alarmed, as if he had not thought of this as a possibility or he had assumed Lafarge would keep his role in the scheme secret. The man was either arrogant or dumb. Lafarge thought the former, the arrogance that comes with those in uniform who are the victors.

"I don't think that would be a good idea Chief Inspector. Who do you think the authorities are more likely to believe? On the one hand the word of a French policeman, who served the Vichy administration, against mine, a decorated soldier.

"I think you may be on a loser there," he added smiling his crooked smile.

"I am just wondering Sergeant, why you are willing to take a risk on behalf of a mass murderer. Not so long ago the forces he commanded were killing your comrades. He must have promised you something pretty special," said Lafarge.

"That is none of your business Chief Inspector. For all you know I am doing it because I believe, like he does, those who are in uniform deserve to be shot not hanged," replied Malinowski.

"I have to go before it gets dark. I don't want to risk being attacked and them stealing this. So what is your answer?" asked Malinowski, his tone suggesting that a negative answer would not be well received.

Lafarge did not appreciate Malinowski's aggressive manner but he too wanted him gone.

"I will do it. It may, though, as I said take time for me to obtain the capsule," he said.

Malinowski did not look best pleased and tapped his watch. The huge time piece looked as if it had come from the black market or more likely from Goering. He recognised it as a B-Uhr, a watch worn by Luftwaffe pilots. He had once been offered one in Paris by a black market acquaintance of his.

Even with a discount, which Lafarge had earned for turning a blind eye to his contact's operation and pointing the finger at his rivals instead, the price was prohibitive.

"The quicker you find one the better Chief Inspector. The

execution date has yet to be set but they are sure to be soon. The appeals process is not like other courts which can take months even years.

“These will be dealt with at pace. So it is in your best interests that you track down someone with a capsule.”

Lafarge sighed and nodded.

“Good. I will be at the Hexenhausle every evening at 1800 hours. I prefer to organise the rendezvous now rather than you leaving a note at the courthouse or asking for me. That could lead to questions being asked and things becoming messy,” said Malinowski.

Lafarge nodded and stood aside indicating Malinowski was free to leave.

He reluctantly shook his hand as he left and then sat on his bed, cradling a drink and thinking furiously about who might be the best and most discreet person to approach about the capsule.

Given his limited contacts -- Faure was quickly eliminated from the list – it did not take long to run through them but in any case there was one obvious candidate who might possess one and might be willing to hand it over – his favourite waiter Nikolay.

*

He wandered down to the bar at the beginning of the evening shift – which was when Nikolay usually worked. He realised he was relying on instinct but to Lafarge his logic was unimpeachable. Not that that had always proved correct or to his advantage.

However, he reckoned that of all the people who needed to retain cyanide capsules it was the likes of Nikolay and the prissy desk clerk. They might be employed for the moment by the Allies but they could also at any time be turned over to the Soviets especially if one of the latter did chance by the hotel or indeed were denounced.

Biting down on a capsule would be life-changing for sure but it would be markedly more painless than being taken back to Moscow and worked on by the Soviet secret police before a show trial and ultimately execution.

The main problem he faced was how to raise it with the

taciturn Nikolay. They got on well enough but only within the limits of waiter and customer -- a very good and reliable one at that – and conversations had never gone too far in terms of 'so what did you do?' in the war.

Thus it was going to be quite a leap in ordering a cognac and adding by the way Nikolay could you throw a cyanide capsule in on the side.

However, he had little choice but to act quickly. He did not doubt that the Allies wanted to carry out the sentences as quickly as possible. Other trials were due but as Faure had said the majority of the present group of lawyers and judges wanted to return home and leave behind the wrecked city and the misery and hatred of the residents.

To his relief he saw the bar was empty and Nikolay was lounging over by the gold topped counter, smoking a cigarette and drawing or writing something.

He swallowed deeply and thinking he might as well be bold wandered over and smiled at Nikolay. The Russian smiled back, though, he had a wary look in his eyes. He reached behind him and poured Lafarge a large cognac.

"Have one yourself Nikolay," said Lafarge.

Nikolay looked surprised but gratefully poured himself one too. However, after clinking glasses with Lafarge and sipping from it he placed it out of sight of any other customers who might wander in. Smoking was permitted but drinking openly was frowned upon by the more senior officers. Mind you they rarely left a tip either.

Lafarge came straight to the point.

"Nikolay I know you fought with Vlasov and you are one of the lucky ones to have escaped to the west," said Lafarge.

Nikolay stared back at him. His expression was blank but he did not protest.

"I don't want you to worry. I am not threatening you or your colleagues with exposing you to your compatriots. I know that you live with the fear of that happening and being taken back home.

"I sympathise with you. I am also living in fear of discovery and I was hoping you could help me. Provide me with something that can give me reassurance should I be tracked down by the people looking for me," said Lafarge.

He hoped his story sounded convincing. To a certain extent he was just gilding the lily, for although there had been no further attempts on his life since de Blaeckere had taken his walk into the unknown that was no guarantee of his security.

Nikolay looked at him, as if he was measuring him up.

"You have a gun do you not Chief Inspector?"

Lafarge grinned.

"Yes, I do Nikolay. However, I am talking about something that one can use if one is disarmed. Something you probably were supplied with when you switched sides. Or at least I hope you were," said Lafarge.

Nikolay fixed him with one of his by now trademark hard stares, then slapped his forehead and laughed.

"Ah right. You mean a cyanide capsule? One of these?" he said opening his mouth and indicating to Lafarge a molar.

"The great thing about this is if it accidentally became dislodged and I swallow it, it would pass through my body without poisoning me. Of course I would have lost it but …" he added shrugging nonchalantly.

"The lack of concern in your voice suggests you have others to replace it," said Lafarge unable to suppress his excitement.

Nikolay gave him a knowing look.

"It will cost you Chief Inspector."

"How much?" asked Lafarge although he was prepared to pay anything given he required it as quickly as possible.

"I will sell it to you for a hundred dollars."

Lafarge whistled and shook his head, hoping Nikolay would reduce his price. He had the money but he did not wish the Russian to think he was a push over. Otherwise he might raise it.

"I will not sell it for anything less than a hundred dollars," said Nikolay sternly.

Lafarge shrugged his shoulders.

"Okay Nikolay you have a deal," said Lafarge sounding resigned and held out his hand.

Nikolay laughed mirthlessly.

"I don't carry them around in a bag Chief Inspector. I sometimes get searched when I come to work. There is a limit to their trust," he said.

"You will have to meet me where I live and we will exchange then."

Lafarge sighed.

"Well what time does your shift end? You must understand I need it as quickly as possible," said Lafarge sounding suitably desperate.

Nikolay breathed in deeply and took a final gulp of his cognac.

"I don't finish till one in the morning. We should be fine going to my lodgings but you will have to mind yourself on the way back," he said.

"I will be fine Nikolay. Besides I will have the capsule," he smiled.

*

"I have what you want Malinowski. Have you brought the bracelet?"

Malinowski looked up from his table at the Hexenhausle pleasantly surprised to see Lafarge had obtained the treasured capsule within a day.

He gestured for Lafarge to take a chair opposite him. The bar was as popular as ever which meant their conversation could take place without anyone eaves-dropping on them.

Lafarge had had no problems making his way back from Nikolay's – the extra twenty dollars he had slipped the Russian had earned him an escort for the return journey. They had encountered a bunch of urchins scavenging among the ruins. The youngsters had thought they would get rich quicker by taking on two adult males, who at the late hour were likely to be drunk.

However, they were sent packing once Lafarge produced his gun and they saw the glint of Nikolay's knife. He would check as soon as he had completed the exchange with Malinowski whether Nikolay had made it in for his shift, as perhaps the urchins with their pride wounded had felt emboldened when they saw him wandering back on his own after dropping Lafarge at the hotel.

Malinowski ordered Lafarge a Mass --which contained a litre of beer -- and made idle chit chat as they waited for the waitress, an attractive buxom middle-aged woman with a little bit too much make-up for Lafarge's taste, to return.

"Helga has come down in the world," said Malinowski noticing Lafarge had followed her walking back to the bar to place their order.

"How so?" asked Lafarge, trying to sound genuinely interested although he was keener to get back to the reason why two men who would normally not be drinking companions were sitting together.

He hoped neither Devries nor Guillemot happened to walk in as both were of sufficient intelligence to ask questions as to how Lafarge and Malinowski had become acquainted.

"Her husband was captured at Stalingrad and she became Streicher's mistress. Not an easy one to imagine that. However, the Jew baiter and hate-mongerer had lots of money and she put up with his perverted sexual predilections," said Malinowski with clear distaste.

"Why is she allowed to work here then? Should she not have been sent away to prevent any potential conflict of interests like what happened with my predecessor," said Lafarge.

"She has her uses," said Malinowski.

"Word is that she provided plenty of damaging evidence against Streicher in return for her being able to keep an apartment he had bought for her. There are also rumours she conducts a black market ring out of here but that she is protected by a US Army colonel.

"I think his protection comes with an eye on finding where Streicher's fortune is hidden. Best to have Helga working here where he can keep his eyes on her. He would move in with her if he could but the fraternisation laws being as they are still he is given a free pass to spend the odd night there but a more permanent arrangement would be frowned upon and he would risk being sent back to the States."

Lafarge laughed at the cynicism of it all. The watch word for post war was protection whether it be Zilberstein trying to escape the guillotine in France or heavily made-up Helga the former courtesan of the malodorous and pervert Streicher.

"This colonel must have a lot of influence to be allowed such leeway," Lafarge said drily "He is the son of a senator."

Lafarge groaned.

"Indeed," said Malinowski as Helga deposited their beers and gave them a warm smile.

Lafarge could see how she had won herself a winning hand in the black market. She must also have a ruthless streak too. She did not look like someone who would have too many worries even when the colonel did finally get recalled. Whether her future plans involved her husband was a moot point Lafarge conjectured as there was little likelihood of an early release.

He had little sympathy for the Germans but he still shuddered at what their treatment must be like in Soviet gulags especially as the Nazis had meted out savage punishment to the hundreds of thousands of Red Army soldiers they had taken prisoner.

No wonder Nikolay and others had switched sides when the Nazis had the upper hand. Thinking of Nikolay focussed his mind on what he was there for.

"So are you ready to exchange Sergeant?" Lafarge asked.

Malinowski wiped the foam of the beer from his lips and licked his fingers.

"Yes. However, let us finish the beers and then we can exchange it in a more discreet place than a public bar. Aside from not wanting Helga to think there are black market activities going on in her workplace which are nothing to do with her, there are also plenty of plain clothes spooks who make it their business to sit in bars and observe," he said.

Lafarge was a bit jumpy and this plan made him uneasy.

"If you say so, but I would like a simple quick exchange as we say good night to each other when you go back to the prison," said Lafarge.

Malinowski laughed.

"I don't think you trust me Chief Inspector! Listen all I am interested in is to pass the capsule to Goering and then get my papers home so I can return to the small town life I once despised but which after these past few years of hell I now yearn for," he said.

Lafarge grinned and held his hands up in apology.

"What about you Chief Inspector? What is it you want after this is over?"

Lafarge sighed. Malinowski had posed a decent question. One he was not sure what the answer to was. He rather envied the certainty of Malinowski and what he wanted. The only constant for Lafarge had been his job but that was now far from sure he would be offered it back or indeed if he would want to continue.

Le Troquer may have gone and he had performed his duties well in Nuremberg -- though they had not been demanding – but a conviction of Zilberstein might be a suitable way to bow out.

He owed Aimee and Ancil a calmer life. He had the jewels as a failsafe financial insurance and could sell them. If he did that he could retire making Luizet and Pinault's lives less stressful and it would allow Aimee to develop her acting career. She deserved that chance and he hoped it would progress to her working with greater talents than Rene Delacroix.

"I think Sergeant I am of the same opinion as you. A quiet life would be most welcome," said Lafarge.

Malinowski smiled and drained his Mass.

"Right let's go," he said.

They wandered back towards the courthouse to make the exchange, both men in a hurry to get it over with.

"Are you not afraid of the capsule being discovered before you hand it to Goering?" asked Lafarge.

Malinowski grunted.

"We are not searched like the prison staff or the prisoner's lawyers," said Malinowski.

"By God we should be but there is some naïve belief that being American and given the heavy responsibility we have we would not dare dishonour the uniform nor the flag," he said laughing humourlessly.

"Victor's privilege," said Lafarge drily.

"Indeed Chief Inspector. Indeed. In this case it is a bonus but you should see what some of my colleagues have accrued for taking back home. Those two who were murdered were very small fry in the greater scheme of things," said Malinowski.

"So you are not involved yourself?"

Malinowski stopped in his tracks and turned to Lafarge.

"This is a one-off transaction Chief Inspector. Admittedly it is one with enormous ramifications for all of us, especially if we are caught. However, I am not involved in the black market. Aside from the risks involved I find it distasteful," he said.

"You don't find this equally distasteful? Perverting the course of justice? Helping an architect of mass murder cheat and have the last laugh at the judges?" asked Lafarge.

Malinowski light up a cigarette and waited until he had exhaled the first intake of tobacco before replying.

"The man has no morals; his acts and crimes are appalling but in my book wearing military uniform entitles someone to be executed by a firing squad. We are hardly breaking him out of jail nor altering his sentence. He is going to die," said Malinowski.

Lafarge felt reassured by Malinowski's argument in their defence. In fact he reproached himself for suddenly becoming so morally supercilious about the whole thing. As Malinowski said their means meant the same end for Goering that the court had designated him.

"Very well Sergeant. In a way the last laugh is on Goering in any case," said Lafarge as he handed the capsule over to Malinowski.

"Oh and why is that Chief Inspector?" asked Malinowski as he withdrew the package from his pocket and pushed it into Lafarge's hand.

"This is going to save a Jewish man's life. I am not sure Goering would appreciate the irony of his last transaction being responsible for that, but if you feel like it please tell him. I would love to see his reaction," said Lafarge.

Both men began to laugh uncontrollably. Whether it was the release of having completed the exchange or simply the effects of the Mass neither knew. They drew surprised looks from those that passed by shortly afterwards.

"There is little to laugh about these days. Clearly those 'Amis' cannot hold their drink. What a waste of good Bavarian beer," muttered one middle-aged German man to his companion as he walked past.

Chapter Nineteen

"So you and this Staff Sergeant found it a laughing matter?" Miller sneered when it became clear Lafarge had finished his confession.

"It seemed amusing at the time," said Lafarge shrugging.

Miller did not look amused in the least, but he did not object when Lafarge lit another cigarette. The room was now so filled with smoke that the bare bulb and the limited light it emitted was like a weak sun covered by a dense fog.

"There is one big hole in your story Lafarge," said Miller.

"Which is what Sergeant?"

"Staff Sergeant Malinowski will be unable to confirm your version of events."

Lafarge was bemused by how confident Miller was. Malinowski had sworn he would accept his part in the scheme. He had said he had little to lose as he was leaving the Military Police. He had made the solemn promise as they parted that night.

Lafarge had no reason to distrust Malinowski as he had played fair throughout and indeed he felt they had formed a bond and he rather liked him.

"I think you will be proved wrong Sergeant. Please can you bring him here and you can ask him yourself," said Lafarge.

"I have no need to. This piece of paper will tell you why," said Miller smiling smugly as he handed Lafarge a piece of A4 sized white paper.

Lafarge held it and read the hand-written note which was in German.

"I would have had no objection to being shot," it began and immediately Lafarge knew whose hand had penned this.

"However, I will not facilitate execution of Germany's Reichsmarschall by hanging! For the sake of Germany, I cannot permit this.

"Moreover, I feel no moral obligation to submit to my enemies' punishment. For this reason, I have chosen to die like the great Hannibal."

Lafarge smiled thinking Goering could not resist a final egotistical flourish comparing himself to the great Carthaginian army commander, who had traversed the Alps with his elephants. There was little comparison between the avaricious sociopath and Hannibal save the solution to their problems at the end. He doubted very much that such a line would be supplied to the international media.

Lafarge looked at Miller and held out his hands.

"Congratulations for bullying me into a confession Sergeant. This makes for interesting reading for an historian or for the investigating officer looking into the lax security at Nuremberg but it hardly implicates me," said Lafarge.

"Turn it over Lafarge," growled Miller.

Lafarge flipped over the page and gulped. Goering had added a PS.

"No doubt there will be uproar and an investigation into how I came to obtain the cyanide capsule. I can absolve all the guards within the prison. They have made my life bearable for the past year. Some have even treated me with the respect my rank merited.

"I owe my final debt of gratitude to a man who I met only a few days ago. His sudden appearance was like that of an angel of mercy, certainly to me in my predicament.

"Fortunately I had in my possession something he dearly wanted. That is always much needed when you have a desire to barter as I have found down the years. Sadly I had nothing to offer the court in similar fashion. I understand when the crimes are so enormous.

"However, clearly this man needed this beautiful bracelet to solve a crime of rather less importance than the ones I was investigated for. I then knew I had a solution to my problem. I was not to be disappointed either. I thank the Chief Inspector for his service.

"I hope that once he has sorted out his considerable problems with the Allied authorities it is not too late for him to save the life of the man he is so desperate to prove innocent."

Lafarge closed his eyes and swallowed deeply. He really

needed more than ever now a shot of cognac.

He could imagine Goering chortling and enjoying writing this, even if it was only perhaps minutes or hours before his chosen moment for death.

The gargoyle features on full display as he deliberately pinned all the blame on Lafarge and there could be only one reason he had chosen to do this. It may not have been written down but Lafarge could read it in the underlying message.

Goering was putting two fingers up at him as he knew the bracelet was required to save a Jew's life. Whether he even realised it was Rosenberg was a moot point. He doubted Goering remembered many names of those he had trodden on in his remorseless ruthless pursuit of power and art works.

Malinowski may have told him the reason thinking why not twist the screw into Goering's ego as he could not do anything about it now the exchange was done. Sadly Malinowski had misunderstood the ability of Goering to wreak vengeance when he thought he had been made a fool of.

He had spared Malinowski, though. However, this may have been – and here Lafarge was surmising wildly – because he placed the suicide note with Malinowski in case there was a final sweep of his cell on the night of the executions. In that case he did not want Malinowski to read it and see he had been named for then the Staff Sergeant might have turned the tables on him and had the capsule seized.

Lafarge was more interested in the here and now, and wanted Malinowski to be questioned.

"So as you can see Sergeant I have not lied to you. I have been honest and accept my part in this. I do not feel ashamed at all. I think Malinowski will also be of the same opinion when you finally make the effort to go and get him," said Lafarge.

"We have committed no crime. The reason I am being held and Malinowski too I imagine is because we exposed an alarming deficiency in the security apparatus in a prison containing a host of notorious war criminals."

"That is a very fine defence Lafarge. However, as I told you Malinowski will not be able to either support or contradict your version of events," said Miller grinning as he looked down eying his dirty fingernails.

"Why is that Sergeant?" asked Lafarge.

"He is due on a train out of here to Berlin in the next few minutes I believe," said Miller.

"Well I suggest Sergeant you get one of your lackeys to drive to the station and pick him up," said Lafarge.

Miller shook his head.

"You don't understand Lafarge and that I sympathise with as English is not your native tongue, so the nuances escape you," said Miller, who appeared to be enjoying every second of Lafarge's discomfit.

"I will spell it out for you very simply so you understand. WE," he said tapping his uniform and for added emphasis then his helmet "do not want one of our own to be implicated so he brings shame on the service. It is bad enough as you have so eloquently pointed out that such a lapse in security has been exposed.

"Andrus is seething and seeking scapegoats. The first thing we had to do was to get Malinowski out of here. Thus Lafarge you will be the only person accused of whatever charge they see fit to bring," said Miller.

"There is nothing preventing me bringing Malinowski's part in it into the public domain at the trial," said Lafarge.

"Traducing the name of a war hero would not be in your best interests Lafarge. I don't think it would be very wise to do so when the Military Police will be responsible for your security," said Miller, the menace in his message clear in his tone.

Lafarge groaned. He could not see any way out of this. The Americans had him, the French had washed their hands of him and Malinowski was on his way home. Fear about his safety and future began to take him over. He had been in many tight corners but this one appeared to be the one where extricating himself would be impossible.

He hugged the overcoat tighter round him. The setting alone was enough to cast oneself into a deep depression. The cold was biting. The dim light and the smoky atmosphere plus the malodorous Miller all pushed down on him.

"So what is the next step? You cannot keep me here now that

I have confessed. You should charge me and place me in a cell. I take it that there are several empty ones after this morning's activity," said Lafarge finding some reserves of dark humour.

Miller did not smile but scowled instead and twirled his baton.

His pock-marked face was not much used to smiling wagered Lafarge. Hailing from Tennessee no doubt he had a dark past of chasing black people through the streets with a baton or a gun with live ammunition. He probably favoured a Confederate flag hanging outside his house than that of the Star Spangled banner.

"I know what I would like to happen to you Lafarge. I thought you were ok when we chatted in the court but in fact you are no better than the Nazis. You and Malinowski think you are above us and can play God with people's lives. That it is all a game," said Miller.

"I hope they punish you severely. Malinowski is fortunate he is leaving the service. I am pessimistic about the reference he will receive from the Army if he asks for one when he applies for a job.

"At least he has his medal. You, though, a former detective under Vichy well that won't be in your favour," added Miller laughing.

Lafarge could have come back at Miller with a double volley of his medal won for bravery despite the collapse of the French Army in 1940, and his relatively clean record under Vichy which had seen him passed fit for service again post the Liberation. However, he was exhausted, cold and resigned to his fate whatever that might be. All he really wanted was to be let out of this room and fed and then locked in a cell on his own.

The oppressive silence that followed -- both had grown tired of each other's company but Miller was following orders to keep Lafarge in the room till the next step was decided upon - was finally broken with a sharp knock at the door.

Miller looked relieved and opened it. Lafarge could not see who it was nor hear their conversation as it was conducted in hushed tones. Miller's body language suggested it was a tense discussion. The sergeant kept clenching and then unclenching his meaty fists.

At one point it became heated and Miller told Lafarge to stay where he was whilst he stepped outside into the corridor and closed the door. Lafarge felt like retorting where Miller thought he might go. However, he bit his tongue.

He stayed seated and chain smoked as the conversation or argument went on. He could not be bothered to steal up to the door and listen. What will be will be he mused to himself.

As the minutes dragged on he did get up and walk around, restoring some feeling to his legs and gaining a bit of warmth. He quickly resumed his seat when he heard the door being unlocked -- Miller's obsession with security a bit late – and in walked the sergeant looking not best pleased.

There again to Lafarge that was nothing new. However, he realised why Miller looked so sour when in behind him walked Guillemot and Devries. They looked grim-faced and Guillemot in particular avoided Lafarge's gaze.

Lafarge wondered what the hell was going on. He guessed salvation was at hand and the glacial greetings he received from his subordinates were so they were not to be seen to be gloating in removing him from Miller's authority.

Miller stood to one side of the room, whilst Devries took centre stage. Lafarge moved towards him and Guillemot but Devries held up his hand to stop him.

"Chief Inspector Gaston Lafarge you are charged with the murder of Inspector Hector Bonville on September 2 this year," said Devries.

Lafarge was stunned but nevertheless protested only for Devries to tell him to be quiet.

"You are to be taken from here and returned to France where you will stand trial at a date to be determined by the investigating officer in consultation with the magistrate," he said curtly and nodded at Guillemot.

Guillemot looked none too enthusiastic but walked over to Lafarge and hand-cuffed him. He once again avoided eye contact with Lafarge, who protested to Devries he was innocent and the handcuffs were unnecessary.

"I suggest Chief Inspector you take it up with whoever is the investigating officer in Paris. The charge is serious enough for you to be hand-cuffed and you are also considered to be a threat not only to us but to yourself. Who is to say you don't have another cyanide capsule on you," said Devries.

Lafarge flashed him an angry look and then shook his head disdainfully.

"Devries really do you think I would murder a colleague? I wonder at your sanity," said Lafarge.

"I am just doing what I am told Chief Inspector. I am following procedure," he said coldly before motioning to Guillemot to remove Lafarge.

The only satisfaction Lafarge took as he left was that Miller looked almost as upset as he was.

"I would be very worried if I were you Sergeant. Andrus is running out of options as scapegoats. You may regret letting Malinowski go. For sure the officers will escape being called to account so that leaves you as the senior rank … hmmm," said Lafarge enjoying the moment briefly before being ushered out by Guillemot.

Lafarge felt a blow to the back of his legs and buckled. All he could hear were swear words aimed at him from Miller as the sergeant beat him and beat him. Guillemot stood to one side and Devries peered over Miller's shoulder and for some reason he was smiling -- that was the last thing he recalled before he passed out.

*

Lafarge came too, the relief he felt at still being alive was tempered by the searing pain he felt through his body. He tried to sit up and take in where he was for he was not lying on the dirty floor where he had fallen under the incessant blows wielded by Miller.

Instead he was lying in a comfortable bed with clean linen and in a room with a view onto the ruins of the castle and the Hexenhausle. Having a drink was the last thing on his mind even if it proved strangely comforting to have the sounds from the inn's clientele drifting through the open window.

However, the winter cold was bitter and he wanted to get out of bed and close the window. The effort of trying to do so wore him out before he had even set foot on the floor.

"I will do that Chief Inspector," said a familiar voice from behind him.

He turned astonished to see Malinowski, who had been seated to the side of his bed.

He grinned at Lafarge and patted him on the shoulder as he made his way over to close the window.

He offered Lafarge a cigarette and pulled up the pillows so the Chief Inspector could sit up, before resuming his seat.

"I apologise for the open window but the smoke was clouding up the room. I had to do something whilst waiting for you to regain consciousness," said Malinowski.

"I am relieved to see you immediately trying to get up and do something. I thought you were dead when I found you. Guillemot was trying to pull Miller back but the thug threw him off and kept on beating you."

Lafarge coughed harshly on inhaling the smoke, his ribs ached.

"I thought you had left. That is what Miller told me. They wanted you out of here as quickly as possible," said Lafarge.

Malinowski smiled.

"I am no nearer going home than I was when you last saw me. In fact there is a chance they may keep me on for the next trial. It fills me with gloom," he said sourly.

"But Miller said....why am I not handcuffed and being guarded?" Lafarge asked.

"Miller is dead as are Devries and Guillemot," said Malinowski.

"I shot them with a little help from your resourceful Russian barman Nikolay."

Malinowski said it in such a matter of fact way that it took Lafarge a few seconds to register what he had told him.

Lafarge was aghast. He could see the hangman's noose in front of him. Aiding Goering's suicide was serious enough but probably not a capital offence. Three dead policemen certainly were even if he had been unconscious.

"Why did you shoot them? Regardless of Miller lying to me and beating me I was under arrest and I had confessed," said Lafarge.

"You were no more under arrest than I was on my way to

Berlin and home," said Malinowski.

"You would have been loaded onto a train and thrown off it once it left Nuremberg."

Lafarge could not believe what he was hearing and clearly there was much more to come. He felt like a drink now and asked Malinowski if that was possible.

Malinowski grinned and withdrew from his pocket Lafarge's hip flask. However, he only allowed him a nip of it. Lafarge smacked his lips in satisfaction. The familiar taste of cognac had revived him a bit.

It also served to get his mind clicking into gear. The clouds were beginning to clear of the set-up. However, he needed Malinowski to confirm it.

"They were all mixed-up in the black market here. I would not be surprised if it was them who murdered the two GIs," said Malinowski.

"They thought you and I were trying to take some of their business. Miller saw us together at the Hexenhausle and chatting to Helga. Well rather he saw me talking to her before you turned up.

"He followed us and saw us exchange the capsule and the bracelet. By the way I re-acquainted you with that. Miller had it in his pocket.

"Miller was intelligent and devious. He put a lot of things together after Goering's suicide and he got them right. The two young MPs he brought with him to the hotel had no idea he was acting on his own and they proved co-operative.

"They were still in your room when I came looking for you. As I was leaving the Grand Nikolay approached me and said he thought he knew where you might have been taken. He had overheard Devries and Guillemot talking in the bar.

"Nikolay reckoned you were being held at their lodgings. He knew it from having delivered something there for Bonville on one occasion.

"He was right too, the canny old goat. We got there just as they were playing out their rather convincing handover. There is a basement with a cellar and that is where they kept you for a couple of days."

Lafarge was surprised Guillemot was involved but then greed as he had seen many times over proved tempting to even those of great probity.

"Guillemot does not fit in. I saw the photo of him with a yellow star," said Lafarge.

Malinowski nodded.

"He was as innocent as you or I in terms of the black market. Devries and Bonville, who we think was the ringleader, applied peer pressure to him. His experiences during the Occupation impacted too. Having survived and regained his place in the police he probably shut his eyes to their extra-curricular activities and enjoyed some of the benefits," said Malinowski.

"The alcohol primarily, and who can blame him," said Lafarge.

"Indeed. Well whatever his motives or knowledge of the plan surrounding you he fired back at us even after we identified ourselves," said Malinowski.

"How did Nikolay identify himself? He has no authority," said Lafarge.

"Quite but these guys have no rules so therefore we have to be creative too," said Malinowski.

"Nikolay took one for the team too. But do not worry it was a superficial wound.

"Miller did not die immediately. He was still breathing, or rather gurgling, when the firing stopped."

Lafarge was relieved to hear Nikolay was okay but he wondered what was to come via a vis Miller for Malinowski suddenly looked ashamed.

"So what did you stand over him till he died?"

Malinowski placed his head between his hands and rubbed his cheeks vigorously.

"I held his nostrils together till he expired," he said, his voice shaking.

"It is the first time I have killed someone in such a personal and close-up manner. Also killing someone wearing the same uniform plays on your mind afterwards even if he was a thug and a criminal."

Lafarge sympathised with Malinowski. He had murdered

several people and it had required looking them in the eyes but he did not regret any of them. They had all deserved it.

The reason he felt sorry for Malinowski was because he had not been obliged to kill Miller. He could have left Lafarge and hoped that the black market ring were satisfied with killing the Frenchman and would spare him. However, an innate sense of decency had propelled Malinowski and Nikolay to come and save him.

"Well I owe you and Nikolay in a way I feel I will never be able to repay," said Lafarge.

Malinowski brushed it aside.

"Think nothing of it Chief Inspector. I believe knowing your cussed nature you would have done the same thing," said Malinowski.

Lafarge smiled.

"Do you know how long I will be here? Are we to be questioned?"

Lafarge felt like apologising for the rapid fire questions but he did not know how much time they had alone. For surely there would be investigators waiting outside the room impatient for him to regain consciousness so they could interrogate him.

Malinowski shook his head.

"The blame for the cyanide capsule has been placed on Miller's head. We helpfully left a few beside Devries's bed which have been collected by the investigating officers.

"They surmise that Goering paid them handsomely for doing him this service and are of the opinion that having benefited from his largesse they were prepared to supply other defendants in future trials with similar capsules.

"I plucked not only the bracelet but also Goering's suicide note from Miller's body. That was a masterful touch by him and in fact the first part is word for word what he wrote.

"The authorities have the original of course but there is no need for flies in the ointment as the British are fond of saying.

"From what I overheard our docs say you will be fit to leave pretty soon. They just wanted to ensure you were not suffering from concussion. You need to rest. The bruises and the aches may last for a while but there is no lasting damage.

"Yes don't look surprised you are being cared for by the US Military's finest medical staff. Staff Sergeant Malinowski would not let a compadre be treated by anything less!" he grinned.

"I am duly honoured Staff Sergeant," said Lafarge giving a mock salute.

Malinowski returned it and gave him a second nip of cognac.

"Honoured you shall be Chief Inspector. Nikolay tells me he overheard Faure in the bar mulling over with another of his legal team whether you deserved a medal of some sort for getting to the bottom of the black market ring," said Malinowski laughing heartily.

Lafarge too laughed. Though it hurt like hell he could put up with the pain as once again it appeared the Gods were smiling on him.

Chapter Twenty

"Gaston I toast you. You have achieved a miracle and I owe you everything," said Rosenberg raising his champagne glass.

Lafarge waved him off and looked embarrassed. If Rosenberg owed anyone it was Malinowski.

Things had moved fast once Lafarge returned to Paris. The bracelet had indeed proved crucial. Suddenly Zilberstein lost the protection he enjoyed. Being financially linked to Goering did not sit well with the ministers and senior policemen who had blocked Lafarge previously.

Lafarge and Gilbert were pretty much able to model the case against Zilberstein as they wished. Meissner's murder fell into that category. Zilberstein protested his innocence forcefully and insisted it was Madame Rosenberg. The problem for him was that officially Madame Rosenberg was dead.

There was also a strong case for him to answer in betraying Leon Reinach and his son in the mistaken belief Beatrice would fall into his arms with her fortune. However, once she rejected him he persuaded Otto Abetz along with de Brinon to deport her as well with her daughter and they could share the spoils.

Goering of course had wanted his pick of the art among the paintings Auguste Renoir's Le petite fille au ruban bleu -- a portrait of Beatrice's mother Irene Cahen d'Anvers as a child.

The formidable sexagenarian – who had escaped deportation due to having converted to Catholicism decades before and a second marriage to an Italian nobleman – had come across it in a collection of looted art.

As the keys turned in Zilberstein's cold damp cell Rosenberg had been released without charge and the gallery was being returned to him.

Lafarge and Aimee had agreed they would move out of the apartment. Rosenberg said they could stay as he was putting it on the market. He could not live in an apartment which reminded him constantly of the wife who had betrayed him.

A compromise solution was Rosenberg said he would offer

the flat at a knockdown price to Lafarge. He had privately thanked Lafarge by giving him a painting by the surrealist Yves Tanguy which was his favourite.

Nikolay had heard correctly for Faure had recommended Lafarge be honoured for his services in cracking the black market ring. He had tried to persuade Faure otherwise and that both Malinowski and Nikolay were as worthy. Faure had refused to listen. Typical lawyer Lafarge had retorted jokingly and accepted the Chevalier of the Legion d'Honneur.

Nikolay had got his reward by being brought back as part of the French delegation and awarded French citizenship. Malinowski as he had feared had been ordered to stay in Nuremberg, his hopes of returning to small town life dashed for the time being.

However, the blow had been softened by promotion to lieutenant and the Distinguished Service Cross. Special circumstances had permitted the award as it was usually for courage against an armed enemy.

Lafarge was now enjoying a celebratory lunch post the ceremony at his favourite local bistro 'Presque Mort'. It had been the black humour of the name chosen by the owners Jean-Luc and Julie Giraud which had first attracted him as it lay a few hundred yards from the Pere Lachaise cemetery.

However, the quality of the food and the drink had proved a more binding attachment and he had enjoyed some of his happier moments there. The Girauds had kept a fine menu throughout the Occupation, thanks in part to strong links with the black market. Lafarge too had protected them. He had persuaded his father to have them re-opened when they were shut down once by the police for suspected resistance sympathies.

Thus now he was enjoying a rich feast with Rosenberg, Aimee, Gilbert, Durand, Pinault, the lawyer Henri Gerland and most pleasing of all for him his old comrade from Limoges Broglie. He had remained in Limoges and deservedly had been made Chief of Detectives which largely revolved round him staying behind his desk and ordering younger types to do the legwork.

Luizet had come to the ceremony but had made his excuses afterwards. Pinault was only too happy to tag along as it gave him a rare moment to relax away from the immense pressure of the Denoel investigation.

Gilbert had told Lafarge discreetly that word was Pinault was going to be forced to step aside unless the case was resolved by the end of the year.

The lunch was winding down and Lafarge realised they would expect a speech from him.

He rose to his feet and went through the usual weak jokes and tributes before coming to the part he knew would be the most testing.

"It is the right moment surrounded by my closest colleagues, friends and my wife to tell you I am resigning," he said.

There were gasps of surprise, a supportive smile from Aimee, and he held up his hands to calm them. He noticed that his hands were shaking and he remarked that he was finding it more difficult than he had thought it would be.

"I have discussed this with Aimee and I feel that it is only right having received this honour today that I should stand down and hand in my badge. After all I can break the habit of a life-time and go out on a high note as I am renowned for fouling things up when everything is seemingly perfect," he said smiling.

"I owe Aimee a lot. I will not go into why and that will remain between myself, her and Broglie. However, as she has recommenced her career I feel it is a good time for me to end mine, admittedly extremely prematurely, but hers requires a lot of effort and single-mindedness as well as talent.

"Long hours are a compulsory part of it too. To a certain extent it sounds like our job! Thus I can now lounge around at home and explain to Ancil why his father is such a sloth!

"So boss you will need a new Chief Inspector but I think the right man for the job is sitting not too far away from you," added Lafarge nodding towards Gilbert.

"Besides he is cheaper as he prefers beer to cognac and on that note ...." Lafarge with a lump in his throat raised his glass of cognac and saluted his friends.

*

"Pinault was genuinely upset you are leaving Gaston. I swear I saw a tear or two even when he warned you not to get bored and become a private detective," said Aimee as they walked up the stairs of their building.

Lafarge laughed.

"Yes he sounded genuine when he said you are a tough stubborn bastard but at least you were my tough stubborn bastard. He made it sound as if he feels threatened by me being out on the market," said Lafarge.

"The trouble is some people just don't want to believe I am capable of speaking the truth."

Aimee giggled.

"Well why do you find that so surprising ex-Chief Inspector," she said playfully.

Lafarge grabbed her round the waist now that they had got to just outside their door and tickled her before planting a kiss on her lips.

The door opened behind them and Lafarge froze. Madame Rosenberg was standing there. Her look was glacial. She raised her finger to her lips and with the other hand gestured with her two middle fingers a walking motion and pointed downstairs.

Lafarge nodded as subtly as he could given his head was resting on Aimee's shoulder. He was more alarmed as to whether she had harmed Ancil.

Aimee turned and saw Madame Rosenberg too. However, there was no surprise in her reaction. Lafarge soon learned why.

"Ah I am sorry we took longer than I thought. I hope Ancil has been a good boy. This is my husband. Gaston this is Madame Leclerc who very kindly offered to look after Ancil," said Aimee gaily.

"She was a make-up artist on my film," added Aimee by way of explanation.

Lafarge had not waited for the babysitter to arrive that morning due to having to be early to the venue for the ceremony. He politely shook Madame Rosenberg's hand before pushing past her to go and see Ancil.

His heart was pounding but he was reassured to see Ancil curled up in his cot sound asleep.

Lafarge kissed him tenderly on the cheek and shut the door. His jolly demeanour and his optimism about the future were now just a front so as not to worry Aimee.

"Do you live far away Madame Leclerc?" he asked.

Madame Rosenberg nodded.

"I am in Convention. A very nice apartment my husband and I rented just after the Liberation but sadly he died," she said.

Lafarge felt like saying 'really he looked very much alive a few minutes ago' but kept his mouth shut. He did not want to endanger Aimee or Ancil and would play her game for the moment. He just wanted to get her out of the apartment as quickly as possible.

"Well perhaps I can drop you home then. It is dark and the metro no doubt is intermittent at best," he said fetching the car keys from the table beside the front door.

Madame Rosenberg did her best at putting up an objection but Aimee said it would be no trouble.

Lafarge clasped Aimee tightly and mouthed I adore you as he opened the door and left with Madame Rosenberg.

Once the door was closed Madame Rosenberg gestured for him to step to the side. She patted him down for weapons but found none. He had left his gun in the flat as he expected her to search him. Fortunately she missed the small pistol he kept strapped to his sock.

She then whispered to him to descend the stairs in front of her.

Lafarge tried to think of where would be best to take her out. However, he then felt the press of a gun muzzle in his back. They then proceeded past Madame Grondon's concierge lodge.

Her lights were off which further reduced Lafarge's options.

Once they were out on the street she told him curtly to turn left. Then she said for him to turn the corner.

Lafarge regretted now that on returning from Nuremberg he had agreed with Pinault the detective watching the building was no longer required.

Lafarge was glad she kept conversation to a minimum as he

did not feel like talking. He needed to try and focus. However, whether it was a mix of the drink and the shock of Madame Rosenberg turning up at the apartment the thoughts were simply not feeding into his brain.

She motioned towards a powder blue Delahaye Cabriolet and pointing towards the boot handed him the keys.

Nobody passed them and he could not see anyone walking towards them dashing hopes of causing a scene and attracting attention to them.

He turned the key in the boot and opened it. But as he turned to hand her back the keys he made his move thinking he would catch her off guard.

He swung his arm but it only met fresh air. She had moved to the side and it was then he glanced down and saw she had fitted a silencer to the pistol.

He swallowed deeply and rubbed his mouth nervously with his hand. He was sweating despite the freezing cold.

Only one question came to his head.

"Why?"

Madame Rosenberg smiled and pressed the trigger. Lafarge fell back neatly into the boot.

Darkness descended as Rosenberg shut it.

*

Lafarge lost track of time as the car trundled along. He spent the journey mulling over where he was being taken and who was waiting for him. He clung to those thoughts which offered him some hope of living because if Rosenberg had intended on killing him she would have hit him with the bullet instead of deliberately firing into the road.

She had achieved her aim of getting him into the boot as he took evasive action but she was too good a shot to have missed him from that range.

Of course there was the possibility that he was being too optimistic and all she was doing was taking him to a deserted spot where he could be executed without attracting attention and his body could lie there for days before being discovered.

It was clear from sharing the boot with a couple of suitcases that this was Madame Rosenberg's farewell to Paris. After all she had nothing to keep her there now. Whatever money she had managed to obtain from the gallery and Zilberstein would have to suffice for that channel was now cut off.

But was it his farewell for good too? If that was the intention he thought the odds were improving for him escaping. She had become over-confident failing to tie his hands, the trip was sobering him up fast and he still had the pistol.

The car finally came to a stop. He could hear her getting out of the car and then returning before starting the car up again.

This was far from comfortable compared to the previous part of the journey as the car bounced up and down on a rough surface -- his head hit the roof of the boot several times -- and he was delighted when the car again came to a stop.

He waited and waited for the boot to be opened. He reached down to his sock and thought about freeing the pistol and firing at Rosenberg or whoever finally released him.

He quickly withdrew his hand as he heard feet scrunching on gravel. The boot door swung upwards and he looked up to see a middle-aged man staring down at him.

"Come on out you get," he said gruffly.

Lafarge clambered out and allowed himself to stretch.

The man did not bother with the niceties of introducing himself and Lafarge did not insist as his host had a gun in his hand.

Instead he took in his surroundings in as much as he could with it being dark. Fortunately light shone out of a farmhouse which was two storeys high. He was ushered inside into a large hallway which had a staircase straight in front and three doorways off it.

He could hear voices to his right but he was pushed into a room to his left. It was a study with bookshelves full to overflowing, two armchairs and a wooden chair which was situated behind a French Empire desk made of mahogany wood and a leather top.

His guard indicated for him to sit in one of the armchairs before he left shutting the door behind him.

Lafarge looked round the room hoping he could spot a drinks cabinet but there was none.

He felt in his pocket and found a scrunched up packet of Gitanes and compensated for the lack of alcohol by lighting one.

Just as he exhaled the door swung open and in walked to his astonishment Pierre-Yves de Chastelain.

"What the hell is the meaning of this de Chastelain! This is outrageous!" Lafarge shouted.

He rose from his seat and moved towards de Chastelain. However, de Chastelain pushed him back into the chair and took the seat opposite him.

De Chastelain looked none the worse for his visit to Dr Petiot mused Lafarge. However, he kept his joke to himself as it was clear de Chastelain was not in the mood for pleasantries. He still had the same dark saturnine good looks and whilst thin he had good colour in his face.

However, the expression on his face was anything but warm. It was pure hatred.

Lafarge made sure he did not cross his legs for it would expose the gun.

"You owe me an explanation de Chastelain," said Lafarge.

De Chastelain removed a cigar from the top pocket of his tweed jacket and lit it.

He rolled the smoke round his mouth before blowing it in Lafarge's direction.

"I think it is you who owes me one Lafarge. I believe I can dispense with Chief Inspector," said de Chastelain.

"It is just as well you have stepped down of your own volition because I would have ensured you had to."

Lafarge realised that Gerland had not exaggerated when he had told him de Chastelain, far from believing he had saved his life, thought he had sent him to Petiot to be murdered.

The irony that he had thought he was genuinely saving de Chastelain for he was ignorant of Petiot's dastardly scheme was not lost on Lafarge. He had also salved his conscience because if he had delivered de Chastelain to Bousquet he would have been executed for a crime Lafarge had committed.

Lafarge told this to de Chastelain. Well at least the first part.

The trouble for Lafarge was that the lawyer knew all about the second part.

"At one point Lafarge I was willing to give you the benefit of the doubt," said de Chastelain.

"I thought if it was a choice between you and Bousquet's complicity in mass murder then you deserved a second chance. Admittedly a pretty low bar.

However, when I learned of Petiot's unspeakable crimes it got me thinking again.

"I decided why should I be a sacrificial pawn in a bitter personal battle between yourself and Bousquet.

"Oh yes Lafarge. I returned to France at de Gaulle's behest in early 1944 to better orchestrate resistance cells. I finished the job poor Moulin had been sent to do.

"I had the good fortune to meet Madame Rosenberg in one of these cells. I saw in her the killer instinct that I could use to get my revenge. I came close to giving up but Madame Rosenberg persuaded me to keep going and she has delivered you to me at last."

Lafarge rubbed his chin. He was cornered and denial was pointless.

Killing collaborator Drieu la Rochelle should have gained Lafarge some currency but it did not as de Chastelain had been close friends. Such was the complexity of France in the dark days that those on opposite sides could remain friends but the Resistance had been renowned for petty rivalries even leading to betrayals.

"So de Chastelain what is it to be for me? Is Madame Rosenberg waiting outside the door? That man who brought me in is he waiting with a shovel to dig my grave? You will stand there smoking your cigar and be the audience? You are not the type to pull the trigger yourself," said Lafarge bitterly.

"You learned well from the Nazis."

De Chastelain shot him a dismissive look.

"Oh I have shot people Lafarge, better ones than you. Like I am sure in reverse you have allowed less deserving humans than Marguerite to live.

"However, you are fortunate. I have had enough of death. My blood lust I hoped would last till I achieved my long-term goal which was you. However, I am exhausted by it. Hate has eaten me up for too long.

"I am content that I succeeded in frightening you that you would never see your family again. I am happy you will have gone through hell in the boot of the car."

De Chastelain stood and it was clear that Lafarge should follow suit.

They went out back onto the gravel driveway where Madame Rosenberg was standing by the car.

De Chastelain went and opened the passenger door. Lafarge breathed a sigh of relief he would not be returning to Paris in the boot.

De Chastelain went round and whispered to Madame Rosenberg, who nodded.

Lafarge had benefited from the brief hiatus to stretch his legs, which had still not fully recovered from the cramped journey down, and paced up and down smoking.

Finally de Chastelain returned to Lafarge's side of the car and he took his cue to get in.

He indicated for Lafarge to wind down the window.

"I may not be going to kill you but I am going to punish you. Lafarge you are being sent into exile," said de Chastelain coldly.

Lafarge felt his stomach churning and his throat constricted. He wanted to jump from the car but de Chastelain pushed against the door.

"Madame Rosenberg is going to drive you to Madrid. Well she rather fancies a spell there and she is on the run although I will put in a good word for her in Paris," sad de Chastelain.

"From there I believe you once tried and failed to get to Argentina. Perhaps that would be a suitable destination? You have the family of your first wife there after all.

"Of course they may not appreciate that you have a second family.

"But then they won't be joining you. For you are forbidden to contact them. You may think that will be easy to circumvent but I should tell you that I am no longer a lawyer. I have used my contacts from the resistance spell to move into intelligence.

"I therefore have the power to tap your phone in Paris and

have the post monitored.

"To all intent and purposes you will be dead to them. I will stop short of posting such a death notice in the paper but be assured if you try to make contact then I will do it.

"If you persist after that then I will consider what other measures should be taken."

Lafarge felt a mixture of fear, torment and anger. He reached down to his left ankle for the pistol but he was prevented from doing so as Madame Rosenberg grabbed his arm. She then bent down and removed the pistol.

"This is a death sentence de Chastelain. I would prefer you pull me out of the car and shoot me," he said.

"I am a Chevalier of the Legion d'Honneur for goodness sake. How are you going to explain my disappearance when it is raised? You may have influential friends but I do as well. Pinault, Luizet and Faure to name a few will be pestered by Aimee to find out what has happened to me.

"What about my other son? Think of him he has no one. Who will visit him? What will he, Aimee and Ancil live off?"

Any further chance of being heard for the moment was drowned out by Madame Rosenberg firing up the engine.

"It is a death sentence Lafarge but it is one which I will get more pleasure from. For I will wake up every morning and enjoy a moment thinking how much torture you must be going through," he said with the most glacial of smiles.

"As for your son in St Anne well I may see he is cared for. He did after all do me a great favour in shooting your girlfriend Berenice. Your hypocrisy in going out with a woman whose private life resembled Marguerite is astonishing. The irony of your union with her was not lost on me Lafarge.

"Aimee and your other son's welfare are none of my concern. They shall pay for your wickedness.

"In case you think you can jump Madame Rosenberg on a stop on the way think of Aimee and Ancil. Their lives are in danger till the moment I receive a phone call from Madame Rosenberg telling me you are both in Madrid."

Lafarge was beaten, although, he never liked to admit as such.

He was out of fight and arguments but he did not feel contrite and to say he was would have felt like begging and that was one thing he would not lower himself to.

He had won his battle with Bousquet.

Even if de Chastelain thought it was tawdry to have used Suchet as a pawn to Lafarge she had served her purpose.

Murdering her had hastened the downfall of the evil person that was Bousquet. His departure had brought in the vile anti-Semite Darnand but he lacked the energy, vigour, organisational skills and shameless ambition of Bousquet. Lafarge had allowed his personal hatred of Bousquet to perpetrate some terrible crimes. However, he judged them worth it in ridding France of Bousquet.

"What am I going to wear? I need to brush my teeth at some point," he said plaintively reduced to bartering for basic necessities.

"I have a little money on me but I need to buy things, including what will be an expensive ticket to Argentina as you so kindly recommended I do."

De Chastelain laughed.

"You have a suitcase packed with your necessities in the boot of the car. Madame Rosenberg spent the time you paid her to babysit to pack for you," he said.

De Chastelain then snapped his fingers and Madame Rosenberg put her foot down.

Lafarge wrapped his coat round him not just for warmth but to feel the only reassuring thing he could cling onto – Marguerite Suchet's jewels.

In that moment as he sped down some country lane to a life of lonely exile he found succour in a line from Alexandre Dumas' classic *The Count of Monte Cristo*, "All human wisdom is contained in these two words – Wait and Hope."

Printed in Great Britain
by Amazon